Praise for *A...*

'*An Academic Affair* is absolut... romantic, and brimming with si... to-lovers romance sparkles fron... misses!' **Natalie Murr...**

'A delightful dive into the messiness of love, academia and everything in between.' **Saman Shad, author of *The Matchmaker***

'A brilliantly innovative and witty enemies-to-lovers romance that combines a virtuoso knowledge of literary studies (and wine) with a devastatingly honest portrait of the higher education sector. Love wins against the modern managerial university!' **Dr Hsu-Ming Teo, Professor of Literature and Creative Writing, Macquarie University**

'If you want something done right, you go to an expert. A doctor of romance penning a rivals-to-lovers, marriage-of-convenience rom-com set in academia? . . . I gobbled this up like a heathen. Hot, funny and so full of heart.' **Clare Fletcher, author of *Love Match***

'*An Academic Affair* is rom-com perfection! The chase in *An Academic Affair* builds and builds and builds, leading to a climax so good that once you've finished, you'll want to experience it all over again.' **Michelle Upton, author of *Emergency Exit Only***

'I loved this book! I was swept into a world of tweed, family drama, wine and love. Jodi McAlister is a genius at writing page-turning love stories.' **Steph Vizard, author of *The Love Contract***

'*An Academic Affair* is a story that will have you giggling and kicking your feet . . . and leave you absolutely begging for more. I'm already counting the days for book two in the series!' **Melanie Saward, author of *Love Unleashed***

'*An Academic Affair* made me believe in two impossible things – true love, and careers in academia. This is a perfect romance that I didn't want to ever end.' **Patrick Lenton, author of *In Spite of You***

'Sadie and Jonah might just be my new favourite fictional couple. I can't stop thinking about them, or this book. Jodi McAlister writes romance like she invented it.' **Karina May, author of *That Island Feeling***

'I fell in love with this gorgeous novel the moment I read the first footnote. Sharp, clever, crackling with chemistry and deeply romantic, I absolutely loved it.' **Nina Kenwood, author of *The Wedding Forecast***

'Rivals to lovers, fake marriage, he falls first, Anne and Gilbert vibes – can this book get any better? Yes, it can. Sadie and Jonah are their own special magic. And who can resist an academic romance? Not me!' **Amy Matthews, author of *Someone Else's Bucket List***

'Who knew footnotes could be such sexy fun? With snappy banter and an intelligent heart, too, this book made me laugh and cry. Jodi McAlister is brilliant at all she writes.' **Dr Catherine M. Roach, Distinguished Research Professor of Gender and Cultural Studies, University of Alabama**

'Deeply emotional and incredibly hot. Jonah is now one of my favourite book boyfriends. Jodi McAlister has done it again.' **Abra Pressler, author of *Love and Other Scores***

'With scorching banter and sizzling chemistry, McAlister has delivered an addictive romantic triumph that's as emotionally deep as it is delightfully steamy. I'm officially obsessed.' **Amy Hutton, author of *Love from Scratch***

'Joyful, poignant, playful and wise about things that matter – from the power of popular fiction to love itself, in many forms – this is the kind of book that made me start the (very real) *Journal of Popular Romance Studies* . . . Jodi McAlister knows her stuff, and she makes it sizzle.' **Dr Eric Murphy Selinger, Founding Editor of the *Journal of Popular Romance Studies*, DePaul University**

'The premise – fake marriage to gain secure employment in academia – is not far-fetched! But *An Academic Affair* goes well beyond a trope – it's a sweet, sexy, smart, genuine and funny romance. It will win a lot of hearts.' **Angela Meyer, author of *Joan Smokes***

An
Academic
Affair

Jodi McAlister

**SIMON &
SCHUSTER**

London · New York · Amsterdam/Antwerp · Sydney/Melbourne · Toronto · New Delhi

First published in Great Britain by Simon & Schuster UK Ltd, 2025

1 3 5 7 9 10 8 6 4 2

Simon & Schuster UK Ltd, 1st Floor
222 Gray's Inn Road, London WC1X 8HB

For more than 100 years, Simon & Schuster has championed authors and the stories they create. By respecting the copyright of an author's intellectual property, you enable Simon & Schuster and the author to continue publishing exceptional books for years to come. We thank you for supporting the author's copyright by purchasing an authorised edition of this book.

Simon & Schuster Australia, Sydney
Simon & Schuster India, New Delhi

www.simonandschuster.co.uk
www.simonandschuster.com.au
www.simonandschuster.co.in

The authorised representative in the EEA is Simon & Schuster Netherlands BV, Herculesplein 96, 3584 AA Utrecht, Netherlands. info@simonandschuster.nl

Simon & Schuster strongly believes in freedom of expression and stands against censorship in all its forms. For more information, visit BooksBelong.com

A CIP catalogue record for this book is available from the British Library

Paperback ISBN: 978-1-3985-5136-7
eBook ISBN: 978-1-3985-5137-4
Audio ISBN: 978-1-3985-5138-1

Printed and Bound in the UK using 100% Renewable Electricity at CPI Group (UK) Ltd

MIX
Paper | Supporting
responsible forestry
FSC® C013604

Prologue

Jonah

In my fifteen years of fighting with Sadie Shaw, we only had six ceasefires.

The first five, we broke.

Ceasefire #1 – Second year undergrad
Thirteen years ago

Our unit chair for Eighteenth and Nineteenth Century Literature made two pedagogical decisions that Future Jonah, who would go on to teach classes of his own, would find utterly fascinating in their sadism:

1) Group work was the best possible way to assess individual students' understanding of the libertine novel.
2) Pairing the two students who, over the year and a half they'd known each other, had spent every seminar passionately disagreeing with each other would lead to excellent results.[1]

---

1   I want to believe the unit chair's sadism was intentionally ironic, given one of the authors we were studying was the Marquis de Sade, but that would definitely be an overreading.

'Truce, Fisher,' nineteen-year-old Sadie said, long red hair spilling over her shoulders as she marched across the seminar room towards me. 'The grade we get on this assessment is more important to me than the fact I can't stand you.'

She held out her hand for me to shake.

I looked at it.

'Well?' she demanded.

'. . . Fine. Truce, Shaw,' I said. 'Our grade is the most important thing.'

I shook her hand. Her skin was soft against mine, the way I had imagined it might be, but her grip was secure, assertive, assured.

Mine wasn't.

I loved arguing with Sadie in seminars. Everything I could think of, she always had an answer to – sometimes a completely unexpected one – and it was entirely, utterly thrilling.

This was our fourth semester of undergraduate Lit Studies at Eastern Sydney University. Every semester, I made sure we were in the same seminars,[2] because I liked arguing with her so much. Every week, I looked forward to the hours we spent together: to those productive, fruitful, generative debates; to the way our commitment to one-upping each other made us both better students; to the glint in her eyes as she turned her gaze on me across the room; to whatever it was she would say next.

Before I started undergrad, I had been determined not to follow in my father's footsteps. I had no desire to do what my brother Elias was doing, to try to become the sequel to Professor Christian Fisher, Eminent(ly Unbearable) Scholar. Yes, I loved reading. Yes, I loved learning. Yes, I was even going to do my degree at ESU, where my dad worked – but that was as far as I was going to go.

---

2   Even if they were at 8am, which should really tell you something.

Under no circumstances would I become an academic, not if it meant becoming someone like him.

Arguing with Sadie had changed my mind about everything I'd imagined for my future.

But she didn't feel the way I did. At all.

Sadie Shaw couldn't *stand* me.

That's probably why I was the one who broke the first ceasefire, by picking a fight about what theoretical framework we should use to examine *Les Liasions Dangereuses*. It was incredibly immature of me, but it was far easier to make myself unlikeable than to try and understand why the girl I'd been psyching myself up to ask to be my date to my sister Fiona's farce of a wedding hated me so much.[3]

Ceasefire #2 – Graduation (undergrad)
Ten years ago

Because we were both compulsive overachievers, we each did a double bachelor's degree[4] and then an Honours year. By the time we graduated, Sadie and I had been arguing with each other for five years.

Tensions had ratcheted up between us after that first broken ceasefire,[5] and they ratcheted up even further in our Honours year.

---

3 This assignment marked the only time I ever received less than a High Distinction in my entire undergraduate career. I don't have her transcript in front of me, so I can't cite this claim, but there is zero doubt in my mind that the same was true for Sadie.

4 Arts/Law for her; Arts/Economics for me. I put this in the footnotes because while it is interesting, it is not especially relevant: our second degrees never mattered again.

5 Never underestimate the power of a young man with wounded pride to double down on the behaviours that will ensure his unrequited crush forever remains unrequited.

What had been a simple classroom rivalry turned into an all-out battle for supremacy, because now there was something to *win*.

Sadie and I never said it out loud, but we clearly had the same idea. We were both going to get first-class honours – that went without saying – but whichever one of us got the higher overall grade and won the University Medal for Outstanding Academic Performance in Literary Studies would also be the winner of . . . well, us.

But there was to be no winner, no loser, no satisfying conclusion that would let us both walk away and bury our feud as the youthful hostilities of two people too competitive for their own good, because we got the exact same score – across coursework, across our theses, across everything – making us the first ever dual University Medallists.

'Can we be civil today, please?' I murmured to Sadie, as we followed the student procession into the graduation hall. Everyone else was ordered alphabetically to receive their degrees, but because we'd won the medal, we had to be beside each other, right near the back. 'I'd rather not have a screaming argument with you in front of my parents.'

'Oh, damn,' Sadie said. 'I'll have to take that off my schedule. I had it pencilled in for about two thirds of the way through the ceremony.'

I looked at her.

I had buried my crush a long time ago, but there were still times – usually when that long, wild red hair of hers was loose the way it was that day, vibrant against the crisp black lines of her robes and mortarboard – that I couldn't help but notice how beautiful she was.

'Please.' It was the closest I'd come to admitting weakness to her since that first insecure handshake.

If she realised, she didn't press the issue – which meant that she hadn't realised, because Sadie Shaw would *always* press the issue. 'I have as much interest in causing a scene as you, Jonah. Do you think I fought this hard just to ruin today by having some stupid argument with you?'

That stung. Our arguments were many things, but never, ever – I thought, anyway – stupid.

'Your parents must be proud,' I said, because it seemed like a polite, civil sort of thing to say.

'I don't have parents.'

I blinked.

'My mum died when I was sixteen. Cancer. My dad was a piece of shit who left when she got sick.'

'I'm sorry. I didn't know.'

'When I said I fought hard for this, Fisher,' Sadie said, 'I didn't just mean I fought you.'

Her robes brushed against mine as we took our seats. 'My sister Chess is here, though,' she added, 'and saying she's proud is a profound understatement.'

It was Chess who ended up breaking the second ceasefire. My dad was vocally displeased that I hadn't won the University Medal outright, and Chess overheard, interpreting his disappointment in me as a slight against Sadie,[6] and . . . well, if there had been even the slightest possibility of Sadie and me staying in touch and maybe even developing some sort of friendship, then the huge, embarrassing scene the two of them caused utterly obliterated it.

---

6 Probably accurately.

Ceasefire #3 – The share house
Eight years ago

We took different paths after graduation. I stayed at university, continuing straight on into a PhD. Sadie left, going out into the real world to make some money.

A great deal of the pleasure I found in university bled away without her there. No other sparring partner came close. On an intellectual level, I missed her, deeply and profoundly.

But I was glad too, because without her there, every day, finding new and fascinating ways to disagree with me, I was finally able to *actually* put that crush of mine to rest, once and for all.

All right, sure, every so often[7] I would wake up in the middle of the night in a cold sweat, paralysed with anxiety over some of the stupid shit I'd said to her.

And sure, once, when I was marking essays for that same unit on eighteenth- and nineteenth-century literature Sadie and I had taken all those years ago, and a student had quoted Lizzy's line, 'I know I shall probably never see him again, but I cannot bear to think that he is alive in the world and thinking ill of me', my first instinct had been to scribble *RELATABLE CONTENT* and not *THIS LINE IS FROM THE 1995 MINI-SERIES, PLEASE READ THE BOOK NEXT TIME.*

But for the most part, I did not think about Sadie Shaw – and I hoped that wherever she was and whatever she was doing, she wasn't thinking about me either. That would be better than her hating me.

In the interest of getting out of my parents' house, I moved in much too quickly with my new girlfriend, a Screen Studies PhD student I met at a postgraduate mixer. About eighteen months into the relationship, though, when she started saying things like 'marriage' and 'children' and 'why don't you ever tell me you love me, Jonah?', I realised I'd made a terrible mistake, broke it off before I

---

7 Weekly. Minimum.

did any more emotional damage, and found myself in the market for somewhere new to live.

After looking at a lot of truly awful and wildly expensive places,[8] I found the perfect share house. It wasn't too far from campus and it was huge: six bedrooms, three bathrooms, with a spacious kitchen I could actually see myself cooking in and a big backyard with a covered deck that would be perfect for studying on sunny afternoons. It was cheap, too, because so many other postgrad students and early career researchers lived there. The couple who interviewed me (Van: sociology; Annie: philosophy) told me there were seven housemates living across four of the bedrooms, and they were looking to add to that number by renting out the other two.

If you have any sense of story progression then I'm sure you can see where this is going, but I did not generally expect my fairly staid, dull, quiet life to follow narrative rules, so imagine my shock when I turned up on moving day, struggling under the weight of a stack of Norton Anthologies – only to run into Sadie in the hallway, red hair piled messily on her head, sweat beading on her collarbone, halfway through moving in her own stuff.

Neither of us was willing to give up the house. Not with that kitchen, not with that backyard, definitely not in the broken Sydney rental market. 'Where am I supposed to go, back to the woman whose heart I just broke?' I demanded. 'Be realistic, Shaw.'

'Oh, yes, I'm sure her heart is just shattered, losing a prince like you, Fisher,' Sadie retorted. 'What about your rich parents?'

'I would rather live with your sister.'

'What's that supposed to mean?'

'That on the one occasion I met her, your sister screamed that I was an entitled prick from a line of entitled pricks, and I would *still* rather live with her than with my parents. Although I'm sure she'd

---

8   Sometimes awful, sometimes expensive, usually both. Nothing will break your spirit like renting in Sydney.

much rather live with you, so how about you move in with her and I'll stay here?'

'No.'

'Why not?'

'Um, I don't know, because she's a thirty-year-old lawyer who doesn't need her kid sister sponging off her anymore?' Sadie folded her arms. 'I'd suggest you move in with your siblings, but you have *only child* written all over you.'

'Oh wow, is Sadie Shaw drawing broad conclusions based on insubstantial evidence? I'm the youngest of three. I've got a brother and a sister.'

'Congratulations. Move in with one of them.'

It went on like that for a long time. A *long* time. We were lucky it was the middle of the day and most of our new housemates were on campus, because if they'd overheard us, they definitely would have asked us both to leave.

Eventually, though, we reached the only possible stalemate for two people as stubborn as we were.

'It's a big house,' Sadie said. 'Will you agree to stay out of my way?'

I took her proffered hand. 'If you'll agree to stay out of mine.'

She'd changed over the years, her style evolving, more freckles covering her face, but her handshake was just as secure as ever.

My breath caught in my throat.

I found myself hoping, in a way that was deeply, *deeply* emotionally unhealthy, that instead of staying out of my way, she would throw herself into it. That she would break that third ceasefire with me, over and over again.

'You can let go of my hand now, Jonah,' Sadie said tersely. 'You're not going to intimidate me by trying to crush my bones to dust.'[9]

---

9   I can't remember precisely what I said next, but it was something along the lines of: 'If you're intimidated, that says more about you than it does about me, Shaw.' So this particular ceasefire lasted about three seconds.

Ceasefire #4 – Graduation (postgrad)
Four years ago

Sadie had moved into the share house because she was starting her own PhD and wanted to be close to campus. I'd started mine a solid eighteen months before her, but when I went part-time for a bit and then intermitted for a year so I could take up a prestigious but time-consuming (and soul-destroying) research assistance gig,[10] she caught up to me fairly quickly.

That meant two things:

1) We were competing *constantly*: for internal grant funding, teaching work, marking work, opportunities for research collaboration – literally everything.
2) Once again (inevitably, really) we graduated in the same ceremony.

'Fisher, I know we tried this last time and it went terribly,' Sadie said as we stood in front of the long mirror in the robing room beforehand, volunteers fussing around us and all the other graduands, making sure the satin linings of our doctoral hoods were draped appropriately, 'but can we be cool today?'

'You mean I have to scrap my plans to stand up when they read your name and announce that I have an objection like I'm Mr Briggs at Jane and Rochester's wedding?' I replied. 'Oh no.'

Sadie rolled her eyes. 'If you could stop your dad from declaring the existence of an impediment, that might be nice.'

She was being sarcastic, but her worries weren't entirely unjustified. My dad had made it very clear he had no respect whatsoever

---

10 I love a lengthy tangential footnote, but if I told the story of that particularly dark time in my academic career (working with that particularly awful scholar and his particularly awful other RA), there would be a whole horror novel down here.

for Sadie's research area, which was popular fiction. I dreaded it whenever he turned up to her sessions in the Higher Degree Research seminar series almost as much as when he turned up to mine. Professor Christian Fisher was the undisputed king of the passive-aggressive, long-winded, wire-barbed *this is more of a comment than a question.*

'If it's any consolation, he's got other people to be a dick to today,' I said. 'My siblings flew in for the ceremony. He'll be too busy bullying my brother Elias for not having a permanent academic job yet, and my sister Fiona for spoiling his three-kids-three-PhDs clean sweep.'

Sadie looked at me strangely.

'What?'

'So you *do* admit your dad's a dick.'

'Of course I admit my dad's a dick. I have eyes. Ears. The memory of growing up in his house.'

'Yet all the times he's come at me,' Sadie said, 'you haven't said a fucking word.'

'And make it look like you need some knight in shining armour to fight your battles for you? Of course I haven't said a fucking word.'

Sadie made a facial expression I couldn't quite read – a raising of the eyebrows, a quirk of the lips – but said nothing.

'Anyway,' I said, 'you hold your own against him perfectly well, Shaw. You don't need my help.'

I put my PhD bonnet on. It pushed the frames of my glasses uncomfortably into my ears. 'Is your sister going to object when they read out *my* name?'

'Chess promised she'd be on her best behaviour.'

'So a fifty-fifty chance, then?'

'About that, yes.' Sadie put her own bonnet on.

Then, to my surprise, her expression softened a little. 'I like that a doctorate isn't really something you can beat someone at, though,' she said. 'There's no, like, super-doctorate. No ultimate academic championship belt. Not today. There's just this.'

Her eyes met mine in the mirror as she gestured to our regalia. 'Today might be the first day in our whole careers that neither of us needs to try to win.'

Speak for yourself, the part of me that had grown up around the Fisher family dinner table wanted to say. *Don't get complacent*.

But I was an adult now.

'Congratulations, Dr Shaw,' I said.

Sadie smiled at me.

It wasn't the first time she had smiled at me. She had done that plenty of times, a predatory smile that said, *I have set a trap and you have fallen right into it, fool.*

It was the first time she had smiled at me like this, though – open, unguarded, warm.

'Congratulations, Dr Fisher.'

The tassel of her PhD bonnet was tangled in her hair. What might happen, I wondered, flexing my fingers, if I reached over and untangled it?

After the ceremony, when we had our testamurs in hand, my eyes met those of the newly minted Dr Sadie Shaw across the wine reception.

She raised her glass to me. I raised mine to her.

'Jonah, pay attention!' my dad snapped. 'I'm trying to help you network!'

He'd pulled over the Head of Humanities from one of the other Sydney-based universities, a man with immense power over staff hiring.

I saw the expression on Sadie's face change.

Her sister came up behind her and said something in her ear. Sadie replied. Chess's eyes flicked to me, and the venom in them was unmistakable. *Entitled prick from a line of entitled pricks,* I heard her snarl again.

I looked away.

And the next day, when Sadie and I ran into each other in the share house kitchen, everything was the same as it had always been, except now it was Dr Shaw and Dr Fisher fighting instead of Ms and Mr.

Ceasefire #5 – English 101
Two years ago

Here's a piece of advice about academia: if you're interested in secure and stable employment with career progression that pays you a living wage, don't go into it.[11] The year Sadie and I graduated, a grand total of five full-time permanent academic jobs in Literary Studies were advertised across the entire country. The next year, it was three. The year after that, four.

Between applying feverishly for these jobs, Sadie and I were working hard in the huge, amorphous body of scholars called the precariat.[12] We were cobbling together our respective livings through casual teaching gigs at as many universities as would have us, frequently competing for the same meagre hours, reapplying for the same work semester after semester. Before graduation, our PhD scholarships had provided a safety net.[13] Afterwards, getting casual work was quite literally a matter of survival.

---

11 Seriously. Don't.

12 Precariat (*n.*): an underclass of insecurely employed academics; too over-qualified to do anything else. (See also: 'sunk cost'.)

13 PhD scholarships are below the poverty line, but you can at least see it from there.

At ESU, our reputations preceded us, so we were only ever hired to teach into different units. Other Sydney-based universities, though, had no knowledge of our lengthy feud – which was how Bass University accidentally hired us to co-teach their big first-year core literary studies unit.

It was a huge deal. Casual staff didn't often get the opportunity to lecture, especially not to this many students, but the unit chair had got some big grant and all his teaching had been bought out for a few years. Sadie and I were hired to teach three seminars each and split the lecturing fifty-fifty.

'This is too big a payday for us to ruin by fighting,' I said, as we sat down at the share house kitchen table to plan our approach. 'Can we agree to be professional about this?'

'Firstly, don't patronise me,' Sadie said. 'Secondly, I'm always professional. You're the one who starts the fights.'

'That's not true and you know it.'

'Keep telling yourself that, Fisher. Let's just alternate lecture weeks. I'll take odds, you take evens.'

'Fine.'

That plan might have worked if we hadn't had to attend each other's lectures in order to maintain the continuity of the content. Sadie didn't like the way I framed Aeschylus's *Prometheus Bound* in my week two lecture, so at the beginning of her week three lecture, which was supposed to be on *Frankenstein*, she had a section entitled *Prometheus Bound: An Alternate Perspective*. I retaliated in week four, with *Another Look At Frankenstein*, and so it went on, the fifth ceasefire broken, week after week.

Oddly enough though, our repeated shattering of the ceasefire led to incredible student satisfaction ratings. Students could be cruel in end-of-unit surveys, but we got raves across the board. *Is it weird*

13

to say that I learnt more from Dr Shaw and Dr Fisher disagreeing with each other than anything else? one student wrote.

My favourite thing was watching Sadie during Jonah's lectures, another wrote. *She was practically vibrating with how badly she wanted to fight him. I kept waiting for her entrance music to hit, professional-wrestling style.*

We got hired back to co-teach English 101[14] for the next two years while the unit chair was on research leave – a very lucrative opportunity in the cut-throat world of the precariat. My dad had warned me multiple times that my feud with Sadie could be career-limiting – "you don't want your name associated in any way with *that* kind of scholar," he kept infuriatingly telling me – but it turned out he did not, in fact, know everything.

Ceasefire #6
Now

We were wrapping up our third and final year of teaching English 101 – and were thus about to be flung back headfirst into the endless knife-fight for teaching work that was casual academia – when the sixth ceasefire occurred.

It was the last day of October, which meant it was my thirty-second birthday. My father had called me earlier and told me[15] that he and my mother would be picking me up at seven and we would be going to dinner. 'And I mean seven, Jonah,' he said sharply. 'We don't have time for you to be late.'

I was supposed to be at a pretty crucial union meeting, but there was no point arguing with the man who had taught me how to argue. 'Yes Dad.'

---

14 Read: *make a complete farce of our ceasefire.*

15 My father never asks. He always tells.

I was ready and waiting in the living room by six forty-five, adjusting the cuffs of my shirt, when Sadie got home. 'Where are you off to?' she asked, glancing at me as she hung her keys on the hook marked 'S' by the door. 'You look like you're about to elbow some peasants aside to get into the last lifeboat on the Titanic.'

'Not your best insult. Low-hanging fruit. What happened at the union meeting?'

'If you'd bothered to turn up instead of getting all dressed up to go and grind the faces of the poor, you'd know.'

'Shaw.'

'What we all knew was going to happen.' Her tone was light, but I could see the tension in her jaw. 'More budget cuts. Casual jobs the first on the chopping block. A wonderfully bright future of unemployment for us all that the union probably won't be able to do shit about. What's so important that you couldn't come and hear the good news for yourself?' She gestured at my suit. 'Hot date?'

'Ha ha. Birthday dinner with my parents.'

Sadie rolled her eyes – possibly at my reason for not attending the union meeting, possibly a reflex at the invocation of my dad, probably both. 'Happy birthday.'

Before I could parse that there was a nice sentiment underneath the facial expression, she'd already disappeared down the hallway.

And let's be honest: it wasn't *that* nice. 'Happy birthday' is not the kind of phrase you have to put any effort into. It's inherently citational. It's always a quotation, reliant on such a distant echo of meaning that it practically means nothing.

It was still the nicest thing anyone said to me all night.

'Jonah?'

I looked up from where I was slumped over the kitchen table in the dark. I'd taken my glasses off, so the figure of Sadie standing in the doorway was blurry. She was backlit by the hall light, wearing pyjamas,[16] hair tied up in a topknot that was listing to the left, and she was holding her comically enormous tea mug, the one with the C.S. Lewis quote on the side that said, 'You can never get a cup of tea large enough or a book long enough to suit me.'

'Ignore me.' I went back to resting my forehead on my folded arms.

Her footsteps shuffled across the kitchen. Water ran. There was a click as she flicked the kettle on, a rustle as she found herself a teabag.

'You know you have a bedroom, right?'

I made a vague noise.

'Unless you're so broke you're subletting it. In which case, the rest of us have to sign off on that.'

The kettle started to boil, softly bubbling.

'And if you're that broke, surely your parents—'

'Don't.'

My tone was sharp, bordering on aggressive, but when I looked up, Sadie just raised an eyebrow. 'Birthday dinner went that well, huh?'

I put my head down again.

There was a gentle susurrus as she poured water into her mug, then a heavy clunk as she set it down on the kitchen table. 'Are you all right?'

I looked up again.

---

16 Even without my glasses, I could tell it was a pair she wore a lot: long, striped cotton pants and a dark blue camisole which clung to her collarbone in a way that— Never mind.

She was standing, one hand curled around the top of a chair. In the dim light, she was like an image from an old black-and-white movie, hair and eyes and clothes dark against her pale skin, my bad vision putting her in low resolution.

'No,' I said.

'Do you want a cup of tea? There's that disgusting ginger one you like.'

'No. Thank you.'

She paused. 'Do you want to talk about it?'

No, I should have said. I had spent fifteen years doing my level best never to show weakness to this woman. In that moment, I had no armour, no defences. I was nothing but an open, gaping wound.

'My family is poison,' I said. '*I'm* poison.'

She blinked.

'You can say *I told you so*,' I added bitterly.

She didn't.

Instead, Sadie sat down across from me. 'I know I devote the better part of my life to being a bitch to you, but surely you don't think I'm *that* bad.'

'This isn't a question of good or bad. It's a question of accurate and inaccurate. And in this case, *I told you so* would be extremely accurate.'

'Jonah, what happened?'

I sighed, reaching for my glasses and putting them back on. 'It's my sister.'

'The one who incurred the wrath of your dad by daring not to get a PhD?'

I stared. How did she remember that?

'I listen when you talk, Fisher,' Sadie said. 'How else am I supposed to dismantle your arguments?'

God. Her mind was a fucking steel trap. 'Yes. Fiona.'

I stood up, the intimacy of sitting across from her suddenly too much. 'When we got to the restaurant tonight, my dad argued with the sommelier for ten minutes over what bottle of wine to order.' I found my ginger teabags in the cupboard, topped up the kettle, and flicked it back on. 'Then he spent another five minutes mansplaining to my mother why she was wrong to want to order à la carte and that we should get the tasting menu. And then, just as the waiter was pouring the wine, my dad casually mentioned that Fiona's shithead husband Matt has left her for his secret second family and is refusing to pay any child support.'

It was too polite a way to say it, too euphemistic, too kind. *I hope things are looking up for you on the job market, Jonah,* my dad had said, swirling the wine in his glass, tasting it, making a face, but then eventually nodding in approval to the waiter. *Now Fiona's gone and ruined her life and come begging for money, we're not going to be able to catch you if you fall.*

What do you mean? I'd asked, mouth going suddenly dry. *What's happened to Fiona?*

'Oh, Jonah,' Sadie said.

'Fi had no idea.' The kettle started to boil. 'No clue at all that anything was wrong. Matt just sat her down one day and said, "Surprise, my investment bank actually *doesn't* need to fly me to Melbourne every week, I have another life and another wife and other kids there, and I like them more than you, bye."'

I just don't understand how she didn't realise, my father had said, after he'd interrupted my mother about twelve times as she tried to – considerably more sensitively – outline the story for me. *I know Fiona was never the brightest spark, but surely this kind of thing isn't that difficult to spot.*

'What a complete fucking arsehole,' Sadie said.

I choked on a sound somewhere between a laugh and a sob as

the kettle boiled. 'Thank you for being the first person to have an appropriate reaction to the situation.'

'What other reaction is there?' She got up, took the kettle out of my shaking hands, and poured hot water into my mug for me. 'Your poor sister. Is she okay?'

'I don't know.'

'What do you mean, you don't know?'

'She didn't tell me.' I took my mug from her and put it back down on the kitchen table, almost collapsing into my chair. 'This is how I found out what happened. From my dad making some offhand comment about money. Fi hasn't said a fucking thing to me.'

I had never seen Sadie Shaw lost for words before. Anything I had ever said to her – anything *anyone* had ever said to her – she had a response to. This, though, her brilliant mind couldn't seem to even remotely compute.

'I tried to call Fi as soon as I got home, but she didn't answer,' I said. 'Which isn't surprising, I guess. She's got three kids, and they can be a handful. She'd probably already collapsed in exhaustion.'

That was what I was telling myself, anyway. What if Fiona was staring at my name on her phone screen, worrying that I was calling to rub it in? To tell her that she deserved this somehow?

'What about your brother?' Sadie sat back down across from me. 'Did she tell him?'

'I haven't been able to get hold of him yet – he's on a fellowship in Germany – but I don't think so.'

Elias, at least, would have told me if he knew. Wouldn't he?

Sadie let out a long breath. 'If anything like this ever happened to me, I would go running to Chess so fast there would be scorch marks on the ground. Why hasn't she told you?'

'Because my family is absolutely fucking *fucked*, Shaw.'

I rubbed my hand over my beard, hoping that the room was dark enough, and my glasses were disguise enough, that she wouldn't see the tears beading in the corners of my eyes. 'Elias and Fiona and I aren't like you and your sister. We don't— We aren't— Sometimes I'm so fucking jealous of you, did you know that?'

Sadie raised an eyebrow.

'I know, I know. I sound exactly like a poor little rich kid. Fuck, I *am* a poor little rich kid. But . . . you remember our first graduation? When your sister got into it with my dad?'

'Of course I remember. I was so embarrassed I didn't think I'd be able to look you in the eye ever again.'

She'd been *embarrassed*? That was new information – and a concept I wasn't even remotely in the right headspace to process.

'Well, I was jealous,' I said. 'Because my siblings and I were raised to fight each other, not fight *for* each other. There's not a person on this planet who would fight for me the way Chess did for you.'

I wrapped my fingers around my mug. 'The very first thing I ever learned was how to argue,' I said. 'Dad drilled it into all three of us. There was this game he used to play at dinner – if one of us expressed some kind of opinion, he'd point at another one of us and say 'devil's advocate!' and we wouldn't be allowed to leave the table until we'd debated it out. Fighting each other was like our family sport.'

I took a long sip of tea, but it didn't help the lump growing in my throat. 'Fiona was the only one who ever resisted. Sometimes, when Dad pointed at her, she'd just say no and walk away. And sometimes she tried to protect me, too. She's three years older than me, and . . .'

I swallowed reflexively. I'd only been seven when my dad took my teddy bear away and told me I could have it back when I'd constructed a persuasive enough argument as to why I needed it.

I'd been completely distraught, but he'd been unmoved (*tears, Jonah,* he'd said, *do not constitute a thesis statement*).

Then two days later, Fiona had materialised in my bedroom in the dead of night. *Here,* she'd whispered, handing me my bear. *I stole him back for you. Find a better hiding place for him than Dad did, okay?*

'She tried to protect me,' I repeated, 'but when she needed me to support her, I turned my back on her instead.'

'How?' Sadie asked. 'What did you do?'

'Let's just say that I was really, *really* unsupportive of her decision to get married.'

I remembered vividly what it had been like when Fiona announced she was dropping out of uni, moving to Tasmania, and marrying an older man. My mother – who was normally quiet and deferential – had snapped, calling her decision stupid and shortsighted. My father had agreed, saying that a choice this foolish made her worse than a failure. Elias had just shaken his head and said, *come on, Fi, don't be an idiot.*

Then Fiona had looked at me.

She was making a terrible decision. I, eighteen years old and newly enamoured of university life, was very confident in that. But she'd just had three other people tell her that exact thing. She didn't need to hear it again.

Yet instead of having her back, I'd cocked my chin, looked her in the eye, and said, *can you explain why this* isn't *the worst choice anyone has ever made in the history of the world?*

Fiona had looked back at me for a long moment, and then turned on her heel and walked out the door.

It wasn't like we'd been on bad terms in the fourteen years since. I'd been a groomsman at her wedding. I sent presents to her kids on their birthdays and chatted to them on Zoom sometimes.

We'd spent some perfectly acceptable family Christmases together. I loved my sister.

But something had broken between me and Fiona that day, something that had never, ever been repaired.

'Sounds like you were right about that,' Sadie remarked, 'given how her marriage ended.'

'Being right's not the point, though.'

Sadie blinked, clearly surprised. I didn't blame her. That wasn't a sentence I ever expected to come out of my mouth either.

'No wonder Fi didn't tell me about Matt leaving,' I said numbly. 'She wouldn't have thought there'd be any point. That I'd just laugh and say *I told you so* and make her feel worse than she already does.'

I took off my glasses and scrubbed my hand over my eyes. 'And when I think of her all on her own in Hobart,' I said, voice hoarse, 'so alone, so isolated, having everything me and my family ever said about her marriage be proven right – having to crawl to my fucking arsehole of a dad for money so she can look after her kids . . .'

I had to stop. The lump in my throat was so large it was making me feel almost nauseous. My eyes were burning with all the tears I was trying not to shed. I was on the verge of completely falling apart.

And Sadie Shaw, the woman who had devoted the better part of her life to breaking me?

This blessed woman just leaned back in her chair, eyeballed me, and with a tone as dry as a desert said, 'So what I'm hearing is that this isn't the greatest birthday you've ever had.'

My laugh was so sudden it surprised me, like she'd reached past my conscious mind and pulled it straight out of my body. 'You know what? I don't think either of my parents even remembered to wish me happy . . . What are you doing?'

Sadie was on her feet, reaching on tiptoes to grab a mug from a cupboard that was slightly too high for her, and then disappearing into the pantry. 'No one should have a birthday that shit, Fisher. Even you.'

She emerged with flour, cocoa and sugar under one arm. The flour bag hadn't been sealed properly, and there was a white smudge of it on her camisole. 'The eggs in the fridge are yours, right? Can I use one?'

'What for?'

She took that as a yes. 'Chess used to make this for me when I was growing up, whenever I had a shitty day. It's the epitome of cheap and cheerful. It's not going to be up to your *Superchef* standards, but you should have at least a little bit of cheer on your birthday.'

Sadie poured the ingredients into the mug, mixed vigorously, then put it into the microwave. The proportions were definitely wrong, but I bit my tongue. 'This really isn't necessary,' I said instead.

'Shut up, Jonah. Let me be nice to you for a second.'

'You're never nice to me.'

'It's your birthday. There's a special provision in the treaty.'

'Really?'

'There's also a special provision for talking shit about your dad. I'm happy to do that whenever you want. *Whenever.*'

I was treated to a flash of her brilliant smile before the microwave dinged. 'I'm not sure it's all the way cooked, but that's fine,' she said, wobbling the mug experimentally. 'I always liked them a bit under anyway. More of a gooey centre.'

She set it down in front of me, along with a spoon. She'd made me a chocolate mug cake, rising lopsidedly out of the mug, listing to the left, just like her topknot.

The lump swelled anew in my throat. The only person who had ever done anything even remotely like this for me before was Fiona.

'Go on, then, eat,' Sadie said, sitting back down, as casually as if she were sitting opposite any of our other housemates. 'If you're waiting for me to sing "Happy Birthday", you're going to be waiting a long fucking time.'

'Good,' I managed to say. 'I've heard you singing in the shower. I definitely don't need a private show.'

'You should be so lucky.'

I took a bite of the cake. I'd been right about her mixing up the proportions. There was way too much cocoa, way too little sugar, and it was incredibly bitter. 'This is delicious,' I said. 'Thank you.'

Sadie eyeballed me for a few seconds before she reached across the table. She didn't hold her hand out for me to shake, like she had during some of our other ceasefires. Instead, she laid it on top of mine, her palm warm against my knuckles.

'Truce?' she asked.

I turned my hand over so we were palm to palm, my fingers loosely clasped around hers.

'Truce,' I said. 'Thank you, Sadie. Tonight . . . You . . . Thank you for listening.'

'You're welcome.'

She squeezed my hand gently, in a way that made it feel like her fingers were closed around my heart. 'I know I'm probably the last person you'd ask for help, given our history, but if there's anything I can do to help your sister . . . well, I've got a soft spot for sisters.'

'Thank you.'

She squeezed my fingers again. I was terrified, suddenly, that she might let go.

'I don't want to fight anymore, Sadie,' I said. 'I know academia pits us against each other all the time – that we pit ourselves against each other all the time – but I don't want to do that anymore.'

For a long time, she was silent.

'I've been fighting for so long I'm not sure I know how to stop,' she said, 'but I'll try if you will.'

And so our sixth ceasefire was forged, the one I thought would be our last. The final binding agreement between Dr Sadie Shaw and Dr Jonah Fisher. The contract we would never break, a mature end to our immature rivalry, the tentative beginnings of something that might one day become a friendship. White flags waving. Weapons down.

The job was listed the next day.

NOVEMBER

Chapter One

Sadie

I wrote my PhD thesis on a concept called eucatastrophe.

People always think I spent a bunch of years wallowing in something really depressing when they hear this, but nothing could be further from the truth. Eucatastrophes are *good* catastrophes.

The term was coined by J.R.R. Tolkien in a lecture called 'On Fairy-Stories', which he gave in Scotland in 1939. The first time I read it, it struck a chord deep inside me that never really stopped thrumming.

Eucatastrophe, in Tolkien's words, is 'the good catastrophe, the sudden joyous "turn"'. In mine, it's the moment in a story where, when it seems like all is lost, that things are going to be awful forever, that the only possible endings are full of misery and despair, *something good happens*.

My favourite example of eucatastrophe comes from one of my most beloved childhood books. An enterprising school librarian had seen me, a disadvantaged little redheaded girl who loved books and learning, and pressed *Anne of Green Gables* into my hands. I loved it so much I cried when I had to return it, so Chess, then in her early teens, had begged, borrowed and eventually stolen to get me a boxset of all the *Anne* books from the school book fair.

I loved and treasured them all, but the third book was my favourite: *Anne of the Island*, the one where Anne goes away to university. Near the end of the book (spoilers, sorry, but this book came out in 1915) it's revealed that Gilbert Blythe, Anne's one-time-rival/eventual-friend/sort-of-ex-because-she-rejected-him-earlier, is dying of typhoid.

And Anne has a horrible, awful realisation. She is in love with this man – and now she's going to lose him.

The next morning, steeling herself for the worst possible news, Anne tremulously asks how Gilbert is.

Gilbert is better. His fever broke. He's not going to die after all.

Eucatastrophe.

I can remember the first time I read this so clearly. I was nine years old, sitting on my bed in the late afternoon in the tiny bedroom I shared with then-fourteen-year-old Chess. I started tearing up when Anne found out Gilbert was dying, but I tried to keep quiet – Chess was sitting on her own bed, studying, and I didn't want to disturb her.

But then Anne found out Gilbert wasn't going to die and I couldn't help it – I burst into tears.

'What's wrong?' Chess was beside me in an instant, her text-books hitting the floor.

'Nothing,' I sobbed. 'It's just—it's just so—'

'It's just so what?'

'It's just so *nice*!'

It took half a second for Chess to put her arms around me, a full second for her to start laughing. 'You scared me to death,' she said. 'Next time you start crying, can you send me some sort of signal that it's just because of a book?'

There were lots of very solid, serious, scholarly explanations as to why I wrote about eucatastrophe in my PhD thesis, but the real reason was that I'd been chasing the feeling I'd had that day ever since: that euphoric moment of joyous relief; that sense that for once, finally, things were going *right*; that sunbeam penetrating the darkness.

I had grown up in that darkness. I had grown up trapped. There were only two things standing between me and the grim realities of a terminally ill mother, an absent-at-best father and crushing poverty: my sister and my books.

Outside the pages of those books, there had been no eucatastrophe for Chess and me, no sudden joyous turn. There had only been a series of long, slow battles. Our mother's against her illness, until she died. Ours, against our father, until he finally stopped coming back. Chess's, to succeed in corporate law, to ensure that we never, ever experienced that kind of poverty again.

And mine, to carve out a career in academia, one of the most competitive and cut-throat industries in the world – and to do it by studying the books that had been my escape, even though a huge percentage of the scholars in my field had no respect for them at all.

It was a battle that, in recent times, I'd started to accept I was going to lose.

It had been years since I'd graduated, and yet I felt like I'd made no progress. I'd published a monograph and a lot of articles and book chapters, and for now, I was managing to find enough teaching work to survive semester to semester, but I was still stuck, stagnating, in the precariat. I was making no progress at all towards anything real, anything solid, anything that would *last*.

There were hardly any permanent academic jobs advertised in Literary Studies, but every time one came up, I applied. I'd only made it to one interview. I thought it had gone well, but then, when they emailed me my rejection, one line jumped out immediately: *your research into popular fiction, while strong, does not fit within our current programme.* I might be a good scholar – a brilliant one, even – but it didn't matter at all if no one respected my object of study.

I kept marching forward. One thing I had never managed to learn was how to surrender.

But no matter how hard I worked – no matter how hard I fought – no matter how many union campaigns I was a part of – it was becoming clearer and clearer that this march I was on was Sisyphean. No universities were hiring. They were all firing – and casual academics like me were always the first to be sacrificed. I could fling myself into the boulder as hard as I liked, but there was no way to stop it from crashing back down on me.

I had just about admitted to myself that it was over, that despite all the years and years I'd sunk into becoming a scholar I was going to have to find another career path for myself—

And then the job was listed.

My heart only leapt a little when I saw the ad in the university jobs email digest: *Lyons University, Lecturer in Literary Studies, Level B, permanent, full-time.* I was too wise and too weary to hope too hard.

But then, when I saw the desired research specialisations, a blinding wave of joy hit me. *The successful candidate will have expertise in one or more of the following areas: modernist literature, early modern drama, popular fiction.*

The tears welled up in my eyes. I blinked them away so I could check I hadn't read it wrong, that this wasn't a hallucination caused by wishful thinking.

Popular fiction.

The sob escaped me before I could cover my mouth, a loud, choked sound, embarrassingly high-pitched. I grabbed a pillow off my bed and bit down on it, so none of my housemates would hear me low-key having a breakdown.

There's a line in 'On Fairy-Stories' that I love so much I got it tattooed on my foot. Eucatastrophe, Tolkien writes, gives us a glimpse of a joy so powerful it's mythic: *'Joy beyond the walls of the world, poignant as grief.'*

Sometimes, even though it seems all but certain, Gilbert Blythe *doesn't* die.

Sometimes, the ad for your dream job wants someone with your ironically unpopular specialisation.

Sometimes, despite all the odds, *something good happens*.

It took me a while to compose myself after that first ecstatic white-hot moment of hope, but eventually, I took some deep breaths and sat back down in front of my laptop, telling myself to be sensible. The job ad might be asking for a popular fiction specialist, but I was far from the only one of those in the world. Some other Sadie was probably sitting in some other bedroom in some other share house, screaming into *their* pillow at the thought that their dream might not be dead.

There's another word that Tolkien coins in 'On Fairy-Stories': dyscatastrophe. That one actually does mean what it sounds like. If eucatastrophe is the good catastrophe, dyscatastrophe is the bad one.

The first hint of dyscatastrophe came when I clocked where Lyons University actually was: Hobart. If I got this job, I'd have to leave Sydney.

That was all right, though. I'd always known that if I was going to get a permanent academic job, I'd probably have to move. And it wasn't like I had much keeping me here. I had friends, sure, but I worked so much that those bonds were tied pretty loosely, even though I lived in the same house as most of them. Really, the only person in my life I absolutely couldn't live without was Chess, and she had money now. She could visit whenever she wanted.

Still. The thought of moving hurt more than I thought it would. I rubbed my chest absently.

I read through the selection criteria again. PhD in a relevant discipline: yes. Excellent teaching record, including curriculum design: yes. Strong publication record: yes (I'd tried to combat the bias against popular fiction studies by taking the academic maxim 'publish or perish' very, *very* seriously).

Expertise in one or more of the following areas: modernist literature, early modern drama, popular fiction.

It was still there. It still said *popular fiction*.

But I'd been so excited by that – so automatically drawn to those words – that I'd hadn't processed the other desired specialisations.

Early modern drama. The exact research specialisation of my nemesis. The man I had only last night agreed to stop fighting with.

I owed more to Dr Jonah Fisher than I would ever, *ever* admit. There were a few reasons for this – pride, for one – but primarily, it was because my debt to him wasn't rooted in anything he'd done for me, exactly. It was what he meant. What 'Fisher' stood for, in the grand narrative of the universe of Sadie Shaw.

It's hard to fight a battle when your enemy is amorphous, nameless, faceless. You can't defeat something you can't see.

And when, in a first-year poetry seminar, a boy with scruffy dark hair and thick-framed glasses and the beginnings of a beard had disagreed with my reading of Wordsworth's 'To Joanna', not backing down even a little when I fought back, he became the face of my enemy.

Ugh, Chess had said to me, turning the fan on our rickety table towards me when I told her about it that evening, sweltering in the shitty little un-airconditioned granny flat we'd been sharing since our mother died. *Fucking privileged little private school boys. They're a plague in the law faculty. They think they know everything.*

I don't think anyone's ever told him he's wrong a day in his life, I'd replied, wiping the sweat off my brow with the back of my hand.

That, I would learn several years later, listening to Professor Fisher eviscerate Jonah in a PhD seminar, was not even remotely the correct reading of his family dynamic.

But symbols were powerful. Jonah had been the face of everything I was fighting against for too long for me to change my mind. And besides, even if his dad told him he was wrong every single day of his life, Jonah was still his father's son. Professor Fisher certainly wasn't introducing *me* – whose research he had once described, to my face, as 'specious, frivolous and pointless', centred on 'a childish interpretation of deus ex machina' – to any senior academics who could offer me work.

Jonah Fisher was my yardstick. He was my benchmark. If I could keep pace with him, then there was still a chance that I could make it in academia. The fact that he too – with all his privilege and connections and acceptably 'literary' area of study – was still insecurely employed and living in a share house in his thirties was one of the few things that let me keep hoping.

Jonah Fisher, though, was also a person.

I wasn't sure exactly when I'd started to divide him into two different people in my mind, but it had crystallised at our PhD graduation, when he'd casually revealed that *of course* he knew his dad was a terrible nightmare person who made a habit of being deeply and offensively unfair to me – and that the reason he had never pushed back was that he didn't want to undermine me.

Anyway, you hold your own against him perfectly well, Shaw, he'd said casually, adjusting his doctoral bonnet in the mirror, like he wasn't forcing me to fundamentally reconsider his place in my personal universe. *You don't need my help.*

So now there were two Jonahs. Tweed Jonah and Cardigan Jonah.

Tweed Jonah was the symbol of everything I was fighting against. The institutional privilege of the ivory tower, determined to keep me and my specious, frivolous, pointless, childish research out.

Cardigan Jonah, though, was the human. The one I'd lived with for years now, and who, despite the fact we argued about *everything*, might not actually be that bad.

That's who I'd sat with, in the darkness of the kitchen. The least tweedy, most extremely cardigan version of Jonah there was. The Jonah who loved his sister, the most relatable, humanising emotion in the world to me. That was who I had agreed not to fight with anymore.

But now there was this job ad – which could not be more perfectly designed to pit us against each other, more bitterly than ever.

✏

It was unrealistic of me to hope that he hadn't seen the job ad, but . . . well, I've never really been a huge fan of realism.

My hope was shattered almost immediately. It was always going to be, given how many early career researchers lived in our share house. 'Jonah!' Van said jovially, as the man in question walked into the kitchen later that night. 'You saw the Lyons ad, right?'

Jonah set his satchel down and got himself a water glass. He had to reach past me – I was standing at the stove cooking myself dinner – and his sleeve gently brushed against my ear, the merest whisper of a touch. 'I saw.'

'That's only the third Lit Studies job that's come up this year, right?' Van said.

'Second,' Jonah and I said at the same time.

Involuntarily, I glanced at him. He must have had the same reflex, because he met my eyes, offering me a tight, profoundly joyless smile. It was a Tweed Jonah smile, one he'd given me a million times before, a smile which usually meant *there is no socially appropriate way for me to say this at present but please know that everything you are saying is wrong.*

'What do you think of the location?' Van asked. 'Tassie's pretty far away.'

'I'd move,' I said.

'My sister Fiona lives in Hobart,' Jonah said. 'So I'd quite like to move there, actually.'

Oh *fuck me.*

And I thought *I'd* had a moment of eucatastrophe. When Jonah had seen the ad and realised that not only did they want someone with his specialisation, not only was it hundreds of kilometres away from his awful dad, but it was in the same city as his sister – his newly-abandoned sister, the one he was desperate to mend his relationship with! – he must have just about died with happiness.

Had he experienced a moment of dyscatastrophe too, when he'd realised that 'popular fiction' was hiding there behind 'early modern drama'? Anger? Frustration, maybe, that his annoying upstart redhead nemesis was going to fight him for something *again*, or—

'I think that's burning, Sadie,' Jonah said.

I took the pan off the stove moments before my dinner became entirely unsalvageable. 'Just because you're better at cooking than me doesn't mean I want a lecture on it,' I said tightly, putting it into a bowl and leaving the kitchen as quickly as I could, because I didn't want to look at him.

In my room, I opened my laptop and pulled up the selection criteria again. I took a bite of my barely edible chicken stir-fry and started ranking myself against Tweed Jonah.

PhD: even. We'd held that degree exactly as long as each other.

Teaching record: probably even. There was a time when I would have awarded the point to myself – my enthusiastic embrace of popular culture meant I had a reputation as Not A Regular Teacher, A Cool Teacher – but seeing the student surveys from English 101 at Bass had made me understand that Jonah had his own appeal. I might be the cool one, but he – with the glasses and the dark hair always falling in his eyes and the beard and the apparently endless collection of knitwear – looked like the archetypal hot young English professor from every student's dark academia fantasy.

Strong publication record: probably also even. I'd published more overall, but he'd published in higher-ranked journals – not that I hadn't tried, but Shakespeare and friends were a much easier sell to the establishment journals than my work. If he'd kept dragging his heels on turning his PhD thesis into a monograph I might have had him – mine, *Joy Poignant as Grief: Reading Popular Fiction in Interesting Times*, had come out fairly quickly after our graduation – but his, *No Hate Lost Between Us: Relationships on the Jacobean Stage*, had been published about a year ago, and already had the same number of citations as mine.

Not that I checked or anything. I definitely didn't have any Google Scholar alerts set up.

Expertise in modernism, early modern drama or popular fiction: even. Obviously.

I probably had him on the criterion about impact and engagement – I was a fairly regular media commentator on romance and fantasy fiction. He had me on the criterion about grant income, though – he'd taken an intermission during his PhD to do a research assistantship, and it had landed him a spot on a research team that won a major national grant.

The last criterion was 'proven ability to establish good working relationships with colleagues'.

Ha fucking ha.

Well, at least we were even on that one too.

I ate the last bite of burnt chicken. When it came down to it, there was only one thing on which we were not even.

But also, when it came down to it . . . it was a pretty big thing.

'No,' Chess said to me the next night. 'No, no, no, no, no. Absolutely not, Sadie.'

'It's his *sister*, though. How am I meant to look past that?'

'*No*.'

She swallowed a mouthful (a perfectly cooked, unburnt mouthful. I went round to Chess's apartment in North Sydney twice a week for dinner, and she always ordered something delicious from somewhere expensive). 'This is not something you're seriously considering.'

'How can I not consider it?'

I took a long sip of my wine (also delicious: Chess's love of wine had started out as a way to accrue cultural capital in the fancy law firm she worked for, but now it was just a genuine love of wine). 'Who does it make me? If I sit there and listen to him tell me that awful story about his sister, and then the perfect opportunity comes along for him to be able to go and help her out, and I say, "no, actually, that's mine, I'm taking that"?'

'Sadie,' Chess said, 'do you want this job?'

'Of course I do, but—'

'Are you qualified for this job?'

'Yes, but—'

'Do you deserve this job?'

'Yes, but—'

'Has the clause after "but" in your last three yeses been some version of "but so does he"?'

'No.'

Chess raised her eyebrows.

'But so does he,' I said, 'and a bajillion other people. There are far, *far* more people with PhDs than there are jobs. That's one of the reasons the academic job market is so fucked.'

'Forget about the bajillion other people. You're not considering throwing away this dream opportunity for them, are you?'

'No,' I admitted.

'Who has everything on his side? The privilege? The connected daddy? The more academically acceptable specialisation?'

I sighed. 'Jonah.'

'Given all this, if another job came up, who would stand a better chance at getting it?'

'He would. But it's *this* job, Chessie. In Hobart. Where his sister lives. There are only two universities in Tasmania, and—'

'How would you feel,' Chess said, holding a finger up, 'if you didn't apply for this job, which has your name written all over it, so he could sail in and take it – and then he didn't get it?'

That answer was easy. 'Gutted.'

'What about if he did get it?'

I bit my lip, trying to imagine a world where Jonah had moved on, ascended to the higher plane of secure employment, and left me behind.

'You would feel like he beat you,' Chess said, 'and you didn't even put up a fight.'

She tapped her fingernail against the table. 'You're a fighter, sweetie – and you're not going to give up now.'

There had been something liquid in Jonah's eyes when he'd sat across from me in the kitchen. *I don't want to fight anymore, Sadie,* he'd said, his fingers tight around mine.

I've been fighting for so long I'm not sure I know how to stop, I'd replied, *but I'll try if you will.*

I was both a truth-teller and a liar. I didn't know how to stop fighting. And I wasn't going to try.

'No,' I said, on a long exhale. 'Of course I'm not going to give up.'

'Of course you're not,' Chess repeated. 'And you never were.'

She leant back in her chair, swirling the wine in her glass. 'If you were seriously considering not applying, you never would have told me about the job in the first place. The whole reason you laid out this dilemma for me was because you knew there was no way I would let you self-sabotage.'

Not for the first time, I thought about how other lawyers must feel when they came up against Francesca Shaw. They must be absolutely fucking terrified.

'This is what you've always wanted,' she continued. 'This is what you've been working for, all these years. And if you think I'm going to let some skinny little private school boy take it away from you because his sister is sad . . . well, I know you're smarter than that.'

'It's his sister, though. His *sister.*'

Chess reached across the table and took my hand. She, of all people, knew why Jonah's story had affected me so much.

But then, 'I don't care how sad his sister is,' she said. 'If he – or she – or anyone – makes you get in your own way, I'll have them assassinated.'

There's not a person on this planet, Cardigan Jonah had said heavily, voice hoarse and throaty, *who would fight for me the way Chess did for you.*

'I love you, Chessie,' I whispered.

She squeezed my fingers. 'You too, sweetie. To the end of the universe and back again.'

Then she let go. For all that Chess was a bulldozer, she knew exactly where the lines were – specifically, the lines that, if she bulldozed past them, would make me cry. 'So that's sorted,' she said briskly, topping up our wine glasses. 'Did you bring me any new books?'

'Of course I did.'

I reached under the table for my bag. Every time I came around to Chess's for dinner, I brought her a couple of new romance novels, sourced from my extensive network of online second-hand bookshops. Chess loved romances – I wasn't the only Shaw sister to enjoy it when things turned out all right in the end – but she had stringent requirements that made her difficult to cater to. There was a fairly detailed list of tropes and plot points she point-blank refused to tolerate.

'I'm going to pre-warn you that these two are pushing it a bit,' I told her. 'But there are valid reasons for their inclusion in the Francesca Shaw collection.'

Chess narrowed her eyes and took another sip of wine. 'I'm listening.'

'This one,' I slid *A Marvellous Light* by Freya Marske across the table, 'is probably going to make you have some contract law feelings.'

The first romance trope that Chess just Could Not with was problematic paperwork. Her lawyer brain simply did not allow her to move past things like 'sex contracts that people apparently definitely have to stick to *or else*' or 'wills that mean two people have to cohabitate for a year or else risk losing their inheritance'.

If I ever write a romance novel, it's going to be about a lawyer who goes around getting people out of these contracts, she'd told me once, at one of our boozier dinners. *She'll charge through the nose and she'll barely have to work, because none of this is in any way legally enforceable so it'll only take her, like, two minutes per client.*

Who will the love interest be? I'd asked.

She'd stopped, wine almost sloshing over the rim of the glass she'd been waving around. *I haven't thought about that part yet.*

Chess picked up the book and examined it suspiciously, like it was an envelope that had a strong chance of containing anthrax.

'But it's a magical contract,' I said. 'It's set in Edwardian London, but, like, magical Edwardian London. Given the world of magic presumably has a whole other legal and judicial system, I'm hoping you can suspend your disbelief, because this book is so good.'

She pursed her lips. 'If you say so.'

I slid *Lovelight Farms* by B.K. Borison across the table. 'This one is fake dating, but—'

'No,' Chess groaned.

Chess hated fake-dating books. We'd had many, *many* conversations about realism and how it wasn't always the most useful barometer when reading romance, but something about fake dating completely set her off. *This is the least sensible way to solve your problems,* she'd said to me the last time I'd given her a fake-dating book. *I can think of at least forty-seven better ways these two* – she'd smacked the book so hard I thought I saw it flinch – *could have solved their problem than pretending to be in a relationship.*

I told Chess pretty much everything, but one thing I'd kept carefully hidden from her was the existence of Goodreads. If she ever took to writing reviews, she would definitely make some people cry.

43

'Why are you doing this to me, Sadie?' she asked.

'I wouldn't give you this book if I didn't think you'd like it,' I replied. 'It's fake dating, sure, but it's so cute and it absolutely works.'

She narrowed her eyes. 'What problem are they trying to solve by fake dating at it?'

'I'm not going to tell you. Spoilers.'

'You're lucky I love you,' she grumbled, taking the book from me. 'The things I do for you. Honestly.'

It was a deeply unserious exchange, but it made me think about Jonah again. If he loved his sister even a fraction as much as I loved Chess, how far would he go to get this job?

Later that night, sitting in front of my computer, the selection criteria open in front of me again, my gigantic tea mug full, I was still thinking about it.

I had every right to apply for this job.

I was *going* to apply for this job.

Chess was right. I had fought too hard for too long. With all the budget cuts going on, I wasn't going to be able to survive much longer in the brutal world of the precariat: it wasn't like I could just wait around for the next job listing. And on top of that, opportunities like this – ones where they actually *wanted* popular fiction specialists – were so rare that if I threw it away, I would almost certainly be throwing away my last chance at an academic career.

I was not going to do that. Not for anyone. Jonah – every version of him, tweed, cardigan, symbolic, human or otherwise – was going to have to fight really fucking hard if he wanted to rip this job out from under me.

But if it had been Chess in Fiona Fisher's shoes – if it had been my sister, abandoned a thousand kilometres away, alone, vulnerable, hurting – and this wonderful, golden, eucatastrophic opportunity had appeared in front of me . . .

I would burn the whole world down before I let anyone get in my way.

Chapter Two

Jonah

My brother Elias was surprised – to put it mildly – when I emailed him to ask for help with my job application. I'm happy to provide feedback on your draft, but I'm not sure why you're asking me, he replied. I don't work in your field.

You're a historian, I sent back. That's close enough. And you're clearly good at job applications. This is your fifth fellowship now, right?

Still no closer to an actual permanent job, though. Why not ask Dad?

Because he has no idea what the current job market is like and he refuses to learn.

This was true. When my dad got his job, back when dinosaurs roamed the earth, he had one (1) scholarly article on his CV. I had tried to explain to him many times that the academic job market worked differently now, but his belief in Shut Up, It's Not That Bad, You're Just Not Trying Hard Enough was practically religious.

It wasn't the only reason, though.

My dad might not appreciate what it was like, being on the modern academic job market, but he'd sat on a lot of hiring committees.[17] He could help me write a killer application.

---

17 Don't ask me about the cognitive dissonance this must require, because I can't explain it.

But it would be one more thing that I had that Sadie didn't.[18]

And much as I wanted – *needed* – this job, and much as the thought of being in the same city as Fiona so I could finally be a halfway decent brother to her had made it feel like a divine sunbeam was shining down on me when I saw the job ad, I couldn't do that to her.

I don't want to fight anymore, I'd said, and I'd meant it. It might already be too late, but in case it wasn't, I didn't want to be the kind of man my father was.

'I'm going to be blunt with you,' Elias said, when we Zoomed to discuss my application. 'Do you even want this job?'

I blinked. 'Of course I do. Fi—'

'Forget Fi.'

'What the fuck do you mean, *forget Fi*?'

Elias sighed. 'I didn't mean it like that. But a sob story isn't going to get you this job, Jonah. *My sister's piece of shit husband left her high and dry for his secret second family* isn't going to do anything for a hiring committee that want to know how your research will count towards their metrics and how much external income you have the capacity to bring in. And the draft you sent me is, frankly, weak and unconvincing.'

'Thanks, Reviewer 2.'

'If you want this job, you don't need me to coddle you. The job market doesn't care about your feelings. The job market is a gladiatorial arena.'

I sighed. 'I know.'

'I know you know. How many jobs have you been shortlisted for?'

---

18 Okay, sure, Sadie also didn't have a brother in academia, but given a) Elias was yet to secure a permanent academic position despite years of trying, and b) she *did* have a terrifying sister, the scales on that one felt a bit better balanced.

'Three.'

'Then you must be able to sell yourself better than this. So, answer the question: do you even want this job?'

I sighed again. There was a feeling settling in the pit of my stomach, a complex concoction in which the two primary ingredients were guilt and exhaustion. 'I've told you about Sadie before, right?'

'The name sounds familiar. Was she the girl in your PhD programme that Dad hated?'

'It's more complicated than that.'

And I spilled the whole story. The years of rivalry, punctuated by only a few ceasefires. All the things I had that she didn't. The way her research specialisation – the one that Dad made a habit of dunking on, every chance he got – lurked there in the job ad, right after mine.

The promise we'd made, my hand in hers across the kitchen table. *I don't want to fight anymore.*

Elias was quiet for a long time when I was finished – so much so I thought the screen had frozen and I'd just been spilling my feelings to thin air.

But then, 'She's your Julia,' he said.

'Julia?'

'You're not the first Fisher to have a nemesis.'

Elias ran a hand through his hair. 'I lost a job to her, seven or eight years back. The same kind of job you're going for: Level B, permanent, full-time. At Lyons, actually.'

I stared.

'And I lost it because she got in my fucking head,' he said, pointing at me through the screen. 'Now it's years later, and I'm still bouncing around the world on whatever fellowships I can find, no closer to any kind of security.'

And if he hadn't lost it, Elias would be living in Hobart. Fiona would have someone. Fishers might be terrible siblings, but at least she wouldn't be alone.

I didn't want to fight anymore.

But I had to. I couldn't let Sadie get in my head, not if I wanted to help Fi.

'I know my claims in the application are under-evidenced,' I said. 'Do you have any suggestions for how I can beef them up?'

I submitted the application the day before the deadline. *Never wait until the last day*, Elias had counselled me. *You know how shit university IT systems are; you never know when they'll have an outage.*

'You get your app in?' I dared to ask Sadie when she came into the kitchen as I was cooking dinner.[19] We hadn't spoken more than ten words to each other since the job was listed, but something about hitting *submit* had given me hope that maybe – just maybe – we could return to the terms of the sixth ceasefire, if only for a little while.

'Yes,' she said shortly. 'You?'

Well, that hope was short-lived.

'Yes.'

She nodded – an acknowledgement, nothing more – then took her gardening gloves off the hook next to the kitchen door and slid her feet into her gumboots.

'Good luck,' I said.

'I'm going to work in the veggie patch, not off to war.'

---

19 As a general rule, the more I was trying to paper over my feelings, the more complicated recipes I attempted. Consequently, that day I was making Beef Wellington. For one.

'No, I mean—' She knew perfectly well what I meant, why was she leaving me to flail like this? 'With your application.'

The pause she left before she spoke again was excruciatingly long.

'You don't mean that, Jonah.'

The kitchen door snicked close behind her before I had the chance to reply.

Which was a good thing, really. Because she was probably right.

There would be dozens – potentially hundreds – of scholars applying. The competition would be vicious. There were many, many people standing between me and this job.

But Sadie Shaw had a way of narrowing my focus, ensuring that the only thing I saw was her.

DECEMBER

Chapter Three

Jonah

The day I got the email was the day I finally told Fiona.

She was surprised when I asked her to Zoom with me. She was always surprised, even though I'd made a point to chat with her and the kids at least once a week ever since I found out what Matt had done, and every time, that surprise was like a little knife in my heart.

'I don't want to get your hopes up, Fi,' I told her, after I'd said my hellos to my twin seven-year-old nieces Rosie and Georgia and my eleven-year-old nibling Lex, 'but I've just been shortlisted for a job in Hobart.'

Fiona pressed her hands to her face. The internet connection crapped out for a second and she was frozen there, like Edvard Munch's *The Scream*.

'Really?'

'It's not a guarantee. Obviously it's not. I've been shortlisted for jobs before and not got them. But they're after an early modernist, and Elias and my old PhD supervisor both told me my application was strong – please don't cry!'

'I'm sorry.' She wiped tears away with her wrist. 'It's just . . . God, Jonah, this is such good news. Everything's such a mess – Matt's totally gone off the grid and I don't have *anyone* – and – and . . . I could really use you right now.'

For one perfect moment, my heart swelled in my chest. I *could* do this. I could mend what I'd broken, all those years ago. I could help my sister.

And then reality sank in, and I realised that I'd made an awful error of judgment.

I'd considered it carefully before I'd told her. If Fi knew I was up for this job – if she was counting on me – then I would *have* to keep my eyes on the prize. There could be no letting Sadie get in my head if the prospect of letting Fi down was this real.

That was a decision I'd made to manipulate my own feelings, though. I hadn't realised, not really, not properly, not until she started crying, the actual weight of Fiona's.

'I don't want you to get your hopes up,' I said again.

But it was hopeless, because 'I don't want you to get your hopes up' was not a magical phrase. I couldn't just tack it on the front of good news and expect Fi to say, 'Oh, okay then, note taken. I won't allow this to affect me emotionally in any way.'

Of *course* she was going to get her fucking hopes up. I was the worst brother in the world.

'It's no guarantee,' I said desperately. 'I know one of the other scholars who got shortlisted and she's brilliant. Unbelievably brilliant.'

'Is it Sadie?'

I blinked. 'How do you know about Sadie?'

'You've been talking about her constantly for fifteen years. Like, *constantly*. Painfully intelligent, never lets you get away with anything, the bane of your existence even though you defend her every time Dad's like "ew, popular culture, how lowbrow", right?'

I blinked again. 'I mentioned her to Elias and he barely knew who she was.'

'It's hard to get a word in edgewise with our family when you don't have a PhD,' Fi said, 'so I spend a lot of time listening.'

The pit of guilt that had been sitting heavy in my stomach since that horrible birthday dinner deepened.

'How do you feel about her being shortlisted?' Fi asked.

I rubbed my hand over my beard. 'I'd have been surprised if she wasn't. Offended on her behalf, even.'

'Those are all how you don't feel, Jonah. What about how you do feel?'

'I . . .'

I thought for a long moment, reaching for my water glass and taking a sip to give myself time to formulate a reply. 'I don't really know how to answer that question.'

It wasn't that I didn't have any . . . *feelings* about Sadie getting shortlisted. I did. A lot of them.

But I'd just sort of assumed it would happen. That either both of us would get shortlisted, or neither of us. It was difficult to imagine a world where we weren't in the trenches of the precariat together, trying to clamber over each other to get out.[20]

And anyway, it didn't matter how I felt.

I had to get this job. I had to get it so I could help Fi, and then all my feelings about Sadie would be irrelevant, because I would be in Hobart, and she would . . . not.

✎

___
20 I realise that, in this metaphor, we would be clambering over each other to rush headlong into enemy fire, but given the crushing workload pressures faced by most academics and the bloating of non-academic middle management focused on profits over people, I stand by it.

'No,' Elias said, pointing his finger at me as we Zoomed to do a mock interview and I cautiously expressed my inability to imagine no longer being in Sadie's orbit. 'This is not helpful. This is not productive. This is exactly the kind of thinking that will kneecap you.'

'I don't know how to stop, though.' I took my glasses off to clean them. 'I can make sensible arguments to myself all day long. There's something in me that just doesn't want to listen.'

'It's your dick, Jonah. Don't romanticise it.'

I nearly dropped my glasses.

'Oh, don't look so scandalised,' Elias said. 'I've been exactly where you are, remember. I'm not going to let you make the same mistakes I did.'

I let out a long breath. 'Fine. What do I need to do?'

'Avoid her. Out of sight, out of mind.'

'I live with her!'

'In a house with doors, presumably. Use them.'

Elias leant back in his chair. 'And whatever you do, no bonding on the interview trip. That's how she'll get past your defences. You'll end up having a drink at the hotel bar and somehow the first civil conversation you ever have will turn deep and meaningful and then she'll tell you something like "I'm thinking about leaving my husband" and your brain will dissolve into porridge and she'll waltz right past you into the job you want.'

Oh wow. Next time I saw Elias in person, I needed to get him drunk and make him tell me the Julia story.

'I would have noticed by now if Sadie had a husband.'

'The detail doesn't matter.' Elias pointed at me again. 'This is not the time to get soft or nostalgic or anywhere within shouting distance of sentimental. Give a Julia an inch and she'll take a mile – and then she'll win and you'll lose. Focus on yourself, Jonah.'

The memory of that night in the kitchen drifted across my mind. The feeling of Sadie's fingers, cool against mine. The sound of her voice when she'd called our final truce.

But I couldn't think about Sadie. I had to think about Fiona.

I dug my knuckles into my thigh and forced myself to imagine what it would feel like, telling Fiona that I was sorry, but I didn't get the job. How much she would cry. How *alone* she would feel, having the promise of support ripped out from under her – even more alone than before.

How much it would be my fault.

'Focus on myself,' I repeated. 'I can do that.'

The university was flying us both to Hobart to interview. Sadie and I agreed, in the longest conversation we'd had in over a month,[21] to share an Uber to the airport.

My headphones were on their last legs, but I'd brought them with me anyway, to provide a symbolic buffer between us.

I needn't have bothered. Sadie put in her earbuds the second we got in the car and didn't take them out again until we got to the airport.

We were silent as we went through security. Her laptop was covered in stickers. I'd seen them from a distance many times before – in seminars, in lectures, in meetings – but the security line was moving slow, so I had a chance to catalogue them when

---

21 Transcript of this incredibly lengthy conversation:
   SADIE: We should share Ubers to and from the airport. It'll be cheaper.
   JONAH: All right. I'll use my account for the trip there, you use yours for the trip back?
   SADIE: Okay.
   Practically a three-volume novel.

she put it in the tray to go through the scanner. Broadly, they fit into three genres: bookish (*smart girls read romance,* read one); pop-feminist (*smash the demon lizard patriarchy* was surrounded by three different coloured *end period poverty* stickers); and union. I only had two stickers on my laptop, but she had the exact same two, prominent despite all the sparkly distractions: *casual academics are always the first casualties* and *only 1 in 4 university workers have secure jobs.*

I saw her notice when I put my laptop in the tray behind hers. Her gaze flickered to mine briefly, and she gave me a look that might have been approval.

But then our trays disappeared into the scanner, she blinked, and it was gone. 'Our flight's not for an hour,' she said, when we got to the other side. 'I'm going to grab a drink at the bar.'

I could murder a glass of wine.

'I'm going to buy a new pair of headphones,' I said, and fled.

Focus on yourself, I told myself, staring blankly at a wall of electronics.

I did not buy a new pair of headphones. Everything was blurring together. I might need a new prescription for my glasses. Or possibly to re-learn how to read.

I did, however, get that glass of wine a little while later, when we were on the plane. It was cheap,[22] but I didn't care. I would have necked the entire bottle if they'd put it front of me.

I had an aisle seat. Sadie was two rows in front of me on the opposite side of the aisle. She had her laptop out and was working on a PowerPoint presentation.

---

22 One of the downsides of growing up with money and then steadfastly refusing to take any of it once you became an adult was that you could tell the difference between cheap and expensive wine but had no way to obtain the good stuff without compromising your integrity.

She must be polishing her job talk. That was one of the components of the interview process: we had to present a thirty-minute overview of our research and teaching philosophy to the department before we did the interview itself with a smaller selection panel.

I'd put the finishing touches on mine last night after a practice Zoom with Elias. He'd advised me to describe our combative battle-lecturing at Bass as 'an innovative and successful example of team teaching, resulting in extraordinary levels of student engagement'. I wondered how Sadie was framing the fact that we stood in front of a hundred and fifty students every week and tried to destroy each other.

As if she could hear my thoughts, she turned around and looked at me.

Fuck.

I could completely understand how Elias had let Julia take his legs out from under him the night before their job interview. I had a doctorate in literary studies, but I did not have the words to explain what it felt like to be looked at – to be *perceived* – by Sadie Shaw.

I drank the last of my wine, instinctively licking my lips to get the last precious drops of cheap nectar.

She turned around and, pointedly, angled her laptop away from me.

The lenses in my glasses are about eight feet thick, Sadie, I wanted to say. *Do you really think I could copy your homework from this distance?*

She would respond. That old, familiar argumentative carousel would start spinning. I might even enjoy it.

But I couldn't let myself get distracted. Everything was riding on this.

I had to focus on myself.

59

I woke up early the next morning to sun streaming through the thin hotel curtains and a message from Elias on my phone. Big day. How are you feeling?

You'll never guess, I sent back. Sadie sat me down in the hotel bar last night and told me she's thinking of leaving her husband???

Hilarious. Elias attached a GIF of an eye-roll.

Don't worry, I followed your instructions. We barely said two words to each other. I'm feeling good.

He sent back a thumbs up. It's the middle of the night here so I'm going to bed, but send me a message when it's done and let me know how you went, ok?

Out of nowhere, a lump appeared in my throat.

Thanks so much for all your help, I replied. I really appreciate it.

He didn't respond.

I dressed formally for the interview, tweed jacket over a shirt and tie, but I realised my mistake the second I stepped outside the air-conditioned hotel. It was much hotter than I'd expected – wasn't Tasmania supposed to be perpetually freezing? – and the wind was so strong I instinctively grabbed at my glasses to stop them falling off my face.

'Fisher!' Sadie was standing beside a cab, skirt of her green dress held tightly in one hand in an effort to avoid a Marilyn Monroe situation. 'Get in the car!'

I obeyed, sliding in beside her. 'Thanks.'

'Don't mention it.'

Then she put her earbuds in again. Hostilities resumed.

The driver didn't have the radio on, and without my own headphones, I could faintly hear what Sadie was listening to. She was clenching and unclenching her fist over and over again and mouthing along to 'My Shot' from *Hamilton*.

Oh God.

What if one of us really did get this job? What if one of us moved to Hobart and the other stayed in Sydney, alone in the house we'd shared for so many years? What if one of us got to be an academic and the other got forced out of the profession entirely? What if one of us finally *won*?

'Stop looking at me, Jonah,' Sadie said suddenly.

'I'm not – I wasn't – I was looking out the window.'

Her nostrils flared, just a little. 'I'm not going to let you psych me out.'

She went back to staring straight ahead, drumming her fingernails against her laptop.

I closed my eyes for a moment, taking a deep breath. I should follow her example. No letting her psych me out. Focus on myself.

Focus on Fi.

The cab dropped us off at one of the campus gates, about halfway up a steep hill. It wasn't a long walk to the lecture theatre where we'd be giving our job talks – and, thankfully, it was down the hill rather than up – but it was enough to get a sense of the campus.

It was wildly different from the universities we'd worked at. ESU and Bass were both classic city campuses, a mixture of new steel-and-chrome buildings and brutalist architecture from the 1960s and 1970s.

The Lyons campus, though, was sprawling, crawling up into dark green bush at the top of the hill and down to the Derwent River sparkling at the bottom, the buildings a mismatched combination of convict-hewn sandstone and 1980s brick. From where we stood, we had a panoramic view across the river to where Hobart's other university lay in the shadow of the mountain.

'Is my hair okay?' Sadie asked me abruptly.

I glanced at her. She'd pinned her hair back tightly, much more severely than she usually would.

I didn't like it. The last time I'd seen her wear this green dress, it had been at some ESU Faculty of Arts holiday party. She'd had her hair out then, fiery red waves rippling down her back, and it had made me want to find a dark corner to weep in.

'You've got a pin sticking out.' I gestured to the back of my own head.

'Here?'

'No, it's . . . Can I?'

She paused for a moment, then nodded. Her hair was warm as I pushed the bobby pin back into place.

'Thanks,' she said.

Oh God. Oh no.

I flexed my hand, trying to get the feeling of her sun-warm hair off my fingers. This was exactly what Elias had warned me about. It might be more subtle than *I'm thinking of leaving my husband,* but Sadie was too smart to use a sledgehammer when a stiletto would do. She'd slid it right between my ribs and—

'Your hair is not okay, by the way,' she said sharply. 'Make sure you look at yourself in a mirror before you give your job talk.'

'Oh, um . . .'

She was walking away before I could get the *thank you* out of my mouth.

The other two candidates were already there when we arrived at the lecture theatre. 'Jonah!' one of them said, standing up and shaking my hand enthusiastically. 'Nice to see you here, mate!'

I doubted I'd hear a bigger lie that day. Rory Worland was another early modern scholar. When I'd intermitted my PhD to take a research assistantship, he'd been the other RA, and he was *not* a fan of mine.[23] 'Nice to see you too,' I said, extricating myself.

---

23 Nor was I a fan of his. If you want to hear some stupendously bad takes on the city comedies of Thomas Middleton and Ben Jonson, then call Dr Rory Worland.

'And hello to you too.' He turned his grin on Sadie. 'You are . . . ?'

'Going over there.'

Sadie walked away, sitting down a healthy distance away from the fourth candidate – a modernist scholar, I guessed, given she'd brought along a copy of *Lolly Willowes* by Sylvia Townsend Warner as a job talk prop – and put her earbuds in again.

'Nice girl,' Rory said. 'Friend of yours?'

'Not really.' If he thought Sadie was somehow allied with me, he'd spend the next twenty minutes trying to either make her life miserable or win her over to Team Rory's Garbage Arguments. 'Excuse me.'

Sadie had been right about my hair. The wind had done a number on it. I combed water through it in the bathroom with my fingers, trying to get it to lay flat, but it wouldn't, a lock near the front falling stubbornly in front of my left eye.

There was a buzz from my satchel. I fished my phone out. FIONA flashed up on the display.

I hesitated. I probably shouldn't take it. I should do what Sadie was doing outside, get myself in the zone, hype myself up.

But I didn't have it in me to deny Fi, not right now. 'Hey,' I said, wedging my phone between my shoulder and my ear as I tried unsuccessfully to get my hair out of my eyes again. 'How's everything?'

'The same.' Her voice was businesslike, but I could hear the quaver underneath it. 'I just wanted to wish you good luck.'

'Thanks, Fi. I'm going to do everything I possibly can. I promise.'

'I don't suppose you have time for a coffee afterwards?' There was a note in her voice, something between wistful and hopeful. 'Or to pop round to the house? Bellerive's not far from the Lyons campus, and the kids would love to see you. I would too.'

'I wish I did.' Why, why, *why* was I constantly letting my sister down? 'But we have to head straight to the airport after we're done here.'

'Oh, okay.' I could feel, rather than hear, her sigh. 'No problem.'

'I'm so sorry. I asked Lyons if I could stay a couple of extra days and take a later flight back, but since it's so close to Christmas, airfares are getting ridiculously expensive and they wouldn't fork out for it.'

'Don't worry about it.' She laughed shakily. 'You'll be here for good soon enough.'

'Don't get your—'

'Hopes up, I know, I know. But I can't help it, Jonah.'

I swallowed.

'The kids are so excited that you might be moving here,' she added.

My blood ran cold.[24] She'd told the kids? She'd got *the kids'* hopes up?

'Me too,' I said faintly.

After we hung up, I bent over, clutching the edge of the sink.

I had to get this job. *I had to get this job.* I had to fight like my fucking life depended on it, or I was going to let her down worse than I ever had before. If I didn't get his job – if I didn't—

'Don't panic,' I told my reflection in the mirror fiercely. 'Don't you dare panic, Fisher.'

Too late.

        ✎

'I, um, first of all, I'm so delighted to be here.' My fingers were sweaty, my eyes refusing to adjust to the lighting of the lecture theatre, putting everything and everyone in a blur. 'It's . . . it's a

---

24 The part of me that was a scholar knew this was not true. The idea of blood running cold comes from the Galenic notion of the four humours, something which comes up regularly in medieval and early modern literature. Blood was considered to be hot, so the idea of blood running cold was a way of expressing that your humours were out of whack and you were seriously ill.

I knew this, and still it felt like my blood very literally ran cold.

privilege to be able to talk to you today about, um, my research into Jacobean drama, and . . . and my broader teaching philosophy.'

It was all right, I told myself fiercely afterwards, sitting in the anteroom. Everyone in there knew how high the stakes were. They'd understand why I was so nervous. The content of my job talk was good, even if the delivery was shaky. I knew that. I *knew* that.

I couldn't seem to get enough air into my lungs. I resisted the urge to put my head between my knees.

Rory came out of the lecture theatre. When the door swung closed behind him, he leapt into the air and punched it, like he was some kind of sportsperson celebrating an epic goal. 'Yes!' he exclaimed.

Sadie cast her eyes up to the ceiling, shaking her head slightly.

I wanted to laugh.

I wanted to cry.

At least if neither of us got this job, we'd have a new point of agreement. We could sit in the kitchen late at night again, drink tea, and talk about how much we hated Rory Worland.

'Dr Shaw?' one of the selection panel said from the door. 'We're ready for you.'

Sadie rose to her feet. Her footsteps were even and measured as she followed the woman into the lecture theatre, her chin high, everything about her body language as secure and assertive as it had been that day of the first ceasefire, when she shook my hand and told me that our grade was more important than the fact she couldn't stand me.

That was the moment I knew, deep down, that I had lost.

I could take Rory Worland. Even on my worst day, with my worst material, I could take Rory Worland.

But even on my best day – even if I produced my very best scholarship, even if I delivered my presentation flawlessly, even if I answered every interview question perfectly, even with all the advantages I had at my disposal – there was still a good chance Sadie Shaw would come out ahead.

✎

Afterwards, I tried to keep my hopes up. It went ok, I texted Elias in the Uber back to the airport. Job talk was a bit wobbly but think I did well in the interview.

And the interview's the most important part, I told myself in the Hobart airport bar, nursing another glass of wine. *That's what they really care about.*

'I did my best,' I told Fiona on our next Zoom call, back in my room in the share house. 'Now we just have to cross our fingers.'

'You've got this, Jonah,' she replied, and I made myself smile, made myself ignore the gnawing feeling in my belly, made myself lie and lie and lie – to myself, to my siblings, to everyone – just in case I was wrong.

But I knew.

I knew long before I got the email, a few days before Christmas. *Dear Dr Fisher, Thank you for your interest in the position of Lecturer in Literary Studies at Lyons University. Unfortunately, we regret to inform you . . .*

I knew before I heard Sadie's scream of ecstatic joy, echoing as loudly around the house as if she'd put speakers in every room.

I knew who the winner was, after all these years.

Chapter Four

Sadie

Chess and I were both tactile people, but she hadn't hugged me this long and this hard since our mother's funeral.

'You're cutting off my circulation,' I said, voice muffled against her shoulder. We were the same height, but she was still wearing her heels from the office, so I felt like a little girl again, being hugged by her quite-literally-big sister.

'I don't care.' Chess somehow managed to tighten her grip on me. 'I'm so proud of you. I'm so thrilled for you and I'm so devastated that you're leaving Sydney, and – oh God.'

'Don't you dare cry. Then I'll cry, and I've already cried so much I think I'm at risk of dehydration.'

She drew back at last, framing my face between her hands. 'I am *so* proud of you, Sadie. You've worked so hard. You've earned this.'

'I don't know about that. Everyone I know works this hard, and—'

'No.' She pinched my cheeks. I felt like an even littler girl. 'We're not letting in impostor syndrome. We're not letting in survivor's guilt. We're not even letting in the fact that it's going to break my heart when you move. Tonight, we're celebrating.'

Chess let go of me and picked up the bottle of champagne she had resting in an ice bucket, taking the wire cage off with a few quick twists. 'We're celebrating the fact that you're brilliant.' She popped the cork. 'And that academia has finally recognised it.'

Despite my best efforts, my bottom lip started to tremble. 'I love you, Chessie.'

Her eyes were soft as she looked at me. 'I love you too, sweetie. To the end of the universe and back again.'

That was something she'd been saying to me since I was five years old. She'd been doing my kindergarten reading with me – Mum had been off somewhere appeasing our father, leaving Chess, aged all of ten, to look after me – and she was helping me sound out the words in a picture book: *I love you to the moon and back.*

I was clearly already a budding literary critic, because I was putting pressure on my reading material before I could even properly read. *If I wrote this book, I'd say I love you to the* sun *and back,* I announced. *Mrs Wilson told us the sun is further away than the moon.*

There's heaps of stuff further than the moon, Chess had agreed. *The stars are even further than the sun.*

The front door had slammed closed so hard the walls of our house shook. Mum was saying something in a pleading tone. Our father was yelling over the top of her.

I'd put my arms around Chess. I used to do that a lot as a kid – whenever I was scared or sad or overwhelmed, I'd cling to her like she was a teddy bear. *I love you to the stars and back, Chessie,* I'd whispered.

Chess had hugged me back. *Well, I love you to the end of the universe,* she'd declared, *and back again.*

Adult Chess had just passed me a glass of champagne when I lost the battle with tears. 'I never could have done this without you, Chess.'

'Oh, Sadie.' She drew me into another hug – one-armed, this time, so neither of us spilled our wine. 'You did this all on your own. All I've ever been is moral support.'

I laughed, trying not to let this turn into a full joy-poignant-as-grief weeping jag. 'That's absolutely not true, but I know better than to have this argument with you.'

'Damn straight.' She grinned. 'You'll lose.'

She took a sip of her champagne. 'Although you do have a point. I'm your legal counsel as well as moral support. Make sure you send your employment contract over to me, okay? I don't want you signing anything that I haven't gone over with a fine-tooth comb.'

'I wouldn't dare.' I sipped my own champagne and tried to swallow down how much I loved her, and how terrified I was to be leaving her, before I completely fell apart.

Chess unboxed a cheeseboard which must have cost her an absolute mint, especially last minute in the pre-Christmas rush. 'How did the private school boy take it?'

'I don't know. I haven't seen him yet.'

Jonah hadn't come out of his room. I knew he was in there – I could see the strip of light underneath his closed door – but I hadn't heard a single peep.

'If it's going to be awkward, living with him for this last six weeks before you go to Hobart,' Chess suggested slyly, 'you could always move in here with me.'

I pointed a piece of brie at her. It started melting in my fingers, and I swiftly rescued it with a cracker. 'Nice try.'

This wasn't the first time Chess had suggested moving in with her. Or the second. Or the hundredth. *You don't need to live in a share house with eight thousand different people. I've got a spare room. I've got all this space. Save your money. Stay here.*

There wasn't much I could resist her on, but this was a boundary on which I'd held firm. She loved me so much, and she'd look after me forever if I let her – which meant I absolutely couldn't let her, not if I ever wanted to be an actual independent adult in my own right.

We were both in our thirties now. That five-year age gap between us that had fundamentally shaped our dynamic when we were kids shouldn't matter anymore. And more than that: I should be the one looking after Chess sometimes – even if I was never, *ever* going to be able to even the scales.

✎

When I found myself in front of Jonah's bedroom door later that night, I told myself that was why I was there. I couldn't pay Chess back, so I was going to pay it forward instead, by making a very mature, olive-branch-y offer to check up on his sister once I moved to Hobart.

Even though, if the shoe had been on the other foot, and Jonah had turned up at my door to say, 'Well, I *suppose* I could have coffee with your sister once or twice, if that would make you feel better,' I would probably have put two hands on his chest and pushed him down the stairs.

But after that night in the kitchen – where, even in the ambient lighting, I'd been able to see how tight and drawn the corners of his mouth were when he talked about how he'd failed Fiona – it felt like I had to say *something*.

Apologise, perhaps.

'. . . please don't cry, Fi,' Jonah said.

I stopped, hand poised to knock.

His sister said something I couldn't really hear, but even through the door, there was no disguising the sound of sobs.

'I'm so sorry,' Jonah said. 'I tried. I really did, but . . . sometimes other people are just better.'

He must have turned the volume up, because Fiona's response came through loud and clear this time. 'No. Don't think that, Jonah. I don't want you to think that. I don't want you to beat yourself up.'

'It's too late for that.'

I recognised the note in his voice. It was the one he used when our students would come to us right at the end of semester. *I know I haven't been to any of the classes and I didn't submit the first assignment, but is there any way I can pass the unit?* they'd say, and he'd look them in the eye and say gently but firmly, *I'm sorry, but it's too late for that.*

'No,' Fiona said. 'This isn't your fault. This is my fault. You told me not to get my hopes up, and I did anyway, and—'

She started crying again, but I thought I heard *I'm sorry, Jonah* in there.

'Fi, please.'

This note I didn't recognise. I'd never, not once in fifteen years, not even that night in the kitchen, heard Jonah Fisher sound desperate.

'Maybe I can figure something out,' he said. 'There's nothing keeping me in Sydney, not really. All the unis I work for are cutting back their casual staff numbers massively. Maybe I even have a better chance of getting teaching work in Hobart. Sadie might throw me some, if I ask her nicely.'

I, like many workaholic thirty-something women, had persistent jaw issues from clenching too much. My masseters were so tight that the myotherapist I saw whenever I could afford it told me it was amazing I could open my mouth at all.

My jaw still dropped to the floor.

'Or I could try for something outside of academia,' he went on. 'My career is on its last legs anyway. Maybe I can move to Hobart and find some other job I can do.'

I fled, as quickly and quietly as I could. This was none of my business. *None.*

Sometimes, when I read particularly dense (*cough* French *cough*) theory, my brain would just slide over the words on the page. I would understand the meaning of every word individually, but my mind simply would not absorb the meaning of the sentence. I would have to go back and read it six or seven times before it came close to sinking in.

The idea of Jonah Fisher coming to me, hat in hand, begging for casual teaching work, was like reading Deleuze.

The idea of him no longer being an academic was like reading fucking *Derrida*.

No. Worse. I could at least get there with Derrida in the end. But I couldn't even imagine it: me, blithely building an academic career, while he was . . . what would he even be? Some guy who worked some nine-to-five in some office? All that work – all that knowledge – all those arguments we'd had – just . . . gone?

What would happen if I ran into him in Hobart, this unimaginable, defanged, non-scholar version of Jonah? What would we even *say* to each other? *Oh, hello, nice to see you, how about this weather we're having?*

I'd won. After all these years we'd been fighting, I'd won. That meant something.

But who would I even be without him to measure myself by?

JANUARY

Chapter Five

Sadie

I avoided Jonah over the Christmas break. It was a childish thing to do, but I'd rather be childish than have to go through a conversation when he ran his hand awkwardly through his hair then did the verbal equivalent of getting down on his knees and begging me for whatever crumbs of labour I could provide him – or, God forbid, told me he was also moving to Hobart so he could help his sister, and giving up academia together.

It was strange, given how much time and energy I'd devoted to trying to defeat him over the years, but I didn't want my victory to be my last memory of him. We'd got to a place you could almost call nice, that night we'd sat across from each other and agreed not to fight anymore. A place with a sense of resolution to it. It wasn't a eucatastrophic ending – far from it – but it had had a satisfying sense of closure about it. Fifteen years of conflict, tied up at last with a bow.

If that was our ending, I could deal with it. It might be anticlimactic, but it was mature.

So in the interest of being adult, I childishly dove out of any room there was even a hint of him entering – which meant I basically declared the kitchen Jonah's territory and never went in there, because he always seemed to be standing in front of the stove cooking something or other – and focused on getting things organised instead. I might have several weeks before I had to move, but there were still things I needed to do. Talk to my various bosses and let them know I would not be available for casual teaching anymore. Start bringing home books from the tiny corners of office space I'd managed to carve out for myself. Familiarise myself with Hobart on Google Maps, work out where would be best to live.

Although I might not have the luxury of being picky. Blithely, I'd assumed that a small city like Hobart would be infinitely cheaper to rent in than the notoriously expensive Sydney, but when I started browsing through real estate websites, my eyes almost fell out of my head. I'd had every intention of living alone once I moved – that seemed like what you did when you had an adult job with an adult income – but if I was going to do that, I'd be spending a truly massive chunk of said adult income on rent. I was going to have to find myself another share house.

I tipped my head back and groaned. When I inhaled again, the delicious smell of whatever it was that Jonah was cooking in the kitchen filled my nostrils, a pointed reminder that the chances of me finding a place as good at the one I'd shared with him for the past eight years were negligible at best.

I rubbed the heel of my hand over the developing anxious tightness in my chest. It was early January, which surely had to be a shit time for rental listings. Maybe more would go up in the next few weeks. Perhaps I should focus on the actual moving, rather than precisely where I would be moving to.

I googled moving companies – and once again, my eyes almost fell out of my head.

They cover moving costs in my contract, right? I texted Chess. Otherwise I might need to sell a kidney.

She was at work, so her response didn't come for a few hours, during which I'd dug more into potential rental listings and worked myself up from mild anxiety into proper panic. Yep, moving costs covered up to $3K, plus accom for the first two weeks. That should be plenty, but if it's not – I've got you. ☺

I tried to focus on the good news – the money for removalists, the fact I had more time than I thought to find a place – rather than the fact that, despite my firm policy around not taking money from Chess no matter how much she tried to force it into my hands, I was sorely fucking tempted.

I took a deep breath. No. I was an adult. I was going to work this out on my own – *how* was the delicious smell of Jonah's cooking still lingering?

My phone vibrated again. Nearly finished going through your contract. There's a few clauses I'd like to see if we can get some wiggle room on, but it mostly seems fine. Only thing that jumped out at me as slightly unusual was partner hire, but that's not relevant in your case.

I blinked.

And we're DEFINITELY having a conversation about salary negotiation. I know you've told me a thousand times that universities don't work like that, but there is ALWAYS room to negotiate.

Ok. Thanks Chessie! Love you xx

You can repay me in romance books ☺, she sent back, then presumably marked a six-minute block as 'pro bono' on her calendar and moved on.

I, however, did not.

I went into my email, dug out my contract, and hit ctrl-F. *Partner h*, I typed.

I read through the relevant section. Once. Twice. Three times.

I read it like someone had put hardcore French theory in front of me and told me I had to explain it to undergraduates.

Then I opened a new tab on my web browser. Did some googling. Fell down some Reddit rabbit holes.

'No,' I murmured. 'That won't work.'

I shut my laptop decisively. No. I'd thought – for a moment – but no.

Only 1 in 4 university workers have secure jobs, the sticker on the lid said.

Only one in four, and I – Sadie Shaw, a girl who came from nothing and nowhere – got the job. Not the Shakespeare bro. Not Dr Jonah fucking Fisher, scion of a scholarly dynasty. *Me*.

It had been a nice thought, but if it was that easy, everyone would be doing it.

I rolled my desk chair over to my bookshelf so I could distract myself by finding some new romance reading for Chess. Once I moved into whatever Hobart share house I ended up in, she was going to have to give up her love of physical books and get herself an e-reader. I was going to be spending so much money on rent that there wouldn't be a single cent left over to pay for posting print books regularly from Tasmania.

I picked up *The Devil in Winter* by Lisa Kleypas for a second, but then swiftly discarded it. Chess usually liked historicals – she could suspend her disbelief better – but given her hatred of both fake dating and problematic paperwork, there was no way I could give her a book which was a—

I stopped.

For a long moment, I sat there in front of my bookshelf, hand still resting on the cover of the Kleypas book, the last faint scent of Jonah's cooking in my nostrils, in the thrall of a truly cursed idea.

I opened up my laptop again. All my tabs were still there, as was the PDF of my contract, the *partner h* of *partner hire* highlighted in blue.

I wasn't seriously considering this.

No.

I was *not* seriously considering this. Chess would kill me, then laugh hysterically at me, then lock me in her spare bedroom for between fourteen and twenty-eight business days until I came to my senses.

Plus, I didn't even like the man! One civil night versus fifteen years of arguments didn't exactly even the scale.

I slammed my laptop shut again. *No.*

But there were those union stickers, sitting there, taunting me, full of whole new subtexts now I finally had a permanent job. *Casual academics are always the first casualties (you class traitor).*

And then there was that desperation in his voice, that note I'd never heard before, when he'd been talking to his sister about how he might give up on academia so he could move to Hobart to help her.

I bit my lip hard, worrying it between my teeth until I could taste blood.

It had been hot, that day we interviewed. Way hotter than it should have been. Walking from the campus gate to the lecture theatre had been like walking through a fan-forced oven.

Somehow, though, Jonah's fingers had been even hotter, shaking against my scalp as he gently pushed that stray bobby pin back into my hair.

He'd been so nervous.

If he hadn't been – if the stakes hadn't been so astronomically high for him – would we even be in this situation now? Would he be the one panicking over the cost of renting in Hobart, or – or . . . ?

I closed my eyes and repeated Chess's words to myself. *We're not letting in impostor syndrome. We're not letting in survivor's guilt.*

'I deserve this,' I whispered to myself.

But I wasn't the only one who did.

I picked up my laptop.

'Come in!' Jonah called, when I knocked on his door.

He looked shocked to see me, but he modulated it down to surprise quickly. 'Hi,' he said, tucking his hands into his armpits. He was wearing navy pyjama pants and a grey T-shirt that had been through the wash so many times it was halfway to transparent, the faint shadow of his chest hair just visible beneath it. 'Happy new year, Shaw. I've been meaning, um, I've been meaning to congratulate you. I'm sorry it's taken so long. I don't want you to think I'm a bad sport, it's just—'

'Shut up,' I said, forcing my eyes back up to his face.

'Oh. Okay.'

The fact that he did what I said without even the slightest protest almost broke me.

This was not the Jonah Fisher I knew. This was not Tweed Jonah, the Jonah who would argue every little point, fight every little fight, who might unroll a scroll at any moment containing a hundred-thousand-word manifesto entitled *Why You Are Wrong About Everything*, complete with another thirty thousand words in footnotes.

This wasn't even Cardigan Jonah, sitting across from me in the dark of the kitchen, vulnerabilities on full display.

This was some other, third Jonah. Broken Jonah. Defeated Jonah. Armourless Jonah.

I almost turned on my heel and ran out of the room.

This was a terrible idea. This was an idea so bad it would probably send me straight to the hitherto-unexplored tenth circle of hell, the one Virgil had decided against showing Dante on the grounds that seeing all the heretics and fraudsters and traitors and whatnot was quite enough for one day and there was no need to go to the worst circle of all.

Jonah was looking at me.

I bit my lip again.

It had been nice, that night before the job was listed. It had felt right, in a way that things had not felt right in a long time. When I'd put my hand on his and said *Truce?* and he'd turned his palm to face mine and said *Truce,* and somehow, out of nowhere, we'd been sitting there at the kitchen table, holding hands . . .

That had felt like a step forward. A real step – an adult step – when I had been stuck in the same place for so long.

'This is going to sound insane,' I said, 'but I was wondering if you'd like to marry me.'

Chapter Six
Jonah

Sometimes, when you're cooking, your ingredients will defy all the laws of chemistry and physics and do something completely unexpected.

Once, for example, I was making dinner for a girl I was seeing. It was our third date and I wanted to impress her, so I was making Roquefort soufflés. It's a difficult recipe, but I'd mastered it – I'd made it dozens of times before – so I was smugly confident that once I put my beautiful, evenly risen, golden soufflés down in front of her, she'd be so impressed we wouldn't even make it to the macarons I'd made for dessert.

They collapsed the second I took them out of the oven.

I'm so sorry, I'd said. *I don't understand what happened.*

Jonah, it doesn't matter, she'd replied. *I bet they're still delicious.*

No. I can't let you eat these. I have to remake them.

My next attempt failed too. She left halfway through my third attempt, and I ended up sitting miserably at the kitchen table late into the night, shoving my face full of macarons, trying to work out how this rock-solid recipe I'd used so many times could have possibly failed.

Up until this moment, the Roquefort Soufflé Incident was the most incomprehensible, inexplicable thing that had ever happened to me.

'. . . I'm sorry?'

'I'm wondering if you want to get married.'

It didn't make any more sense the second time.

'I recognise this sounds insane,' Sadie said again.

I was fairly sure I was having some kind of out-of-body experience, which is the only excuse I have for what I said next. 'I didn't know you felt like that about me.'

'Oh, fuck off, Jonah.'

'You just asked me to marry you!'

'No, I asked if *you* wanted to marry *me*.'

'What makes you think I want to marry you?'

'Just – shut up, okay?' Sadie snarled. 'I am not in love with you. Believe it or not, I have managed to use my powers of deductive reasoning over the past fifteen years and have also figured out that you're not in love with me. This is a business proposition.'

She sat down on my bed – *Sadie Shaw* was sitting on my bed, that was infinitely more unlikely than me fucking up those soufflés three times in a row – and opened her laptop. 'My contract has a provision for partner hire.'

She turned the screen towards me. She'd highlighted the relevant section. I tried to read it, but it was like my astigmatism had suddenly got a thousand times worse.

'They'll consider partner hire where relocation is involved, and the partner is suitably qualified for employment at the institution,' Sadie said. 'You were shortlisted. You're suitably qualified.'

No I wasn't. Suitably qualified people for the role of Lecturer in Literary Studies could presumably do things like 'read' and 'speak'.

'I thought maybe we could fudge it by being like, "Hey, you already know that we live at the same address, look at our applications," and then we could pretend that we, you know, "live together".' She put scare quotes around it with her fingers. 'But that wouldn't work. I did some research, and they make you sign a statutory declaration about the nature of your relationship. Chess told me once that you can go to jail if you lie on a stat dec, so we'd have to get married.'

'What?'

She gave me a look that was the equivalent of her snapping her fingers in my face and saying, *come on, keep up.* 'If we sign a stat dec that says "we've lived together for several years, and recently got married", none of it will be a lie.'

I stared.

'Like I said, it sounds extreme,' she said, 'but I genuinely don't think it would be that big a deal.'

That – the most ludicrous in a series of cascadingly ludicrous statements – finally broke through the white noise. 'Not that big a deal?!'

I stood up, but I had nowhere to go. My bedroom was tiny and there was barely enough space for me to squeeze into my chair between my desk and the bed Sadie was currently sitting on. If I wanted to leave, I'd have to jump over her legs.

I faced the wall instead, running a hand through my hair and tugging so hard at it that it was astonishing half of it didn't come out.

'Think about it, Jonah.' How did she sound so calm? 'It wouldn't have to change anything. We already live together here. Why not live together there too? It'd solve a problem for me, honestly. Hobart rent is bonkers expensive, and this way I won't have to try and find another share house.'

'Are you asking me to marry you so you can have a *flatmate*?'

'Obviously not. Don't be ridiculous.'

'Only one of us is being ridiculous.'

'I'm trying to help you!'

'I don't need your help!'

I turned around. 'I don't need your help,' I repeated, trying to keep my voice down so our housemates wouldn't come running to try and separate us. 'I don't need your charity, and I don't need your pity. Please leave.'

Sadie stood too. It brought her topknot level with my eyeline. Just like that night in the kitchen, it was listing to the left.

'Jonah,' she said, 'think about your sister.'

'Why do you care about my sister? You don't even know her.'

'I know, but – look, can we sit down? You're looming over me. I hate it.'

We sat, me in my desk chair, her on my bed again. The fabric of my pyjama pants brushed hers as our knees touched.

'Like I told you,' Sadie said, 'I have a soft spot for sisters.'

She made a sound that was somewhere between a sigh and a laugh. 'Not that Chess would ever need anything or anyone.'

That, I believed. Sadie's sister was terrifying.

'So I know what it feels like,' she said, 'to love your sister, and feel like there's nothing you can do for her.'

I put my hands underneath my thighs, sitting on them so I didn't have to find something to do with them.

'I know we've had our differences, Jonah.'

That was putting it mildly.

'I know that's putting it mildly.'

Beneath my thighs, my fingers twitched.

'But the thought of you not being able to help your sister – of me being the thing that stands between you and her – I hate that. And I'm not sure I can live with it.'

The room was bright. Too bright, really. The globe in my desk lamp had burnt out, so I had the overhead light on. It was harsh, bluish-white light, the kind that did nobody any favours.

Despite that, it felt like we were in the kitchen again. In the quiet, still darkness, the remnants of that terrible mug cake on the table in front of me, Sadie's hand on mine as she asked, *Truce?*

'And honestly, I feel like you have to appreciate the genius of the scam,' she said, tone lighter now. 'What a way to outsmart the managerial classes and get more casuals into permanent jobs, right?' She tapped one of the union stickers on her laptop.

'I'm not sure how popular arranged marriage would be as a conversion strategy with the rank-and-file,' I said tightly.

'This isn't arranged marriage.' Sadie looked thoughtful for a second. 'This would typically be called marriage of convenience. Maybe marriage-in-name-only. When romance was serialised in women's magazines in the mid-twentieth century, it was such a popular trope that they used to call it MINO as a shorthand, and—'

'I don't need the lecture.'

She raised her eyebrows.

'I'm sure it's a very interesting lecture,' I amended. 'But – think about this, Sadie. Think about what you're proposing. Literally, down on one knee, proposing.'

I expected her to snap back at me, but her voice was almost gentle. 'Do you really think I would come to you with a proposal this extreme if I hadn't thought it through?'

'Look, I might not have always shown it, but I have every respect for your intelligence,' I said. 'But no, I don't think you've thought this one through. You said yourself that it was insane.'

'I said that it *sounded* insane. Not that it was.'

'Do the semantics really matter?'

'Of course they do.'

Only Sadie Shaw could turn a discussion about her *literally proposing to me* into an argument about close reading.

'It's not insane,' she said. 'Nothing about our relationship or our living situation changes. You get a job you deserve just as much as I do, with the bonus that you get to help your sister and I get to sleep at night. All that's different is that we sign a piece of paper.'

'It's a pretty important piece of paper. Would you call that,' I gestured to my framed doctoral degree, 'just a *piece of paper*?'

'Of course not. You had to earn it. Anyone can get married.'

'What if the university caught us?'

'How would they catch us? The marriage will be legal. Everything we'll put on the stat dec will be true. They'll have no way of proving any different.'

I paused.

'Doesn't this—' I struggled to find the right words. 'Doesn't this mean something to you, though? You read all those romance novels.'

'So that means I'm dreaming of a white dress and a picket fence and a Prince Charming?'

I'd heard this sharp, clipped note in her voice before. It usually meant she was going to tear someone[25] a new arsehole.

'I'm a woman in academia, Jonah. I'm familiar with all the research on how marriage benefits men and disadvantages women. All the stuff about division of domestic and emotional labour. I've read all those books by all those pale, male, stale scholars where they casually mention in the acknowledgments that their wife typed the manuscript and did like ninety per cent of the research.'

She probably didn't know it, but she was very accurately describing my parents.

'Love – now that means something to me,' she said. 'Marriage, not so much.'

---

25 Usually me.

Sadie put her hands on the bed behind her, leaning back slightly. I studiously did not look at what that manoeuvre did to her breasts in her thin camisole.

'Not that I'm suggesting we actually stay married until death do us part,' she added. 'Just until we both pass probation. We'd be much harder to fire then.'

I wasn't considering this – no, I absolutely wasn't considering this – but the unfriendly lighting was catching fiery highlights in her hair, and—

'How long is probation?' I asked.

'Three years.'

'Three *years*?' My voice hadn't hit a note this high since before it had broken.

She shrugged. 'We've lived in the same house for eight years already and managed to not kill each other. What's another three?'

How was she so nonchalant about this?

'Although it doesn't have to be the full three,' she added. 'That's for your protection, not mine. No skin off my nose if you want to end it earlier.'

I could hear my own heartbeat pounding in my ears. 'Come on, Shaw. You haven't thought this through. Not really.'

She gave me a pointed look. 'When, exactly, over the last fifteen years, have I given you the impression that I don't think things through?'

'There are so many reasons why this is a bad idea,' I said. 'What if . . . What if we got married and you fell in love with someone else? What would you do then?'

'Who says we can't have an open marriage? We could be the Lit Studies equivalents of Sartre and de Beauvoir.'

'Sartre and de Beauvoir weren't married.'

'I *know* that, Jonah.'

She exhaled through her teeth. 'Listen, I relate to your sister more than I'd like to, okay?' she said. 'I especially relate to her kids. I know what it's like to be abandoned.'

I remembered what she'd told me all those years ago when we won the University Medal. Her mother dying. Her father leaving. The look in her eyes when she'd said, *When I said I fought hard for this, Fisher, I didn't just mean I fought you.*

'My dad was an abusive shithead birthed directly from Satan's arsehole,' Sadie said. 'Leaving was the best thing he ever did for us, but it still hurt.'

She folded her hands in her lap, lacing her fingers together. 'It wasn't my mum's fault, but when she died, you can bet that felt like being abandoned too.'

I couldn't even imagine what that was like.

For all that my parents were terrible – for all that they'd pitted Elias and Fiona and I against each other – they were always there. Even when my dad had made that awful, *awful* crack about not being able to catch me if I fell because Fi had come begging for money, I knew he didn't actually mean it.

If I fell, he would never let me hear the end of it. That dirtiest of words – *failure* – would be wielded against me like a weapon for the rest of my life.

But there was a reason Fi had set aside her pride and gone to them when Matt refused to pay child support. She'd fallen, and – financially, at least – they'd caught her.

'There's only one person in my life that hasn't abandoned me,' Sadie said. 'My sister.'

She took her listing topknot down. That glorious hair of hers fell wild around her shoulders. I swallowed reflexively, hoping she hadn't heard the way my breath caught in my throat.

'I'll never be able to pay Chess back for everything she did for me. Not in a thousand years. The only thing I can do is pay it forward.'

Then she paused. 'Your sister is going through a nightmare,' she said. 'But if we can pull this partner hire thing off, and you can show up for her, be there for her, the way that Chess was for me, then . . . then in the middle of that nightmare, *something good happens.*'

I swallowed again.

I knew – I *knew* – this was a terrible idea.

I knew what I should say.

This is unbelievably generous of you to offer, Sadie, and I don't want you to think I don't appreciate it – but I can't.

'All right, Shaw,' I said instead. 'Let's get married.'

Chapter Seven

Sadie

If this was a movie, there would be some kind of smash cut between Jonah looking me in the eye and saying *all right, Shaw, let's get married*, and our wedding. A montage of us getting dressed, jumping in a car, and then suddenly he'd be sliding a ring onto my finger and someone – probably an Elvis impersonator – would be saying *you may now kiss the bride*.

But it wasn't a movie, so what actually happened was that we spent the next twenty minutes quietly researching what you had to do to get legally married in Australia. 'Basically, we need to fill in this form, sign it in the presence of an authorised witness, and get a celebrant to lodge it,' Jonah said, showing me his screen. We were both sitting on his bed now, cross-legged, leaning against the wall, computers in our laps. 'Then, once it's lodged, we can get married in a month.'

'A *month*?' That would mean us getting married at the beginning of February, only a few days before I – we, if we pulled this off – started at Lyons. 'What do they have to do, call the banns?'

'There's a provision for cutting it short, but I don't think we qualify.' He ran a hand over his beard. 'I guess it's to make sure people really think things through.'

Jonah tipped his head back against the wall, looking up at the ceiling before turning to look at me. 'This is probably a good thing. If we got married like *that*,' he snapped his fingers, 'and then the uni was like, "sorry, no partner hire for you", then you'd be stuck with an entire husband you didn't want.'

'Then we'd go to Plan B.'

'What's that?'

'I kill you, inherit all the money your parents are going to leave you, and start a new life as a wealthy widow who solves murders on trains.'

Jonah chuckled. I could feel his breath, hot against the side of my face.

Then he sighed. 'We don't know if this is even *possible*, Shaw. Your contract says that they'll consider partner hire, not that it's a guarantee.'

'I'll email HR at the uni and set up a meeting so we can figure it out. But if getting married really is a month-long process, then we need to get the ball rolling. If we need a celebrant to lodge the form, let's find a celebrant.' I opened up a new tab. 'Any preferences?'

'Not really.'

He turned his head back to the ceiling. 'You know, for the better part of the last millennium, you could get married simply by declaring that you were married. You didn't even need any witnesses. You could just say, "you're my husband", "you're my wife" and boom, married.'

'I know,' I said absently, scrolling through celebrant listings. 'I was at your talk in the seminar series about it.'

I'd been interested, too – almost against my will. He'd been using speech act theory to talk about the marriage ceremony and the problems it presented when depicting weddings on the Renaissance stage. Phrases like *I take you to be my lawfully wedded wife* were the kind of speech acts that changed reality – you said it and then you were married – which made it tricky for actors to say them to each other, even though everyone involved was male and it was four hundred years before the legalisation of gay marriage.

Although getting married wasn't quite as simple as just saying the words. *Marriage in England in the early modern period came down to two things*, Jonah had said, gesturing at his PowerPoint. *A verbal contract which began the marriage, and a physical union which consummated it.*

One of the downsides of being a redhead is how obvious it is when you blush. At the memory of his lips curving around the word *consummated*, I felt the flush start somewhere near my belly button, creeping up towards my face.

'Is that celebrant's website seriously Going-to-Gretna-Green-dot-com?' Jonah was looking at my screen. 'I've changed my mind. I do have preferences. I want that one.'

I glanced at him, surprised.

'If we're going to go through with a plan this absurd,' he clarified, 'then we might as well have the thing solemnised by someone with a sense of humour.'

The celebrant had a Calendly on their website, so I made us an appointment for the following afternoon. 'We should fill in the Notice of Intended Marriage form now, so we can hit the ground running.'

'Okay.' Jonah tabbed back over to it. 'We'll need an authorised witness to our signatures – a justice of the peace, a lawyer, a doctor, someone like that. The celebrant can probably do it, unless you want your sister—'

'No.'

He looked at me again.

'I don't want to tell Chess. Not yet.'

There was a long pause before he spoke again. 'This is none of my business, but if you're really going to be my wife, Sadie . . .'

The words *my wife* coming out of Jonah Fisher's mouth made me feel a lot of things, none of which I intended to interrogate.

'. . . can I ask why?'

'Because it might not even work. We might get a flat no from the uni on partner hire. This,' I gestured between us, 'might be nothing. I don't want to worry her until there's something to actually worry about.'

Jonah didn't say anything.

It was the exact same move he used in our lectures, when he asked a question and none of the students were brave enough to answer. I had a bad habit of cracking and filling in the gaps, but he wasn't afraid to let a silence get uncomfortable, to guilt students into responding.

It was unsurprising, then, that I broke first. 'Chess is going to hate this.'

'Because she hates me.'

'I might not have always been very flattering about you.' That was putting it *extremely* euphemistically. 'And then there was that incident with your dad when we won the University Medal.'

It was one of the few times in my life I'd been genuinely angry with Chess. *What the fuck do you think you're doing?* I'd snarled at her when I'd finally managed to yank her away from Professor Fisher, my face tomato-red with embarrassment. *Do you know who that man is? Do you know how powerful he is in our department? Fuck the five-year plan, I'll probably have to wait for him to die if I want to do a PhD here now!*

That'll be soon, Chess had snarled back, *because I'm going to kill him.*

She bared her teeth. *He called you an upstart overrated nobody and said that your marks had probably been elevated because it would look like nepotism if his son won alone.*

I'd looked back over my shoulder. Jonah had his hand on his dad's chest, holding him back, face as red as mine under his mortarboard.

And pure, unadulterated loathing had filled my heart, because now I was going to have to wonder *for-fucking-ever* if what Professor Fisher had said was true.

'I really am sorry about that day,' Jonah said, knee brushing against mine. 'I know it was a decade ago, but in case I haven't said it before . . . I'm so sorry.'

The main benefit of moving into the share house had been the gradual discovery of this man: Cardigan Jonah, Jonah the human, Jonah who was not simply the second coming of his shithead father. I was forever leading with my fists, and I could win an Olympic medal in grudge-holding, but even I had eventually ended up in the kitchen that night, telling him I didn't want to fight anymore.

Chess, though, steadfastly refused to believe in the existence of Cardigan Jonah. For her, it was simple. There was only Tweed Jonah, the son of a Tweedier Jonah. Every humanising thing he did should be interpreted as some kind of trick, just another attempt to defeat me.

I might win a medal in grudge-holding, but Chess would win the gold.

Jonah let his head thud back against the wall. 'I suppose the fact that I hate my dad too probably wouldn't change your sister's mind.'

'Probably not.'

It definitely would not. *That's exactly what he wants you to believe*, she'd hiss at me, *so he can ride your coat-tails.*

I was going to tell Chess about this wild, absurd marriage plot of mine. There was no way I could not tell her. I didn't know *how* I was going to tell her, but I was going to tell her.

But there was no point in breaking my brain in half trying to figure out how I could possibly explain this to her until I knew it was something we could actually *do*.

Right?

The celebrant's office was in Bondi Junction, and we stopped by the mall the next day before our meeting. 'I think they'll know we intend to get married by the fact we've filled out the forms,' Jonah grumbled. 'This doesn't need to be a whole big charade.'

'I'm not saying it does, Fisher,' I replied, herding him along, 'but we need to make ourselves at least *somewhat* believable as a couple.'

He made a sound somewhere between exasperation and resignation. 'Sweetheart.'

I stopped in the middle of the mall walkway and stared at him.

'What?' he said. 'I'm contributing! A real couple wouldn't spit surnames at each other. They'd use pet names, wouldn't they?'

'Not that one,' I replied. 'That sounds like something you'd call a little girl.'

'I'm assuming *baby*'s off the table too, then.'

My mind completely refused to process the notion of Jonah Fisher calling me *baby*.

'Honey,' he tried, as we started walking again.

'What am I, a sixties sitcom wife? Because I can tell you right now that I'm not cooking for you.'

'You better not. I've tasted your cooking.'

'Well, fuck you too.'

'I'll cook. You can grow the vegetables.'

This was, I grudgingly had to admit, a pretty good deal. I loved gardening, and eight years of living with him – for all I'd tried to avoid him – had taught me that Jonah was an excellent cook.

'We just need a few little things,' I said. 'Things that will suggest to people that we're a couple without us having to make a big song and dance about it.'

'What are you thinking, dear?'

'That I'm not a hundred and eighty years old. Not *dear*.'

I tucked a stray piece of hair behind my ear. 'People always over-complicate this when they do fake dating in romcoms. They over-perform. They don't pay attention to what actual couples do in real life. Actual couples don't go around making out in public, or dragging 'just married' signs and a string of tin cans behind them, or wearing 'I'm with stupid' and 'I'm stupid' T-shirts. They do little things. Holding hands, kissing each other on the cheek, those kinds of things. Things we can definitely manage.'

Jonah nodded, looking contemplatively into the middle distance.

'But the easiest, most obvious one of all,' I added, grabbing his wrist and pulling him into the Barbie-pink shopfront of a cheap jewellery store, 'is rings.'

The engagement ring we chose was cubic zirconia, set in sterling silver. A green stone was surrounded by smaller faux diamonds, spiky rather than smooth, like little shards. It cost the princely sum of $27.99, which Jonah insisted on paying: 'I'm all for radically revised gender roles in the heteronormative institution of marriage, but I should still pay for my wife's engagement ring.'

There was that word again. *Wife*.

'I'll buy the wedding bands, then.' I turned away, browsing through the trays. 'Here – does this one fit you?'

He gave me his hand. I slipped a ring onto his finger, still wired to a flimsy piece of cardboard with the price tag attached.

I'd never looked properly at Jonah's hands before. I'd seen them, of course, but I'd never really *looked*. He had the fingers of a violinist, long and slim and nimble.

I had a sudden, vivid flashback of what it had felt like, that night in the kitchen. Those fingers, wrapped around mine.

I shivered.

'Darling,' he said softly.

Oh no. Had I accidentally said something out loud?

'Darling,' he repeated. 'As a pet name. What do you think about *darling*?'

'I, um . . . I don't hate *darling*, actually.'

I took the ring back off his finger. 'Not *darl*, though.'

'Agreed. Never *darl*.'

'What about the ring?' I brandished it at him. 'Are we agreed on this?'

'I never really imagined my wedding ring would come in a pack of three.'

'So much the better. You've got spares if you lose one. Or if the gold finish rubs off. The fact that these are three for twelve dollars doesn't give me a lot of faith in their staying power.'

I threw the packet of rings up in the air and caught it again. 'Not that they'll need much staying power. Three years isn't that long.'

'Yes it is.'

'We can buy two packets, if you're worried.'

'No, that's not what I . . .'

Jonah exhaled. 'You know there's no way I can ever repay you for this, right?' he said at last.

I opened my mouth.

'Don't pretend I'm talking about the rings. You know what I mean.'

He took one of my hands in both of his. Another shiver shot up my spine, and it took every skerrick of willpower I had not to let him see it.

'Thank you, Sadie,' he said.

'It's fine.' Deeply uncomfortable with his level of sincerity, I tugged my hand free before he could see that all the hairs on my arm had stood up. 'It's not that big a deal. We wear a couple of rings and stay flatmates for a few years. Then we can get divorced, go on our merry way and spend the rest of our lives pretending to be bitter exes.'

I shepherded him over to the cash register. 'Imagine how easy it'll be working together then. We already have so much practice fighting.'

Jonah made a harsh, barking sound in the back of his throat that might have been a laugh.

'Let's face it, Fisher,' I said, tapping my credit card against the reader. 'I was born to be your ex-wife.'

The meeting with the celebrant turned out to be simple. She was a tall South Asian woman with curly hair and a bright smile, and she talked us through everything we needed to do calmly but warmly, her signature on our forms as our witness an authoritative scrawl. 'I assume you picked us because you want the full Going to Gretna Green experience – getting married as quickly as possible, but with minimum fuss,' she said. 'I'll get everything sorted, and we'll get you married before you need to leave for your new jobs. You don't need to worry about a thing.'

The meeting with HR at the university, though, was not so simple. 'We were not aware that this was your situation, Dr Shaw,' one of the people on the Zoom call said coldly. 'Or yours, Dr Fisher.'

Jonah had his arm around me – half so we'd pass as a couple, half so we could both fit into frame. I could feel him shaking.

I took a deep breath and tried to channel Francesca Shaw, The Lawyer Who Eats Lawyers. 'When would it have been appropriate for us to disclose our relationship? During the hiring process? When it would substantially disadvantage our chances?'

'Sadie's chances in particular,' Jonah said. His arm was still shaking, but his voice was steady. 'There's plenty of research demonstrating the internalised bias hiring committees hold against married women in their twenties and thirties, because of the assumption they'll take time out for maternity leave.'

'This can hardly be an un-anticipated circumstance,' I added. 'Your contract has an express clause around partner hire where the partner is appropriately qualified.'

I reached up and laced my fingers through Jonah's where they rested on my shoulder, trying to provide him with some steadiness and show off my engagement ring all at the same time. It was an attempt to visually suggest something I did not want to – and that my inner Chess absolutely would not let me – put into words: that if they didn't use the partner hire clause to hire Jonah, they would lose me too.

'No one could be more appropriately qualified than Jonah,' I said. 'The fact that he was shortlisted for this job is ample evidence of that.'

We put up a good fight and the university reps tersely agreed to look into it, but afterwards, neither of us were convinced that it was going to work.

'Well, it was fun while it lasted,' Jonah said heavily. 'Thanks for trying.'

'Don't despair just yet,' I said. 'Maybe they just have terrible personalities.'

He smiled, but it was humourless. 'I don't think I'm going to get a eucatastrophe this time, Shaw.'

I sighed. I didn't either.

And even though that would be awful, I was also kind of relieved. If they turned us down – if they sent us an email saying, *LOL, nice try, but permanent academic jobs aren't just lying around for anyone with a wild scheme and a ring to scoop up* – then I wouldn't have to tell Chess about any of this.

I was at ESU, tying up some loose ends, when I got the email from Jonah. FW: Employment contract (Lecturer, Level B) was the subject line.

Then a text, two seconds later. It worked.

Followed swiftly by another. So I guess we have to start telling people?

/

We bickered over the details of the plan, but the way forward was clear.

Academia was a small, incestuous world. The more people who knew our relationship existed somewhere between 'sham' and 'scam', despite its technical legality, the likelier it was that Jonah and I would find ourselves not just unemployed but unemployable.

We had to sell this to *everyone*.

Firstly, there were our housemates. Jonah thought they knew us too well for us to lie to them. 'Maybe not all of them, but we've lived with Van and Annie for eight years!' he protested, sitting on my bed, the soft glow of my lamp catching the few strands of grey in his dark hair and turning them silver, the fairy lights above him giving him a starry crown.

'Do you know how many times they've asked me when you and I are going to bang it out?' I demanded.

He immediately turned bright red.

'It'll be easy,' I said. 'We'll just be like, "Oh no, the thought of being separated made us realise that we've actually been enemies-to-lovers all this time, and now we're rushing to the altar so we never need to be apart again."'

He exhaled, pinching the bridge of his nose behind his glasses.

'Plus,' I said, unable to resist needling him, 'what do you think they *think* we've been doing in each other's bedrooms recently?'

He gave me a withering look, as he turned even redder. 'Cute, Shaw.'

'I thought so.'

'What about your friends?'

'What about the Van and Annie plan did you not understand?'

'Your other friends.'

'Like our PhD cohort? They know what we're like. The enemies-to-lovers line will totally work on them.'

'No.' Jonah ran his hand through his hair, the silver strands shifting and sparkling. In this kind of lighting, it was difficult not to notice that he really was quite a handsome man. 'I mean – your other friends. Your non-university friends.'

'Fisher,' I said, jamming the pad of my thumb into the cubic zirconia spikes of my engagement ring, 'we work about the same number of hours a week, right? Are you out there maintaining a whole host of non-uni friendships? Because if you are, I give you permission to lecture me about time management.'

Then there were our siblings. 'If it's all right with you, I'd like to let Fiona think we're real,' Jonah said, once we'd finished arguing about our non-existent friends.

'Are you sure?' I asked sceptically.

'I'm going to tell Elias the truth, but Fi's already carrying so much. The last thing I want to do is add *my baby brother is entering a loveless marriage just so he can move closer to me* to the pile.' Jonah took off his glasses and started polishing them. 'Plus, she's terrible at keeping secrets. She told her kids I was moving to Hobart before I'd even interviewed.'

Fuck me. No wonder he'd been such a nervous wreck that day.

'When are you going to tell Chess?' he asked. 'I assume you're going to tell her the truth.'

'Obviously,' I said. 'I just need to find the right moment. But let's talk about the biggest bridge we have to cross. How are we going to tell your dad?'

Jonah closed his eyes for a second, exhaling audibly. He hadn't put his glasses back on yet, and for a moment he looked very young, and very scared.

'It doesn't need to be *we*,' he said. 'I'll tell him.'

'I don't suppose you could get your mum to . . . soften him up for you?' Not that I could wrap my head around what a softer Professor Christian Fisher would look like.

'My mum was one of his PhD students who dropped out to have his babies and be his unpaid research assistant.' His tone was sharp. 'Just how effective do you think that would be?'

I held my hands up. 'Sorry.'

He sighed, putting his glasses back on. 'No, I'm sorry. That was uncalled for. It's just . . .'

He didn't need to finish the sentence. I was not in the habit of being particularly sympathetic towards Jonah Fisher, but it didn't take much to imagine just how poorly his dad must have taken it when he lost the Lyons job to me – and how much worse he was going to take this.

'What if we don't tell him the whole story?'

'Shaw, I plan on telling my dad that we're the greatest pair of lovers since Heloise and Abelard. If he found out we were pulling a scam like this—'

'Not that.'

I shifted in my desk chair, uncrossing and recrossing my legs, trying to find a comfortable way to sit. 'I mean about the partner hire. What if we told your dad that Lyons had a sudden change of heart and decided to hire us both, and wow, wasn't it convenient that we fell in love along the way?'

'No.'

'It's okay. Really. He's going to be an arsehole about you marrying me anyway, right? If letting him think that we both got the job on merit will take the edge off—'

'*No.*'

Jonah looked me dead in the eye. 'My dad has been trying to cut you down for years,' he said. 'Do you think I would really take away your opportunity to rub his nose in what you've accomplished?'

I was suddenly very uncomfortable in my chair again.

Then he made it a million times worse by reaching over and touching the back of my hand with one finger, pressing lightly between my knuckles.

'Thank you, though,' he said, 'for offering.'

''sokay,' I managed.

My body was determined to react, but I repressed it as forcefully as I could. God, I was going to have to get myself under control, and fast, or Jonah was going to notice.

'My dad needs to respect your achievements, Shaw,' he said. 'That's worth more than my pride.'

🖉

A couple of nights after Jonah broke the news to his parents that he was marrying an upstart overrated nobody and moving to Tasmania with her on a partner hire, we went round to the Fisher family home for dinner. 'They insisted,' he told me apologetically. 'They seem to think I'm playing some kind of practical joke.'

'Are you a practical joke kind of family?'

He snorted. 'What do you think?'

I was genuinely very curious to see where Jonah had grown up. Considering how often his dad liked to use the words 'vulgar' and 'cliché' when he described the books I studied, the Fisher family home should have been an elegant *Grand Designs*-esque architectural wonder.

It wasn't, though. The house our Uber pulled up to in Watsons Bay was a garden-variety McMansion, no different from the other McMansions on the street.

We were both wearing our own variety of armour. I'd pulled my hair back severely, put on my favourite don't-fuck-with-me black jumpsuit, and sung *Vigilante Shit* quietly to myself as I applied eyeliner sharp enough to kill a man. Jonah had combed his hair back, trimmed his beard and put on a tweed blazer with leather elbow patches.

It was a sultry summer evening – far too hot for him to be wearing tweed. I didn't think it was the heat, though, that was making him look faintly sweaty as he rang the doorbell.

His dad answered. He stood there for a long moment, looking us both up and down. Instinctively, my right hand curled into a fist.

'Jonah,' he said. 'Ms Shaw.'

'*Dr* Shaw,' Jonah and I said at the same time.

Over his dad's shoulder, I caught his mum's eye. She, at least, had the good grace to look apologetic.

I looped my hand around Jonah's bicep. Thank God he'd turned down my offer to minimise my accomplishments, because I didn't think I had it in me not to dunk on this man. 'Considering I'm marrying into the family, Christian, you can call me Sadie.'

A muscle in Professor Fisher's jaw twitched. I resisted the urge to smirk.

'It's nice to meet you, Sadie,' Jonah's mum said, offering me her hand to shake.

That was the most pleasant thing either of them said to me for the entire night – and, notably, pretty much the only thing his mum said at all. If I'd doubted anything Jonah had told me about his family being poison before, I sure as hell didn't now. No wonder Fiona had ended up where she was. In her shoes, I too might have married the first man who offered if it meant not having to sit around this table.

'So, tell me how you were hired over my son, *Sadie*,' Professor Fisher said as we sat down to dinner.

It was impressive, really, the way he could make my name sound like an insult. He was a hair's breadth away from bellowing *are the shades of Pemberley to be thus polluted?!*

'She has an outstanding research track record and exemplary teaching performance,' Jonah said.

'Did I ask you, Jonah?'

I was tempted to parrot exactly what Jonah said back into his dad's face – *I have an outstanding research track record and exemplary teaching performance* – but in the interest of being an adult, I opted for a slightly more conciliatory approach. 'Lyons was looking for a popular fiction specialist.'

That muscle in Professor Fisher's jaw twitched again.

'They don't see popular fiction studies as specious and point-less,' I couldn't resist adding, 'unlike some other, more short-sighted institutions.'

'I thought they were looking for an early modernist,' Professor Fisher said to Jonah, turning his head to make it very clear I was no longer being addressed.

'It was one of the other desired specialisations.' Jonah passed me the beans. 'Rory Worland made it to interview too.'

That must be the Shakespeare bro who'd leapt and punched the air when he walked out of his job talk, in the single most transparent attempt at psyching out the competition I'd ever seen.

'Perhaps that split the vote in the hiring committee,' Professor Fisher mused. 'That happens sometimes, when they interview two people with the same specialisation.'

'Or perhaps,' Jonah said, 'they hired Sadie because she was the best choice.'

His dad ignored him. 'I know the Head of Humanities at Lyons. Sofia Vargas. Awful woman. Terrible scholar.'

Professor Vargas had been the head of our hiring committee. I'd liked her immediately – and, reading between the lines of this particular tirade, she'd probably been the one who made sure 'popular fiction' appeared on the list of desirable specialities.

'An old chum of mine started there last semester, though,' Professor Fisher continued. 'Lachlan Petrovski. You should mention my name to him, Jonah. He'll look out for you – when he's not too busy sorting out Sofia's messes, anyway.'

'I don't need looking out for, Dad,' Jonah said. 'I'm an adult. I don't need a babysitter.'

'Is that so? Because maybe if someone had been babysitting you a bit more, you wouldn't have got *distracted*.' The last word was a snarl, accompanied with a dismissive gesture directed at me. 'The same thing happened to your brother. He got distracted by a girl and now he's unemployed.'

Oh, fuck this.

'Elias is not unemployed,' Jonah said. 'He's on his fifth—'

'Oh wow, Christian,' I cut in, laughing. 'I didn't know you had such great respect for my intelligence.'

Professor Fisher's glare refocused on me.

'A scheme like that,' I went on brightly, 'convincing Jonah to fall in love with me at just the right moment so I could swoop in and steal this job from him – that would take meticulous planning and an incredible level of skill to execute.'

I reached over and took Jonah's hand where it was resting on the table, lacing my fingers through his. 'Of course, in your universe, where I'm a Machiavellian genius, I'm not sure why I'd actually marry Jonah after stealing the job that was rightfully his, but thank you for giving me so much credit.'

Could I, I wondered, actually make Professor Fisher's head explode, if I pushed hard enough? The vein pulsing in his forehead was very much suggesting that I could.

'You should be grateful, Dad. Happy, even.' Jonah's fingers tightened around mine, so tight it hurt a little, pressing my engagement ring uncomfortably into my knuckle. 'However it happened, I've got a permanent job now – and I'll be able to help out Fiona and the kids.'

'Fiona—'

'Don't.'

It was the same way he'd said it that night in the kitchen, when I'd blithely strolled in, found him collapsed over the table and made some crack about him being so broke he'd need to take money from his parents. *Don't*, he'd snarled, venomous even by our standards.

'And on top of that,' he went on, 'you're getting one of the most brilliant early career researchers in the country as a daughter-in-law.'

Oh. Goodness.

Did he really think that?

The hairs on the back of my arm were standing up again, but more importantly, Professor Fisher's jaw was twitching so hard it was practically humming, and I'd lost my battle with restraint.

I leant over and pressed my lips to Jonah's jaw. 'You're so sweet,' I said, rubbing my nose performatively against his cheek. 'I can't wait to start a life with you.'

His dad looked apoplectic.

Slowly, Jonah smiled. 'Me neither, darling.'

His words were warm against my lips as he turned his head towards mine. This time, as his nose brushed mine, I couldn't suppress the shiver.

Neither of us spoke in the Uber home afterwards. Dinner had been a tense, unpleasant encounter, and we were both silent as we processed it.

Well, Jonah was probably processing. I was . . . thinking.

Specifically, I couldn't stop thinking about reaching out and touching his beard. He kept it quite short – not that far removed from stubble, perhaps a three- or four-day shadow – and I'd always thought that it would feel rough, like one of those scratchy doormats.

Against my lips, though, when I'd kissed his cheek, it had been soft. Had that been real, or just adrenaline?

And then there had been that thing he said. *You're getting one of the most brilliant early career researchers in the country as a daughter-in-law.*

That couldn't have been real. That he had some level of respect for my intelligence I could believe – but that? No. Surely not.

He'd said it, though. With his whole chest. To his *dad*.

I rubbed my hands up and down my arms, telling myself it was the air-conditioning that had given me goosebumps.

'Can you handle another Fisher tonight?' Jonah asked abruptly.

Perhaps it was because I'd been thinking about stroking his beard – or perhaps it was because I'd read far too many romance novels – but my brain heard the words 'handle' and 'Fisher' and took them to a much more literal place than he'd intended.

'What do you mean?' I asked, glad the darkness of the car was concealing the inevitable scarlet flush creeping up my collarbone.

'How would you feel about calling Fiona with me? I should tell her myself. Before my parents do.'

Oh. Okay. That made sense. With the way he'd found out about her husband and the second family debacle and whatnot. Yep.

'All right,' I said, trying to repress the part of myself that had illogically decided to feel slightly stung.

When we were home, in his room, we bickered half-heartedly for a few minutes about the best approach to take before we sat down in front of his laptop, his arm around my shoulders. 'Hi, Fi,' Jonah said, when she answered the video call. 'There's someone I'd like you to meet.'

Fiona didn't look like I'd imagined her. I'd seen what my father had made of my mother, how worn and beaten down and broken he had left her. I expected to see a woman who had been crushed.

I wasn't wholly off-base. Even through Zoom, there was no disguising the fatigue writ large across Fiona's face. But there was light too, bright behind her big brown eyes – so similar to Jonah's, even with his glasses – a capacity for joy that I had simply never seen in my mother.

Her hands flew to her mouth when Jonah explained everything. 'You're joking.'

'We're not. We, um . . .'

He looked at me, that unfamiliar desperation behind his eyes.

'Fell in love,' I finished for him.

'Oh God,' Fiona said. 'Oh *Jonah*.'

'It's fast, I know,' he said, 'but once we finally figured it out, the thought of letting this job tear us apart . . . well, with the partner hire and everything, getting married just made sense.'

'So you're moving? Here?'

'Yes. We've got to tie up some loose ends here in Sydney – like actually getting married – but then we're moving. We'll be in Hobart in a few weeks.'

Fiona burst into tears.

'I'm sorry,' she sobbed. 'I'm so sorry – God, Sadie, what must you think of me?'

'It's all right,' I said. 'Really, it's fine.'

'You just . . . You can't even know what good news this is to me.' She rubbed her sleeve roughly across her face. 'Everything's been so hard, with Matt gone, and – oh, Jonah.'

A fresh wave of sobs overtook her. Beside me, I felt Jonah start shaking.

But his voice, when he spoke again, was firm. 'You're not going to be on your own anymore, okay, Fi? I'm going to be there to help you.'

'We.'

Jonah glanced at me.

'We're going to be there to help you,' I said. 'Both of us.'

'I know I've only just met you, Sadie,' Fiona said, smiling tearily, 'but I think I love you.'

Something blossomed in my heart; warm, golden tendrils snaking their way through my veins.

There. That look on her face.

Eucatastrophe. Joy, poignant as grief.

'How did two people as miserable as your parents produce Fiona?' I asked Jonah a little later, after we hung up the call. 'She's a human ray of sunshine.'

'I don't know.'

He laced his fingers together, stretching his arms over his head. 'There are a lot of things I don't know about my sister anymore,' he said, 'but I'm looking forward to learning.'

It was such an earnest thing to say.

Sincerity, my research had taught me, was often seen as a vulnerability. To earnestly express a feeling was a weakness. It was part of the reason people – including, but not limited to, Professor Christian Fisher – liked to hang shit on romance novels. There was something inherently earnest at their heart: a sincere love and hope and joy that readers often reacted to with the same feelings, a delicate flower that provoked some people to want to crush it.

The part of me that led with her fists should have seen this earnestness, and made a joke of it.

But there was still a honey-golden warmth snaking through my bloodstream, so, 'That's really nice,' was all I said.

Jonah looked at me, and he smiled, the way he had at the dinner table.

My face heated at the memory of his nose brushing gently against mine.

'If you want,' he said, 'I can help you tell your sister.'

It was like a bucket of ice water had been thrown over me.

'No,' I said firmly, standing up. 'I need to do that on my own.'

I had dinner with Chess the next night. 'Okay, I'm really pushing your boundaries here,' I said, sliding *Roomies* by Christina Lauren across the table to her as my heart pounded a million miles a minute. 'I've never given you a contemporary romance with this trope before, because it's kind of fake dating and problematic paperwork all wrapped into one, but it's good, I swear.'

Her eyes narrowed. 'What's the trope?'

I swallowed. 'Marriage of convenience.'

She groaned. 'Sadie, no!'

I didn't tell her.

A few days later, she took me to a fancy new wine bar. She got deep in conversation with the bartender about tannins and tears, and I psyched myself up to tell her. Sure, she hated Jonah, and sure, she was going to hate the idea of me marrying him, even if it was only on paper, but it was a public place. How apocalyptic could her reaction be?

I didn't tell her.

Dinner at her place the next week. *Obviously* I couldn't tell her in the wine bar. Chess had no problem making scenes in public places. The one she'd made at graduation with Professor Fisher was proof enough. At her place, then.

Right before I walked through her door, I took off my engagement ring and put it in my handbag.

I didn't tell her.

'We're getting married in a week, Sadie,' Jonah told me exasperatedly. 'You have to tell her. Let me help you.'

'No. I'm having dinner with her tomorrow. I'll tell her then.'

I didn't tell her.

FEBRUARY

Chapter Eight

Sadie

'I can't believe you're leaving me in two days!' Chess exclaimed. 'God, Sadie. This has all gone so fast.'

The movers had come that morning. Almost all the worldly goods Jonah and I owned were now somewhere in a shipping container en route to a storage facility in Hobart, ready for us to unpack once we found a rental. The rest of my stuff was in a carry-on suitcase, sitting in Chess's spare room. I was going to spend tonight and tomorrow at her place before our flight.

Tonight, I'd be spending the night as an unmarried woman. Tomorrow, though . . .

My left thumb went instinctively to my ring finger, looking for the spikes of my ring. It had become a tic over the last month, a grounding technique, jamming the pad of my thumb into them.

But this time I found nothing. My engagement ring was in the inside pocket of my handbag with the three-for-$12 packet of wedding rings, one of which I was due to slip onto Jonah Fisher's finger at 4pm the next day.

And I still hadn't told Chess.

One of the things you had to do all the time as an academic scrounging for jobs and fellowships and grants was craft the narrative of your research career. It was usually called ROPE – Research Opportunity and Performance Evidence – and you had to talk about how much you'd achieved relative to the opportunities you'd had.

I'd taken that concept a step further and crafted a narrative for myself, one that I'd told to myself, sold to myself, over and over again.

It was the story of the ultimate underdog. Sadie Shaw had come from nothing and been excellent despite it. Sadie Shaw had created opportunities where there were none and made much more than the most of them. Sadie Shaw had kicked down the doors of the ivory tower and made everyone who told her she couldn't do it rue the day they'd crossed her. Sadie Shaw was a badass.

But she was a badass who was very, very scared of what her big sister was going to say when she found out about the wedding.

'How soon is too soon for me to come and visit?' Chess asked. She'd pulled an especially fancy bottle of wine out of the cupboard she liked to refer to as her 'cellar' and was rummaging around for a corkscrew. 'I don't want to be clingy – I know you're going to need time to find a place and get settled and everything – but I'm genuinely worried I'm going to fall apart without you nearby.'

'Um . . .' I lectured to hundreds of people regularly, and yet my voice sounded like a scared eight-year-old's. 'When were you thinking?'

'I've got a ton of leave saved up.' Chess deftly levered the cork out. 'I could come whenever you want. I could even fly down next week and help you house-hunt, if that would be helpful.'

I had a sudden, horrifying vision of what that would look like. Chess, crashing on the couch of the serviced apartment the university was temporarily putting Jonah and me up in. Her, me and him, in the same space.

'The next few weeks will be a bit chaotic,' I said. 'Starting work and all.'

'You just let me know when you want me to come and I'll be there.' She sniffed her wine, then took a long sip before making a sound of satisfaction. 'God, that's so good.'

'What is it?' I asked, because I was the world's biggest coward, taking the easy way out of a difficult conversation as soon as it presented itself.

'This is the Bibliophile Noriko, their reserve pinot noir.' Chess turned the bottle around and showed me the label, which had an artfully drawn picture of a messy stack of books on it. 'I first picked up a bottle of theirs a few years ago because the label reminded me of you, but their wine is so good that I joined their wine club. I get a half-dozen sent to me every three months.'

I took a sip. It might have been the best wine in the world or the worst. I couldn't tell. My whole mouth was numb.

'Bibliophile is Tasmanian, actually.' Chess smiled at me over the rim of her glass. 'Based in the Coal River Valley. Super close to Hobart. Maybe I'll surprise you one day. Turn up on your doorstep and kidnap you so we can go wine-tasting.'

It was the smile that broke me.

She'd smiled that smile at me a million times before. *Don't worry, sweetie. Everything will be okay. I'll make sure of it.*

And she would.

She'd cleared the way for me. She'd swept all the debris out of the path between me and the ivory tower, fought all the monsters, cheered when I finally kicked down the door like she hadn't done anything at all.

She would do anything in the world for me. She *had* done every-thing in the world for me.

'Chessie,' I whispered.

I was choking on how much I loved her. How much I would never, ever be able to repay her. Suffocating on it.

'Oh God, don't cry!' She was beside me on the couch in an instant, an arm wrapped around my shoulders. 'If you start, I'll start.'

I put my wine down. I was going to contaminate it with my tears otherwise, or spill it all over Chess's beautiful floor, the floor she'd worked so hard for, to make sure we never went hungry or thirsty again.

'Can you, um, can you . . .'

'Can I what? What do you need?'

'Can you get out of work early tomorrow?'

'Of course!' she said, almost laughing. 'I'll have to rearrange some meetings, but that's okay. I could take the whole day off, if you like.'

'I . . .' My thumb went to my ring finger again, searching. 'I, um, have plans. But I . . . I . . .'

Chess put her wine down too and turned to face me on the couch, taking my hands in hers. 'What is it?'

I looked at our hands. If I looked at our hands, I didn't have to look at her face.

'Could you meet me in the park tomorrow at four? The one near the share house? Under the fig tree? Do you know the one?'

'I know the one. Do you want to have a picnic? I could order another one of those fancy cheeseboards.'

'No.'

I swallowed once, twice. If Chess hadn't had such a firm grip on my fingers, I would have reached for my glass and knocked all that expensive wine back like a shot of tequila.

'I'm getting married,' I whispered.

Chess went completely still.

'What?' she said at last.

'I'm getting married. At four. Tomorrow. In the park.'

Another moment of silence.

'Sadie,' she said, 'I don't understand.'

'Remember how you looked at my contract?' I still couldn't look at her. 'And there was that provision for partner hire?'

'Ye-e-es.' She stretched out the vowel sound. Her fingers were completely motionless in mine. 'But that doesn't apply to you. You don't have a partner.'

'What if . . .' I swallowed again. 'What if I did, though?'

'Well, first I'd ask why you didn't tell me sooner. You've introduced me to every boyfriend you've ever had. Or at least I think you have.'

'I have,' I said miserably.

'Then what's going on?'

She let go of one of my hands and tipped my chin up, forcing me to look her in the eye. 'Whatever's going on, you can tell me.'

The words came out in a rush. 'Remember how I told you about Jonah's sister?'

It took a second – maybe two seconds – but an entire novel played out on Chess's face as she put the pieces of the story together.

'Tell me you're not serious.'

'It's not romantic.' Now that I'd started talking I couldn't stop, an avalanche of words pouring out of me. 'Obviously, it's not romantic. But what was I supposed to do, when I heard that story? I couldn't just do nothing, not when I could do *something*. And it's not going to be any different from how things already are between us – I mean, we've been housemates for years, and trust me, it's going to make living in Hobart so much cheaper and easier – and there are so few permanent academic jobs, this is kind of like putting one over on the system, and—'

'Stop.'

I stopped.

Chess let go of my hand and folded her fingers in her lap. 'What have you signed?'

'The wedding's not until tomorrow, so not much, not yet.' Why was she so calm? 'The Notice of Intended Marriage form. A stat dec for the university.'

'What did you say on the stat dec?'

'That we've lived together for eight years and now we're getting married.'

She let out a long breath. 'Okay. Okay. Not great, obviously, but we can work with that.'

'What do you mean, "we can work with that"?'

'I can get you out of it.' She reached for her wine, took a long sip, then set it down again. 'There are a couple of approaches we can take. There's irreconcilable differences, obviously, but if you really do feel badly enough about the thing with his sister that you're willing to undergo an entire ridiculous charade to ensure that this man gets a job he doesn't deserve—'

'He does deserve it. Just as much as me.'

'No, he doesn't, or *he* would have got the job,' Chess snapped. 'But if you're determined to do a solid for him, you don't have to marry him. There's no way anyone can legally prove whether you are or aren't engaged.'

'Lyons would get pretty suspicious when we kept postponing our wedding. Plus, we already made it pretty clear that we'd be married by the time we got there.'

'Sadieeeee.' My name came out of her in a groan. 'Why did you wait until the last minute to tell me? You must have filed the notice of intent weeks ago! Why are you only telling me now?'

She pinched the bridge of her nose, hard. 'This would have been so much easier to get you out of if you'd just *told* me.'

'I don't want you to get me out of it.'

'So you actually want to do this?'

I didn't know how to respond.

'You actually want to marry him.' It was a question that sounded like a statement. 'This man. This fucking private school boy. That's who you want to marry.'

'He's not that bad. He's . . . he's . . . he's nice, really, once you get past all the tweed.'

Chess scoffed.

'And it's not that I *want* to marry him, exactly. It's . . . it's—'

'Sadie, if you want to fuck him, just fuck him.'

My mouth fell open.

'I'm serious.' Chess drank the remaining half of her glass in one gulp. 'Arguing is friction. Hate sex is a real thing. If it'll help you get it out of your system, I will sacrifice one of the last two precious nights I have with you so you can go and fuck him.'

'I don't want to fuck him!'

'But you want to marry him?'

'Stop lawyering me!'

I wanted her to shout. It would have been easier if she'd shouted.

Instead, though, she reached out and pushed a stray strand of hair behind my ear. When she spoke, her voice was soft. 'Sweetie, I'm just trying to look after you.'

'Stop!'

There were no spikes for me to push my thumb into, so I had to clench my fists instead, driving my fingernails into the palms of my hand. 'This is why I didn't tell you!' I exclaimed. 'I'm an adult now, Chess! I'm thirty-one years old! I know what I'm doing! But you still treat me like I'm a little kid you need to look after!'

'I'm your *sister*.' There was a sharp edge in her voice now. 'And I love you.'

123

'Too much!'

I knew – even before I saw the words hit her like a slap to the face – that I'd said something unforgivable.

But the brakes were off now, a month's worth – years' worth, a life's worth – of pent-up feelings pouring out of me. 'I love you, Chess, and I appreciate everything you've done for me. But I'm not a little girl anymore, and sometimes – God, sometimes being loved by you is exhausting.'

Francesca Shaw always knew what to say.

That had been true my whole life. Chess knew what to say. Chess knew what to do. No matter what the situation was, Chess knew how to handle it.

Silence fell.

Chess sat there, on the couch, still as stone, and said nothing.

'I, um . . .' I stood, legs shaking beneath me. 'I think maybe I should leave.'

She didn't stop me.

Chapter Nine

Jonah

My parents weren't attending the wedding. 'If you'd given us more notice, perhaps we could have figured something out, Jonah,' my dad had said sharply, 'but as you're well aware, this conference trip has been planned for months.'

I didn't mind. A wedding without them – without my dad lobbing grenades at Sadie or her sister, who would probably punch them out of the air and directly back into his face – sounded infinitely more pleasant than one with them there.

Plus, with my life and furniture all packed up and being shipped across the country, it meant I had a place to stay for my last couple of nights in town that blessedly didn't have them in it.[26]

---

26 Our brief engagement had gone smoother than it had any right to, but perhaps the only truly awkward moment had come when my mother called me, said 'Don't tell your father about this, but—' and offered to pay for a honeymoon suite in a fancy hotel for our wedding night. Obviously I had to tell her no – newlywed or not, there was no way Sadie was spending our last night in Sydney anywhere but with her sister, and I couldn't run the risk of someone reporting it back to Mum if I stayed in the suite alone – but trying to come up with an explanation as to why my new bride and I would *absolutely* prefer to spend our first night as a married couple together under my parents' roof rather than drinking champagne at the Ritz-Carlton was legitimately harder than my PhD.

I spent the night before my wedding in my childhood bedroom, the suit I'd rented for the ceremony hanging in the wardrobe next to my old high school blazer. I slept poorly, and consequently slept late. The sun was streaming in through the windows by the time I shuffled down to the kitchen to scrounge up some breakfast—

Only to be greeted by the rich aroma of freshly brewed coffee, and my brother standing in front of the toaster.

'Elias!' I exclaimed. 'What the fuck are you doing here?'

'Surprise.' He grinned. 'What do you think I'm doing here? You're getting married!'

I didn't know how to name the feeling that started – not to sweep over me, like a wave, but roll over me very gently, like a cloud moving across the sky.

It was . . . warm. Pink. There were notes of surprise: surprise that he was here, but also that the thought of coming here had even occurred to him. Something like satisfaction, too, like when the lid finally pops off a hard-to-open jar.

'Please tell me you didn't fly all the way from Germany just for my wedding. That's so much money. And it's not even a real wedding!'

'I've got one return flight built into my fellowship funding. I figured I might as well use it while Dad is somewhere else.'

'You should have gone to see Fi.'

'I did. I spent the last couple of weeks in Tassie.'

I blinked. I'd talked to Fiona almost every day since Sadie and I told her we were getting married, and she hadn't said a thing about Elias being there.

'She didn't want to ruin the surprise,' Elias explained.

Or, the Fisher part of my brain translated, she didn't want to risk him and me falling back into old Dad-established patterns and ruining this fragile new bond the three of us were building by over-exposing us to each other. Elias had been nothing but helpful[27] since I reached out to him about my job application, but our devil's advocate programming ran deep. Supportive siblinghood didn't happen overnight.

Two pieces of toast popped out of the toaster. Elias slid them onto a plate and passed them to me. 'Bridegroom first. I'll make more.'

I'd been dreading spending the day alone, given the million-plus possible ways for me to drive myself into an anxiety spiral, so having Elias there helped. We lingered for a long time over breakfast, talking about his fellowship, my new job, what a piece of shit Matt was for refusing to pay child support even though he'd somehow managed to financially support two families for more than a decade, how Fi's eldest kid Lex was like a tiny adult now, how devastated Rosie and Georgia were that they weren't going to be at the wedding because their sole ambition in life was to be flower girls. 'I'm under strict instructions to film every second of the ceremony,' Elias said, reaching for the almost-empty jar of Dad's fancy marmalade. 'Fi's just as sad as the girls that she won't be there. She's given me a list of requested angles and everything.'

I'd been about to fight him for the last of the marmalade, but I let him take it. 'Do you think it's the right thing to do? Not telling Fi that Sadie and I aren't real?'

'Do I think it's a great idea? No. But would telling her be a worse idea? Absolutely.'

He spread the marmalade on his last piece of toast. 'One, she doesn't need more things to worry about, not right now. And two, she might not be a scholar, but she's still a Fisher. She's as competitive as we are. If she knew you were faking a whole marriage for her, who the fuck knows what she'd try to do to one-up you?'

---

27 Blunt – combatively blunt, even – but helpful.

It was hard to argue with that logic.

'Besides,' Elias said, taking a bite, 'the marriage *is* real. History is full of people who were married to each other for reasons other than love.'

That phrase, casually uttered over breakfast, ricocheted repeatedly around my brain as the day went on, the volume turning steadily up and up as the time came for me to start getting ready.

I am not in love with you, Sadie had snapped at me, the day she'd come to me with this scheme, this madness with some method in it. *I have also figured out that you're not in love with me.*

But she was still going to marry me.

In the eyes of everyone – the law, the world, the university, my sister – Sadie Shaw was going to be *my fucking wife.*

'Your Gretna Green package didn't come with any flowers, did it?' Elias said, poking his head into the bathroom.

'No,' I replied, trying and failing to get a rogue piece of my hair to lie flat as I stood in front of the bathroom mirror in my shirt-sleeves. 'We went with one of the cheapest packages they offer. It includes the ceremony, the paperwork, half an hour with a photographer and that's it.'[28]

'Then I didn't risk incurring Mum's wrath by picking some of her precious roses for nothing. Or ruin my algorithm forever by searching for "how to make a boutonniere".'

Elias had pinned a yellow rose and a spray of greenery to the lapel of his suit. 'I think yellow roses have traditionally meant

---

28 We'd had an argument about whether we needed the photographer, which Sadie had eventually won. 'It's like the engagement ring,' she'd said. 'If we've got a couple of wedding photos on our desks at work, it's an easy way to signal that we're legit without having to act like a couple of horny teenagers in public.'

'But—'

She'd sighed. 'Which one of us knows more about romantic comedies, Fisher?'

platonic love,' he said, helping me into my jacket, 'but the language of flowers is outside my particular area of historical expertise.'

'Sadie might know.' I took the boutonniere he handed me and turned it over idly in my fingers, surprised and touched by the gesture. 'She likes gardening.'

It had been a familiar sight in the share house, Sadie putting on her gardening gloves and going off to work in the vegetable patch she'd established in the backyard. When we'd sat down one night and written our wish list for rental properties in Hobart, she'd scribbled 'green space' under the Would Be Nice column. *It's not a must,* she'd said, *but if we could find somewhere I could make a garden, I'd like that.*

Gardens didn't happen overnight.

Sadie Shaw and I were going to make a *home* together.

Elias took the boutonniere back from me and pinned it to my lapel. 'I'm looking forward to meeting her. It's a rare woman who'd have the gall to do something like this.'

What an incredibly profound understatement.

'Can I ask you something?' I said.

'Mm-hmm.'

I hesitated.

'When you were in my shoes,' I said at last, 'if Julia had come to you with an offer like this . . . would you have done it?'

'Yes.'

Elias's demeanour was distracted as he tried to rearrange the greenery to best showcase the rose, but his voice was certain. 'She wouldn't have even had to finish the sentence. If she'd mentioned that partner hire was an option, I would have been down on one knee.'

I might not know my brother as well as I should, but I didn't think he was just talking about the allure of secure employment.

'Unfortunately for me, though,' he said, 'Julia already had a husband.'

'Do you still think about her?'

It was hard to describe the look that came over him. Wistful, maybe.

'Yes,' he said. 'Every day.'

Then he slapped me on the shoulder. 'But today's not about me. Let's get you wed, little brother.'

We got to the park half an hour early. I'd been worried it was going to rain, but the grey clouds of the morning had cleared to a cool, crisp afternoon, the leafy debris under the fig tree crunching, rather than squelching, beneath my feet.

Ten minutes later, the celebrant and the photographer arrived, and five minutes after them came Van and Annie, who we'd asked to be our witnesses. 'Still can't believe this is happening, man,' Van said, giving me a bro hug I had to step back from lest I crush my boutonniere. 'You and Sadie. *You* and *Sadie*.'

'Me and Sadie,' I echoed vaguely.

'She was getting ready when we left,' Annie said. 'She looks beautiful.'

I blinked. I'd thought Sadie was spending the night with her sister. Oh God. Had she not told her sister?!

'As soon as the bride gets here, we can get started,' the celebrant said. 'Do you have any questions for me?'

I shook my head. She smiled, patted me like you would a dog about to go into the vet's office, and went back to chatting with the photographer, casual and cheerful and calm, like she wasn't about to fundamentally change my life.

In less than an hour, I was going to be married.

I was going to be a husband. I was going to have a wife. We were going to say some words that would change reality, and no matter how we felt about each other, I would be married to *Sadie Shaw*.

Unless she chickened out. Because if she hadn't told her sister . . .

I took a few steps away from everyone, deeper into the sheltering shade of the fig tree, and took some deep breaths.

Four o'clock came. Four o'clock went.

Four ten.

Four twenty.

'I'll need to charge you extra if the bride is much later, Dr Fisher,' the celebrant said to me. 'I have another wedding at six.'

I nodded numbly.

What a way this would be for Sadie to cement her ultimate victory. To really, truly, profoundly humiliate me. *And you thought beating Elias for a job was good,* she'd cackle to Julia, in some bar where the clientele was solely made up of Fisher nemeses. *Let me tell you about how I beat Jonah for a job – and then left him at the altar.*

'Look!' Annie said suddenly. 'There she is.'

As a scholar, I had been trained not to make sweeping generalisations, but I'm fairly confident this is true: everyone who has ever got married feels like the time between laying eyes on your partner on your wedding day and them reaching your side is endless. No walk is longer than a walk down the aisle.

In our case, the walk itself was long. The path across the park was much longer than your standard aisle. The way time stretched as my bride walked towards me, though, was not simply geographical.

Sadie was wearing a white knee-length sundress, the skirt fluttering slightly in the breeze. So was her hair, pulled half back.

Her handbag was over one shoulder, a bunch of supermarket flowers sticking out of it. With her other hand, she was pulling a cherry-red carry-on suitcase.

She was so beautiful.

And even at a distance – even with my terrible eyesight – I could plainly see that she wasn't okay.

'I'll go and help her,' Annie said.

'No,' I said. 'I'll go.'

Sadie relinquished the suitcase to me without argument, a clear sign that something was terribly, horribly wrong. 'I'm sorry I'm late,' she said, her voice coming out high-pitched, fast-paced, a bubbling fountain of words. 'It took me longer to get ready than I thought – and then I was like *flowers*, I need flowers, the photos will for sure look fake if I don't have a bouquet, and . . .'

'Shaw, slow down.'

I caught her wrist with my free hand, pulling her to a halt.

She looked up at me. She'd done a good job on her makeup – God, she was beautiful, no wonder teenage Jonah had had such an enormous crush on her, I would compare her to a million summers' days – but the whites of her eyes had a pinkish tinge to them. She'd been crying.

'Your sister . . . ?' I asked.

She shook her head.

'Did you tell her?'

I couldn't marry her if she hadn't. That I knew, deep in my bones.

'I told her. She, um, she . . . I don't think she's coming.'

Oh fuck. *Fuck.*

I didn't want to ask the question, but I had to. 'Do you still want to do this?'

Sadie closed her eyes and took a deep breath.

I braced myself. *I'm sorry, Jonah, I can't.*

But then she opened them again. Her spine straightened, and when she spoke, her voice was as certain as her handshake.

'What I want,' she said, 'is to get this over with.'

✎

And so I married Sadie Shaw at four thirty on a Tuesday afternoon, in the shade of a hundred-year-old fig tree. Elias held the cheap bouquet of slightly wilting pink roses she'd bought, so Sadie could hold my hands. Van and Annie watched, her bags sitting at their feet.

'I call upon the people here present to witness that I, Jonah, take you, Sadie, to be my lawful wedded wife,' I dutifully repeated after the celebrant.

'I call upon the people here present to witness that I, Sadie, take you, Jonah, to be my lawful wedded husband,' she echoed.

My hands were shaking as I slipped a ring onto her finger; shaking worse as she slipped one onto mine. Standing this close to her, I could see that her dress was actually a very pale green, like the stone from her engagement ring had bled into it, ever so slightly.

'Let us hope this day will form a milestone in your lives, one that you will look back upon with much joy and happiness,' the celebrant said. 'It therefore gives me great pleasure to pronounce you husband and wife. You may now both kiss, if you wish.'

Our eyes met.

We'd talked about this. *We don't have to kiss, if you don't want to*, I'd said. *There's a reason they say 'if you wish'.*

It'll look weird if we don't, Sadie had replied. *Plus, the photographer'll probably make us kiss later anyway. I can handle one little peck, Fisher, if you can.*

She didn't look like a person who could handle it.

I cupped her face in one of my hands, lightly, slowly, giving her every opportunity I could to push me away.

Her fingers travelled up to clutch my lapels. I felt the weight of it, emotionally and mentally, but also physically. My jacket was pulling taut across my shoulders.

Sadie Shaw was clinging to me.

What I want, I saw again, in her pleading eyes, *is to get this over with.*

So I kissed my bride.

Gently. Softly. Chastely. One little peck. That was all.

I drew back.

But she was still clinging to me.

The pull of her hands curled in my lapels kept me close. Our noses brushed together as we shared the same air. Her breath – my breath – our breath – was coming quick and hot.

Van whooped. Something snapped. Sadie sprang back.

'Congratulations,' the celebrant said warmly, as if my bride hadn't just jumped away from me like I was on fire. 'Now let's get the marriage certificate signed so we can make this legal.'

It took less than a minute for everyone to sign the papers that would irrevocably change who we were to each other – so short a time, so small a gesture, for so big a change. 'Okay, let's loosen up!' the photographer declared. 'You're married! Let's celebrate.'

'Are you all right?' I whispered to Sadie, as the photographer made us pose with our foreheads leaning against each other, fingers intertwined.

'What does it look like?'

The acid in her voice should have unknotted something in me. That was the Sadie I knew, caustic, acerbic.

It didn't, though. The knot twisted itself even tighter, guilt shooting through me like an electric current.

'Let's try something old school romantic!' the photographer said. 'Jonah, I want you to kiss Sadie's hand. Make sure we can see that beautiful ring!'

Sadie had goosebumps all up her arms, I noticed, as I pressed her knuckles to my lips. 'Are you cold?'

'A little,' she admitted.

I took my jacket off and wrapped it around her, the smallest possible way I could placate my conscience. 'It'd be a pretty bad start to our marriage if I let you get hypothermia in the first fifteen minutes.'

It was a weak attempt at a joke, and the laugh she gave was weak in response, as the photographer kept clicking away ('Oooh, yes, lovely, very romantic!'). My boutonniere was looking a little worse for wear, the petals of the yellow rose bruised from where she'd curled her fingers into my lapels when we'd kissed.

My wife. I'd kissed my *wife*.

Once the photographer had taken a few more shots and then left with the celebrant for their six o'clock wedding, and we'd waved Van and Annie goodbye, Sadie took off my jacket. 'Thanks for this,' she said, practically throwing it back at me and then slinging her handbag over her shoulder. 'I'll see you at the airport tomorrow. Text me when you get there and I'll let you know where I am, okay?'

I caught her wrist. 'Sadie, wait.'

'What?'

'You, um . . . When we talked about how this night would go before, you said you'd stay with your sister. But . . .'

She pulled her wrist out of my grasp, fished in her handbag for an elastic, and tied her hair back. 'Another night on the share house couch won't kill me.'

'Come on, don't be ridiculous. You're not going back to the share house.'

'You will note,' she said tersely, pulling out the handle of her carry-on, 'that nowhere in the contemporary marriage service does it say I have to obey you.'

'What would Van and Annie think? We're newlyweds, and yet you're running away from me to crash on their sofa?'

She shrugged. 'They'll probably think we had our first fight.'

'Come home with me.'

She looked right through me.

'My parents are away. It's just me and Elias, and he knows that we're . . . you know.'

'Spend some time with your brother, Jonah.'

'Oh, his brother has plans,' Elias said, sticking his head into the conversation. 'I'm off to dinner with an old colleague. Nice to meet you, by the way, Sadie. Welcome to the family.'

'We can order a pizza,' I said, as Elias strode away.[29] 'You can have Fiona's old room for the night.'

Sadie bit her lip. It left a fleck of lipstick on one of her front teeth.

It felt like a sign she might be wavering, so I played my trump card. 'You don't even have to talk to me if you don't want to.'

'Fine,' my wife said.

I thought she was going to take me up on it. She disappeared as soon as we got back to the house. The pipes groaned as she took a shower so long I was vaguely concerned even my parents' state-of-the-art hot water system would run out. Finally, there was silence for such an extended period of time I thought she'd gone to bed.

But then she emerged, wearing a familiar pair of pyjamas,[30] wrapped in a huge olive-green cardigan. 'Were you serious about pizza? I'm starving.'

---

29 I would put the odds of Elias *actually* having plans at about fifteen per cent: possible, sure, but terribly convenient.

30 You know the ones.

'Sure. The usual?'

She nodded. One of the few things we'd never fought over was our pizza order. Sometimes, despite that promise we'd made when we moved into the share house to stay out of each other's way, we'd both be conscripted into a pizza night, and whenever that happened, she and I always split the same thing – pesto chicken pizza, side of garlic bread. I'd eat my share in one sitting, but she'd always save one or two pieces of pizza and have them for breakfast the next day.[31]

'I hope your sister doesn't mind me borrowing this cardigan,' Sadie said. 'It was hanging on the back of her desk chair.'

It was actually my cardigan – Fi had stolen it from me years ago, back when we were still close – but I wasn't about to tell Sadie that. 'She won't mind. Want something to drink? I can raid my parents' wine cellar.'

'No. That's okay.'

Then she rubbed a hand over her face. 'Actually, you know what? Yes. Maybe a drink will help.'

'Any preference? White? Red? Rosé? Sparkling?'

'Not red,' she said, a little stiffly. 'Anything else is okay.'

I second- and third- and fifteenth-guessed myself before I finally decided that no, it wasn't too much to choose a bottle of champagne.[32] 'They won't notice,' I said, when Sadie protested. 'They order cases of it from France on the regular.'

'I don't care what they think. It just seems like a waste. I probably won't drink more than a glass.'

'Elias can drink the rest when he gets home.' I popped the cork. 'We should celebrate.'

---

31 Despite the fact that pairing pizza and coffee was objectively disgusting. That we *had* fought over.

32 If we couldn't go to the Ritz-Carlton, then . . .

She made a noise somewhere between a scoff and a disdainful snort.

'We're both gainfully employed.' I poured the champagne too fast and it started fizzing wildly, so I had to stop before the glasses overflowed. 'And we're pioneers of a bold new strategy for casual conversion. Future higher education union heroes. That deserves celebration.'

The pizza arrived as I finished filling up our glasses. We carried it to the lounge room, setting everything down on the coffee table. 'They won't give a shit about the wine, but this, my parents would care about,' I said, passing Sadie a plate. 'There's a strict no-eating-on-the-couch policy in this house.'

'Sometimes I wonder why you are the way you are, Jonah,' she said, 'and other times it makes perfect sense.'

I wasn't entirely sure what that meant, but I had a strong suspicion that if I tried to find out, it would lead to an argument – and much as that would signal a return to normalcy, it didn't seem like the most auspicious beginning to a marriage, even one like ours.

So I raised my glass instead. 'Cheers, wife.'

Sadie rolled her eyes, but she clinked her glass against mine. 'Cheers.'

We drank. 'Want to watch something?' I nodded my head at the TV.

'Okay.'

I helped myself to a piece of pizza. 'Any preferences?'

'As my wedding gift to you,' Sadie said, tearing open the foil wrapper of the garlic bread, 'I'll let you choose.'

She broke off two pieces before passing the bread to me. 'Within reason, anyway. No documentaries. And nothing about men doing violence and not having emotions. Preferably something where women at least speak, even if it doesn't technically pass the Bechdel test.'

'Noted.' I took a bite of pizza, chasing the cheese, before turning on the TV. 'Just for clarity, my "within reason" excludes all reality TV apart from *Superchef*.'

'You're such a fucking snob, Fisher,' she said, but there was no venom in it.

I almost picked *Suits*, which I'd been vaguely intending to watch for a while, but stopped myself just in time. Given the pointed absence of her sister at our wedding, and the fact that Sadie was here and not with her, a show about hotshot lawyers seemed . . . not ideal.

We ended up with some gentle small-town drama, set somewhere green and mountainous. The protagonists were both kind and competent, the stakes were low, the scenery was pretty. It didn't require a lot of attention. The overall effect was somewhat meditative.

'Top-up?' I asked Sadie.

'Maybe just half.' She wrapped my old green cardigan tighter around herself.

I obliged, adjusting the air-conditioning so it'd be a couple of degrees warmer as I went to put the champagne bottle back in the fridge.

I'd been psyching myself up for a good half hour to ask what had happened with her sister when I realised Sadie was asleep. She'd burrowed into the corner of the couch, face pillowed on one of her curled hands, hair loose around her face.

People were supposed to look younger when they slept. I'd read more than enough books to know that. Sadie didn't, though. In repose, she looked like she'd been holding her burdens at bay all day, only for them to collapse in on her now she was unconscious and unprotected. Twin worry lines cut deep furrows between her eyebrows. My fingers itched with the need to reach out and smooth them away.

The noise from the TV stopped. *Are you still watching?* popped up on the screen. I turned it off.

I could fall asleep here too. It would be easy. It was warm and cosy. The couch was soft. The two glasses of champagne had partially liquefied my bones.

If I fell asleep here, next to her, and it were a few hundred years earlier, it would count as the consummation of our marriage. Once you spent the night alone in the same room as someone, that was it. There was no going back after that for regretful newlyweds in the early modern period, no take-backs on the vows you'd spoken. You were *married*.

I ran my thumb over my wedding ring. I'd never really been a jewellery guy, and wearing it felt strange. Not wrong, exactly, but strange.

Then I exhaled. 'Shaw.'

No response.

'Sadie.'

'Mmmm . . . ?'

'Time for bed.'

'Mmmm.'

'Come on. Up we go.'

She didn't resist as I worked one arm beneath her knees and the other under her shoulders. Her own arm draped bonelessly around my neck as I picked her up, her head lolling into my chest.

My bride was heavy in my arms as I carried her upstairs, over the threshold of Fiona's old bedroom, the one next to mine. I couldn't resist stroking some of those loose fiery strands out of her eyes as I tucked her into bed, cardigan and all. 'Sleep well, okay?'

'Mm-hmm,' was all she said in response.

I went back downstairs. I cleaned up, putting the rest of the pizza in the fridge so she could have it for breakfast. I wiped down the coffee table, poured the dregs in our wine glasses down the sink, put a spoon in the neck of the champagne bottle and left a note about it on the kitchen bench for Elias.

I made myself a cup of the ginger tea Sadie hated so much and stared out the kitchen window for a long time, trying to resist the urge to twist the unfamiliar ring round my finger. I didn't want the cheap gold finish to wear off too quickly, even if we did have spares.

Eventually, I went back upstairs. It took me a while to fall asleep, given the way my thoughts were stumbling and tripping over each other, but I managed it.

I awoke in the grey pre-dawn.

It took me a while to realise what had woken me. I was not and had never been a morning person. My brain didn't really turn on properly until I'd had several cups of coffee.

But on the other side of the wall, my wife was weeping.

Chapter Ten

Sadie

The morning after our wedding, Jonah made me breakfast.

His fingers were dextrous around the handle of the frying pan. His wrists flexed as he flipped the pancakes expertly, sleeves pushed up to his elbows. His attention to detail as he poured syrup and fanned out carefully-cut strawberries was mesmerising. The plate he slid in front of me looked like a magazine cover.

In another, better world, where Jonah set this plate in front of another, better wife, this would be a perfect epilogue. Obstacles overcome. The promise of the marriage plot fulfilled. The first day of a happily ever after.

'This looks beautiful,' I said, throat scratchy. 'Thanks, Fisher.'

He didn't blush, but his cheeks went a little pink above his beard. 'I was going to make you eat cold pizza, but Elias ate it all when he got in last night, the arsehole.'

He slid into a chair opposite me. 'Besides, you know my opinions on combining pizza and coffee, and starting the day off with a fight seemed like a terrible idea.'

Sun was streaming in through the kitchen window. It winked off the gold finish on his wedding ring. Even though I'd just about cried myself hoarse, a tell-tale lump started to grow in my throat again.

This was not that other, better world.

I'd done it. I'd gone through with it.

I was Mrs Jonah Fisher. He was Mr Sadie Shaw.

The rings might be fakes, but their significance was not. No matter how many of our collection of spare wedding bands we went through – no matter if every piece of cubic zirconia fell out of my engagement ring – we were still bound together now, in a very real way.

And Chess hadn't been there.

Hardly anyone had. We'd asked Van and Annie to be there as our witnesses, but we'd invited the rest of our housemates as well, current and past. None of them had been able to make it.

We'd invited some colleagues from the various universities we'd worked at too. None of them could make it either. *That's academic culture for you,* Jonah had said to me, shrugging, when we realised just how small our small wedding would be. *Everyone's always working. Tuesday afternoon isn't exactly the most convenient time.*

But Jonah's brother had come. The brother who lived and worked in Germany, the brother who he'd been raised to fight instead of fight for, the brother he had freely admitted he didn't know particularly well – Elias had come.

And Chess hadn't.

There was a theorist called Zygmunt Bauman who wrote about 'liquid love', the idea that late capitalism had 'liquified' a lot of connections between people. When the world is a marketplace, he argued, we don't want to tie ourselves tightly and permanently to people. Instead, we always have one eye on the market, always on some level considering trading people in for a better, newer, shinier version.

Mostly, when I used Bauman in my work, it was to critique him. The enormous ongoing popularity of the marriage plot and the happily-ever-after, I'd contended in an article in the *Journal of Popular Romance Studies,* signified a strong attachment to the idea that we could find someone we would never want to trade in, and who would never want to trade us in.

But maybe I'd been a bit unfair to old mate Zyg, because, when I looked at my life, he clearly had a point.

I was thirty-one years old, and Chess was the only constant in my life. Everyone else was impermanent. Whether I untied the ties that bound us together or they did, the threads always came undone in the end, unravelling and drifting free.

It had never been something I'd minded. I'd been laser-focused on my career, not my interpersonal connections, and no one had ever made me care enough to mind. When my first boyfriend had tried to talk me into being in love with him – *Don't you love me, Sadie? You love hanging out with me and going out with me and having sex with me. I think you* are *in love with me, and you're just too scared to say it* – I'd cut the thread right there without a moment's regret.

Did you love those things? my therapist had asked me.

Sure, I'd replied, *but I didn't love him.*

How do you know?

Because I know what love feels like, I'd said. *I love Chess.*

That was the one great unshakeable truth of my life. People would come. People would go. Mothers would die and fathers would leave and friends and boyfriends and housemates would drift in and out, but Chess was always there. It didn't matter that all the other bonds that bound people to me were liquid, tied loosely, destined to come undone. She was my anchor. I was tied tight to her.

Then I'd said those awful, unforgiveable things.

I hadn't just cut the thread. I'd hacked through it with a machete, frayed ends all over the floor.

No wonder no one had turned up to my wedding. No wonder the closest thing I would probably ever have to a real partnership was this fake, temporary sham with my long-term nemesis. Why would anyone want to be tied to me?

'More coffee?' Jonah asked.

This, now, was the only tie I had binding me to another person. This, a tie solemnised with a three-for-$12 piece of costume jewellery, consecrating fifteen years of animosity with only a thin veneer of civility over it, his desperation to help his sister drizzled on top like he'd drizzled syrup on those pancakes.

'No.' I stood. 'I'm going to pack.'

Everything I owned was in a carry-on suitcase. He knew that. He'd wheeled it across the park for me yesterday.

He knew that the upstart overrated nobody he'd tied himself to was a coward and a liar.

Upstairs, sitting in the desk chair that had once been Fiona's, I sent a stream of messages to Chess.

> Chessie, I'm sorry. I'm so, so sorry.

> It was the heat of the moment, and I said things I didn't mean.

> I love you.

> I'm in Watsons Bay for the rest of the day – I'll drop you a pin with the address.

> Our flight's at 7pm. I already emailed you my flight details, but I'll forward them to you again just in case.

> Please come by. I need to see you.

> I love you.

None of them were answered.
And Chess didn't come.

✎

Elias insisted on driving us to the airport. 'It's not a very good wedding present, but it's the best I could do on short notice,' he said, kissing me on both cheeks in farewell as Jonah got our luggage out of the boot.

'Us not having to pay cab fare is a great present,' I said, only half paying attention. 'There's still a couple of weeks before that steady pay cheque kicks in.'

Elias slapped Jonah's back in one of those aggressive hugs that men give each other where they simultaneously want to express affection and are terrified of doing so. 'Be good, little brother.'

'Thanks so much for coming.'

Jonah's voice was gravelly, in a way I'd only heard once before: that night in the kitchen. *Elias and Fiona and I aren't like you and your sister. Sometimes I'm so fucking jealous of you, Shaw.*

Chess should be here. She should *be here.*

Elias slapped Jonah's back again. 'I wouldn't have missed it.'

I took my phone out again. At the airport now. Please come. We can't leave it like this, Chessie.

'I might, um . . .' I was dimly aware of Jonah saying. 'At work. If I run into . . . do you want me to . . . ?'

'No,' Elias replied. 'Let those sleeping dogs lie.'

Then he slapped Jonah's back a third time. 'Look after Fi, okay? Tell the kids Uncle Elias said hi.'

'I will.' Jonah turned to me. 'Ready to go?'

I wasn't. Not even remotely.

I nodded, pulling the handle of my carry-on bag up.

The security line was moving at a glacial pace. I was probably the only person who was glad about it. Every step forward felt like a piece of bamboo being jammed under my fingernails, right into the veins that led to my heart.

'I think we should get a car,' Jonah said abruptly.

I glanced up at him. 'What?'

'I know we decided not to.' We shuffled forward another few increments in the line. 'But I think we need to revisit the conversation.'

Conversation was a euphemism. It had been an argument, one of the more intense ones we'd had during our month-long engagement. If our housemates had overheard it, they would have assumed we were either on the verge of breaking up or ripping each other's clothes off.

'Hobart's not like Sydney,' he said. 'There's so much less public transport, especially when you get out of the city centre. I'm telling you, Shaw, it makes sense to buy a car.'

'Have you magically found some buying-a-car money lying around? Because I sure haven't.'

'We could get a loan together. What if Fi needs us to pick up the kids or something? How are we going to do that without a car?'

The line moved forward a few more steps. Suddenly, I was completely, utterly exhausted.

'Okay,' I said.

'What?'

I held up the finger with my engagement and wedding rings on it like I was flipping him the bird, the closest thing to resistance I could muster. 'In for a penny, right?'

He ran a hand over his beard. 'I, um, thought that would be harder.'

I didn't have the energy to respond.

There was still no sign of Chess by the time we'd cleared security, no matter how hard I craned my neck looking for her while Jonah got pulled aside for a random bomb check.

'I'm just going to go to the gate and sit,' I told him when he'd been given the all-clear. Surely, if Chess did come, that would be the first place she'd go. 'Feel free to wander. I can look after your luggage, if you want.'

'That's okay. I'll come with you.'

'Suit yourself.'

We were running early – despite my earlier attempts to delay in the hope that Chess would turn up at the house, the Fisher brothers had overruled me on the importance of beating the traffic, two to one – so our gate was mostly empty, but I guided us to seats as far away from the boarding area as possible. If we had our backs to the wall, I theorised, we'd be able to see everyone that walked towards us.

What was I going to do if Chess didn't come? How was I supposed to get on this plane with *you love me too much* being the last thing I'd said to her?

Chessie, please, I texted her. If you won't come, please call me. I need to hear your voice.

This was the longest I'd ever gone without talking to her. Even when I'd been overseas for conferences, or she'd been working monstrous hours, Chess and I talked every single day.

I jammed my thumb into my engagement ring, scraping it against the unfamiliar pressure of my wedding band. What the fuck was I going to do?

Jonah nudged me with his elbow. 'I'll be back, okay?'

I barely registered it. My body nodded automatically in acknowledgment. He got up and walked away.

And I was alone. Just me and our luggage and the pressure of the spikes of cubic zirconia against the pad of my thumb, and the horrible, horrible weight of what I'd done.

How could I leave if she didn't come?

I couldn't. I *couldn't*.

Chess would be furious with me. *You've worked your whole life for this opportunity!* she'd shout. *What do you mean, you threw it away?*

But it would be a different kind of fury. A familiar fury. There was nothing in the world that made Chess angrier than the thought I might not achieve my dreams. It would be a fury I knew how to manage, a fury we could find our way to the other side of.

Unlike this. This horrible, pointed, suffocating silence that I had no idea how to manage at all.

I bit my lip, hard enough to draw blood.

When Jonah got back from the bathroom, I was going to tell him. *I'm sorry, but I can't,* I'd say. *You go. I have to stay. Lyons only wanted one Level B lecturer anyway, right? You'll do as good a job as me.*

He'd protest, but I'd insist. *Good luck with Fiona. I hope you two can get close again, I really do. And don't worry, I'll get Chess to help us figure out the legalities of a quickie divorce.*

I pressed my thumb harder into my engagement ring. I'd gotten used to wearing it, this past month. It would feel strange not to have Jonah's ring on my finger – naked, almost – but there was nothing that would make me feel as utterly and entirely stripped bare as having this awful, *awful* hole in my heart where Chess should be.

I almost jumped out of my skin when Jonah tapped me on the shoulder, ricocheting wildly between surprise and hope that he was Chess and disappointment that he wasn't and guilt for feeling disappointed because he had done nothing wrong, nothing at all. All he'd done was treat me kindly and carry me to bed and make me the world's most beautiful pancakes and be the most cardigan-y version of himself and I was going to pull the rug out from under him anyway.

'I got you something,' he said, sitting down beside me, just as I was opening my mouth to tell him that I was sorry, but I couldn't.

He handed me a white paper bag with the logo of the airport bookshop stamped on it in navy ink. 'A wedding present. Sorry about the lack of wrapping.'

I took the book out of the bag. It was *Codename Charming* by Lucy Parker.

'I hope I read the paratext right,' he said, tapping his finger against the two cartoon figures on the front cover. 'If this is actually some kind of heart-wrenching saga where everyone dies horribly in the end, I can take it back and exchange it. I kept the receipt.'

'You read the paratext exactly right,' I replied numbly. I had a copy of the exact same book in my handbag, intended to be my plane reading. 'Um—'

'And I got some snacks. It'll probably be too late for dinner by the time we get to Hobart.'

He handed me a bottle of water and a packet of nacho cheese Doritos – my junk food of choice when I was either deeply stressed or on my period.

Oh God. Oh *God*.

'Jonah,' I said. 'Jonah, I . . .'

But he wasn't looking at me anymore. His gaze was fixed on a point over my left shoulder.

I turned to see what he was looking at, and—

'Chess,' I breathed.

I was on my feet before I was conscious of it, propelled towards her as if by gravity. 'Chessie,' I said. 'I'm so glad . . . I'm so sorry . . . I'm—'

'Not you,' Chess snarled, striding straight past me. 'You. Private school boy. With me. Now.'

My heart fell out of my body, landing with a wet splat on the terminal floor.

I couldn't move, couldn't breathe, couldn't do anything as Chess towed a clearly unwilling Jonah away, fingers fastened around his wrist like a manacle. She yanked him to a halt in front of the bookshop – the same bookshop where he must have bought *Codename Charming* for me – and jabbed her finger into his chest, once, twice, three times.

She was facing away from me, and her voice didn't carry, but it didn't matter. Her body language and Jonah's facial expression did not require years of study in close reading to interpret.

Chess curled her fingers into Jonah's lapels and yanked him into her, like a mafia boss in a movie seizing someone by the collar and telling them that if they didn't deliver in one hour, they'd be thrown off a bridge in concrete shoes.

I had done the same thing yesterday. The celebrant had told us to kiss, and I had clutched at his lapels as the weight of what I'd just done collapsed onto me – *I got married, and Chess wasn't there* – and his lips had brushed against mine, and even though it felt like the ground had turned to the ocean beneath my feet, Jonah had held me up.

I'd crushed the rose of his boutonniere when I'd grabbed at his lapels. I had not taken enough care, interested only in what I wanted, what I needed, and the delicate flower had been ruined.

Chess let him go suddenly. Jonah stumbled back a few steps, face white, and she turned on her heel.

I thought she was going to walk straight past me – she didn't slow down – but then she stopped abruptly, looking at me.

I couldn't say anything. After sending her flurries of messages all day, now I was completely frozen.

'Good luck, Sadie,' she said.

And then she was gone.

She was nearly out of sight by the time I managed to galvanise myself into action, the book in its paper bag falling to the floor. 'Chessie, wait!'

She stopped.

I wanted so badly for her to say something. Anything. Even something combative – *don't you have a plane to catch?* – would be something, a place to start.

She didn't say anything.

'I'm so sorry,' I said. 'I'm so, so, so sorry.'

Nothing. Nothing and nothing and nothing, nothing to use as a springboard, nothing to cling to, nothing left.

'Chessie, please.'

Francesca Shaw, who always had something to say, said nothing.

Panicked, I scrabbled in my handbag. 'Please,' I said, pressing my original copy of *Codename Charming* into her hands, the one I'd brought to read on the plane. 'You'll really like this author. This one has fake dating but when she's done that before there's always been a really good reason so maybe it'll be okay.'

Chess said nothing. She held the book like I'd handed her a too-hot cup of coffee and it was burning her fingers.

'I'll send you more. As many as you want. Every day.'

'No.'

One word. One syllable. A knife, directly into my heart.

'I'm so sorry, Chess.' It was a plea. 'I love you so much. I didn't mean it.'

She put the book into her handbag, snapping the clasp shut decisively.

'I know you're sorry,' she said. 'And I love you too. To the end of the universe and back again. Always.'

I had one split second of molten, golden relief before she looked me in the eye.

'But you meant it, Sadie,' she said. 'And I need some time to work out what that means for me. Alone.'

I don't know how long I stood there, frozen, staring after her as she disappeared into the distance, before there were gentle fingers on the small of my back. 'Come on,' Jonah said, propelling me forward, out of the path of a family with an absurd number of wheelie bags. 'Let's sit down.'

He bent down to pick up the copy of *Codename Charming* I'd dropped as he led me back to our seats. 'Do you want this?'

I nodded, taking it from him and clutching it in white-knuckled fingers, so hard that I would probably bruise the pages.

He sat me back down. 'Here.' He took the lid off the bottle of water he'd bought and offered it to me.

I shook my head wordlessly.

'I'm so sorry, Sadie. This is all my fault.'

I wanted to scream.

I wanted to scream right in this man's face, this man whose face I had screamed in plenty of times before, this man who was being so fucking *nice* to me. I wanted to scream and scream and scream, and I wanted to never stop screaming.

'Just shut up, Jonah,' I said hoarsely. 'Please.'

He should have got up and left.

Instead, he hesitated. Then he put his arm around my shoulders and pulled me close.

I should have pushed him away.

But this was the only tie I had left now, the last bridge I hadn't burnt – so I reached up and, even though I had no right to, even though there was no one watching, I clung to my fake husband's hand like a lifeline.

Chapter Eleven

Sadie

'Not long to go now,' Jonah said, hoisting my bag down from the overhead compartment and then reaching for his own. 'You'll feel better when you've had some sleep.'

That was fundamentally untrue, but I didn't have the energy to argue. I'd tried to doze on the two-hour flight to Hobart, but my mind wasn't kind enough to let me. Every bone in my body felt like it was melting.

And we were supposed to show up to campus tomorrow, two scholars finally delivered to the promised land of secure employment. God.

'I don't think anyone will be expecting big things of us tomorrow,' Jonah said, reading me as easily as if I were written by Shakespeare. 'They're hardly going to make us lecture three hundred students and draft a grant proposal on our first day.'

I nodded, turning off airplane mode on my phone as the people a few rows ahead of us started to file off the plane. Nothing from Chess.

It's late, I told myself. *She's probably asleep. She'll feel better in the morning too.*

It wasn't a convincing story, but I clung to it.

My knees creaked as we walked across the tarmac and into the terminal. 'Let me just find our driver,' Jonah said absently, craning his neck to look, 'and – oh God, Sadie, I'm sorry about this.'

'There he is!' someone exclaimed.

Two cannonballs slammed into him, wrapping their arms around his waist. 'Uncle Jonah! Uncle Jonah!'

'Hi girls.' Jonah's eyes met mine apologetically over their heads. 'What are you doing here?'

Two identical sets of wide brown Fisher eyes looked up at him. 'Mummy said we could stay up late to pick you up!' one declared.

'It's *way* past our bedtime,' the other one said.

'Well, then, hello Rosie, hello Georgia.' He smoothed their hair down, one hand on each head. 'How nice to see you.'

'Are you Auntie Sadie?' the first one – Rosie? – demanded of me.

My mouth was suddenly dry. *Auntie* was not a word I had been prepared for. 'I, um . . .'

'Yes,' Jonah said. 'This is Auntie Sadie.'

'We made a sign for you!' Georgia (?) exclaimed.

'Then you made Mummy carry it,' Fiona said, coming up behind them. 'And Mummy did not consent to being covered in so much glitter. Hi, Jonah.'

She leant over her daughters' heads to kiss Jonah on the cheek, hugging him one-armed, a pink piece of cardboard with WELCOME UNCLE JONAH AND AUNTIE SADIE written in big glittery letters in her other hand. 'I hope you don't mind us turning up like this, but we were all so excited to see you.'

She turned her attention to me. 'And to meet you!' Fiona handed the sign to her third, older child and wrapped her arms tight around me. 'Hi, Sadie!'

I nearly burst into tears.

All I wanted was my sister. All I wanted was Chess to have somehow made it to this airport before me and to be here with a big glittery sign saying WELCOME SADIE, I LOVE YOU TO THE END OF THE UNIVERSE AND BACK AGAIN AND EVERYTHING IS GOING TO GO BACK TO NORMAL BECAUSE I DID THAT ETERNAL SUNSHINE SURGERY AND EXTRACTED THE MEMORY OF WHAT YOU SAID TO ME STRAIGHT OUT OF MY BRAIN and to put her arms around me until I complained about not being able to breathe but still not let go.

'It is *so nice* to meet you properly.' Fiona drew back and beamed at me.

'You . . . you too.'

'This is Lex.' She ushered the tweenager now holding the sign forward.

'Hello,' Lex said, their tone a mixture of polite and prickly. 'Nice to meet you. I use they/them pronouns.'

Jonah had warned me Lex could be a little touchy around new people – *Matt didn't react as sensitively as he could have to them coming out*, he'd told me, *which in retrospect, maybe should have been a warning sign* – but they were coming in with about a tenth as much energy as their sisters, and I felt immediately grateful. 'Nice to meet you too, Lex. She/her is fine for me.'

Lex gave me a look that was uncannily like one of Professor Fisher's when he was watching me give a seminar paper, a penetrating stare designed to find the weaknesses in my arguments.

But then, unlike their grandfather's, it morphed into approval. 'Cool. Hi Uncle Jonah.'

'Hi kiddo.' Jonah bumped Lex's proffered knuckles with his own.

'I hope this is okay, but I sent your driver away,' Fiona said. 'I figured you'd be starving after your flight. I thought we could get some late-night fast food and then I'll run you over to your hotel.'

My bones, which had felt like they were dissolving, suddenly felt like they were made of iron.

Jonah put his arm around my waist. 'Food sounds great, Fi. But we'll have to make it quick. I really want to catch up properly, but we've got a big day tomorrow, and I need to get Sadie to bed.'

'I'm sure you do.' Fiona's eyes sparkled.

Jonah immediately turned crimson, but, 'That would require a level of energy neither of us currently possess,' was all he said. 'Girls, how do you feel about pulling our bags for us?'

Rosie and Georgia, it turned out, were very excited about pulling our bags. 'Look, I'm Daddy, off on a business trip!' one of them declared as we made our way through the car park, which made Fiona look nauseous, and Lex make a scoffing noise, deep in their throat.

Jonah, though, kept his arm tight around my waist, holding me to him and holding me up simultaneously. I looped my arm around his waist too, anchoring myself in the fight against my creeping exhaustion. *To sell the scam,* I would tell him, if he asked.

He didn't ask, though. He just let me lean on him.

He did the same in the fast-food place Fiona drove us to, arm resting on the back of the booth behind me, fingers brushing lightly against my shoulder as he ate fries with his other hand. He carried the conversation too – asking Fiona questions about the kids and what it had been like having Elias stay for a fortnight – while I drooped against him.

'You all right?' he asked me quietly, when Fiona got up to chase down Rosie and Georgia, who were sugar-high on soft-serve.

'Not really,' I murmured, cognisant of Lex sitting in the corner of the booth, engrossed in a book.

Jonah turned his head. The kiss he pressed to my hair was a whisper, so gentle I might have imagined it. 'I've got you, okay?'

I leant into him. 'Thank you,' I said, so quietly that I might have imagined that too.

'Oh God, I'm sorry for keeping you out so late,' Fiona said, coming back to the table with the twins in tow. 'Let's get you two lovebirds to bed before you turn into pumpkins.'

Even with only about a twentieth of my brain working, I could see the tiredness carved into her face too, under the excitement.

The university was putting me and Jonah up for a fortnight in a hotel in the city centre as a stop-gap while we found a place of our own. Fiona dropped us off after making us promise that we would come to dinner on Friday and also send her our wedding pictures as soon as we got them: 'I love Elias, but he's no videographer.'

'Well,' Jonah said, as we watched the tail-lights of her SUV pull away.

'Well,' I echoed.

He kept his hand on the small of my back as we walked inside, as if he somehow sensed that without something tethering me to reality, I would disintegrate. 'Dr and Mrs Shaw?' the receptionist asked.

'Close enough,' Jonah said. 'I'm Mrs Shaw.'

I could barely manage a laugh.

We took the lift up to our floor. The inside was mirrored, an infinite number of Sadies and Jonahs reflected in an endless line. Hopefully, some of those Sadies and Jonahs lived in that other, better world.

He had to swipe the keycard three times before it worked. 'Here we are,' he said, smiling encouragingly at me, the way he had smiled at his nieces. 'Home sweet— Oh.'

There was only one bed.

We'd been promised a one-bedroom apartment, with a bedroom and a separate living room. I'd been saving the last vestiges of my energy to overrule Jonah when he insisted on taking the pull-out couch.

What we had, though, was a studio: a single large room with an ensuite bathroom, a tiny kitchenette with a dining table and two chairs in one corner, two uncomfortable looking armchairs in another – and one king-sized bed.

I wanted to cry until I laughed.

If Chess read this in a book, she would throw it out the window of her twenty-sixth-floor office. *That's a ridiculous coincidence. And what, they couldn't just go back to reception and get the mistake corrected? What hotel are they staying in, the inn on Jesus's birthday?*

'I'll go downstairs and get this sorted out,' Jonah said.

'No.'

'It's okay, Sadie, I can deal—'

'No, I mean . . .' I took my hair down from the topknot it had been in all day, shaking it loose around my shoulders so I could tie it up again. 'I'm tired. You're tired. Let's just go to bed.'

He looked at me for a long moment. 'Are you sure?'

'I'm going to pass out within the next eight seconds, Fisher. I think your virtue is safe from me.'

Something in me wanted to make him blush that brilliant crimson colour, but his cheeks only went a little pink. 'Do you want to grab a quick shower and wash the plane off?' he asked me. 'You can go first.'

The hot water should have finished the job that the physical and emotional fatigue had started. I fully intended – and expected – to be fast asleep by the time Jonah got out of his own shower.

But, it turns out, there are different kinds of exhaustion.

There's the exhaustion you've earned. The exhaustion they write about in fantasy all the time, a sort of wholesome tiredness, where it's been a hard day's march on your quest, and you've got another hard day's march tomorrow, but you've dined simply on the bread and cheese that always sounds so delicious on the page and sunk into a deep, dreamless slumber.

Mine was the other kind. The kind that feels like a parasite, robbing you of your energy, robbing you of your will, even as it forces you to keep going.

There was a brief flash of light and burst of steam as Jonah came out of the bathroom. He was briefly illuminated – hair standing up at weird angles from being towelled dry, wearing those same pyjamas as on the night I proposed to him – before he turned the light off, plunging the room into darkness again.

He swore under his breath as he tripped on something. There was another brief flash of illumination as he sat down on his side of the bed and plugged his phone in, a soft clunk as he put his glasses on the bedside table, a rustle of covers as he lay down next to me. 'Night, Sadie,' he said softly.

He clearly thought I was already asleep, so I didn't reply.

I looked over at him. In the dim light coming from the strip under the apartment door, I could just make out the outline of him.

Jonah Fisher liked to sleep on his front. His head was turned towards me, hand resting beside it on the pillow. The air-conditioning had not caught up with our presence, so he only had the covers pulled up to his waist. His back was a long, smooth line in the darkness, a straight line that was somehow also a perfect curve, a line that, in that other, better world, his other, better wife would surely be unable to resist tracing with her fingers.

'Shaw,' he murmured, 'go to sleep.'

'I am asleep.'

His chuckle came from a place low in his belly, pressed against the mattress.

Silence. We breathed together.

'Do you want to talk about it?' he asked.

Yes. No.

'I don't know how to,' I whispered.

How could I put into words what it felt like, this hole in my chest where the ties that bound me to Chess had been hacked away? And how could I explain to him – this man who had held me up and held me together and had turned his entire world upside down to help his sister – that I had cut the ties myself?

'I'm really sorry,' Jonah said.

'It's not your fault.'

'It is, though.'

There was a rustle of bedding as he shifted slightly. 'I know your sister is angry with you for marrying me,' he said. 'And I know how important she is to you, so I'm sorry, Sadie. I'm really, *really* sorry. If there's anything I can do to help make it right – anything at all – please tell me. I'll do it. In a heartbeat. Even if—' He paused for a moment. 'Even if you decide you want to end this – this marriage, that's completely fine. The ball's in your—'

'Stop.'

He stopped.

'Jonah, none of this is your fault. Really. You haven't done anything wrong. And . . .' There was a lump in my throat so large it was difficult to get the words out around it. 'After everything we've gone through to get here, do you really think I'd ditch you? Just like that? Especially after meeting your sister?'

'We're not talking about my sister,' he said softly. 'We're talking about yours.'

I sniffed.

'If you want to talk about her, that is,' he added.

I swallowed several times, but the lump in my throat wouldn't go away. 'We had a fight. I . . . I said some things. Awful things. Things I don't think she can forgive me for.'

Silence again. My breath felt like it was caught behind the lump in my throat, like I might suffocate, right here in bed in the middle of an air-conditioned room.

'Don't be ridiculous, Shaw,' Tweed Jonah snapped. 'That's the stupidest thing you've ever said to me. Including when you tried to convince me there was a direct line between nineteenth-century bardolatry and BookTok.'

'Excuse me?'

'Your sister loves you unconditionally.' The tone in his voice was sharp. 'Any fool can see that. You are, theoretically at least, an intelligent woman. Do you really think you could fuck that up in one fight?'

'You don't know what I said to her!'

'It doesn't matter what you said to her! She loves you. She'll get over it. Do you really think people march into airports and shirtfront the husbands of people they're planning to wash their hands of forever?'

She . . . had done that, hadn't she?

She hadn't replied to any of my messages. She hadn't wanted to talk to me.

But Chess had still marched into the airport and delivered what I was sure were some extremely detailed threats to Jonah.

She *had* come.

'You're underestimating how much she loves shirtfronting people,' I said, because it was easier to fight than to concede.

But Jonah gave no ground. 'You're underestimating how much she loves *you*.'

A tear leaked out of my left eye. I sniffed, wiping it away with the heel of my hand.

His tone was gentler when he spoke again, tweed giving way to cardigan. 'I said some awful things to my sister too, once upon a time,' he said. 'Things she absolutely shouldn't forgive me for. But . . . well, you've met her.'

'It took you *years* to get past it, though. Years and years.' The thought of this ache in my chest lasting more than a decade made me want to scream into the pillow and never stop.

'Yes, it did, because I was young and dumb and didn't apologise. Surely you of all people remember what I was like when I was younger, Shaw.'

I sniffed again.

'You're much smarter than I was,' he said.

He wasn't wearing his glasses, but somehow, unerringly, the pad of one of his fingers found the space between my knuckles in the dark, a feather-light touch. 'If Fiona and I can sort out our shit, then you and Chess can definitely sort out yours. Just give her some time to calm and down and adjust to' – his finger tapped between my knuckles, once, twice, three times, making my heart skip a beat in its haste to match his rhythm – 'this.'

A long breath escaped me. It felt so urgent, the need to fix things, the ache in my chest so awful – but of course, along with everything else, I owed Chess what she'd asked for.

Time. Alone. Without me.

I inhaled and exhaled again, long and slow.

Then I turned my hand over on the pillow, so I could lace my fingers through Jonah's. Hopefully, he would understand why – but if not, I'd come up with an explanation in the morning, once my head was clearer.

'Thanks for yelling at me, Fisher,' I said quietly. 'I needed it.'

His fingers clasped mine, dextrous and certain.

'Any time, Shaw,' he murmured. 'Any time.'

Chapter Twelve

Jonah

I woke the next morning to the soft trill of my alarm. Light was streaming through the gaps in the curtains, a sunbeam hitting me directly in the eye, and my wife was sprawled across my back, dead to the world.

I had not moved in the night. I didn't like sleeping on my front, but the terror that I'd wake up beside Sadie with a visible erection had apparently paralysed me even in slumber.

She, though, had moved. Our fingers had been the only part of us touching when we'd fallen asleep. At some point, however, she had decided that my bony back was a superior cushion to the many hotel pillows, and draped herself over me like a quilt.

Her head was resting just above one of my shoulder blades. I could feel all ten of her fingerprints where they rested against my skin, one hand on the nape of my neck, the other on my waist. Her body was angled at a diagonal to mine, her breasts squashed directly into the middle of my back.

And if I thought too hard about that fact, then Project Control Your Inner Teenager, Jonah, Absolutely No Boners would be a complete disaster.

'Shaw,' I whispered, twitching my shoulders to rouse her and reaching over with one arm to turn the alarm off.

'Mmm?'

There were a few more glorious, sleepy seconds of her warm weight pressing me down into the bed before she leapt off me like I was made of knives. 'Oh, fuck, Jonah, I'm sorry!'

I sat up slowly, reaching for my glasses on the bedside table, wishing her eyesight were more like mine, because surely, *surely* it was written all over me how little I had wanted her to move. 'It's fine. Don't worry about it.'

Thankfully, she told me to take the first shower ('I need to pick the right first-day outfit'). I managed to escape to the bathroom before she noticed that Project Control was in catastrophic failure. I could only hope she didn't hear the strangled sound I only managed to swallow half of when it failed completely in the shower – or if she did, she'd just assume I'd stubbed my toe on something.

We were going to have to find a place of our own *soon*, I decided, flicking through rental listings on my phone when it was Sadie's turn in the bathroom, earmarking a few with Friday evening inspections that we could take a look at before dinner at Fi's tomorrow. How was I ever going to be able to concentrate at work when I knew that I would be going to bed with my wife that night?

Sadie had clearly had the same impulse as me when it came to picking her outfit: armour. I'd put on my lucky tweed blazer, the one I'd worn to all my job interviews.[33] She was wearing a black jumpsuit, cinched at the waist, which I'd seen her wear at milestone events before: our PhD completion seminar, a TV interview she'd done on romance fiction for Valentine's Day two years ago, a union meeting where we'd voted on whether to strike, dinner with my parents.

---

33 Given I was zero for four on job interviews, 'lucky' might be something of an overstatement, but emotional attachments are not always rational.

'You look nice,' I offered, instinctively standing up when she came out of the bathroom like we were in a nineteenth-century novel and then immediately feeling awkward about it.

She cast a critical eye over me. 'You look like you're going to be hot. It's supposed to be a million degrees today.'

I chuckled self-consciously. 'And here I thought my wardrobe was going to be perfect for the Tasmanian climate.'

I was prepared for her to take aim at my arsenal of tweed and knitwear and pull the trigger, but she didn't. Instead, she bit her bottom lip, brow furrowed slightly.

No, no, no, no. If she started thinking, she'd immediately sink into the pit of angst that had consumed her yesterday – and if she did that, the pit of guilt I'd been sinking into would consume me too. 'Let's go down to breakfast. You're clearly hungry, if you're eating your lipstick.'

Her hand flew to cover her mouth. 'Good idea.'

'You know,' I said, opening the door for her, 'I don't think you've ever said those words to me before.'

'If you had more good ideas, then maybe I would.'

It was a half-hearted bit of repartee, but I let myself ascend a rung on the ladder out of the pit of guilt anyway.

It didn't last, though. The minute we sat down at a table together, having made ourselves plates at the buffet, Sadie sank back into herself, and I slid straight back down.

I had thought a lot about marriage. You couldn't study early modern theatre and not think about it. Whether it was the joyous fifth-act weddings and fêtes of comedies like *Much Ado About Nothing* or *A Chaste Maid in Cheapside* or the messy couple drama of tragedies like *Macbeth* or *The Duchess of Malfi*, marriage was a constant preoccupation. Given I'd written my thesis and then my monograph on the depiction of relationships on the Jacobean stage, I'd probably spent years of my life musing on marriage.

What I hadn't really thought about was my own.

Love – now that means something to me, Sadie had said, that fateful night when she'd proposed to me. *Marriage, not so much.*

One of the reasons I'd said yes to this absurd scheme was that I felt – well, no, perhaps not exactly the same way. There were nuances. Similarly, though.

Marriage to my father had turned my mother into a shadow of herself. I, like the rest of my family, had been convinced that Fiona was throwing her future away by getting married – and shitty as I felt about it now, I ultimately hadn't been wrong. By all logic, the ring on my finger should be nothing but a costume for me.

So why was it that all I'd been able to think about since the day I'd kissed my bride was making her happy?

'Why are you staring at me, Jonah?' Sadie asked abruptly, fork halfway to her mouth. 'Do I have something on my face?'

'Oh! I, um . . .' I had a PhD in words – why was I so frequently lost for them? 'Sorry. You're just in my line of sight.'

She raised an eyebrow. It was obvious disapproval, but it was also pure, unadulterated Sadie Shaw: original flavour, not its recent miserable shadow.

It buoyed me enough to try the move again that had not worked in the security line yesterday. 'There's some rental places we could look at tomorrow evening, if you want,' I said, taking out my phone and quickly starring a couple I knew she'd hate before I handed it to her. 'I'm sure you're not interested in using me as a pillow long-term.'

'Oh, ha ha,' she said dryly, starting to scroll. 'You're a real comedian.'

I leant back in my chair, grinning at her over my coffee. 'I try.'

'Not well.'

There was that acerbic note in her voice. There she was, there was the woman that had said "I can't stand you" to teenage Jonah and ground his pride and his heart into a bloody pulp. 'Please tell me this is a joke.' She turned the phone around, displaying one of the places I'd just starred.

I put my foot on the next rung of the ladder out of the pit of guilt and hoisted myself up. 'What's wrong with it?'

'What's wrong with it?!' A flush was creeping up her chest. 'What's *wrong* with it?'

That argument carried us all the way through breakfast, and all the way back upstairs so she could fix her lipstick. 'What part of "green space" was ambiguous to you, Fisher?' she demanded, sticking her head out of the bathroom, lip-liner in one hand. 'How am I supposed to grow the vegetables for your gourmet cuisine in three square centimetres of concrete?'

'One, at no point did I insist on you doing that. We're living in Australia's fucking larder now, you don't need to farm the land and provide for us. Two, if anyone could get whatever the gardening term is for blood from a stone, surely it would be you, Shaw.'

She made a familiar noise of frustration, but her eyes were alight. She was enjoying herself.

One of the lesser-known genres of Jacobean drama was the domestic tragedy.[34] The most famous example was Thomas Heywood's 1603

---

34 Lesser known because Shakespeare didn't write in it. It had been a point Sadie made to me when she'd tried to convince me that nineteenth-century bardolatry (where a bunch of critics decided Shakespeare was a million times better than all his contemporaries) could be considered a loose analogue to contemporary BookTok discourse, because it elevated a particular author above all others for reasons that, from an outside perspective, could be very difficult to see.

I didn't think she was right, but I'd been surprised to learn that she'd absorbed so much about Renaissance literary cultures. I hadn't thought she paid that much attention to my research.

play *A Woman Killed With Kindness*, which I'd written about extensively because it told the story of a marriage.

There were not a lot of lessons to take from it. If you boiled it down to the bare bones of the plot, it was about a man who was allegedly too kind to his wife because he sent her away instead of revenge-murdering her when he caught her cheating on him (leading to her longer, more agonising death by guilty starvation).

Perhaps, though, there was a lesson for me in the title.

In the airport, Chess had grabbed me by the collar and made what she expected of me very, very clear.

I'm not going to tell you not to lay a finger on her, she'd snarled. *Sadie's an adult. She can do what she wants. Fuck who she wants. Marry who she wants.*

Then she'd yanked me in closer. *But you have ridden her coattails into a job you do not deserve,* she'd said, kicking me face-first into the pit of guilt with steel-capped boots. *And if you do one single thing to drag her down – if you hold her back, even a little – I will ruin you.*

I had tried kindness. It had worked a little, but not a lot. Too much, perhaps, would smother Sadie, at a time when she could not afford to be smothered.

What she might actually need was not a pillow but a punching bag, somewhere to put all those pent-up feelings.

And much as I did not want to fight anymore – I had to give my wife what she needed.

I owed her that much.

✎

Unlike being married, I *had* imagined having a permanent academic position. Many times.

One of my favourite things to do, if I was neck deep in marking or needed to head off an anxiety spiral about my ongoing insecure employment, was to decorate my dream office, the one I would have one day when I reached the promised land.

My dream office, like my dad's real one at ESU, would be lined with bookshelves, so full they looked a bit dangerous. Unlike his, though, my office would also be comfortable, welcoming, inviting. Instead of the confrontational lone chair he had in front of his desk to interrogate people, I'd have a couple of comfortable, cosy chairs in a corner, perfect for conversation. Maybe even a couch, with a blanket, in case I or someone else needed to take a nap. A bottle of some kind of dark liquor in my desk drawer – that was my dad again – but two glasses instead of one, drinks shared collegially or compassionately where necessary.

'Well,' Sadie said faintly, as we stared into the sixth-floor cupboard we were apparently going to be sharing.

'Well,' I echoed.

I traced a finger over the nameplate. All the other nameplates in the corridor were engraved metal, but ours was paper: *Dr Sadie Shaw* typed in a sans serif font, *Dr Jonah Fisher* scribbled underneath in blue pen.

All the other doors in the Literary Studies corridor were locked. We'd followed the directions in the first-day email we'd both received and had encountered a lot of people in our first couple of hours of gainful employment at Lyons University – the people in faculty services who had taken our photos for our new staff cards, the IT people who'd given us the work laptops we both had under our arms, the security people who'd handed us the envelope with our office keys inside – but we had not encountered a single one of our new academic colleagues.

The lights in the corridor were on motion sensors. They'd

winked on as we exited the lift. As we stood there, staring into the tiny space we were supposed to share, they winked off again.

'This is worse than the bed,' I said, at the same time as Sadie said, 'This is going to be really awkward when we get divorced.'

We glanced at each other.

'First day and you're already fucking up, Shaw,' I said.

She arched an eyebrow. '*I'm* fucking up?'

'The only d-word you should be uttering at work,' I said, nudging her lightly with my elbow, 'is *darling*.'

She rolled her eyes.

We entered our office, something which should have felt like a huge metaphorical leap taking barely a single step. There was hardly enough room for us to stand side by side.

Most academic offices had the desk facing the door, so the occupant could look up from their work and see who was there. To orient a desk that way in this office, though, would require the occupant to vault over it to get to their chair, because there would be no room to walk around it.

Instead, our desks were against the perpendicular walls – although 'desk' and 'against' were imprecise ways of putting it. They were more white laminate planks than desks, long and narrow, attached to the walls by metal frames.

Sadie put her laptop and her handbag down on the left plank, which was only just wide enough to hold them, and experimented with the winder on the metal frame. 'At least they go up and down, I guess,' she said, glancing over at me. 'That's something.'

I held her gaze for one beat. Two.

Then we both started laughing.

'I never thought I'd ever be nostalgic for hot-desking,' I said, setting my laptop and satchel down on the right plank and trying to wedge myself into my desk chair, 'but at least that involved actual desks.'

She chuckled again, but then her expression got more serious as she tried to sit down and our chair wheels immediately got tangled. 'How are we going to get any work done when we're practically sitting in each other's laps?'

'Not a fucking clue,' I said, forcing teenage Jonah – summoned by the phrase *sitting in each other's laps* – back down, lest Project Control enter a new level of disastrous failure. 'What if one of us needs to have a confidential consultation with a student? What are they supposed to do, stand awkwardly in the doorway while the other one of us puts headphones on and pretends they can't hear?'

Sadie exhaled. 'We're going to have to scope out the campus cafés before semester starts. We'll have to hold all our office hours there, so we might as well do it at whichever one has the best coffee.'

'Do you want to start now?' I asked, half-rising from my chair. 'It's not like there's anyone else here to notice if we go on a coffee—'

'Oh, there you both are!'

Half-sitting, half-standing, all-the-way-jumping in surprise, my foot got caught in the wheels of my chair and I tripped. My glasses fell off my face, landing on the carpet – and, as if I were a character in some farce by Molière, I fell straight into Sadie's lap.

'Well, this is quite a re-introduction, Dr Fisher!' the woman standing in our doorway said cheerfully.

Then she wagged her finger playfully at us. 'I know you two are married, but no hanky-panky in the office.'

She was clearly joking, but my face must have been beetroot red as I righted myself. 'Professor Vargas,' Sadie said, her own blush starting to creep up her chest as she handed back my thankfully-unbroken glasses. 'Lovely to see you.'

'Sorry about that,' I said. 'You startled us. We didn't think anyone else was here.'

Professor Sofia Vargas was a tiny woman, less than five feet tall, but she had a massive voice that far outsized her. *You know those stories about Tolkien teaching at Oxford and basing Treebeard on C.S. Lewis after hearing his voice echoing down the halls?* Sadie had said to me after the HR call about my partner hire, *Vargas has the same vibe.*

'Oh, it's only me here today,' Professor Vargas said. 'We do a lot of working from home at Lyons these days. The corridor does have a bit of a zombie apocalypse feel, doesn't it?'

We both laughed nervously.

At least this would solve our office space problem. We'd still be on top of each other, working from home, but not quite *this* on top of each other.

'Although not now you two are here!' Professor Vargas said, immediately shattering my delusions. 'We're taking full advantage of the fact we've finally got some continuing staff whose teaching hasn't been completely bought out by research grants. You'll be in front of a *lot* of classes this semester!'

Then she paused, regarding our tiny office as if for the first time. 'Lucky you're a married couple. You'd really want to like someone you were crammed into this box with, wouldn't you?'

We both laughed nervously again. 'Lucky,' I echoed, unconvincingly.

'Come down the hall to my office. Let's talk through your workloads somewhere with more space, shall we?'

Vargas's office looked much more like the office of my dreams. Fewer overstuffed bookcases, perhaps, but the windows had stained-glass detailing around the edges, and the little coffee table with a couch and armchairs she had in the corner was more comfort than even my ambitious internal interior designer had dared to dream of. 'This must look horribly unfair, after the closet we've stuck you in,' she said apologetically as she gestured at us both to sit, 'but being the

Head of the School of Humanities does come with its privileges.' She grinned broadly at us. 'Hopefully someone will retire soon and we can get you a bit more square footage, hey?'

There was no other response we could make but to laugh nervously once more.

'All right.' Vargas logged into her laptop then turned it around to face us. 'I know we hired you both on 40-40-20 contracts, and it was my intention to try and honour the spirit of that as well as the letter.'

When you were in the precariat, a 40-40-20 contract seemed both as magical and out of reach as a pot of gold at the end of a rainbow. It meant you were getting paid to work on your research 40% of the time, teaching another 40%, and doing service – committees and admin and various other stuff – 20%.

'But like I said,' Vargas went on, 'the Lit Studies department is in a bit of a staffing pickle at the moment. Your new Head of Department – that's Lachlan Petrovski, you'll meet him tomorrow – and I have had to be a bit creative in planning out your workload.'

Sadie glanced at me. I recognised the unease in her eyes. She clearly hadn't forgotten the name of my dad's 'old chum' either.

But then I registered what the spreadsheet on Vargas's screen actually said, and all thoughts of Petrovski disappeared completely from my mind.

A 40-40-20 contract meant that, theoretically, you were working a lot more than a casual academic – it was full-time, after all, not hourly. Practically, though, it had always seemed like it would be a lot less work, because you were actually getting paid for your research instead of doing it for free on the side in the vague hope it would one day earn you one of these mythical contracts.

That was technically probably still true – but *my fucking God*, the amount of teaching they had loaded us up with for the semester was eye-watering.

All of it was lecturing. And all of it was together.

What they'd done, Vargas explained to us, was manipulate our respective 40% teaching allocations to get us in front of as many students as possible. Sadie and I would be chairing two units each – her, a first-year unit on contemporary literature and a second-year unit on Romanticism; me, a first-year unit on classic literature and a second-year unit on medievalism – but all of the small-group seminar teaching and marking would be done by casual academics. We would be doing the large-group teaching, co-lecturing all four units together ('we know you've been very successful as a teaching team in the past, so we thought – let's lean on that!').

Semesters at Lyons were thirteen weeks long. Lectures went for an hour and took place weekly.

That meant that, between us, Sadie and I were going to have to write *fifty-two lectures*.

The word-count sweet spot for an hour-long lecture for me was between five and six thousand words. I tried to do the maths on the total word count we were expected to produce – apparently, according to the workload calculator, with just one lone hour of prep time per lecture – and my brain started making static noises like an old television.[35]

'I know it's a lot,' Vargas said, smiling apologetically at us, 'but it's a great long-term investment. Once the lectures are written, you'll be able to use them for years.'

'Oh,' was all my bolshy wife – who had never backed down from an argument in her entire fucking life, and who I knew, from being at dozens of the same union meetings as her, had very strong views on staff exploitation – said.

---

35 I did it later. If we split the difference and said 5500 words, multiplied by 52, that was 286,000 words – the equivalent of about three novels.

'I don't suppose the staff previously teaching the unit have notes we could use as a scaffold . . .?' I asked cautiously.

'No, unfortunately. We've had casual scholars giving these lectures in the past, and we've implemented a policy about reuse of their work.'

That was actually a very good, very sensible policy. Universities had a nasty habit of paying casual academics to do work once, then either recording their classes or taking their teaching materials and reusing them in many subsequent semesters without paying them again. Sadie and I had both advocated for the implementation of a similar reuse policy when we were in the precariat.

That didn't particularly help us in the present moment, though. I had to resist taking Sadie's hand and holding on for dear life.

'Don't worry, though! There's also some fun stuff hidden in here!'

There was *more*?

Vargas scrolled down the spreadsheet on her screen. 'We had to do some creative accounting and spin some of this as service, but we've managed to get you both some unit development hours, so you can do some of that work we actually hired you for. We want to put together some new units for the semester after this one: one on popular fiction, one on Shakespeare. And guess who we want to write them?'

She beamed. Sadie looked nauseous. I could only assume I did too.

'You two being an item really was a bit of a blessing, if you ask me.' Vargas leant back in her chair in satisfaction. 'We managed to palm off our new modernism unit on one of our existing staff, but God only knows who we would have got to write the Shakespeare unit if you hadn't been a package deal.'[36]

---

36 The sole piece of satisfaction I took from this conversation, which, due to overwhelm, I did not realise until considerably later, was her strong implication that Rory Worland would not have been in contention.

She gestured from me to Sadie. We both forced another nervous laugh.

We were silent as we walked back down the corridor to our cupboard, Professor Vargas having swept past us to the lift on her way out ('Off to work from home this afternoon!') and a promise to see us at the pre-semester School of Humanities meeting the next day ('Invite should be in your email!').

I opened our office door. Sadie and I both stood in the doorway again, regarding the tiny space, the cell we'd have to spend so much time in, far more intimate and far more permanent than the bed we were temporarily sharing.

'How about we go and get lunch?' Sadie said.

I was fairly sure that if I tried to eat anything, I would throw up, but I agreed anyway.

We found a table in a corner of a café in the next building over. Because semester hadn't started yet, it was quiet, and we sat there in abject, shell-shocked silence for several long minutes, extremely mediocre chicken wraps held limply between our fingers.

'Fuck,' Sadie said at last.

'Fuck,' I agreed heavily.

'What the fuck. *How* the fuck. Just – fuck.'

She put her wrap down on top of its cardboard container and pressed two fingers into the space between her eyebrows. 'Just when I thought this week couldn't get any worse.'

'Hey!' I said, initially repressing but then leaning into the flash of hurt, because even if I was as panicked as she was, I had punching-bag duties to perform. 'You obtained a precious jewel this week, Shaw. How dare you?'

I flipped her the marital bird, the way she had in the airport. She made a sound that was halfway between a scoff and a snort, and I was congratulating myself on some top-notch spousing when she sighed. 'Here are some words I thought would never come out of my mouth,' she said. 'Jonah, you are by far the best thing that has happened to me this week.'

Oh.

Wow.

Her week has been unbelievably shit, I told myself, trying to beat back the rising heat in my cheeks. *It's not like you have any competition.*

Sadie picked up her wrap again and took a bite. 'Imagine how much work they would have tried to heap on me if we hadn't pushed for partner hire,' she said, somehow still the most beautiful woman in the world with a mouth full of chicken and avocado. 'I would have drowned.'

'Now that would have been an achievement,' I managed. 'First person in the world to have drowned in a cupboard.'

The sound she made this time was more distinctly a snort of amusement, but it was followed by another sigh. 'We still might. Fuck, Jonah.'

'Fuck,' I agreed again.

'And the fact they want us to do it all *together*, too!' She took another bite of her wrap, a few crumbs flying out of her mouth. 'What the fuck is that about? I know we're—' she flipped the marital bird back at me, 'but come on. Everyone knows collaboration is more work than just doing it yourself.'

'Maybe it's a strategy.' I took a bite of my own wrap. 'They're hoping we'll drive each other up the wall and split up, so they can fire me.'

She looked thoughtful for a moment. 'That would explain the cupboard.'

It was my turn to snort with amusement.

When we were finished with lunch, we ordered coffees and took them back to our office so we could start making a plan of attack. I swivelled my chair around to face Sadie's desk-plank so we could work side-by-side, me scribing as we both worked off my laptop on a document in the new shared drive we'd just set up, but after the fifth time our chair wheels got tangled, we decided to call it and – like the rest of our colleagues – work from home.

Back in our serviced apartment, we started off sitting at the tiny kitchenette table, tried the uncomfortable armchairs, and eventually ended up spending the afternoon working side by side on the bed. 'So much for not fighting anymore,' Sadie said heavily, loose strands of hair sticking to my shirtsleeve as she looked at the plan on my laptop screen. 'All we're going to do is fight.'

The only way we knew how to teach together was to performatively disagree. Our planning document was a table of weeks and texts and potential arguments we could have over them – arguments which, over the course of the afternoon, had provoked several more arguments[37] – trading off lectures the same way we had for the past few years at Bass.

'Just for work, though,' the part of me that had got stuck on the phrase *Jonah, you are by far the best thing that has happened to me this week* said. 'At home, we can be a team.'

'Thanks, Fisher.'

She glanced at me. I glanced at her. For a moment, I felt exactly like I had at our PhD graduation, when I'd seen that the tassel of her bonnet was tangled in her hair. What would happen if I reached out – gently, gently, ever so gently – and stroked those loose strands behind her ear?

Then her stomach growled, the bubble burst, and we both laughed. 'Dinner?' I asked her.

Sadie nodded, reaching for her phone and opening up one of the delivery apps. 'Let's see what's open around here at – shit, seven-thirty. I didn't realise it was that late.'

---

37 Picked at a ratio of about 3:1 Fisher:Shaw.

'Two and a half hours overtime and it's only day one. What an auspicious beginning.'

It happened slowly, her foot slipping on the ladder above her pit of angst, like it was a slo-mo sequence in one of the action movies my Screen Studies ex-girlfriend had forced me to watch.

'I wish I could talk to Chess about this,' the greyed-out shadow Sadie whispered. 'She'd know how to push back.'

I took a risk. 'Why don't you call her?'

She looked at me like I'd grown a second head.

'I'm serious. I know you're fighting, but one of you is going to have to call the other eventually, right?'

Sadie bit her lip, biting off the last vestiges of her lipstick. 'Okay.'

She did it. *Calling: CHESSIE* came up on her phone screen.

Chess didn't answer.

And Sadie looked completely, utterly crushed.

I was suddenly filled with an overwhelming wave of anger. How dare Chess make Sadie feel like this? Wasn't her whole deal that she would do anything for her? Wasn't this the relationship I'd been so jealous of, the one I'd measured mine with Fiona and Elias against?

I'd been so confident last night when I'd told Sadie that *of course* she could mend things with Chess, no problems. Sure, Chess hadn't come to our wedding, but she'd turned up at the airport to scream threats at me. You didn't do that if you didn't care. She might sulk for a bit, but she'd get over it. She loved Sadie too much not to.

But in reality, I didn't actually know this woman – and maybe her bond with Sadie wasn't as strong and as perfect as it had always looked to me, someone who had spent so many years being an objectively bad sibling. And maybe some part of Sadie had already known that, deep down: after all, *something* had made her so scared to tell Chess we were getting married that she'd waited until we were practically at the altar.

Just how unconditional is *your love?* I should have snarled back in Chess's face, when she'd had her fingers twisted in my collar at the airport.

Maybe then she would have been the one who stumbled back. Maybe she would have been the one begging Sadie for forgiveness instead of the other way around. Maybe I wouldn't have to spend all my time picking petty fights just to give Sadie something else to think about, because suddenly I'd become a devout adherent to a *happy wife, happy life*-esque philosophy: *wife not actively crying, Jonah doesn't feel like he's dying.*

Maybe then I could reach out and trace the long line of that red hair. And maybe then I could draw Sadie to me, cradle her head in the crook of my neck, and I could say – I could say—

I stopped.

I took out my own phone and opened up a delivery app. 'What about pasta?' I said, taking Sadie's phone out of her nerveless fingers and handing her mine instead.

'Pasta is the absolute *worst* food to get delivered, Fisher.' A hint of that familiar acid came back into her voice. 'You know that.'

I did know that.

And I knew, looking at her as she scrolled ('If you insist on noodles, Jonah, then let's get Thai'), that I could no longer relegate the way I felt about her – the way I had felt about her ever since our very first seminar debate, fifteen years ago – to a footnote in my mind, something to be skimmed at best and skipped over most of the time.

No matter how I tried to rationalise it, this wasn't some teenage crush I'd never managed to entirely shake. It was no mere physical attraction, nothing that could be summed up by *it's your dick, Jonah, don't romanticise it*; no simple intellectual fascination that could be explained away by the fact that Sadie was the best sparring partner I'd ever had. Now that I was married to her, I couldn't gloss over it anymore, or argue myself out of what I had always known perfectly well was the truth.

I was in love with my wife.

I loved Sadie Shaw more than words could wield the matter, dearer than eyesight, space and liberty.[38]

---

38 'Where both deliberate, the love is slight:
Who ever lov'd, that lov'd not at first sight?'
- Christopher Marlowe, *Hero and Leander* (1598), lines highlighted by Jonah Fisher one week after meeting Sadie Shaw in first year undergrad, *YES* scribbled beside them.

'The more I strive, I love; the more I love,
The less I hope: I see my ruin, certain.'
- John Ford, *'Tis Pity She's A Whore* (1633), lines highlighted by Jonah Fisher shortly after moving into the share house, *THIS, SHE'LL RUIN YOU IF YOU LET HER* scribbled beside them.

'I know she hates me,
Yet cannot chuse but love her:
No matter, if but to vex her, I'le haunt her still.'
- Thomas Middleton and William Rowley, *The Changeling* (1622), lines highlighted by Jonah Fisher the day after PhD graduation, *RELATABLE CONTENT* scribbled beside them.

I might have relegated my adoration of Sadie to my mental marginalia in an attempt to pretend it away, but that didn't mean it hadn't always been completely obvious to anyone who looked for it.

Chapter Thirteen

Sadie

Jonah was picking fights with me on purpose.

He thought he was being very subtle. 'I can't believe you're drinking caffeinated tea before bed,' he said, folding back the covers on his side. 'You'll never get any sleep, and I don't know if you've noticed, but we have a shit-ton of work to do tomorrow.'

'Not all of us are weaklings who can only tolerate that horrible ginger shit you drink after ten am,' I shot back, and the fight commenced, like we both didn't already know perfectly well how many litres of tea I was capable of drinking, and we both didn't already know exactly what the other one was going to say next.

He'd been doing it all day, finding the pettiest points to quibble over, but it was the things he didn't push on that gave his game away. 'Night, Shaw,' was all he said to me, when I built a wall of pillows between us in bed.

'Night, Fisher,' I replied, turning the light off and lying down on the other side of the barricade that separated me from the most cardigan-y version of Jonah that had ever cardigan'd.

Tweed Jonah was not afraid to sink his teeth into my weaknesses. He relished it, in fact. He'd done it the night before, completely demolishing my argument that I had ruined things with Chess forever.

Today, though, he'd been picking fights as a way of showing me that everything was normal. That the rings we were wearing didn't have to change anything, and, oh, the fact that I'd snuggled up to him in the middle of the night and pressed myself so close against him it must have felt like I was trying to crawl inside his skin? I've already forgotten about it, Shaw, and it's ridiculous that you'd find something so minor and meaningless embarrassing.

He could try as much as he wanted, but I was smarter than that. Cardigan Jonah in Tweed Jonah's blazer was still Cardigan Jonah.

I turned over in bed, exhaling. *Can you both like being taken care of and resent it at the same time?* was a question I should note down to discuss with my therapist.

Although I knew exactly what she would say. *Of course you can, Sadie. Why do you think you said what you said to Chess?*

I checked my phone again, but I already knew there would be nothing there.

First day was INTENSE, I texted her. I know you need some space, but would love to talk about it when you're ready. I love you so much xx

On the other side of the barricade, Jonah started snoring – not loudly, but gently, a comforting low rumble. I put my phone down and let it lull me to sleep.

Mock Tweed Jonah was back at it again the next day, showing me some more completely unsuitable rentals over breakfast, being deliberately obtuse about which building on campus we needed to go to for the school meeting, and never once mentioning the fact that I had woken up sprawled across the pillow barricade with one of my hands on his arse.

I let him do it, taking the bait he was strewing behind him like breadcrumbs. It was a good distraction; from our terrifying workload, from the fact Chess hadn't responded, and from the fact that I couldn't help but notice he had a *great* arse – something which was absolutely, positively none of my business.

It was starting to wear on me though, after, unable to face the cupboard, we spent two hours sitting in a campus café doing some more work on the pedagogical plan for the four (four!) units we were going to be co-lecturing. Some of the points he made about our approach to the Romanticism unit were valid (he was right, for example, that hanging a week on the scandalous exploits of nineteenth-century actor Edmund Kean would be a good idea, even if he was best known for performing Shakespeare), but others were low-key nonsense. 'We absolutely do not need more Wordsworth,' I snapped at him, as we packed up to head over to the school meeting. 'We've got the preface to *Lyrical Ballads*, as well as "Expostulation and Reply" and "The Tables Turned". That's plenty.'

'One, no it isn't, how are you going to teach Wordsworth without teaching "Tintern Abbey"?' Jonah held the café door open for me. 'Two, why did you insist on putting in his two most annoying poems?'

'He's an annoying man! And because they perfectly express that whole books-are-shit-learn-from-trees-you-stupid-bitch thing that's at the heart of all his work.'

'It is not—'

'Don't, Fisher. It's been fifteen years. I'm not prepared to relitigate "To Joanna" with you.'

It should have been a sign for him to back down, but he didn't. 'I can't believe you're resisting the opportunity to put our origin story on the syllabus.'

'To Joanna' had been the subject of our very first fight, back when we were both first-year undergrads. Jonah had argued that it was a deeply romantic poem about a man trying his best to immortalise his mortal beloved by carving her name into a rock, a more lasting tribute than anything that could be captured in print. I'd argued it was the mansplain-y musings of a very pretentious man who couldn't deal with the fact a woman had laughed at him when he took her on a walk and basically had an orgasm at the sight of some trees.

Neither of us had given ground. Further years of study had made me slightly more sympathetic to Jonah's reading of the poem (NB: *slightly*), but at the time, he really had been being a bit of a Wordsworth himself – something which had obliterated the initial thought I'd had, the very first time I'd ever laid eyes on him.

He's cute.

I quickened my pace. Suddenly, I was thinking about his arse again, and all the hairs on my arms were standing on end, and I wanted to make it to the meeting before the blush that was starting to creep up my body made it somewhere visible.

I escaped to the bathroom as soon as we found our way to the conference room where the School of Humanities pre-semester meeting was being held, splashing water on my face and glaring at myself in the mirror. 'Get it together, Shaw,' I whispered at my reflection.

One of the toilets flushed. I adjusted a couple of my bobby pins and smiled politely and – I hoped – professionally at the petite dark-haired woman who emerged from the stall.

'Hi,' she said, smiling back in the mirror as she washed her hands. Then she blinked. 'Sadie Shaw?'

Shit. Was I supposed to recognise her? 'Yes. Hi. Um—'

'You don't know me, don't worry. I recognise you from the photo they sent around when they announced you were the new hire. I've read some of your articles.'

She dried her hands on a paper towel and then held one out to me. 'Julia Scott-O'Connell. I'm in History.'

'Sadie – Lit Studies – but you obviously know that.' I shook her hand. 'I'm flattered you've read me. I didn't know my work would appeal to a historian.'

'I do a lot of work on histories of love, histories of sex, things like that, so I'm very interested in your work on romance.' Julia paused to touch up her lipstick in the mirror, a dark burgundy colour. 'I was delighted when they announced your hiring. I'm one of the co-leads on the interdisciplinary love studies research network we have here. You should join.'

'I would love to,' I said, slightly surprised. 'Thank you.'

Julia smiled at me again. She was one of those people with an innate warmth to her smile, the kind of sparkle in her eye that translated into charisma. 'You're welcome. Shall we get out there? If you sit with me, I'll give you the lay of the land.'

And just like that, I – the reigning queen of liquid love, of bonds tied loosely – had seemingly made a friend.

The school meeting was taking place in a conference room, chairs arrayed in rows in front of a lectern. 'You know Sofia, right?' Julia nodded to where Professor Vargas stood, chatting to two men in suits. 'The Head of School?'

'Yes,' I replied, as we slid into seats about two thirds of the way back. 'She hired me. Then dropped a terrifying amount of teaching on me.'

'That's not surprising.' Julia put her handbag on the floor, took out a box of mints, and offered me one. 'There's been a lot of creative workload accounting going on for the last couple of years. The suits she's talking to are middle managers in the faculty exec team. They don't give a shit about either scholarship or student experience. All they care about is slashing the budget to bare bones in any way they can.'

'Sounds familiar.' This was exactly the same thing that would have forced me completely out of academia if I hadn't got this job.

'Sofia's a good egg. People underestimate her, but she's got an iron will and she's held her ground on a lot of fronts. The fact that we've managed to get some new permanent hires' – Julia nudged me with her elbow – 'is proof of that. But there's only so much she can do when things are coming from above her head. If they start talking about "Renewniversity"' – she put scare quotes around it with her fingers – 'or Phase Three in this meeting, the shit's about to hit the fan.'

'What's Phase Three?'

'The suits have this three-phase plan – the Renewniversity plan – to reduce faculty spending, but given Phases One and Two were both rounds of redundancies, I don't think it's a very complicated plan.'

Oof. I made a mental note to tell Jonah later that we needed to transfer our union memberships over to the Lyons branch ASAP.

Automatically, my eyes sought him out. He was standing talking to a woman in a short-sleeve shirt and a bow-tie whom I recognised from the hiring committee. He caught me looking and gave me a somewhat sheepish – and perhaps apologetic? – wave.

Julia followed my gaze. 'Friend of yours?'

'You could say that,' I said. 'He's my husband.'

It was the first time I'd said those words since our wedding. *My husband.*

A line from one of the books in my treasured *Anne* box-set flickered into my mind. I couldn't remember the exact wording, but it was right after Anne and Gilbert finally got married. Gilbert introduced Anne to someone as 'my wife' for the very first time, and nearly burst with the pride of saying it.

That wasn't exactly the emotional response I was having, but . . .

Well, it wasn't embarrassing, being able to point to Jonah Fisher across a room and say 'See that man? I'm married to him'.

Jonah turned back to his conversation, and – oh no, the line of his blazer was very flattering, and *since when did he have such a good arse?!*

Thankfully, Julia distracted me before I could fall too far down the rabbit hole. 'You managed a partner hire? Here? In this climate? Did you have to promise to sacrifice your firstborn child on the sacred altar of the faculty budget?'

I laughed, absolutely refusing to interrogate the notion that 'firstborn child' was something people were going to assume Jonah and I wanted to have. 'Judging by the amount of teaching they're wringing out of us, they should have hired, like, twelve people.'

'It's still impressive,' Julia said. 'Well done on navigating the two-body problem. That's unbelievably difficult to do. Literally the first thing that happened to me when I got my job here was a divorce.'

Before I could ask her more, Vargas stepped up to the lectern. 'All right, everyone!' she said, tone cheerful despite the two middle managers standing menacingly behind her. 'Let's get this show on the road, shall we?'

Julia interpreted for me as the three-hour meeting got underway, leaning over and whispering explanations of who the various speakers were. The Associate Head of School for Research was apparently a good person to know ('they keep telling us there's no internal funding for research, but she's good at finding it'). The Associate Head for Student Experience meant well but was largely ineffective ('maybe people would listen to her more if they were actually *in* the classroom'). The dean of the Faculty of Arts, who popped in for twenty minutes to lambast everyone for the poor results of a recent staff satisfaction survey, was a snake ('get ready for some hilarious emails about how great he is at supporting *our people* and *our wellbeing,* I like to play a drinking game with them').

Jonah, who was sitting a couple of rows ahead of me with some other men in tweed, took out his phone during this particular speech. I know we have a ton of shit to do, he texted me, but let's move transferring our union memberships to the top of the to-do list.

One thing I had always appreciated about Jonah, even during all the years we were feuding, was that despite his astronomical levels of privilege, he'd always been a staunch union man. Great minds, etc, I sent back.

Didn't know you rated my mind that highly, Shaw.

I sent him back an eyeroll emoji.

The last agenda item of the meeting was an update from all the heads of department – two of whom Jonah had apparently unwittingly sat between. I would have to make fun of him later for being drawn to other tweed bros like they were a swarm of salmon. 'That's Tom Carmichael, my department head,' Julia whispered as one of them stood up. 'He's a piece of shit. Whatever you do, *do not* be alone in a room with him.'

Well, shit. I would have to have a different kind of conversation with Jonah.

The last person to stand up was the tweed bro on Jonah's other side. 'Well, it's wonderful to be making my first speech to you all as the new head of the Literary Studies department,' he said, clapping his hands and then rubbing them together. 'It definitely won't be my last.'

'Lachlan Petrovski,' Julia said in an undertone. 'Only been here six months, but already knifed your old head of department. Different breed of piece of shit to Carmichael – more power-hungry misogynist than active predator – but definitely also a piece of shit.'

I ran my tongue over my teeth in disquiet. Of all the people in the room, Jonah had gravitated immediately to the powerful arsehole who was friends with his dad.

'Let's finish this meeting on a cheerful note, shall we?' Petrovski said. 'I'm happy to announce that we've got not one, but two new hires starting in Lit Studies this week. Jonah, Sadie, will you come up here please?'

My knees ached from sitting so long as I got up. Jonah gave me an awkward half-smile as we walked to the front of the room. I didn't reciprocate.

'Most of you will already know about Sadie Shaw joining us, from the email that went round a few weeks ago,' Petrovski said. 'I'm delighted to tell you all, though, that with some elbow grease and begging to the budgetary gods, we've also managed to hire her husband.'

He clapped Jonah hard on the shoulder. 'I can't tell you how thrilled I am to have Dr Jonah Fisher joining our department. He's a Shakespearean scholar of the highest calibre – and those of us who have been around the traps for a while will be very well acquainted with his father, Professor Christian Fisher, a titan of literary studies scholarship in this country.'

Oh, absolutely fuck this.

I looked for Julia in the audience – surely she would have a hot take on what complete bullshit this was – but she was gazing at Jonah, eyes wide, lips parted, looking slightly stunned.

And that did *not* make me feel a combination of possessive and jealous amid all my disquiet, and did *not* remind me of the whole 'we could be the Sartre and de Beauvoir of Literary Studies' thing I'd said to Jonah when I'd pitched him on the concept of getting married at all.

Jonah and I didn't have a chance to talk after the meeting. When it concluded, no one seemed to have any appetite to get back to work, lingering instead over the tea and coffee and soggy sandwiches. A host of people came and introduced themselves to us, a sea of names and faces I definitely would not remember, pulling us in different directions.

I didn't get to talk to Julia either. 'I have to head off,' she told me as soon the meeting ended, 'but I'll send you an email about the love studies research network, okay?'

She was gone before I could tell her she should send one to Jonah too – given his work centred on relationships, he'd probably be interested – but maybe that wasn't such a bad thing.

It was nearly five by the time Jonah and I extricated ourselves from a long conversation with Petrovski – a conversation which I'd really only been part of on a technicality, given he addressed everything he said to Jonah. 'Our first rental inspection is at five fifteen,' Jonah said, when we were by ourselves at last. 'Do you want to head off?'

I nodded.

He shouldered his satchel. I picked up my handbag. As we started walking, I began an irritated mental countdown. He would pick the next stupid fight in five, four, three, two . . .

But he didn't say anything.

Jonah Fisher was not, in my experience, a brooder. It was one of the few ways he deviated from the dark academia aesthetic to which he was otherwise so wedded. He could be *quiet*, yes – I couldn't count the number of times I'd seen him settled in a corner of the couch in the share house, reading, oblivious to everything going on around him – but he didn't really brood.

Maybe I didn't know him that well, though, because the man inspecting these properties with me clearly had some kind of higher degree in brooding.

He uttered approximately four syllables during our first two inspections. Two of them were 'no', flatly stated. I didn't like the places either so I didn't argue, but when we got to our third and final inspection of the evening, I tried turning his own tactic against him. 'We could make this place work,' I told him, standing in the middle of the horrible kitchen of a horribly expensive tumbledown house.

'You wanted green space for your garden. There isn't any.'

'I could figure something out. Maybe there's a community garden nearby.'

He sighed. 'If you want it, fine. Let's put in an application.'

Having already decided I would rather live in our prison cell office on campus, I promptly had to backpedal.

'Okay, out with it,' I snapped, when my second attempt to start an argument – suggesting we take an Uber to Fiona's place in Bellerive, which was only a few minutes' walk away – resulted in Jonah simply taking out his phone. 'What's up your arse, Fisher?'

He just looked at me.

'You've spent the last day and a half picking the pettiest fights you can think of and now you're like a fucking limp noodle.' Why had I phrased it as *what's up your arse*? His arse was the last thing I needed to be thinking about. 'Out with it. Why are you sulking?'

His expression changed, morphing into a classic Tweed Jonah *You fool, Sadie Shaw, I can't believe you can't see the massive flaw in the argument you just presented* face. 'Why do you think?! You were at the meeting.'

'The one where they were like, "Oh yes, we hired this woman, but let's talk about the really important thing: WE HIRED THIS MAN!"? I was indeed there, watching you sit elbow to elbow with every power player in the room.'

'They sat down next to me! Because of my fucking dad!'

He ran his hand through his hair, tugging hard at the ends. 'For my entire life, the only way anyone has ever perceived me is as an accessory to some fucking better scholar. Christian Fisher's son. Elias Fisher's brother. Sadie Shaw's husband.'

I rolled my eyes.

'And I can't escape it!' He tugged at his hair again. 'No matter what I do, I can't get away from it! I'm never just Jonah Fisher, scholar. I'm permanently stuck in other people's orbits.'

'Grow up.'

'What?!'

'You heard me. Grow up. This is the most ridiculous poor-little-rich-boy shit you've ever said to me.' I put on a mocking voice. 'Oh no, my daddy's friends are going to give me *advantages*, whatever will I do?'

'You don't know what it feels like, Sadie!'

'You're right, I don't! Because no one has ever treated me like that a day in my life! Today included!'

'Did you miss the bit where they were like "Here's Sadie Shaw and here's the man we only hired because he married her"?'

'Did you miss the bit where Petrovski was so fucking excited to talk about how you were joining the department he nearly exploded?'

'Because of my dad!'

'Oh, golly, gee, Jonah, that must be so difficult for you, having all these advantages simply handed to you. However do you cope?'

'How do *you* cope, knowing that you've actually earned all of your accomplishments? Do you have any idea what it's like having to constantly question your own abilities?'

'You are not going to make *me* feel bad because *you* have privilege!'

'I know I have privilege coming out my fucking ears! Do you think that makes it any easier to have a career based entirely on riding people's coat-tails?'

'How did you manage to fit in a Masters degree in feeling sorry for yourself around all your other research? Please, give me some time management tips.'

'If I wanted a Masters, I probably wouldn't have to lift a finger to get it! They'd just give it to me!'

'Oh no, what a tragedy!'

'Hey!' Fiona barked. 'Time out!'

Our argument had, without either of us noticing, carried us to her house. She was standing in her front yard, hose in one hand, watering her garden as the twins played on the lawn. 'Don't make me turn this on you,' she said, flicking the water towards our feet.

Jonah's shoulders drooped. 'Sorry, Fi. We were just . . .'

'Fighting?' Fiona arched an eyebrow.

Jonah sighed. I folded my arms.

It was terrible ruse-selling, but Fiona just shook her head fondly. 'Hey, girls?'

Rosie and Georgia looked up. 'What?' one of them asked.

'How do you feel about being secret agents?'

Their eyes lit up.

Fiona crouched down to their level. 'Your mission, should you choose to accept it, is to help Uncle Jonah relax. He's had a big week, and he's tired.'

'Like Daddy after a long day in the office?'

'Exactly like that.' Fiona didn't skip a beat. 'So he needs a couple of secret agents to take him inside, and sit him down on the couch, and put the TV remote in his hand, and to play where he can see them – *very quietly*,' she dropped her voice to a whisper, 'because it's a *secret* mission. And it has to be undertaken without the super-vision of mission command, because mission command is going to take Auntie Sadie out for a wine.'

What?! No!

The exhaustion of the last week crashed down on me like a pile of bricks. The *last* thing I wanted to do was go out for a drink with Jonah's very nice sister and lie to her about how he was the light of my fucking life and wasn't she lucky to have him back in hers. I had just enough energy to grab him by the hair, put his head through a wall, and kick him up the irritatingly good arse. That was it.

Fuck. Fuck fuck fuck.

Fiona held out her hand to the girls. 'Agents, do you accept?'

Rosie and Georgia conferred. 'We accept!'

'Excellent.' Fiona shook their hands. 'Mission command is putting her trust in you, agents. Don't let me down.'

'We're the *best* agents. Come on, Uncle Jonah!'

The twins each grabbed one of Jonah's hands and towed him into the house. The glance he threw me over his shoulder was terrified.

It was probably because the expression on my face was somewhere between 'if you leave me, I'll kill you' and a simpler 'I'll kill you', but Fiona clearly interpreted it as fear of her daughters, because she only laughed. 'Lex!'

'What?' came from inside the house.

'Come here, please!'

Lex appeared on the doorstep a few moments later. 'What?'

'Let's open negotiations,' Fiona said. 'If I was to bring home, say, two books for you, would you be willing to spend the next hour or so reading in the living room and making sure the girls don't make Uncle Jonah want to run screaming into the night?'

Lex thought for a moment. 'Three books,' they said, 'and you have a deal.'

'Done.'

Fiona and Lex shook on it, then she turned her attention on me. 'Come on, shiny new sister-in-law,' she said, beaming. 'Let's go have a wine and a chat.'

I gritted my teeth and forced myself to smile back. 'That sounds lovely.'

✎

At least one thing went my way. Fiona was a talker. The bar she took me to was on the high street in Bellerive, about a ten-minute walk down the hill from her house ('Walking down the hill is a lot more fun than walking up the hill, let me tell you!'), and she kept up a steady stream of chatter the whole way, pointing out local landmarks and places Jonah and I might like to get coffee or lunch or go on date nights. 'There are a ton of cute places over here, but this one is the absolute best,' she said, pulling open the door to the bar. 'Most people think you have to go over to the western side of the river for nice bars, but this place has immaculate vibes.'

They wouldn't be immaculate for long, if Jonah and I were to attempt something as ludicrous as a date night – screaming arguments tended to ruin the atmosphere – but I nodded politely.

From the outside, the wine bar didn't look like much: just a simple tinted glass window in the little strip of restaurants, with the name – Tsundoku – engraved on it in flowing script.

Inside, though, it was a different story. The space was narrow but deep, bar on one side, a long single row of dark wood tables marching towards the back on the other. A tealight flickered on each of them, giving the place a dimly lit, cosy ambience. The chairs were a collection of mismatched leathers and velvets in browns and reds and greens and ambers, and the walls were lined with chaotically overstuffed bookshelves, the kind where you could entirely believe a rare, possibly cursed manuscript from hundreds of years ago might have languished, buried, until some plucky reader pulled it out.

It was a dark academia wet dream. Jonah would love it.

'What do you think?' Fiona asked.

'It looks like your parents' house.'

'Oh God, don't say that! I love this place too much for them to taint it.'

Well, this was an auspicious start.

I drove the pad of my thumb into my engagement ring and tried to pull myself together. This might be the most poorly timed casual drink in the history of the world, but Fiona wasn't to know that. After all the shit she'd been through, the least I could do was not to ruin her favourite bar.

'Sorry,' I said.

But she wasn't listening. 'Satoshi!'

The man behind the bar turned around. Instantaneously, a broad grin spread over his face.

'No!' He pulled his glasses down his nose so he could exaggeratedly peer at her over the top of the thick lime-green frames. 'It can't be! Surely the long-lost Fiona Fisher has not simply walked into my bar?'

Fiona beamed as he came around to hug her. 'I'm sorry it's been so long,' she said, laughing as he lifted her off her feet. 'It's just been impossible to get away, with the kids and everything.'

'Not to worry. You're here now.' He put her down and turned his attention to me. 'With a new friend!'

'Sadie, this is Satoshi, one half—'

'The better, more handsome half.'

'—of the Tsukamoto wine brothers, the geniuses behind this place. Satoshi, this is Sadie, my baby brother Jonah's wife. They've just moved here for work.'

Satoshi was tall and lanky, somewhere in his mid to late twenties, black hair bleached ashy blonde. He was wearing a tailored dove-grey waistcoat over a crisp white shirt, which would have been a conservative look if it wasn't dotted with brightly coloured pins: little glasses of wine, little stacks of books, a map of Tasmania, the Japanese flag, the progress pride flag, another one I was fairly sure was the pansexual flag.

'Delighted to meet you, Sadie.' He shook my hand. 'Genuinely. Fiona needs some reliable babysitters. My bar is in danger of collapsing without her patronage.'

'Satoshi!' Fiona exclaimed, laughing.

'Welcome to Tsundoku,' Satoshi said, talking to me but wrinkling his nose affectionately at her. 'Let's get you a drink. Inside or outside?'

'Inside, I think,' Fiona said. 'I'll take you out to the back deck another time, Sadie – it looks over the water, it's beautiful – but I love it in here with the books best.'

Satoshi led us to a table under a chalkboard, the specials written up in the same flowing hand as the engraving on the window. 'Are we drinking by the bottle or the glass?'

'Tempting as a bottle sounds, just a glass,' Fiona said. 'I left Jonah alone with the kids, and if I expose him to the girls too long, he will take his beautiful new wife and move back to the mainland before you can blink.'

It was only the leaden weight of exhaustion in my bones that stopped me from saying *fuck it, let's get a bottle, then.* The thought of Jonah being so overwhelmed by babysitting that he packed up and got out of my fucking face had taken on a new appeal.

I'd forgotten it lately, what with all the cardigan-y kindness he'd been showing me, but there was a reason he'd been the face of the establishment to me for so long. No matter how snuggly his knitwear was, strip it off him and there was a tweed bro, having a little cry about how hard it was to have a rich well-connected daddy.

That was who I'd blown up my relationship with Chess for. That – how had she put it? *That entitled prick from a whole line of entitled pricks.*

'We might take home a bottle to have with dinner, though,' Fiona told Satoshi, oblivious to the fact that on the other side of the table, I was imagining dunking her brother's head in the toilet. 'Oh, and I need a few books too, if you don't mind. I had to bribe Lex to run interference if the girls get too . . . themselves.'

'I can provide all those things,' Satoshi said. 'I'll be back. I'm going to pour you something special.'

He disappeared. Fiona turned her smile on me. I tensed, bracing myself for some horrifying question like *so tell me exactly when you fell in love with my brother.*

But, 'I hope you don't mind me commandeering you into coming out for a drink,' was all she said. 'I love my kids to bits, but God, I need a break.'

There simply wasn't anything I could say to that. There was no even vaguely truthful response that wouldn't make me sound like an absolute monster.

'Of course I don't mind,' I said. 'I needed a break too. As I'm sure you could tell.'

Fiona chuckled. 'If there's one superpower I've developed as both a Fisher and a mother, it's knowing when two people who love each other very much need a time out.'

At least she was still buying the ruse.

Satoshi reappeared, setting two glasses down in front of us. 'Isamu finished his special project,' he said to Fiona. 'How do you feel about being the first Tsundoku customers to taste the fruits of his labour?'

'Oh my goodness, honoured!'

'Has Fiona told you much about what we do here, Sadie?'

I shook my head, preparing to ask many follow-up questions. Being dragged around by Chess had given me a passable wine vocab, and every second we spent talking about this bar was another second I didn't have to spend lying to Fiona.

'Tsundoku is one arm of a business run by my brother Isamu and I.' Satoshi poured red wine into our glasses with a deft and practiced hand. 'We're a wine bar, serving wines from many vineyards – as well as selling second-hand books – but we also have our own vineyard, so we like to showcase our wines here, which Isamu makes.'

'He's an incredible winemaker,' Fiona said. 'Seriously.'

'Shhh,' Satoshi said. 'Don't let him hear you. You know how committed he is to never smiling. Anyway, this is his most recent baby, a wine he's been nurturing for a while which I've finally bullied him into letting me pour. Meet Bibliophile's brand new kyoho akai, one of the first wines in Australia made from a Japanese grape.'

Fiona held up her glass, beaming at me again. 'Cheers.'

'Cheers.'

I clinked my glass against hers. We both drank.

It tasted like . . . wine. Nice wine, but wine. I must have heard Chess have a thousand intense wine-bar discussions about bouquets and tannins and 'the nose', but despite my acquisition of the language, I could really only distinguish between three types of wine: wine I liked, wine which was good enough to drink, and paint thinner.

'Wow,' Fiona breathed.

She had practically stuck her whole face into the glass, alternately sniffing and sipping. 'It's amazing. Notes of cherry, notes of chocolate . . . it reminds me of black forest cake.'

'Oh, I like that,' Satoshi said. 'I'm going to pinch that for the tasting notes.'

'Not too sweet, though. It feels like it could really tip over, in the wrong hands, but it's perfectly balanced.'

Fiona and Satoshi started talking – something about skins and residual sugars – but I tuned them out. Something was niggling at the corner of my brain; an irritating, persistent itch.

Then it clicked. 'Bibliophile?'

'That's the name of our wine label,' Satoshi said. 'Tsundoku is the bar. Bibliophile is the wine.'

He showed me the bottle. *Bibliophile* was written on the label in the same elegant script as the window engraving and the chalkboard, underneath a picture of a messy stack of books.

'Are you familiar with it?' he asked.

'A little.' I traced my thumb over the stack of books, that same stack Chess had said reminded her of me. 'My sister is a big fan. She's in your wine club.'

I wanted to laugh and cry at the same time. What were the fucking chances?

I was not a superstitious person. Devoting my life to studying stories had hammered home to me how much people used them to make sense of their lives. There was some innate tendency in humans that made us read our lives like they were books, scripted by some higher power. *A tall, dark, handsome stranger will enter your life,* we might hear, and off we'd go, reading too much into an innocent conversation with the man behind us in the coffee line.

I knew, intellectually, that it was just a bottle of wine. No higher power had guided me here. It was just a coincidence. I *knew* this.

And yet all I could perceive it as was a symbol. A reminder of the sister who loved me so, so dearly – and whose love I had flung back in her face like it was garbage.

'Sadie?' Fiona asked. 'Are you all right?'

'Yes, yes.' I could not fall apart here, *I could not*. If there was one thing I owed this woman it was not to dump more emotional labour on her. 'I'm fine. I just . . . my sister is my only family, and I miss her, you know?'

'Oh, of course you do!' Fiona put her hand on her heart. 'She'll have to come visit. You can bring her here!'

'Name the date and I'll lay on the full Tsundoku experience,' Satoshi said. 'I could even make Isamu come and run one of our meet-the-winemaker nights, if she likes his wines that much. Or you could go out to the vineyard for a weekend. We have a restaurant and a cellar door there and our mother manages a little B&B.'

'Maybe,' I said faintly.

He rapped his knuckles gently against the table. 'I'll leave you ladies to it. Enjoy.'

'Thank you, Satoshi,' Fiona said. 'It's so lovely to be back.'

He smiled fondly at her. 'It's so lovely to have you back.'

Then he was gone and I was alone with Fiona, who was beaming at me again from the other side of the table.

'This place is so nice,' I said, because if she asked me about Chess I was going to cry, and if she asked me about Jonah I might turn into the Hulk. 'How did you discover it?'

'Oh, it's not a very interesting story.' She flapped a hand dismissively. 'Hobart's small. The eastern shore is even smaller. It would have been harder *not* to discover it. I can't even remember the first time I came here, to be honest. Matt and I come here for date nights all the time – well, *came* here, anyway, before . . . you know.'

Nice work, Shaw. Remind the abandoned woman of her shithead husband. 10/10, perfect, no notes.

'Sorry.'

'Don't be, don't be.' Fiona made the dismissive hand-flapping gesture again. 'Matt didn't ruin it for me, that's the important thing.

He might have taken just about everything else, but Tsundoku is still mine.'

Well, that was bleak as hell.

'Cheers to that,' I said, holding up my glass.

She laughed. 'Cheers.'

We clinked glasses and drank again, then Fiona's face turned serious. 'Can I tell you the real reason I brought you here?'

Oh God.

I jammed my thumb into my engagement ring again and squared my shoulders. This was a test. I was good at tests. I had never failed a test in my entire life. If I could handle repeated academic cross-examinations from Professor Christian Fisher without giving a single inch, then surely – *surely* – I could handle one conversation with his significantly less terrifying daughter without having some kind of nuclear meltdown.

'Of course.'

'Well, there's a few reasons,' Fiona said. 'I really was dying to get out of the house. But I also wanted to apologise.'

I blinked. 'What for?'

'For turning up at the airport the other night.' Her sheepish expression was eerily similar to Jonah's. 'I realised as soon as I saw you that I'd made a horrible miscalculation. Of course you'd be exhausted after all that travelling! But I have this nasty habit of getting way, *way* ahead of myself, and I was just so delighted that you and Jonah were here, and I couldn't wait to see you, and the kids were excited too, and . . . I'm sorry. I'll learn to read the room better in future, I promise.'

'Fiona, please don't worry about it,' I said, deeply relieved to be getting out of this conversation so lightly. 'Really. I never want to stand between you and Jonah. Ever. No matter how tired I am. It really should have been him you brought out tonight. I know you have a lot of brother–sister time to catch up on.'

'No, no, it had to be you. Because there's one more thing I need to say to you, and it's a big one.'

Fuck. It would probably be bad if I poured the rest of the contents of my wine glass down my throat, right?

'I was so excited, when you and Jonah told me you were getting married and moving here,' she said. 'But I was apprehensive too, because marriage is a huge step, and you took it so fast.'

'It really wasn't that big a deal.' This, at least, I had a pre-developed script for. 'Would we have done it if not for the partner hire thing? Not this quickly, no. But given the circumstances, it just made sense.'

'I know, but it's still a huge deal. Trust me, as someone in the middle of a messy divorce, getting married is an enormous deal.'

I jammed my thumb even harder into my engagement ring and gritted my teeth. I didn't particularly want to be reminded of that right now.

'You didn't have to marry Jonah, but you did,' Fiona said. 'I know it was mostly so you could stay together, but I'm not an idiot. I know some of it was so that you could bring him with you to Hobart. Where I live.'

She reached across the table and put her hand on mine. 'You took this massive, binding step, to help out a woman you didn't even know. And that's why I wanted to get you on your own, so I could tell you, from the bottom of my heart: thank you. Thank you for loving my brother enough to do this.'

The English language currently has about 170,000 words in common use. It is an embarrassment of words, more than most of us will ever use in our lives.

'Oh,' was the only one I could find. 'Oh – Fiona. Oh, I . . .'

'Not just for my sake. His too, obviously. Do you know I remember the very first time he ever talked about you?'

Fiona leant back in her chair, swirling her wine in one hand. 'It was about a year before I married Matt. Elias had moved out already, but I was still living at home. I would have been twenty-one. Jonah was eighteen, and he'd just started uni. He sat down at the dinner table one night and started talking about some debate he'd had with this girl in his seminar about . . . some poet, I think.'

Fucking Wordsworth.

'My dad went full – well, you've met him. He started quizzing him: "How did you read the poem? How did she? Did you take into account this line? How did she respond to this point? Why didn't you counter with this argument, you stupid boy? You could have demolished her whole case if you'd only raised this point!" Classic Christian Fisher nonsense. I'm sure you're familiar.'

I nodded, teasing my bottom lip between my teeth.

'But I'll never forget how Jonah responded.'

She topped up our water glasses. 'He looked Dad dead in the eye, and said, "Winning wasn't the point. Her reading was so interesting, I just wanted to hear what she would say next."'

I blinked.

'Which is about as close you can come to treason in the Fisher family,' Fiona said casually, as if the ground hadn't just turned to water beneath our chairs. 'I'm sure you've heard all about how we were raised. Winning arguments was practically our religion. I was radicalised at age ten when Dad took Jonah's teddy bear away and told him he could have it back once he made a persuasive enough case for it.'

I couldn't help but picture it: tiny, serious Jonah trying to find a way to rationalise his need for a basic childhood comfort, only to be faced with the unsympathetic brick wall of Professor Christian Fisher. Involuntarily, one of my hands curled into a fist.

'He's, um –' I drank some of my water, trying to clear my suddenly dry throat, '– he's never told me that. About the teddy bear.'

'I'm not surprised. He might be a fully-grown man now, but he's still a *boy*. He has his pride.'

. . . and I'd completely refused to listen when he'd tried to tell me how hard it was to have people only ever perceive him through the lens of his father.

Ever since our wedding, Jonah had been trying to look after me. Some of his tactics had been profoundly irritating, but he'd been doing his best – and then the second he'd needed a bit of looking after in return, all he'd gotten were my teeth. I was as bad as his fucking dad.

'Then,' Fiona went on, oblivious to the crisis I was having, 'I will never forget this either, because it was adorable – he put his chin in his hand and said, "If this is what university is going to be like, I think I've fallen in love with it."'

Oh.

Goodness.

I didn't know what to do with this information. If my mind was a glass full of water, then this week, people had continually been dropping rocks into it, driving the level up and up and up. The fight with Chess was a rock. Getting married was a rock. Moving was a rock. Starting work was a rock. All the lectures that had been dumped on us – fifty-two rocks, right there.

Fiona had just thrown in another handful, and now my mind was overflowing. How many crises could one person have simultaneously?

'Jonah and I haven't been close for a long time,' Fiona said, sipping her wine, eyes crinkling at the corners as she smiled at me, 'but I've always paid attention when he mentioned your name, because I had a sneaking suspicion he might marry you one day.'

Well, at least we didn't have to worry about selling her on our story. Fiona had already gone and written it for us.

I could have left it there. I should have left it there. It would have been so easy. I should have picked up my glass, knocked back my wine, and said something like, *well, speaking of Jonah, I suppose we should get back to him, I know how desperate he is to spend time with you* and then that would be that.

But somehow, without me ever actually deciding to say it, the words, 'Jonah's also kind of the reason I fell in love with university,' were coming out of my mouth.

'Whaaaaaat?' Fiona leant back in her chair, grinning. 'Now this I have to hear.'

I rubbed a hand over my brow. Tsundoku was perfectly temperature-controlled, but I both had goosebumps and felt like I was sweating.

I'd never told this story to anyone. Not even Chess, who'd already formed a very strong negative opinion about Jonah by the time this had happened, due in large part to The Incident at our first graduation ceremony.

'I didn't follow the same academic path as Jonah,' I said. 'I took some time out between Honours and PhD. I grew up poor and I wanted a financial safety net before I fully committed to being broke again, so I took an office job and I told myself I was going to stay there for five years before I went back to uni.'

I started twisting my rings around my finger. 'But I was bored out of my brain. The office was near campus and I used to go there sometimes on my lunch breaks. Visit my old haunts. Remind myself what I was working towards, why I was suffering through all this boredom. Sometimes I'd go to the library and just walk through the stacks and smell that old book smell.'

'Oh my God, you and Jonah *are* perfect for each other.'

I was pretty sure old book smell had a universal appeal, but I wasn't about to gainsay her. 'One day, I was running late to get back to work, and I took this shortcut through the Lit Studies building. I was really legging it – I normally wouldn't risk cutting through that building, because I didn't want to run into your dad – but then suddenly, I came to a screeching halt, because I heard Jonah's voice.'

Fiona put her hand on her heart.

'He was teaching a seminar.' God, I hoped the low lighting in here meant she couldn't see how red I was turning. 'He was standing in front of a whiteboard, and he was leading this discussion about *North and South*, and he was wearing – the same tweed blazer he's wearing today, actually. He's had it for years. I hope he's been getting it dry-cleaned.'

Fiona laughed.

'He was wearing that blazer,' I said. 'His hair and his beard were all scruffy, and his glasses were falling down his nose, and he looked like the most stereotypical academic in the world – and I had this profound moment of clarity. All I wanted was to be in that class-room. All I wanted was to be in his shoes. All I wanted was what he had. I wanted to *be* him.'

It had been such a small thing, but it had felt eucatastrophic, that moment: like a deus ex machina in my own life, stars which had been crossed suddenly aligning, a wild Jonah appearing like a WRONG WAY, GO BACK sign on the highway to put me on the right path.

'And I didn't want to wait anymore, not for another second,' I said. 'So I texted my boss that I'd gone home sick, and I went and knocked on my Honours supervisor's office door to discuss enrolling in a PhD.'

Then I'd gone home and told Chess what I'd decided, omitting all the parts about Jonah, and she'd hugged me so hard I thought my ribs were going to break. *All I want*, she'd whispered in my ear, *is for you to get what you want, sweetie.*

'Anyway, now he's stuck with me,' I finished, forcing out what I hoped was an airy laugh. 'If I hadn't seen him teaching that seminar, I would have been years behind him, academically speaking. He'd have got the Lyons job outright instead of having to marry me for it.'

'Somehow,' Fiona said, 'I don't think he minds.'

She was profoundly wrong about that, but I wasn't about to tell her so.

Thankfully, Satoshi chose that moment to come by with a stack of queer middle-grade books for Lex. As he and Fiona chatted about what wine would go best with what she was planning for dinner, I escaped under the pretext of looking at the bookshelves, so I could take a few deep breaths and calm down.

I simultaneously thought about that story all the time and hadn't thought about it in years. Every time Jonah put on that tweed blazer, I was reminded of it – of that feeling of wanting so desperately to have what he had – but I hadn't considered it in its broader context in a very long time. Certainly not since I'd married the owner of the blazer.

I'd meant everything I'd screamed at him earlier. Seeing academic powerbrokers gravitate to him, the way they always gravitated to him, drove me up the fucking wall.

But wasn't this exactly what I'd tried to tell Chess, and been infuriated that she couldn't manage to hear? That Jonah was a human, under the tweed? Maybe even a good one?

I thought again of his dad taking his teddy bear away and telling him he could have it back once he made a persuasive enough argument. Nice as it must be to have the world falling over itself to do you favours, having them do it because of your connection to a man like that – a connection you did not ask for and could not change – must be galling.

I hadn't been wrong, but I still owed him an apology.

I'd already picked out a couple of romance novels to send to Chess, but I ran my fingers along the spines of the books, looking for something that might pique Jonah's interest.

It took me a while, but eventually, I settled on a dusty old cloth-bound volume entitled *Specimens of the Elizabethan Drama*. Jonah almost certainly owned all the plays it contained – some of the titles sounded very familiar, and there was nowhere else I would have learnt them but from him – but whoever had owned the book previously had filled it with marginalia. Jonah annotated his books like a BookTok girlie, so maybe he'd get a kick out of it.

I took my selection of books up to Satoshi, who was back behind the bar. 'Can I also buy a bottle of your reserve pinot noir?' I asked. 'It's my sister's favourite. I want to send her a care package.'

'Ah, the Noriko! Your sister is clearly a woman of excellent taste.'

Satoshi reached under the counter and pulled out a bottle. I took out my wallet, inwardly wincing. I'd pay any sum in the world if it meant Chess would speak to me again, but this was still going to take a serious chunk out of my as-yet-unaffected-by-my-new-job bank account.

But he just waved me away. 'On the house.'

'No!' I only just resisted the urge to immediately put my wallet back into my bag. 'This is expensive wine. You can't just give it to me for free.'

'The next time you come, I'm happy to charge you full price and aggressively wave the tip jar in your direction, but tonight, your money's no good here.'

Satoshi jerked his head towards where Fiona was sitting, flipping through one of the books he'd given her for Lex. 'She's a good person. There aren't a lot of good people in the world, but she is one. All she does is look after other people.'

His tone was off-handed, casual – and yet the guilt it sent crashing into me was heavy as a truck.

Fiona *was* a good person. Moreover, she was a good person that the world had fed into a woodchipper – and my first reaction when she'd invited me out for a drink was irritation.

Jonah was a good person too. It might not always show, and he might not always get the tactics right, but only someone intrinsically good – intrinsically kind – would treat me the way he'd been treating me.

They had been raised by the worst man in the world and they were still good people. They might not have been close, but when Fiona was in trouble, Jonah's first instinct had been to run to her, to protect her, to look after her.

And I, a person raised by a fierce protector, someone who would do – who had *done* – literally anything for me?

There must be something deeply, profoundly, fundamentally broken in me, to scream, *'You're always trying to look after me!'* at Chess as if that were a bad thing. To be annoyed at a nice woman who just wanted to take me out for a drink. To be completely unable to hear Jonah when he tried to tell me how being viewed through the lens of his father made him feel.

The Fisher siblings were good people, but I wasn't.

No wonder everyone always untied themselves from me in the end.

'The least I can do,' Satoshi said, still looking over at Fiona, eyes tender behind his green-framed glasses, unaware that I was having yet another crisis, 'is give a bottle of nice wine to someone who's going to look after her for a change.'

'That's so kind of you,' I said, words bubbling out of my throat, because if I didn't talk I was going to either cry or run. 'Although I'm not sure how well Jonah and I are looking after her at the moment.

We went and looked at a few potential places to rent before we went round to her house this evening, and we got into a screaming argument. She practically had to turn the hose on us.'

'You need somewhere to live?' Satoshi's gaze refocused on me. 'Because I might be able to help you with that.'

Chapter Fourteen

Jonah

Our new apartment was in Bellerive, the same tranquil small-town-esque suburb that Fi lived in, only a short bus ride away from campus – and it was, by any measure but certainly by comparison to the other places we'd looked at, an absolute miracle. The bedrooms were big enough to fit our desks and our bookshelves. The kitchen made me salivate: wide black stone benchtops and cabinetry, picked up in the tapware and in the industrial-style light fittings throughout. There was a spacious balcony with a view over the river and the cricket stadium, which the outgoing inhabitant – our new landlord, Isamu Tsukamoto – had covered in plants. There had been no doubt that we were going to take it, the Hobart rental market being what it was, but when Isamu mentioned that the internal courtyard of the complex was also a community garden, it was clear we'd gotten very, *very* lucky.

Not to mention that we were getting the place absurdly cheap. 'You're doing me a favour,' Isamu told us when we met him to inspect it. 'I want to lease this place so I can move to the vineyard permanently. Having to list it and spend time vetting potential tenants would mean more time in Hobart.'

'But you don't even know us,' I felt obliged to say.

'I know your sister. She vouches for you. I trust her.'

Presumably Fiona *hadn't* mentioned just how strained our relationship had been until very recently.

'And if the Francesca Shaw I've been sending wine to for the last three years is indeed your sister,' he said to Sadie, 'then I've got collateral. Trash my place and I'll cut her off.'

Sadie laughed, but dejection flickered across her face. 'If I had even the slightest inclination to trash the place, that threat would put me right off.'

If I'd had even the slightest inclination to trash the place, the sight of Isamu – an unsmiling man with black hair pulled back severely in a man-bun and biceps which could crack walnuts – would have put me right off, no further threats required, but I didn't mention it. I just put my hand on the small of Sadie's back instead, in a way I hoped she would interpret as supportive. *I know your sister's still not speaking to you, but I've got you, Shaw.*

We'd found our groove again, after the horrible Friday night fight we'd had on the way to Fiona's. I'd spent ninety minutes sitting on Fi's couch, barely even noticing that the twins had put on *Bluey* and were snuggled up on either side of me,[39] wallowing in my pit of guilt. Was one lone mention of my dad really all it took for me to go full *well, actually, I think you'll find it's* extremely *difficult to be a straight white well-connected man*?

I'd planned to abase myself at Sadie's feet and apologise, but to my great surprise she got in first. 'I'm sorry I was such a bitch to you earlier,' she'd murmured into my ear under the pretence of kissing my cheek when she and Fiona got back from the bar. 'You didn't deserve that.'

Before I could protest, she was reaching into her handbag. 'I got you something.'

---

39 Thank God Lex was there, honestly. I had a long way to go as a babysitter.

It was a book of excerpts from various Elizabethan plays, scribbled on and marked up by some previous scholar. 'You probably have all of these already,' she'd said, 'but I know you love marginalia.'

Thankfully, Lex's squeal of delight over the books Fiona had brought home for them distracted her, or she would have seen me go a brilliant shade of crimson. If Sadie ever found out how often I scribbled *YES* or *THIS* or *RELATABLE CONTENT* next to passages about pining, then . . .

Later that night, back in our serviced apartment, she sat me down on the bed, apologised again for our huge blow-up and, after I'd apologised in return, told me to stop picking petty fights with her. 'I know you've been doing it to distract me, and I appreciate the thought,' she said, 'but please don't.'

'I'm sorry,' I'd replied, somewhere between horror and panic that she could read me that easily. If she could see I'd been doing that, what else could she see?

'I meant what we said that night too,' she said. 'I don't want to fight anymore either.'

I'd nodded. She'd half-smiled. I braced myself for what would come next – probably her saying something flippant (almost certainly an insult) to end the conversation.

But then, to my great surprise, she'd gone up on her knees and put her arms around my neck. 'You're a good husband, Jonah,' she'd said. 'I'm sorry you ended up with such a terrible wife.'

'You're all right, Shaw.' I'd allowed myself to stroke her hair just once. 'Don't sell yourself short.'

Then I let go, because if I let myself get used to the feeling of her close to me, I would say something stupid like *stay there* or *don't move* or *can I kiss you* or *I love you* and this tender, blossoming thing between us – this last, true ceasefire – would die.

Because no matter how badly I wanted to say those things to her, I couldn't. It would be thoughtless and selfish. If there was one lesson I had really taken away from that very first ceasefire of ours all those years ago, it was that Sadie Shaw did not feel about me the way I felt about her. She never had. For fifteen years, I'd adored her; and for fifteen years, she'd abhorred me.

I owed her so much. If I was ever going to begin to repay her for everything she'd done for me by marrying me, the best gift I could give her was not my love, but my silence. She was already miserable. Why make her even more uncomfortable?

So I said goodnight instead, and jammed three pillows between us.

It didn't help. Every single day, no matter how high we built the wall and how clearly we set our boundaries, I woke up with her sprawled across my back.

It was getting harder and harder,[40] spending every second of every day with her. Sitting next to her in a café or our cupboard office or at Fiona's dinner table or on the bed in the serviced apartment, it was unbelievably difficult not to reach out and tease a lock of her hair between my fingers and say, *you are the most beautiful woman I have ever seen.* Watching the dejection slide over her face every time she looked at her phone and there was nothing from Chess, it was painful not to put my arms around her and tell her, *you can yell whatever the fuck you want at me, I'll still love you.* And all those mornings, when I woke with her pressed against me . . . God, it was just about impossible not to turn over, pull her closer, and make an impassioned pitch to her on the idea of properly consummating our marriage.

Thank God we had our lovely new rental lined up. I had survived some extremely difficult tests in my academic career, but

---

40 Yes, literally as well as metaphorically.

nothing – *nothing* – had ever been as difficult as sharing a bed with my wife.

✏

We ended up moving about a week and a half later, on, of all days, Valentine's Day. Despite the teetering tower of our workload – we still had fifty of those fifty-two lectures to write – we took a half-day off work and met Isamu at lunchtime to pick up the keys. 'As discussed, I've left the whitegoods for you,' he said, holding open the door of the apartment for us. 'I've also left—'

'Oh my God,' Sadie breathed.

'—the herb garden.'

The apartment itself was empty now, all cold polished concrete floors and black strips of lighting against the white walls and ceilings, but the balcony was still alive with greenery. It was an incredible tension between order and chaos, leaves spilling wildly from plant pots organised into raked tiers with military precision.

Sadie's face was alight as she looked at Isamu. 'This is amazing.'

One corner of his mouth lifted slightly. 'I saw you admiring the plants when you inspected the apartment, and I have a well-stocked kitchen garden at the vineyard already,' he said. 'We also have some spare outdoor furniture from Tsundoku, if that interests you. All it's doing currently is taking up space in Satoshi's storeroom, so you're welcome to it.'

'Thank you so much!'

I had no right to dislike this man, who had been nothing but extremely kind and unnecessarily generous to us. But as I watched Sadie look at him, starry-eyed – and as I watched him later, biceps flexing as he hauled an outdoor table and chairs up the building stairs for us with no apparent effort – a green-eyed monster took up residence in my heart.

What would I say, if she came to me and said, *Remember how we were going to be the Sartre and de Beauvoir of Literary Studies? I'm off to be de Beauvoir with our jacked winemaker landlord*? How would it feel, sitting in his apartment while he put his hands on my wife?

'Jonah, are you okay?' Fiona asked, tapping on the frame of the propped-open front door. 'You look like you're about to be sick.'

'I'm fine. Just thinking about work stuff.'

That, at least, was a perpetually plausible excuse, and Fiona bought it immediately. 'Your movers are downstairs, by the way. They pulled their truck up on the lawn, which means people are going to start shouting at them any minute, so you might want to go down and help them.'

It was another unusually warm day,[41] and Sadie and I both shed articles of clothing as we helped the removalists haul all the stuff we'd shipped over from the share house up to our apartment. 'Why the fuck did we go into a career that – careful, mind the corner – required so many *fucking* books?' Sadie panted, as we manoeuvred one of her bookshelves into place in her bedroom.

She rubbed the back of her hand over her forehead, leaving a long streak of dust. My fingers itched with an almost uncontrollable desire to reach over and gently wipe it away.

'Jonah?'

'Sorry,' I said, trying to pull myself together. 'I thought that question was rhetorical.'

---

41 Climate change is real, it turns out.

Of course, Isamu – apparently not yet convinced that he had done enough for us – chose that moment to walk in carrying an especially heavy box of my books like it weighed nothing.[42]

Sadie and I had disagreed strenuously over who should get the slightly larger bedroom, but eventually I'd proved victorious, insisting that she, as the person who had actually *got* the job that brought us here, should take it. Thankfully, our removalists were the kind who took apart and rebuilt your furniture for you,[43] and they had put together Sadie's bed and were halfway through mine when Fiona returned from her dual mission of placating our neighbours and getting us coffee.

'Why did you bother shipping two beds over?' she asked, putting the cardboard coffee-tray down on the black stone kitchen bench.

'In case we have guests,' I said, at the same time as Sadie said, 'Airbnb.'

Fiona looked quizzically between us.

'We wanted to keep our options open,' Sadie said.

'Exactly,' I improvised. 'If someone wants to come and visit us, then we've got a spare room. If we need a bit of extra cash every now and then, we can list it on Airbnb. Which one of those coffees is mine?'

Fi passed the one marked *decaf* to me, seemingly satisfied with our comically bad handling of her very simple question. 'I also have a gift for you. Two gifts, actually.'

The first one was from Isamu's brother Satoshi. 'He wanted to welcome you to Bellerive,' Fiona explained, presenting Sadie with a

---

42 It was the one I'd put all my Norton Anthologies in. Anyone who has ever dropped one of those on their foot, and consequently not been able to walk for a week, will understand how deeply galling this was.

43 And doubly thankfully, Isamu had left after hauling that box of books upstairs, because if Sadie had seen the horrifying sight of me trying to wield an Allen key, there was every chance she would have run after him.

beautiful gift box stamped with the Tsundoku logo, which contained cheese, condiments, crackers, and a bottle of riesling. 'And also thank you for taking the apartment, because, in his words, "It'll be a lot harder for Isamu to interfere in my bar from the vineyard than from around the corner."'

Then she handed me a rectangular object wrapped in sparkly pink paper with unicorns on it. 'This one is from me. Sorry for the wrapping. I didn't have time to buy anything more adult.'

I opened it, carefully freeing the tape from the paper so it wouldn't rip. 'Oh, Fi.'

She'd had three of our wedding photos framed. Two of them – one of us with our foreheads pressed together, and one of me kissing Sadie's hand – were in small frames. The third – the one of me wrapping my jacket around her – was blown up bigger.

'I thought these two could be for your desks at work,' Fiona said, tapping the smaller ones, 'and this one could hang right –' she took the larger one from me, 'here.'

There were three hooks on the wall in the living room. Fi hung the picture on the middle one, adjusting it carefully until it was straight. 'I know you got married on the cheap, but your photographer did an excellent job.'

'Yeah, they did,' I agreed vaguely. I was going to have to write a very nice Google review about Going to Gretna Green.

Fi had chosen my favourite of the photos. My fingers were curled tightly around the lapels of the jacket, creating the illusion that I was using it to pull Sadie into me. Sadie was looking up at me, an emotion in her eyes that I knew, realistically, had been gratitude, but which the photographer had translated into something . . . else.

There was movement beside me. Sadie. She didn't take my hand, but her fingers curled around the bare skin of my upper arm, like I was about to escort her into a ball. I stopped breathing.

'I really like that one,' she said.

'Me too, darling,' I murmured.

'It's gorgeous, isn't it?' Fi said. 'It really shows how much you care about each other – oh God, I'm sorry.'

I had to sacrifice the feeling of Sadie's fingers on my skin, because tears had started to stream down Fiona's face. 'Don't cry,' I said, pausing awkwardly for a moment before putting my arms around her. 'It's okay.'

'I know, I know,' she sobbed. 'I'm being stupid.'

'No you're not.' I tightened my grip on her. 'You're not stupid, Fiona.'

Her tears were soaking through the fabric of my shirt. I could feel them pricking at the corners of my eyes too, but I forced myself to hold them back. She had done her best to look after me when I was younger, and now it was my turn.

'You're not stupid,' I told her firmly. 'I know I've made you feel that way before, and I'm so sorry. I was wrong.'

'I didn't *know*, Jonah!' she exclaimed. 'This was going on for years. Years! And I had no idea! What kind of moron misses something this massive?'

'There's nothing stupid,' I insisted, 'about believing someone when they tell you that they love you.'

Fiona looked at me for a long moment, searchingly, before her forehead fell forward onto my shoulder again. 'Sometimes it all just . . . hits me, you know?' she said, voice muffled in my shirt. 'How much I cared about Matt. How little he cared about me.'

I didn't know how to respond to that. I just held her tighter instead.

She let me hug her for a few moments, then she drew back, extricating herself from my grip and scraping her wrist roughly over her eyes. 'If it was just me, then maybe that would be okay,' she said.

'Maybe I could live with that. But he's got those other kids in Melbourne, and he cares about them more than our kids – he won't even pay child support, for fuck's sake, and he's shown no interest in seeing them since he left, and . . . how am I supposed to explain that to them?'

'I don't know.' Shit, what was I supposed to say? My first real test at being a good brother, and I wasn't going to pass. 'I'm sorry. But—'

'You don't need to explain it to them,' Sadie said.

Fiona and I both looked at her.

'My dad was a piece of shit.' Sadie shrugged as she leant back against the kitchen bench, but her fingers were folded around the edge so hard her knuckles were white. 'No one ever needed to explain that to me. It's a cliché, but actions speak louder than words. Your kids are going to be able to read Matt's actions just fine.'

She paused for a second, biting her lip.

'But they're going to be able to read yours too, Fiona. And Jonah's, and everyone else in their lives who shows up for them, and who keeps showing up for them. They're never going to have a single doubt that they're' – her voice cracked – 'loved.'

'Oh God, Sadie,' Fiona said, the tears starting again.

And then the two most important women in my life stood there, in the middle of our new kitchen, hugging, for a long time, while I desperately hoped I could do something – anything – to make sure neither of them felt like this ever again.

I offered to go with Fiona when she had to leave for school pickup – leaving her alone after she'd broken down like that seemed like a terrible idea – but she refused. 'This is not the first time I've cried over Matt, and it won't be the last,' she said. 'Trust me, I'm going to make you both come around to my place all the time – like, *all* the time – but there's no way I'm taking your first night in your new home away from you. Especially not on Valentine's Day.'

She hugged me goodbye. 'Enjoy the wine and cheese. And whichever bed you pick.'

'Fiona!'

She grinned at me. 'And thank *you*,' she said, hugging Sadie again. 'For being here. For bringing him with you. For everything.'

'You don't need to thank me,' Sadie said. 'Really.'

Her eyes met mine over Fi's shoulder. It made me feel so many things that I almost had to turn away.

Almost.

In the fifteen years of our gruelling education, I had never quite learned how to look away from Sadie Shaw.

What was slightly more unusual was the fact that this time, she hadn't looked away from me.

By the time Fiona left, we were still looking at each other. There was a long, extended, agonising silence.

Sadie bit her lip.

And I nearly broke. I nearly broke like a first-year student in a lecture who couldn't handle the quiet after a question. I nearly flung myself at her feet and wrapped my arms around her waist and said *I love you, I love you, I love you, the words are too citational to express how I feel about you but maybe if I say them enough times that'll get the meaning across, and maybe if I keep saying them you won't be able to get the words 'that isn't why I married you, Fisher, get off your knees, you pathetic fool' in edgewise.*

Then Sadie covered her face with her hands. 'I can't believe the first thing that jumped into my mind when she asked us about why we have two beds was *Airbnb*. What the fuck was I thinking?'

'I'll admit,' I said, just barely managing an appropriately jokey tone, 'that I've heard you make slicker arguments.'

'Just laugh at me and be done with it.' She groaned into her hands. 'I might as well have said that the second bedroom was for our good friend Bunbury.'

'I'm sure we'll find some people for you to try that line on. Maybe we can make a game of it, see how long it takes before someone goes, "Hang on, isn't that Algernon's fake friend from *The Importance of Being Earnest*?"'

She glared at me from between her fingers. 'Don't patronise me.'

'I'm not. I'm just refusing to laugh at you. We're not fighting, remember?'

She dropped her hands from her face, exhaling. 'I did say that, didn't I?'

'You did. And there's no walking it back now, Shaw.'

I don't know where I found the courage[44] to flick the tip of her nose gently with my finger, but it made her smile, and that sent some harp-string in me thrumming, a gentle, warm vibration.

'Come on,' I said. 'Let me help you hang your fairy lights.'

The summer sun was setting by the time we'd finally managed to unpack everything, which left us with two fully kitted-out bedrooms, with desks squeezed in front of the windows and books carefully organised, if haphazardly stacked, on the shelves – and a living room which was completely empty, apart from our wedding photo on the wall.

'So we clearly need to buy some stuff,' I said, leaning against the kitchen bench and regarding the empty space. 'A couch, to start with.'

Sadie nodded, taking her hair down, shaking it out and then I assumed tying it up again, although by that point I had averted

_____
44 Stupidity?

my eyes. 'Want to go furniture shopping next weekend, once we get our first pay cheques?'

'We could try looking on Facebook Marketplace. We might be able to get one cheap.'

She shook her head, hair now safely tied in a topknot. 'I love cheap, don't get me wrong, but I've been burnt before with second hand couches. Someone gave my mum one after my dad left. They must have really wanted to rub salt into the wounds, because it was full of bedbugs.'

'Jesus Christ, Sadie.'

'Not interested in your pity.' The acid note in her voice was deeply familiar. 'But I'm not interested in bedbugs either. Besides . . .'

'Besides what?' I prompted, after a few moments.

'It'll be a good test, don't you think?' The expression on her face was almost shy, and it was deeply *un*familiar. 'Seeing if we can get through buying a couch without some stupid argument?'

'You're on,' I said, making up my mind then and there that we were going to pass this test with flying colours. She could have whichever couch she wanted, even if it was neon pink and cost eight million dollars. 'Let's go shopping.'

'It's a date.'

I nearly melted into a puddle at her feet.

Then something in her eyes lit up, and the urge to fall to my knees before her got even stronger. 'I've got an idea. Get your doctorate.'

'My doctorate . . . ?'

'The piece of paper ESU gave you the same day they gave me mine, Fisher, keep up.' She snapped her fingers.

I obeyed, because my brain wasn't working fast enough to argue. She fetched hers too, and then she hung them on the living room wall, on either side of our wedding photo.

'The actual most important day of our lives deserves to be commemorated too,' she said, standing back, regarding the wall.

'Good idea,' I said faintly. 'Looks good.'

I wasn't going to let that sting. *I was not.* I knew, as well as she did, that what we now had on our wall was two truths and a lie.

Sadie laced her fingers together and stretched her arms over her head. I had to avert my eyes again. 'Want to eat that cheese? I'm starving.'

'Sure,' I said, to the black industrial lighting strip on the ceiling.

We didn't own any glassware – like the couch, the wineglasses in our share house had been someone else's property – so we ended up drinking white wine out of tea mugs: hers, the ridiculously enormous one with the C.S. Lewis quote on the side; mine, a normal-sized black one with the logo of the Australian and New Zealand Association for Medieval and Early Modern Studies on it. We took them out to the balcony, setting the cheese platter down on the table Isamu and his incredible arms had brought up for us, and sitting on either side of it, chairs wedged in close to avoid crushing the herb garden.

Sadie put some brie on a cracker and ate it, closing her eyes as she tipped her face up towards the sky. 'This is nice.'

The sun was setting over the river. The light was Aperol Spritz orange. It caught faint freckles on her skin, turning her hair into living flame against the green backdrop of the plants.

'Yeah,' I said, unable to take my eyes off her. 'It is.'

'That was nice before too,' she said, meeting my gaze. 'With Fiona. You . . . she's lucky to have you, Jonah.'

'Thanks,' I replied. 'For saying that – and for saying what you said to her.'

I was never going to tell Sadie how I felt about her. She didn't feel the same way I did, and it would be unfair to make her carry the burden of my feelings. But sitting there beside her in the gentle evening breeze, drinking wine and looking over the river from the balcony of our home, I made a decision.

If I could have this – have Sadie as a real friend, a real ally, a real companion – then even if our marriage would only ever be on paper, maybe, just maybe, I could be happy.

MARCH

Chapter Fifteen

Sadie

Time started to pass.

There was a famous narrative theorist named Paul Ricœur who distinguished between 'clock time' and 'human time'. Clock time was measured in seconds, minutes, hours, days: the things we think of as the basic building blocks of time. Human time, though, was measured in events: the basic building blocks of story – and thus, because humans love nothing more than to narrativize their own experiences, of our lives.

The first couple of weeks of our marriage had been full of milestones, packed to the brim with the eventful stuff of human time, but as we settled into our new apartment, our new jobs, our new (for lack of a better word) relationship, our routines became established, and clock time began to pass.

'The difference between clock time and human time is really the fundamental conceit behind reality dating shows like this one,' I explained to Jonah one night, sitting cross-legged on the couch we'd bought a few weekends earlier as I forced him to watch the season premiere of *Wherefore Art Thou Romeo?* with me. 'They're experiments in prioritising human time over clock time. The central question is essentially, "What happens if we run through all the human time milestones of the romance plot – meeting, liking, dating, kissing, sometimes fucking, committing – in a strictly limited amount of clock time?"'

Jonah had a mouthful of pasta – he'd made a particularly delicious fettucine dish with a green sauce made from Isamu's herbs, which I'd been carefully nurturing on the balcony – but his eyes said everything his mouth could not re: the proposition that reality dating shows were actually Ricœurian experimentation.

'And it works!' I insisted. 'Sometimes, anyway. Three couples came out of the last season of this franchise. Three! I know you're a terrible snob about reality TV, but you can't tell me that on a basic narrative level, you don't find that interesting.'

He swallowed. 'Only for you, Shaw, would I watch something with a title that was such an aggressive misinterpretation of early modern language. You know *wherefore* means—'

'*Why*, not *where*, yes, I know.' I twirled some fettucine on my fork. 'I listen when you talk, Fisher.'

'Then you should know I'm not *that* bad a snob about reality TV.' He nudged my leg with a sock-clad foot. 'If I'm going to watch this with you, then you have to watch the next season of *Superchef* with me.'

I pretended to consider. 'Fine, fine, seems fair.'

'Good.' He pointed his fork at me. 'And I expect the same level of narrative analysis. Going on *Superchef* is my only backup plan if you divorce me and I get fired, so I need all the insight I can get on how to game the format to win.'

The show had started. On the screen, the new lead was having an earnest conversation with the host about what she was looking for in a partner ('I just want someone I can have an intelligent conversation with, you know?').

But I turned away from it to face Jonah. 'You know I'm not planning to divorce you anytime soon, right?'

He was looking at his pasta, negotiating a particularly trouble-some noodle. 'I know you're not planning on it,' he said lightly, 'but you never know when I'm going to piss you off again.'

'Is that a threat?'

I'd intended it jokingly, but his eyes, when he looked at me, were serious. 'Of course not. But I don't exactly have a strong record when it comes to *not* pissing you off.'

I hesitated for a second, then I put my hand on his knee. Beneath his pyjama pants, his skin was warm.

'Fisher,' I said, my own skin starting to heat in response, 'unless you do something really awful – something where I have to, like, report you to The Hague – I'm not going to divorce you before probation is up, okay?'

'No war crimes in the next three years,' he said, smiling faintly. 'Got it.'

On the screen, the host and the lead were still talking. 'Tell me what an ideal date would look like for you,' the host said.

'For a first date, I want the excitement, the theatre, the spark,' the woman replied. 'Let's have an adventure. Let's have a beautiful dinner in a beautiful restaurant afterwards. But once you really get to know someone, once you've built up that level of intimacy . . . ? All I really want is dinner on the couch watching bad TV.'

I snatched my hand away, busily twirling more pasta on my fork. 'Besides, if we got divorced before we passed probation, I'd probably be the one who was fired, not you, given how passionately Petrovski hates me,' I said, trying to keep my tone airy. 'This is delicious, by the way. My compliments to the chef.'

'Thanks,' Jonah said.

He settled back into his corner of the couch. 'So explain to me who these people are, Shaw.' He gestured at the screen. 'What do I need to know?'

'Okay, so . . .'

I launched into an extended explanation. The interruption from the TV had been awkward, but I was grateful for it. If it hadn't happened, there was a chance I might have let the actual truth slip out.

I'm not going to divorce you, Jonah. You're all I have.

After that first couple of weeks in Hobart – and after an incredibly long stream of unanswered texts and calls – I'd stopped trying to contact Chess. She'd asked me for space, and in return I'd bombarded her with messages. If I wanted her back anytime soon, I had to show her I respected her wishes.

But going completely radio-silent was inconceivable. Not speaking to my sister – even if she wasn't speaking back – was something I just couldn't do. How was she meant to know how sorry I was for the things I'd said to her if I didn't tell her?

Every Wednesday evening, Jonah and I would take Veronica and Lin, the two casual academics who were teaching into our courses, out for a glass of wine and a cheeseboard at Tsundoku so we could talk about our plans for the following week (after so many years of being casuals ourselves, we were determined to treat our staff the best that we possibly could). Every time, I'd pick out a couple of books for Chess from Satoshi's very well-stocked romance shelves. Then, after Jonah and I went home, had dinner, and watched *Wherefore Art Thou Romeo?*, he'd retire to his room for his weekly Zoom with Elias, and I'd retire to mine to write Chess a letter.

Dear Chessie,

Do you remember that first veggie patch we cultivated when I was seven, behind our old house? It was such a little overgrown disaster, but I was so proud of it, and you told me it was the best garden in the world.

I babysat Rosie and Georgia today (also aged seven) while Jonah took Fiona out, and they helped me prepare my patch in the community garden for autumn planting – and MY GOD, Chess, was I this bad? I remember you and me spending hours looking after that garden and having the best time, but they got bored after about five minutes and started throwing dirt at each other (and also me). Here's a picture, in case you want to see what I look like with mud all through my hair.

I have an incredibly long way to go as a babysitter. I was also babysitting Lex (Fiona's eldest, they just turned twelve), and completely forgot about them for about two hours because I was so distracted by the twins. Thankfully they were just sitting quietly on the balcony reading, but I felt so awful. Fiona laughed at me when I apologised, but . . . oof. The guilt.

The age difference between Lex and the girls is the same as the one between you and me. I don't think I've ever really appreciated how hard that must have been for you, looking after me when you were only a kid yourself.

I miss you. I love you. And I'm so sorry for the things I said to you.
All my love,
Sadie xxx

Dear Chessie,

I took my friend Julia to Tsundoku yesterday. She lives on the other side of the river – people are really intense about east side/west side stuff in Hobart, it's a whole identity thing – so she'd never even heard of it before.

Suffice to say she loved it. Another convert to Bibliophile! I can't wait to take you here someday.

You'd like Julia. She's a real no-nonsense, no-bullshit type. She's the co-lead of this interdisciplinary research network I joined, and in our meeting the other day, a guy from the Health faculty tried to speak over her. I've never seen someone get so politely but thoroughly eviscerated. It was a thing of beauty. I'm going to have to get her to teach me how to do it, because my boss . . . ugggghhhhhhhh.

Anyway, I found out when we went for drinks that Julia knows Jonah's brother Elias??? More than knows him, if I'm reading between the lines right. 'Remember how I told you the first thing that happened to me when I got my permanent job was a divorce?' she said. 'It wasn't just the job's fault.'

Whatever happened, she absolutely fucking hates Elias's guts. She was pretty sus on Jonah for a while too, but when he declined to join her research network because, in his words, 'It's about time my family connections did me a disservice for a change', she decided he was probably okay.

'I mean, I like you, and you liked him enough to marry him,' she said. 'How bad can he be?'

I know you don't like Jonah either, Chess, but I promise you, he really is okay. We're . . . I guess you could say we're sort of friends now? We're getting along, anyway.

I wish you were here so I could show you. I love you so much, and I always, always will.

Sadie xxx

✎

Dear Chessie,

Uggggghhhhhhhh I wish we were still having dinner twice a week so I could vent. I need your advice on how to deal with my horrible boss.

So it's always been clear that Petrovski doesn't like me, right? Like, from the first time I met him, he thought I was garbage. Julia said it's probably because I was hired by Vargas (his boss) who he hates – he and Carmichael (the sex predator head of history) are gunning for her, and they try to undermine her every chance they get. But I think there's a solid dose of garden-variety misogyny in there too (along with the classic tweed bro anti-pop-fic snobbery). I've never seen him look at a female colleague without contempt in his eyes.

Anyway, Petrovski's hatred of me has mostly been coming out in little ways; e.g. he's always ordering me to take minutes in department meetings like I'm his secretary (which Jonah has been great about, actually – he always volunteers to take them instead). Today, though, really took the fucking cake.

He rocked up to our Romanticism lecture (about twenty minutes in, just to make it extra rude). It was Jonah's turn to lecture, but we're doing this thing where we interrupt each other to clarify or build on what the other person is saying. We got this piece of student feedback when we were teaching at Bass about how they were always waiting for our entrance music to hit when the other one of us was teaching – like professional wrestling – so we've been experimenting with dramatically interrupting each other (sans music) and teaching via argument.

So I got up and interrupted Jonah, just like we planned, and we had this – entirely scripted! – debate about Coleridge's scathing review of Charles Maturin's play Bertram. The students loved it (Bertram is a ridiculous play and Coleridge's review is hilarious, so it was fun to argue about). But then afterwards, as the students were leaving – leaving! not left! some of them were still in the lecture theatre! – Petrovski grabbed my elbow, pulled me aside, and absolutely reamed me out for disrespecting another scholar.

Jonah jumped in immediately and tried to explain our teaching strategy. Our casuals Lin and Veronica were there too, and they backed him up, but Petrovski wouldn't hear it. He just completely ignored the two of them like they weren't even there, and said, 'Jonah, it does you credit to defend your wife like this, but Sadie, this is unacceptable.'

Then – oh yes, there's more! – he had the gall to ask me when to expect my next research output, because unless I achieve the requisite number of research points per year, I won't pass probation.

As if I have time for research at the moment! Jonah and I spend basically every second of every day writing all these fucking lectures!

(Jonah is also subject to the research points thing – we have exactly the same job with exactly the same conditions – but do you think Petrovski asked him where his next output was?)

Jonah and I had a good idea, though. We're going to co-author an article on our professional wrestling-style pedagogy for one of the Scholarship of Teaching and Learning journals (more work, yes, but what's another 8000 words when we already have to co-write, like, 300,000?). At least then, if Petrovski tries to formally discipline me for being a bitch to Jonah in lectures, we'll have a publication to say that I was being a bitch for very serious, scholarly reasons.

I'm going to talk to Julia and brainstorm some strategies for dealing with Petrovski – conveniently, she's also our union rep, so if he REALLY gets out of hand, she'll know all the processes – but God, I miss you, Chessie. Every time I see his horrible little face, I think, 'Chess would know how to handle this. Chess would know what to do.'

I know you need time and space and I respect that (I mean, I know it might not look like it, considering all these letters, but I promise, I do). But when you're ready . . . it would mean everything to me, just to hear your voice. Please call me??
All my love, to the end of the universe and back again,
Sadie xxx

Every week, I slid my letter inside one of the romance novels I'd bought for her – *Honey and Spice* by Bolu Babalola, *Second First Impressions* by Sally Thorne, *Iris After The Incident* by Mina V. Esguerra – and sent it off.

But Chess never replied.

And with every week of silence, I became more and more convinced that I'd lost the one person who I'd thought would love me forever.

APRIL

Chapter Sixteen
Jonah

One chilly Thursday morning, a week or so after Easter, I took a coffee down to Sadie in the community garden and found her standing, arms crossed, frowning at her veggie patch.

She spent an hour or so in the garden each morning before we sat down to get stuck into the next of our fifty-two lectures,[45] and I brought her down a coffee every day. Normally, she barely looked up. I'd get a 'Thanks, Fisher, appreciate it,' maybe two seconds of her attention as she worked out the best place to balance her enormous mug, and then she'd go right back to what she was doing while I made a hasty escape, lest I think too hard about the image of her on her knees.

Not this time, though. 'Something wrong?' I asked her, handing her the mug.

'Not wrong, exactly.' Her breath was coming in little white puffs. 'I just don't have enough room for everything I want to do, that's all. The plot's too small.'

Sadie wrapped both hands around the mug, taking a sip. 'I've got so many ideas for this section' – she indicated the last bare strip of

---

45 We'd written well over thirty of them now. Fifteen years after we'd got our worst grade ever because we were terrible collaborators, Sadie Shaw and I had well and truly learned to work together.

dirt in the patch – 'and they're all tripping over each other. I've got decision paralysis, and I need to get over it before the ground gets too frosty.'

She shook her head, trying to get a stray piece of hair out of her eyes but clearly not wanting to let go of her coffee in the frosty morning air. I wrestled with myself for a few seconds before I said, 'Can I . . .?'

'Can you what? Oh, sure.'

Trying to be as businesslike as possible, I stroked the loose section of hair behind her ear. 'What if we went plant shopping together after work? I don't know shit about plants, but I do know shit about vegetables, so maybe I can help you narrow it down. I could see if Fi will let us borrow her car.'

Sadie thought about it, then nodded. 'Okay.'

'Great. Breakfast in about fifteen minutes, by the way. I'm making those corn fritters you like, so don't dawdle or they'll get cold.'

She took another sip of her coffee. 'Fine, fine.'

'And speaking of cold—'

I took off my cardigan and draped it around her shoulders. She had goosebumps all over her arms.

'No freezing to death out here, Shaw,' I told her sternly. 'There are no good clichés about mysterious widowers solving murders on trains like there are about mysterious widows. I need you alive.'

I half-expected her to protest, but she didn't. 'Thanks,' was all she said. Her cheeks and the tip of her nose were pink with cold. 'I'll do my best not to get dirt on it.'

I made a dismissive hand gesture. 'It'll wash. Fifteen minutes.'

'Fifteen minutes.'

I hoped, as I headed back up to our apartment, that I actually had all the ingredients for those corn fritters she loved. I'd intended to serve a quick breakfast of bircher muesli, which I'd prepared the night before, but it'd keep until tomorrow.

✎

Fi agreed to let us borrow her car, so Sadie and I headed straight to her place after our last lecture of the day. 'Thank God Petrovski didn't pick today to make one of his surprise appearances,' she said, as we sat beside each other on the bus back from campus. 'Can you imagine what colour he would have turned if he caught me teaching *Red, White and Royal Blue* to impressionable first years?'

'Caught *us*,' I said, nudging her with my elbow. 'I was there too. And I'm going to guess a sort of bilious chartreuse.'

'No, that sounds like him about to be sick. It'd be something in the reds, the purples – some real head-about-to-explode colours. And you know exactly which one of us would get the blame.'

I sighed. You didn't need to be paying close attention to see just how much contempt Petrovski had for Sadie. She wasn't the only object of his ire – we'd both been in enough department meetings now to be able to very confidently make a list of who he liked and who he didn't – but the difference in the way he treated us was so stark it would be comical if it wasn't so awful.

'Let's just hope he doesn't start sticking his head into seminars as well as lectures,' Sadie added. 'At least we have enough job security to defend ourselves. Veronica and Lin don't.'

The bus rattled around the sharp corner down the hill towards Bellerive a little too fast. For a second, all of Sadie's body weight pressed into me before she caught herself. 'Sorry.'

'It's fine.' The feeling of her pressed against me would, I knew, fuel my fantasies for many nights to come. 'Look, I worry about Veronica and Lin too. I can't believe I'm saying this, but . . . do you think I should try talking to my dad? See if he can get Petrovski to back off?'

She shook her head decisively. 'We both know that wouldn't do any good.'

I sighed again. I wished I could argue, but she was right.

'Julia told me to start documenting everything Petrovski does, but I already was,' she went on. 'It's the very first thing that Chess would have told me to do.'

Like it always did when she mentioned her sister, a wave of misery swept across her face. And like they always did whenever this happened, three emotions hit me in a precise, rhythmic order: first, a flash of anger; second, a surge of protectiveness; third, a deep, creeping, gnawing guilt.

'That's smart,' I said, keeping my tone businesslike. 'And you know I'll back you up.'

'Thanks, but I'm not sure how much it'd help. You're married to me. They'd probably just assume I – I don't know, withheld sex until you agreed to do what I wanted.'

Did she *have* to mention sex? Could she not have a little respect for the fact that sometimes I wanted her so badly it caused me actual physical pain? I'd thought that now we had our own apartment with separate bedrooms it would make Project Control easier, but if anything, it was only getting harder.[46]

'Speaking of marriage,' I said, carefully angling my body away from hers as we stood to get off the bus, 'I had an idea for what to call our article. What do you think of "Bickering Like An Old Married Couple: Productive Disagreement as Pedagogy"?'

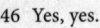

---

46 Yes, yes.

Fi was looking harried when we got to her place, and we offered to take the kids plant shopping with us to give her a break, but she declined. 'Lex is reading, and the girls are at a friend's place this evening,' she explained, pressing her car keys into my hand. 'Getting their shit together to get them *to* said friend's place was a bit of a production – I thought I'd hid it well enough, but they got into their stash of Easter chocolate . . .' She ran a hand through her hair. 'Anyway, this afternoon was a lot, but now it's just me and Lex and a quiet house for a few hours.'

Sadie chewed her bottom lip as we got into the car. 'Do you think we should offer to take the kids one night next week?'

My hand slipped as I went to turn the key in the ignition. 'Like, for the whole night?'

'I know we babysit a decent amount but . . .' Her voice trailed off for a few moments. 'You married me because you want to help Fiona, right?'

'Not just to help Fiona,' slipped out of my mouth before I could stop it.

'Yes, yes, gainful employment, whatever,' Sadie said, breezing right past it. 'But she clearly needs help. More help. So let's help. What if we took the kids one night a week? Gave Fiona a night to herself?'

I let out a long breath, hoping she would assume it was because I was thinking. 'Lex could sleep on the couch, but we'd have to put the girls in my room.'

'Or my room.' She shrugged. 'They'd probably like the fairy lights.'

Oh God.

'But . . . you'd be fine with it?' I asked carefully. 'Sharing a bed with me again?'

'I should be asking you that question. I'm not the one who spent that first fortnight waking up to being groped.'

247

Not helping not helping *not helping*.

I started the car and pulled out of the driveway, more to give myself something to focus on than anything else. I didn't need to look in the rearview mirror to know I had turned scarlet.

'About which I'm sorry, by the way.' She leant her head against the passenger side window. 'But I'm sure I could, like, tie my hands to the bed-frame or something.'

Thank fucking God I was already blushing. The image of Sadie, in my bed, hands tied to the frame, felt like someone giving my brain repeated electric shocks.

'I suppose it would help explain why we keep a Bunbury Suite,' I choked out.

Foolishly, I glanced briefly across at her. She was still teasing her lip between her teeth, and it was a real mercy all my blood was currently in my face.

'I just think it would be a good thing to do,' she said. '*The* good thing to do.'

My mind was in the gutter and here was my wife, looking at the stars.

'Fiona deserves some time to herself,' she went on, as we pulled onto the Tasman Bridge. 'And . . .'

'And what?' I prompted, when the silence stretched out a little too long.

'Nothing, really.' Sadie scrubbed a hand over her face. 'I've just been thinking, lately. About my mother. About how maybe, if she'd had some other adults in her life that had been willing to look after me, then Chess wouldn't have had to.'

There they were again, predictable as the sunrise. The flash of anger. The surge of protectiveness. The wave of guilt.

She let out a long breath. 'It must have been exhausting for her,' she said. '*I* must have been exhausting for her. She was a child, but she had to become an adult so quickly because someone had to look after me, and . . . there's just no way I can balance the scales between us. Ever.'

I couldn't say even a hundredth of the things I wanted to. There was no way Sadie would react well to me telling her exactly how cruel and unfair I thought Chess was being to her, even if it was the truth.

'Rosie and Georgia are the most exhausting people on the planet,' I said instead, 'and I'd still lay my life down for them without hesitation.'

She sighed again. 'I don't know how you became so convinced you were a terrible sibling, Jonah. You're great at it.'

'I've been studying.' I took my hand off the steering wheel for a moment and tapped a finger between two of her knuckles. 'It helps, when you're married to a master.'

The compliment did not hit as intended. Sadie's shoulders slumped.

I gritted my teeth against all the things I wanted to say. It was completely hypocritical of me – a few months of decent brotherhood did not make up for my track record – but I just fundamentally did not get it. If Fiona could let go so easily and so readily and so generously of how awful I'd been to her, how could Chess not do the same for Sadie? How could she just *leave* Sadie like this, when she must know perfectly well how Sadie felt about being left?

There was a common trope in early modern theatre called the bed trick. Someone would think they were going to bed with one person, but, unbeknownst to them, they would end up in bed with someone else.

Early modern theatre was full of unbelievable nonsense, but the bed trick had always struck me as the pinnacle of it. Even if it was completely pitch-black, how could you not know that the person you were sleeping with was not the person you'd intended to?

These months married to Sadie had only reinforced my conviction. I wasn't even going to bed with her anymore, but when she got in one of these moods, I didn't need to touch her or even lie down next to her to know that a bed trick had been played on me. I loved her in all seasons – the heights of joy, the depths of misery, better, worse, richer, poorer, sickness, health, all of it – but it was crushing to see her like this, so far away from the woman she usually was, the woman I had meant to marry.

Because Sadie Shaw was not subdued. Sadie Shaw was not this greyed-out shadow. Sadie Shaw was a torrent of thought and intellect and confidence, a bonfire of a woman, gleefully torching whoever – me, usually – was in her path.

When she got like this, though, it felt like my bonfire of a bride had had water poured on her, only wisps of smoke escaping from a few smouldering coals.

And it made me absolutely fucking furious.

Furious at Chess, for pouring that water on her. Furious at Sadie, even, for continuing to blame herself for her own smothering.

But mostly furious at myself, for my inability to make her feel even a little bit better – and deeply, deeply guilty.

Sadie could insist that the rift between her and Chess was her own fault as much as she wanted, but that argument was as thin and specious as one Rory Worland might make. There was no way she would be this miserable if she hadn't married me.

And now here she was, insisting on looking after my sister when her relationship with her own was in tatters, and all I could do was fantasise about burying my face in her hair and my fingers in the lush curves of her skin and removing my heart from my chest and laying it at her feet.

She was still quiet by the time we arrived, and I had to resist the urge to take her hand or loop my arm over her shoulders as we walked into the giant garden and hardware store. Wedged between anger and guilt was protectiveness, and sometimes I could get away with using the ruse of our marriage to offer her physical comfort. She'd usually accept it, if it could plausibly be read as *look at us, everyone, observe how we're definitely a completely real couple*, even though what I was actually saying was *you mean everything to me and I don't want you to fall apart.*

I had to settle for pushing the trolley instead, and doing some performatively masculine, 'Wife, step aside, what did you marry me for if not to lift heavy things for you?' bits when she tried to pick up a gigantic bag of fertiliser, in an extremely cheap effort to make her laugh.[47]

'So, run me through all these garden ideas of yours,' I said, as we made our way to the outdoor section. 'Give me your dot points. Let's narrow it down.'

She exhaled. I'd written enough lectures with her now to recognise that she was trying to re-focus her attention on the task at hand. 'It really boils down to a dilemma between planting and sowing. Do I want to plant alliums or do I want to sow a crop of root vegetables?'

'Tell me more. What kinds of alliums? What kinds of root vegetables?'

'Alliums, I was thinking especially about leeks. I love leeks. Root vegetables – heirloom carrots, parsnip, maybe beetroot.'

'And you can't do both?'

'Not enough space.'

'All right.' I steered our trolley around to the relevant aisle and started to load it up with leek plants. 'Seedlings are best, right? Or should we be looking for more established plants?'

---

47 This was . . . semi-successful, I'd say? Mostly because I also struggled under the weight of the fertiliser. Isamu Tsukamoto I was not.

'We didn't even make a decision!' she protested, trailing after me.

'Yes, we did.' I put another leek plant on the trolley. 'You said *I love leeks*. I didn't hear you say *I love parsnips* or *I love beetroot*.'

'I do like both those things!'

'But do you love them?'

We had a semi-combative stare-off for a few seconds before she broke. 'Not like I love leeks,' she grumbled. 'Not that plant, Jonah, it looks a bit iffy. This one instead.'

'You should have told me you loved them,' I said, swapping out the plants. 'I'd have cooked with them more often.'

'You already do all the cooking. I don't want to start treating you like a restaurant, where I can just wave my hand and order whatever I want.'

'Shaw, *please* order whatever you want. I really do love cooking. You've given me a gift here. This'll be a fun little project for me, experimenting with exciting new leek dishes.'

She regarded me for a few moments. 'Where did it come from?' she asked. 'The cooking thing?'

'What do you mean?'

'Correct me if I'm wrong, but having been to your parents' house, it doesn't seem like *let's teach our son to cook* would be a big priority.'

I snorted. 'You're not wrong.' At Sadie's gesture, I swapped out a couple more of the leek seedlings. 'I moved out of home after graduation. Our first graduation, I mean. The one with all the . . .'

'Shouting,' she filled in. 'I remember.'

I thought I'd committed a fatal error by reminding her of Chess again, but she still seemed engaged. 'I moved into a place with this girl I was seeing at the time – I'm not sure if you ever met her, but she—'

'Oh yes, the woman whose *heart you broke*?' Sadie clutched dramatically at her chest. '*I can't possibly let you have this share house, Shaw, for I am simply too much of a heartbreaker to find another!'*

'Are you finished?'

She smirked. 'Probably not, but continue.'

'Anyway, when I moved in with her, I was useless,' I said. 'Couldn't cook, couldn't clean, couldn't do anything. I realised quickly that I needed those skills if I was ever going to function as an adult, so I studied.'

She blinked. 'You studied?'

'That, I did know how to do. You wanted some garden stakes too, right?' She nodded, so I started pushing the trolley down towards the garden care section. 'I figured out pretty quickly that Ps make degrees when it comes to cleaning. It just had to be passable. But the better I got at cooking, the happier it made my girlfriend, and . . .'

'Fisher,' Sadie said, 'did you seriously learn to cook so your girlfriend would fuck you?'

'No!' I flushed bright red. 'Get your mind out of the gutter, Shaw. I learnt to cook so she would love me.'

'And it worked.'

I stopped, looking sideways at her. She'd phrased it as a statement, not a question, and I could hear the blood rushing in my ears as everything around us went into soft focus.

'You broke her heart,' she clarified. 'When you – I'm assuming it was you who ended it.'

'Oh. Yes. It was me.'

I turned to face her, resting my elbows lightly against the handle of the trolley. 'I realised, after a while, that with every extravagant dish I cooked her, she thought I was saying *I love you*. But what I was actually doing was cooking her extravagant dishes as a way of getting out of saying it. Because I didn't.'

The answer was right there for her, if she wanted to put the puzzle pieces together. *I didn't love her – could never love her – because I've been in love with you since the day we met, Shaw.*

Sadie looked thoughtful. For a moment, I was terrified she'd figured it out.

'That's really quite emotionally intelligent,' she said. 'For – how old were you? Twenty-four? Twenty-five?'

'About that.'

'Sorry,' she said. 'For making fun of you for breaking her heart. That was dickish.'

'It's fine,' I said, somehow both relieved and disappointed at the same time. 'That water went under the bridge a long time ago. And I did figure out my one true love because of that relationship. Me and cooking have been going strong ever . . . Watch out!'

I grabbed her wrist and pulled her into me. My back went crashing into a stack of plant trellises and Sadie came crashing into my chest, just in time to avoid getting completely flattened by a man barrelling along at top speed, the landscaping supplies piled high on his trolley blocking his line of sight.

He carried on, either not noticing or not caring that he'd nearly just mown someone down. The trellises behind me quaked ominously, and it was only the rough edges of one of them jabbing into my back that kept me tethered to reality.

Every line of Sadie's body was pressed against mine.

'Shit,' she whispered.

She hadn't moved. The words were hot against my skin, her gentle breath tickling the short hairs of my beard.

'You all right?' My voice came roughly out of my throat, like someone had taken sandpaper to it.

She nodded, hairline brushing against my nose. 'Fine. Thank you.'

Her fingers curled into my collar, pulling it taut across the back of my neck. She looked up at me.

And it was our wedding day again. Sadie Shaw was clinging to me, and there was something desperate in her eyes, and the only answer I had was to kiss her.

My head dipped lower . . .

. . . just as she exhaled, forehead coming to rest against my shoulder. 'I think you saved my life,' she said into my clavicle.

I pressed my lips against the top of her head, pretending with everything I had that that was all I had intended to do. 'I like a good garden stake as much as the next person, but they're not worth dying for, Shaw. Get your shit together.'

The words were as much for me as they were for her.

'Come on,' I said, taking her by the shoulders and pushing her gently away from me. 'Let's get out of here.'

The business of checking out and packing all of the stuff safely into the back of Fi's car was blessedly thought-consuming, and then we got distracted by a sudden flash of inspiration for one of our upcoming lectures, so when Sadie brought it up again, as we unloaded all our purchases back home in our garage, it took me by surprise.

'You know, I think I got into gardening for the same reason you got into cooking, Fisher,' she said, her tone casual as she wedged the last of the leek seedlings into the little trolley she used to haul plants down to the community garden, ready for the morning.

'You were also a fully grown adult who realised they had no practical life skills?' I closed the boot and looked at her quizzically. 'Didn't you tell me when we were at Tsundoku a couple of weeks ago that you started gardening when you were, like, six?'

'I was seven. And I thought if I could contribute to the household and help out, my father would stop screaming at my mum and Chess and me that we were all a waste of space.'

I stopped dead.

She sniffed, swallowing once, twice. 'I thought I could make him love us.'

'Oh God,' I said, as tears started to bead in the corner of her eyes. 'Shit, Sadie.'

'Sorry.' She brushed them away roughly. 'I didn't mean to trauma dump on you. My abandonment issues are for my therapist to worry about, not you. I'm fine, really. I just . . .'

She didn't need to finish the sentence, and there was no way I was going to make her. 'I need to take the car back to Fi,' I said, 'but it can wait. We can go upstairs. I can make you a cup of tea. I could even . . . I didn't want to tell you until I got it perfect, but I've been finessing a mug cake recipe. I've got some ideas for some pretty adventurous flavour combinations. You could taste-test them for me.'

'Oh, Jonah, that's really nice of you.'

My heart skipped a beat.

But then she shook her head. 'Take the car back to Fiona, though. I think I, um . . . I think I should just be alone for a minute.'

'Are you sure?'

'Yes. I'm sure.'

Then, to my great surprise, she put her arms around my neck. 'Thank you, though,' she said. 'I appreciate it.'

She kissed my cheek, and maybe that was why I let what I said next come out of my mouth.

'Any time, darling,' I whispered into her hair.

I kicked myself for it every second of the short drive back to Fi's. Mug cake. Fucking *mug cake*. Why the fuck had I offered to make her mug cake? The thing that she'd specifically told me, on the night of the sixth ceasefire, was something that Chess used to make for her?

And I'd tried to kiss her. I'd called her *darling,* even though there wasn't anyone else there to hear it except her. What the fuck was I thinking?

I smacked the steering wheel. Yes, we'd been getting along. Yes, we'd been getting a bit more tactile of late. Yes, we were now even in a place where her hugging me the way she'd just hugged me was . . . normal.

But whenever Sadie reached out to me – whether to put her hand on my arm, or her arms around my neck, or even to sprawl over me in her sleep, as she surely would again if we started babysitting the kids one night a week – I had to remember that it wasn't because she was genuinely emotionally attached to me. It wasn't because I was Jonah Fisher, person she enjoyed spending time with.

It was because she was lonely, and I was *there.*

The basic governing principle of narrative was causation. It wasn't *X happened then Y happened* – it was *Y happened because X happened.*

Sadie had not started reaching out to me because, out of nowhere, she was starting to feel about me the way I'd always felt about her. She was doing it because she and Chess were at odds, and I was the only possible substitute.

I could enjoy it, sure. But I couldn't read into it. And I absolutely – *absolutely* – couldn't take advantage of it.

I sighed, pulling the car to a stop in Fiona's driveway. I had a sneaking suspicion I knew what the right thing to do was, but that didn't mean I wanted to do it. I'd resisted it over the past few months – if there was one thing I knew about Sadie, it was that she could speak for herself – but it was obvious nothing was going to change unless I did something to change it.

It only took about three seconds to find Chess's email address, sitting beneath a stern, unsmiling picture of her on her law firm's website. Dear Francesca, I wrote.

I'm sure you're not interested in hearing from me and I don't blame you at all. Neither I nor my family have ever given you any reason to like me – and you were absolutely correct when you told me I had ridden Sadie's coat-tails into a job I do not deserve.

What I do blame you for, though, is making her miserable.

Despite what you may think, I care very deeply about your sister. You might find this difficult to believe, given our history and the numerous ways I've benefitted from our marriage, but I would not have married her otherwise. Sadie is extremely important to me – and the fact that you're refusing to speak to her is killing her.

I know you had a fight the night before our wedding. I know you probably both said some things, but frankly, I don't care. Are you really going to let me – someone I know you have no respect for – come between you?

Your silence is breaking your sister's heart. If you care about Sadie at all, you'll stop hurting her like this. Just call her. Please.

Regards,

Jonah

'You were sitting out there a long time,' Fi said, when I finally went in to give the car keys back. 'Everything okay?'

'Fine, fine. Just' – I waved my phone vaguely – 'emails. So, Sadie and I had an idea.'

It took a while to sell her on the concept of the kids coming to stay for the night ('Are you sure? All three of them? Are you *sure*? Do you maybe want to start with Lex and work your way up?'), but eventually Fiona agreed we could take them the following Thursday, after our teaching for the week was finished. 'And to say thank you,' she said, digging around in her fridge and then handing me a bottle of Bibliophile fumé blanc, 'take this home to your lovely wife.'

'You don't need to do that, Fi.'

She waved me off. 'Plenty more where that came from. Lex and I stopped by Tsundoku the other day so they could pick up some more books. Satoshi sent me home with a case.'

I accepted the wine-cooler bag she handed me. 'They really love you there, hey.'

'Well, I've spent a ton of money there over the years.' She took a sip from her cup of tea. 'But both the Tsukamotos are such lovely men. You know Satoshi was the first person I told, when Matt came clean about his other family? After he broke the news to me I had a sort of out-of-body experience. I must have walked straight out of the house, because the next thing I knew I was at Tsundoku and Satoshi was taking me out the back and sitting me down in his office and pouring me a glass of wine and listening to me spill my guts.'

My fingers tightened around the bag. 'I'm so sorry you didn't feel like you could tell me, Fi.'

'Oh, Jonah.'

Fiona hugged me. Hesitantly, careful not to hit her with the wine, I hugged her back.

'That was as much my fault as it was yours,' she said. 'More, really.'

'Come on, Fi. You know that's not true.'

Fiona drew back and raised her eyebrows at me.

I sighed. 'Sorry. That instinct to argue . . . it's baked in pretty deep.'

'Tell me about it.' She made a sound that was halfway to a chuckle. 'I liked to think I'd freed myself from all of Dad's toxic programming, but . . . when Matt left, there it was. Pride, so much wounded pride – and this incredible bone-deep embarrassment about how wrong I'd been.'

'I know it probably doesn't mean much,' I said, 'but I hate that we were right. I hate what I said to you, that night you told us you were getting married. You always looked out for me, and when you needed someone to be on your side, I was such a nasty little shit to you. I'm so sorry.'

'You're here now, Jonah,' Fiona said softly. 'And that means the world to me.'

'I missed you, all those years,' I said. 'And . . . I know I've never been good at saying this, but I love you.'

She smiled. 'I love you too, baby bro.'

Then she shoved me playfully in the shoulder – thankfully, because if we kept walking down this very sincere path, one of us was going to cry and it was probably going to be me. 'Though maybe don't throw those words around too soon. See if you still love me after spending the night with my kids.'

My phone buzzed in my pocket as I started the short walk home, leaves crunching under my feet. I know this is your territory, but I tried to make dinner, Sadie had texted. Let's just say it didn't work? So . . . I hope you like toast.

You're in luck, I sent back. I love toast.

Thank God. I was worried you were going to divorce me for disrespecting your kitchen.

I replied with the laughing emoji.

I was about to put my phone away when I saw I had another notification – email, this time. From: Francesca Shaw.

I stopped right where I was. Maybe I shouldn't have been so

quick to say how much I loved toast. There was a serious chance I might throw up.

But it was just an auto-reply – *I am currently on leave* – and a long list of who to contact in various circumstances.

I let out a long breath, letting it whistle through my teeth. Was the reason that Chess wasn't replying to Sadie that she simply wasn't getting her messages?

No. Surely not. She might not be checking her work email, but it was ridiculous to assume she wouldn't have got all those texts and missed calls from when we first moved here. And surely, if she wasn't getting all the books Sadie was sending her, at least some of them would have been returned to sender.

As I started walking again, I thought about whether to tell Sadie about the email I'd sent, but decided against it. Chess's lack of response would tell her nothing she wasn't already dwelling on at enormous length. Plus, she'd likely be livid that I'd reached out without telling her and I was at the end of my strength. I couldn't bring myself to upset her.

Sadie smiled at me when I walked back in, laugh lines deepening in the corners of her eyes. 'Sorry again about dinner.'

'Nothing wrong with toast. Perfect vehicle for marmalade – and I bought a delicious Bruny Island one at Salamanca Market last weekend. Pear, lemon and cardamom. It tastes like sunshine.' I held up the bag in my hand. 'Wine?'

'Please.'

No, I definitely wasn't going to tell her. She'd find out eventually, when Chess finally got over herself and spoke to her again. Sadie could be angry with me for overstepping then, when her sister was finally restored to her position as the most trusted person in her life.

In the meantime, though, she had me, and I would treasure whatever scraps she deigned to give me.

MAY

Chapter Seventeen
Sadie

'Hnnnnrrrrgggghhhh,' Jonah groaned when my alarm went off.

I froze, halfway through sitting up. Usually, on Friday mornings, when we were sharing his bed in the Bunbury Suite so Rosie and Georgia could have mine, he didn't even register my alarm going off in the pre-dawn. He'd sleep straight through me peeling myself off him and tiptoeing out to go and potter around my garden for a bit before the kids woke up, which conveniently meant we never had to talk about the fact that I always ended up sleeping half on top of him.

'Cold,' he mumbled. 'You're so warm, Shaw. Like a hot-water bottle.'

I tucked the quilt around his shoulders. He made a satisfied noise and snuggled into it. As usual, he was sleeping on his front, half draped-over, half hugging his pillow; and as usual, it made me think of three things: the story Fiona had told me about his dad taking his teddy bear away from him; what it might feel like if his arm was around me instead of the pillow; and then the teddy bear again, because I really shouldn't be thinking about the other thing.

'Go back to sleep, Jonah,' I whispered, wrapping my dressing gown around myself. He wasn't wrong about the cold – as winter got closer, the mornings were getting increasingly icy.

'Don't take too long today,' he murmured. 'Got to go to campus after we get the kids to school, remember?'

I suppressed a groan. Fridays were usually what we optimistically and euphemistically called our 'research day'. We didn't have to teach any classes, and getting Lex and the girls off to school was a task that didn't require looking particularly presentable, so we usually spent the day working from home in the most comfortable clothes we owned.

Today was the first Friday we might actually get to look at our actual research. We'd finished writing the new units we'd been tasked with and we'd put the final touches on Lecture 52 the day before, a whole week and a half before we were due to give it. So, naturally, today was also the day that Petrovski had insisted on meeting with us both on campus to discuss our Semester Two workload – which was almost certainly going to involve dropping even more lectures on our heads.

'Parcel came for you yesterday,' he added, just as I was about to sneak out of the bedroom. 'Forgot to tell you, with the kids and everything. I put it on top of the fridge.'

It was probably some books I'd optimistically ordered for the research I was almost certainly going to have to set aside again immediately. 'Thanks. Need anything from the garden for breakfast?'

'Cut me some chives and chervil.' His eyes were still closed, voice half-muffled in his pillow. 'Going to make omelettes. The twins love them.'

Something in my chest started aching. I rubbed at it with the heel of my hand.

'Okay,' I said. 'I will.'

He sent Lex down to the garden a little while later with my coffee. I was always glad to spend time with Lex – now they'd realised I knew a decent amount about the books they liked, we often had good chats about what they were reading – but I always missed Jonah too, on these Friday mornings. The little rituals we'd established, the patterns, the routines . . .

It made sense. I didn't need all my years of therapy to tell me that I craved stability, and it didn't take a genius to see that Jonah was the only one currently providing it to me.

But still. I shouldn't miss him when he was literally just upstairs. Him asking for herbs so he could make his nieces happy shouldn't make me want to cry. I couldn't get too attached to our cosy little domestic arrangement, no matter how surprisingly pleasant it had become. Because even if we still had more than two and a half years of it ahead of us, it was eventually going to end, and if I tied myself too tightly to it . . .

After I'd sent Lex back up to the apartment, I rubbed the heel of my hand across my chest again in the crisp morning air, looking at the snow, which had fallen overnight on the mountain.

Sometimes – usually when Jonah and I were arguing over one of our lectures – I thought about the story Fiona had told me that first night at Tsundoku. *If this is what university is going to be like, I think I've fallen in love with it.*

Sometimes – like when he set a new dish in front of me, designed just for my tastes – it was hard to understand how I'd ever hated him. This man had been raised so coldly, so combatively, and yet every day of our marriage, he'd treated me with such care – me, and Fiona, and the kids. *You're a good husband, Jonah.*

Sometimes – like when I caught a glimpse of him coming out of the bathroom wearing a towel slung low around his hips; or when he was focusing hard on dinner, wrists flexing as he flipped something in a pan; or on mornings like this one, when I woke before my alarm in the Bunbury Suite but pretended to be asleep so I could spend more time sprawled on top of him – I thought about what

Chess had said to me, in that last, awful fight we'd had. *Sadie, if you want to fuck him, just fuck him.*

There had been a moment last month when I'd seriously thought about it. When he'd taken me shopping for plants, and he'd pulled me out of the path of that trolley and against his chest, and his eyes had darkened behind his glasses and his lips had parted and his breath had been hot and uneven against my skin – I'd been this close to saying *fuck it* and jumping him.

But I couldn't risk it.

He was the only thing I had in the world now, and if I let myself have him – let myself close any of the remaining distance between us – let myself get really, truly, properly attached – it was going to destroy me when this ended.

✎

Petrovski was running late for our meeting – not especially surprising, given he had about as much respect for other people's time as he had for women – so Jonah and I took up residence in our cupboard office while we waited. 'You okay?' he asked. 'You're quiet this morning.'

'Fine, fine.' I waved a hand dismissively. 'Just worried about what kind of workload nightmare there is in store for us next semester, that's all.'

Jonah turned his chair around to face mine, as much as he could without our chair wheels tangling. 'No matter what, we're finishing our old-married-couple article first though, right? We've got to get those research points.'

'Trust me, I'm well aware.'

'Sorry. I know you don't need me to mansplain how important research points are. I'm just . . .' He ran a hand through his hair.

'I have nightmares about what would happen if we went through all of this just to fail probation.'

'Yes, imagine,' I said, forcing away the uncomfortable prickle that always went through me when I was reminded of our expiration date, 'having to go through being married to me for absolutely no payoff.'

He gave me a strange look. 'Shaw, that's not what I—'

The lift dinged. 'Good morning, Jonah, Sadie,' Petrovski said, with no acknowledgement it was nearly lunchtime. 'Shall we have that chat?'

This was the first time Petrovski had deigned to invite us into his inner sanctum. His office wasn't as big as Vargas's, but it was still ten times bigger than ours. 'Have a seat.' He gestured to two chairs, set confrontationally in front of his desk. 'I've got some good news and some bad news.'

The good news, apparently, was that our co-teaching this semester had proven to be such a success (despite all the times Petrovski had walked into our lectures and openly disapproved, something he pointedly neglected to mention) that they wanted us to do it again. 'We'll do exactly the same thing for the two compulsory first-year units running next semester,' he said. 'Each of you will nominally chair one, but you'll teach them both together. We'll really bed down that foundation for the years to come.'

Twenty-six more lectures to write. Awesome. Just awesome.

'Now, though,' Petrovski said, making an extremely condescending face as he looked at me, 'comes the bad news. We're putting the new popular fiction unit on hold indefinitely.'

My jaw – tighter than it had ever been, as I hadn't got around to finding a new myotherapist yet – dropped.

'Are you seriously telling me,' I demanded, 'I spent all that time writing that new unit – the whole reason you hired me in the first place – only for you to shelve it?'

'I know this is upsetting, Sadie.' He was talking to me like I was five. 'But the budget is very tight right now, and sometimes, we can't afford to run all the units we want.'

'Then shelve mine,' Jonah said tightly. 'Shakespeare's in plenty of other units. You don't need more.'

'The decision has been made,' Petrovski said. 'In this difficult time for the faculty, it's important that we focus on our core business: providing our students with the high-quality literary studies education that they come to Lyons for. And, with respect, Sadie, the kinds of things you do don't necessarily fall under that remit.'

I was going to punch him. I was going to punch him right in his smug tweedy face. 'Would you like benchmarking data from popular fiction units at other institutions? Because I can provide that. These are consistently high-enrolment, extremely popular units.'

'I hear you.' Now he was talking to me like I was three. 'But the university has a reputation to uphold.'

'And Sadie is a tremendous asset to it!' Jonah said. 'That's why you hired her!'

'Jonah, I appreciate you're defending your wife.' Oh, so now he was talking like I wasn't even in the room. Cool. Cool cool cool. 'But this little foray into the popular was one of Sofia's initiatives, and as she transitions out of her role as Head of School, I'm sure you can agree we need to realign our priorities.'

'What do you mean?' I said. 'Where's Vargas going?'

The evil little smirk on Petrovski's face told me everything I needed to know, even before he opened his mouth. 'She and the leadership team have mutually agreed that it would be better if she explored other opportunities.'

Fuck.

'Professor Carmichael will be taking over as Head of School' – Double fuck. Julia was going to flip a table – 'and I'll be serving as his deputy, as well as remaining in my role as head of the Literary Studies department.'

Had anyone ever had a smile so infuriating?

'To conclude this workload conversation,' Petrovski went on, 'next semester, in addition to the two first-year units, you will also co-teach the two new second-year units: the one on modernism that Dr Henshaw has prepared and the one on Shakespeare that you've prepared, Jonah.'

Twenty-six *more* lectures, on top of the twenty-six he'd already assigned us. Again.

'Why?' I said. 'Jonah's the expert on early modern drama, not me. There's no reason for me to co-teach that unit.'

'And if Dr Henshaw prepared the modernism unit, surely Dr Henshaw should be teaching it,' Jonah said. 'Neither of us have any expertise in that period.'

'Dr Henshaw's workload is at capacity.' Petrovski was getting annoyed now. 'And sometimes we have to teach units we don't particularly want to teach. We all have to do our part.'

He levelled a look at Jonah. 'As the son of such an experienced and celebrated scholar, I would expect you to understand this.'

Jonah stiffened.

'Christian Fisher hasn't seen the inside of a classroom in at least a decade,' I said tersely. 'Even if he had, he would never deign to team-teach.'

Petrovski stood, a clear sign that he wanted us to leave. 'If you have any hope of passing your probationary period, Sadie,' he said, 'I'd suggest you watch your tone.'

'Don't speak to her like that.'

'Jonah,' Petrovski said, 'while—'

'Don't even think about finishing that sentence with something like *it does you credit to defend your wife.*' Jonah stood too, glaring at Petrovski. 'This isn't about the fact that I'm married to her. This is about your total disrespect for her as a scholar.'

'As I was saying,' Petrovski said, meeting Jonah's eyes, 'while I understand you're upset, I'd also suggest watching your tone. Don't think I've forgotten that you're on probation too.'

We rode the bus home in silence. There didn't seem to be much to say.

Jonah got off two stops early. 'I'm going to the shop,' he said, gesturing at our little local supermarket out the window. 'To grab some stuff for dinner tonight.'

'Do you need anything from the garden?'

'No.' His jaw was set. 'I've got it.'

When I got home, the apartment – which just that morning had been a whirlwind of activity, with Jonah and I trying to juggle getting ready for work with getting the kids ready for school – was deathly quiet. I was completely alone.

I dropped my handbag in my room and went to the kitchen, pouring myself a tall glass of water and drinking it slowly. I had to stop. Think. Not panic. Be sensible.

I sent a quick text to Julia about what had happened in the meeting and the fact that Vargas had apparently been forced out of the university. I updated the document I was keeping on my phone of all the ways Petrovski was unfairly targeting me. I emailed Lin and Veronica to see if they'd be interested in taking some more seminars for us next semester. I sent another quick email to Henshaw to see if we could set a meeting time to talk through their modernism unit. If I got very, *very* lucky, maybe they'd have created some preliminary lecture notes that Jonah and I could use as a starting point.

Fuck. Jonah.

Don't think I've forgotten that you're on probation too. I'd led with my fists with Petrovski, and Jonah had come to my defence because he was a good fucking person, and now he was in the shit right beside me.

I poured myself another glass of water and turned around, leaning back against the kitchen bench, trying to take deep breaths and slow my heart rate. The disparate ways that Petrovski treated Jonah and I had never been fair, but still, if he lost this job because of me . . .

I closed my eyes. Me catastrophising wasn't going to help either of us.

When I opened them again, I caught sight of a package sitting on top of the fridge. Jonah had mentioned it that morning, but I'd completely forgotten about it.

I went up on tiptoe to get it down. The weight of it in my hands was familiar. Books.

I found a kitchen knife (one of mine, not one of Jonah's – one of the few spats we'd had since moving in here had been about his precious knives) and slit it open. I pulled the books out and blinked in surprise. I'd been expecting a couple of second-hand research monographs I'd found online for cheap. These were romance novels – a Talia Hibbert, an Alisha Rai, a battered old Jennifer Crusie.

And then I found the note.

Dear Sadie,

First of all, I'm sorry I haven't replied to your letters. I'm so, so glad your life in Hobart is working out well (even if your boss is not – I'm sure you don't need me to tell you to document everything he does, just in case). It makes me really happy to hear that your world is full and that you've built a network of people around you who care about you.

I've been thinking a lot about the fight we had and I want you to know that I took what you said to heart.

As a result, I've taken a leave of absence from work (lucky I had all that time saved up!) and I've gone away for a while to do some soul-searching. You've been my whole world for as long as I can remember. I need to work out who I am on my own, what my life looks like when it doesn't revolve around you.

Because of that, I'm going to be off-the-grid for a while longer. I'm staying with a friend who's holding onto my phone for me, but if you really need me – you can call.

Love,

Chess

PS. Hope you like these books. I don't have your skills in picking them out, and the availability here is a bit limited.

The note fell from my fingers to the floor. I covered my mouth with my hands, but nothing could prevent the awful, strangled sob from coming out.

I want you to know I took what you said to heart.

Those horrible things I'd said to her, the things I would do anything to have her forget. She'd *listened*.

You've been my whole world for as long as I can remember.

I'd been a burden on her for her entire life and when we had that fight, she'd finally realised it.

I need to work out who I am on my own, what my life looks like when it doesn't revolve around you.

I was never going to be able to fix it. I was never going to get her back.

I'd lost her.

I picked the letter up from the floor and read it again, tears blurring my eyesight. *If you ever really need me – you can call.*

But I had been cursed with an excellent education in close reading, and between the lines, I could see all the things she wasn't saying.

All the leave she'd saved up, that time she was going to spend visiting me – that was gone. She was going to be off-the-grid awhile longer – it had been months, and she still couldn't bear to speak to me. I could call her, but only if I really needed her – call me if you need me to bail you out of jail, kid; otherwise, I'm exhausted and I'm done.

The front door closed. I shoved the letter hurriedly in my bra, scrubbing my hands across my face before Jonah saw me. If he knew I was such an awful person that my own *sister* wanted to cut ties with me, then . . .

'I hope you're prepared to eat like a queen tonight, Shaw,' he said, dropping two heavy paper bags on the kitchen counter, 'because I'm about to cook through my feelings, and it's going to get elaborate.'

'Can't wait,' I managed to choke out. 'How about, um, how about I run down to Tsundoku and buy some wine?'

'No need. I already did.' He took a bottle out of one of the bags and put it in the fridge. 'I've got it covered. You don't need to worry about anything.'

Please let me worry about something, I wanted to say. *Please, let me contribute. Please let me look after you in some tiny little way, so I can convince myself I'm not a millstone around your neck.*

'I am so sorry about how that went down today,' he said. 'I can't believe Petrovski's doing this to you. Getting you to put in all that work writing that pop-fic unit and then cancelling it – and the way he was *speaking* to you!'

'You didn't need to—' I swallowed, still perilously close to tears. 'You didn't need to defend me like that.'

'I know you're perfectly capable of fighting your own battles, but – Sadie, are you all right?'

He was looking at me, examining me closely, trying to read my face. If I stood in this room for one second longer, he was going to see exactly what Chess had – that I was a burden, and he was better off without me.

'Still just rattled from the meeting,' I said, forcing a smile. 'I'm, um, I'm going to go do some work, okay? We've got another fifty-two lectures to write, and I want to make sure I'm pulling my weight.'

JUNE

Chapter Eighteen

Sadie

My thirty-second birthday fell on the Sunday after the last week of semester. When it dawned, I was feeling lower than I ever had in my life.

I had been in a slump ever since the letter from Chess arrived, but as the week of my birthday approached, I started to let a little bit of hope back in. Ever since I could remember, Chess had made a big deal of celebrating my birthday. Whether she was spoiling me with some lavish gift or making me a mug cake out of whatever she could find in our shitty little kitchen, she was always, *always* there.

But my hope that she might miraculously appear, arms outstretched and ready to forgive me, had been dashed a couple of days earlier when I opened our front door and nearly tripped over the package on our doorstep. It was a half-case of the Bibliophile Noriko reserve pinot noir, with a note enclosed that simply said: *Happy birthday, Sadie. C.*

It was almost worse than her not acknowledging the day at all. *Hey, remember that expensive wine we never finished drinking that night you told me I loved you too much? Here's enough for you to drown in. Happy birthday.*

Given that, I was in no mood to do anything special for my birthday. I was especially in no mood to do anything wine-related for my birthday – but Fiona had gleefully planned a day trip for us all out to the Tsukamoto brothers' winery, and if I cancelled, it would crush her.

'Just wait until you see it!' she exclaimed, as Hobart's eastern suburbs started to give way to wine country. 'It's so beautiful out here.'

She was driving. Lex was in the passenger seat, headphones in. The girls were in the back, chattering busily over whatever it was they were doing on their iPad, leaving Jonah and me in the middle.

I leant my head against the window. There was something vaguely hypnotic about the straight lines of the vines.

Jonah touched my hand with one long finger. 'You all right?'

I nodded. 'Fine.'

I'd had to tell him about the wine. It was much more difficult to conceal six bottles of wine than it was to conceal a letter, after all. *That's great, though*, he'd said over breakfast that morning. *She's making an effort.*

I suppose, I'd lied. If I told him what I really thought – that Chess ticking a checkbox to double her Bibliophile wine club order for the quarter was so little effort she might as well have said *fuck you* – he'd have argued with me, and I didn't have the energy for that.

So I'd forced a smile when he slid a plate of corn fritters in front of me, and promptly changed the subject. *The finish on your wedding ring is wearing off*, I'd told him, gesturing at it with my fork.

He'd peered at it through his glasses. *Oh, so it is*, he'd said. *Should we switch it out before we leave?*

I'd slid the second of the three-for-$12 wedding rings onto his finger. The corn fritters had made me feel a little better – he knew how much I liked them, and ever since he'd found out about my love of leek he'd been tweaking the recipe to include more of it. But there could be no clearer reminder than the streaked, faded gold finish on his discarded wedding ring that this tie – like all the other ties I'd ever had – was going to come undone in the end.

'No thinking today, birthday girl!' Fiona declared. 'Only drinking!'

Jonah put his hand on top of mine, his palm on my knuckles, his fingers finding the gaps between mine. 'That sounds like a sensible resolution, darling.'

He was an intelligent man. He might not know about the letter, but he'd probably guessed I was thinking about Chess. He had so many other things to worry about, between work and his family, and here he was, worrying about me instead.

I exhaled. No matter how dejected I was, I had to rise to the occasion. If nothing else, I owed him – and Fiona, and the kids – a pleasant day.

So I made myself smile. 'Drinking, not thinking,' I echoed. 'I pledge to be a wonderful example for your children, Fiona.'

She laughed. 'Obviously the whole reason I've immersed myself in wine culture is to make it seem less cool to them. Thank you for joining me in my mission to make them teetotallers.'

Jonah squeezed my hand, smiling back at me. Part of me wanted to snatch my hand away, and part of me wanted to hold on tighter. Caught between the two impulses, all I could do was sit perfectly still.

The winery was on the top of a hill, lines of vines trickling down the slope. 'That's katakana,' Lex said, pointing at the sign next to the gate, which had Japanese characters under the word *Bibliophile*, written in that same trademark Tsundoku script. 'It says *biburio-fairu*. And the ones on the other side of the gate are kanji. They say *Tsukamoto*. Satoshi taught me.'

'He'll be delighted you remembered,' Fiona said fondly.

The man himself met us in the car park, emerging from the building with a grin on his face. 'I had to come down yesterday to talk business with Isamu, so I jumped on one of the wine tour buses,' he said, hugging Fiona hello. 'I thought I could be your designated driver home today, so you can enjoy the wine too.'

'Sometimes, Satoshi,' Fiona said, drawing back briefly to look at him, then hugging him again, 'I think you're an angel sent directly from heaven.'

Satoshi showed us around with obvious pride. 'The actual winery, where Isamu makes the wine, is on the other side of the hill,' he told us. 'That's his domain, so of course the design is all deeply utilitarian and unattractive. Here, though' – he gestured to the tasting room, all white walls and warm wooden beams, where a minibus-full of people was being served – 'I had more input.'

He pointed out the B&B, tucked away around a quiet corner ('It's very peaceful there, if you ever need a quiet getaway,' he said to Jonah and me. 'My mother runs a tight ship.'), before he led us into the restaurant. The same colour palette from the tasting room persisted, but the majority of the walls were glass, offering a panoramic view of the vines.

'Pinot gris,' Satoshi said, pointing out the different blocks of vines, 'chardonnay, pinot noir. There are more varietals down the bottom of the hill and behind the B&B.'

Chess would love this.

The instinct to take out my phone and send a picture to her was almost overwhelming. *At your fave. Wish you were here.*

But I jammed the pad of my thumb into my engagement ring instead. A picture of some vines did not rise to the level of *If you ever really need me – you can call.*

Satoshi led us to our table. *Fisher family, 6 people*, was written on the reservation sign. Jonah draped his arm over the back of my chair, fingers brushing my shoulder supportively, and Fiona beamed at me from across the bread plates, so I pasted the smile back on my face. I might be miserable, but I wasn't going to drag them down with me.

'I thought we'd do lunch a tiny bit out of order!' Satoshi announced. 'Rosie, this is for you – Georgia, for you – Lex, my buddy, my pal, are we feeling in a party hat mood? All right. I'm relying on you all, because I'm a terrible singer. *Haaaaaaaaappy birthday . . .*'

He beckoned to one of the waiters, who put an exquisite birthday cake down on the table in front of me.

Once the cake had been cut and we'd all eaten a slice and the girls were clearly summiting an Everestian sugar high, Satoshi took them outside. 'Don't even think about it,' he said firmly, when Fiona got up to follow them. 'Rosie and Georgia and I are going to take a walk through the sculpture garden and we're all going to criticise how ugly Isamu's flower choices are. Lex, you're going to help, right?'

'Just how much wine have you bought from him?' Jonah asked, as Satoshi let the girls pull him away, one attached to each wrist, Lex trailing after them.

'A lot,' Fiona said, topping up our water glasses. 'Like, *a lot.*'

Isamu came over to our table, setting a white and a red wine glass down in front of each of us. 'I'm going to run your tasting today,' he said in his low growl of a voice. 'We'll move through it slowly, so you can drink the appropriate wine alongside our tasting menu.'

I had a sudden, unsettling feeling. All the hairs stood up on the back of my neck. I turned to look behind me.

'What's wrong?' Jonah asked.

'Nothing, nothing.' There was no one behind me, just the buzzy chatter of people at other tables and the waitstaff bustling to and fro and the serious presence of Isamu, standing in front of us. 'Just – you know when it feels like someone walks over your grave?'

'Thirty-two isn't *that* old, Shaw.'

I rolled my eyes.

Jonah grinned, then pressed his lips to my temple. 'Happy birthday, darling.'

There was a flash in front of us. Fiona. 'You two are the cutest,' she said, showing us the photo she'd taken.

If I hadn't known better, I never would have guessed that the couple in the picture – him smiling into her hair, her trying her best not to do the same into the crook of his neck – were a lie.

The sun was dipping low over the vines by the time we left, deep orange fading into deep blue as the crisp winter day turned slowly into night. In the back, Rosie and Georgia's chatter slid into sleepy silence. In the passenger seat, Lex kept up a conversation with Satoshi for a while, but then they fell quiet too. I was sitting between Fiona and Jonah in the middle, and after a while, both their heads lolled onto my shoulders. They each started snoring softly, slightly out of time with each other.

Satoshi's eyes met mine in the rearview mirror. 'Sugar and booze,' he said. 'A lethal combination. You're clearly made of sterner stuff than the Fishers.'

'. . . 'm not asleep,' Fiona mumbled.

'Sure you're not.'

Jonah didn't stir.

His left hand was resting on my knee, heavy and warm. I traced the line of each long finger and ran a fingertip over the gold band of his ring.

How many times, I wondered, would I have to do it before the finish wore off this one too?

He'd been so good to me. So, so good.

But how long was it going to take before I wore him down, like I'd worn down Chess? Before he realised what a burden it was – how exhausting it was – looking after me? Before this friendship, or this affection, or whatever it was that he'd come to feel for me, turned back into loathing?

'Did you have a good birthday?' Satoshi asked me.

'It was lovely,' I lied. Here was another person who did not deserve my misery. 'Thank you for everything you did to make the day so great. You really went above and beyond.'

'My pleasure. But it was nothing, really. Isamu did most of the work.'

Isamu hadn't been the one babysitting the world's most energetic seven-year-olds, but I wasn't about to say that out loud. 'I guess we're his favourite tenants.'

Satoshi laughed. 'I don't think you're going to have any dramas renewing your lease.'

I brushed my thumb over Jonah's wedding ring again, then, careful not to disturb either of the siblings snoozing on my shoulders, took my phone out.

There was nothing from Chess. No message, no well wishes – just the wine abandoned on my doorstep, and everything that signified.

I bit my lip, hard, until I tasted blood.

Jonah woke when Satoshi pulled the car into Fiona's driveway. 'Come on, Rosie-girl,' he said softly, heaving her sleeping body into his arms. 'Let's get you to bed.'

Satoshi followed him, carrying Georgia. Lex stumbled inside under their own power, and I kept an arm around Fiona's waist, making sure she didn't trip and fall on the way to her bedroom.

'Thanks for letting me bully you into going out to the winery for your birthday, Sadie,' she murmured, flopping face-first onto her bed. 'It was such a nice day.'

'Yeah, it was.' I set a glass of water on her bedside table. 'Sleep well, okay?'

'Mmmm.' She turned onto her side, snuggling her face into the pillow. 'I'm so glad you married Jonah. I love you both so much.'

Something in my chest squeezed painfully tight.

'Me too, Fiona,' I whispered, grateful she'd already fallen asleep.

The night air was blessedly cool on my face as Jonah and I walked home. It was crisp and still and quiet, a few stars visible in the sky, the gibbous moon bright and pearly over the river, even if it was a few days away from its full glory.

'I'm sorry your sister didn't call.' Jonah gestured to my handbag. 'I could tell you were hoping.'

'I was,' I replied quietly. 'But not expecting.'

That was the pattern, after all. Chess had lasted much, much longer than anyone else, but everyone always unbound themselves from me in the end.

I turned to go up the stairs of our apartment building, but Jonah took my elbow. 'I got you something.'

He led me to the courtyard, where the community garden was. 'It's not much. Sorry.'

He gestured to a weedy, overgrown plot, three away from the one I'd taken over from Isamu. 'I figured out whose it was and offered to take it off their hands. So you can have more space for your garden.'

'Oh,' was all I could say.

Jonah ran a hand through his hair, the moonlight winking silver off his scattering of greys. 'I know a patch of dirt is a pretty shitty present, especially given how much work it'll be to clear it, but I'll help. And I'll go to the nursery with you and get you whatever plants you want, and fertiliser and whatever – and God, I just realised I'm offering to buy you literal bags of shit for your birthday. Sorry. But—'

'Stop.'

He stopped.

'I love it. Thank you.'

He smiled, that sheepish Cardigan Jonah smile that I had started, at some point, to treasure. 'I mean, it's a pretty self-interested present. You grow very good vegetables.' He took my hand. 'Come on. It's cold. Let's go inside.'

'Wait.'

I bit my lip again. The taste of blood was salty and metallic in my mouth.

'We need to talk, Jonah.' I looked at his hand in mine instead of at his face. I knew what I had to do, and if I looked him in the eye, I would lose my nerve. 'About how this ends.'

Chapter Nineteen

Jonah

It was not a complicated sentence.

I had spent a great deal of my career poring over complex, obscure, archaic language. If this were a line I were reading, I would skate right by it. It did not take effort to parse.

'I don't know what you mean,' I said anyway.

'Yes, you do,' Sadie said quietly. 'Don't be obtuse. Please.'

Her head was bowed, moonlight kissing the curves of her face in the darkness. There was only a flicker of flame in her hair, where light from one of the other apartments was caught in it. Her breath was a faint puff of white in the cold night air.

In mine, her hand – usually so steady, so certain – was trembling.

'I don't understand, though,' I said. 'Aren't you . . . Aren't we . . . ?'

It would be naive to finish the sentence the way I wanted. Of course Sadie wasn't happy. We might have found something comfortable and companionate and maybe even contented with each other, but there hadn't been a single moment since the day I'd spotted her across the park in her pale-green wedding dress, dragging that suitcase behind her, that she'd been *happy*.

'You haven't done anything wrong, Jonah.'

She looked at me at last. 'I never really dreamed of having a husband,' she said, 'but if I had, I would have dreamed of one like you.'

You have me, I wanted to say. *You've always had me.*

'Have you met someone else?' I asked instead.

She blinked. 'No. When would I have had time to meet someone else?'

'Then why?'

She looked at the ground again, breath coming out of her in a rush.

'If you don't want to do this anymore, that's fine,' I said. 'Of course that's fine. I would never force you to stay married to me if you don't want to be. I would never force you to do anything you don't want to do. But – we talked about keeping this going for three years, Sadie. It's only been a few months. So I just don't understand why . . . now.'

'You don't need me anymore.'

A tear winked like a diamond on her cheek before she roughly thumbed it away. 'You've got what you wanted out of this. You've got your job – and you're probably much more likely to fail probation if we stay together than if we split up.'

'Sadie, no.'

'And you need your job,' she said, barrelling forward, 'so you can stay here in Hobart and help Fiona. You've found this place in her life – this proper, solid place – and I don't want to put that in danger.'

'I'm not the only one with a place in her life,' I said. 'They all adore you. Fi. The girls. Lex.'

'They haven't known me very long, though.' Her voice was hoarse. 'It'll be easier for them if we split up sooner rather than later. The longer someone stays in your life, the harder it is when they leave.'

I was going to kill her sister.

'What about work?' I tried. 'We've got another fifty-two lectures to write. Do you really want to negotiate a divorce, on top of that? One of us having to move out?'

'No! Of course I don't! I . . . I like what we have, Jonah. I like this life we've built together.'

'Then let's keep living it!' I said. 'I like it too, Sadie. I like everything about it. I like coming down here in the morning and bringing you coffee and hearing you talk about your garden. I like sitting down with you after work and having a glass of wine together. Hell, I even like watching that fucking dating show with you!'

She shook her head, thumbing another tear away.

'Nightmarish as our workload is, I like being a lecture team with you,' I said. 'I like co-authoring that article with you. I like it when you disagree with me. I like how you make me think. More. Better. I always have. Ever since the first day I met you.'

'Jonah, please.' Her voice was barely a whisper. 'Don't make this harder than it already is.'

'I don't want to make things hard for you.'

I cupped her face in my hand, tipping it up to mine. 'I mean it. I'm not interested in making your life difficult. Especially not after the way you turned it inside out for me. I'm never, ever, *ever* going to stand between you and what you want.'

She choked back a sob.

'But I want you to know that I'm happy,' I said. 'Here, together, with you – living this little life of ours – I'm happy. And I'll gladly keep doing it, as long as you want.'

Sadie was silent for a long time.

She bit her lip. It was the most difficult thing I had ever done, not to trace my thumb over the imprint left by her teeth.

'I'm a burden on you,' she said at last.

What?

'And you deserve more than this,' she whispered. 'You deserve better.'

'Oh, come the fuck on, Sadie. That's the most ridiculous thing you've ever said to me.'

I dropped my hand and took a few steps away. 'I don't deserve any of this. I never have. I don't deserve my job. I don't deserve this life. I don't deserve you, certainly not after the privileged douche-bag-y way I spent years treating you. And to call yourself a fucking *burden*? When I wouldn't have any of this if it wasn't for you?!'

'Jonah—'

'No,' I snarled. 'You can tell me anything else. You can tell me "I've decided we're getting divorced, that's that, the end, I will not explain my reasoning". That's fine. But you don't get to tell me that you're a burden and I deserve better. You don't get to make such a specious argument and expect me to swallow it.'

'How have you forgotten who I am?!'

Her teeth were bared. Her fingers were clenched. In the cool, still air of the night, Sadie Shaw had caught alight.

'I am not a complex text,' she bit out. 'I am not some onion with layers of subtext and meaning for you to peel back. I am who you've always thought I am.'

I folded my arms. 'And who's that? Please, inform me exactly what I think of you. I'd love to hear it.'

'I'm *awful*.' Her nostrils flared. 'I'm still just that bitch from class who won't shut up or back down and who'll turn the smallest thing into a war. I'm still so profoundly unlovable that I can count my friends on one hand.' More tears were welling in her eyes, but she wiped them away so aggressively it must have been painful. 'Everyone works this out in the end, Jonah. Even Chess did.'

'I don't know what the fuck is going on with your sister,' I said tightly, 'but that is not true.'

'I told her she loved me too much!'

Sadie buried her face in her hands, fingers white as she clawed at her hairline. 'All she's ever done is look after me – put me first, make me the centre of her world – and I told her that she loved me too much! I told her that being loved by her was exhausting!'

'So?'

'What the fuck do you mean, *so*?'

'It's true, isn't it?'

She was stunned into silence.

'It can be exhausting sometimes, being loved by people,' I said. 'My dad, for all his faults, loves me. That's exhausting.'

'Don't compare Chess to your dad.' Her voice was low.

'What about Fiona, then?' I said. 'I love her. I'd lie down on railroad tracks for her. Sometimes, though, when she's turning up to the airport to meet us when we just want to fall into bed, or dragging us out on adventures with her, or asking us for help when we have a mountain of work, I'm a bit exhausted by it.'

'It's not the same.'

'It's not *not* the same.'

'Are you telling me,' Sadie said, 'that you would ever seriously look Fiona in the eye and tell her she loves you too much?'

'No. But—'

'But nothing!' She wrapped her arms around herself. 'That is who I am, Jonah. That is who you're married to. Sure, maybe you're enjoying this little domestic idyll now, but you won't always. I am all fists. I am all teeth. One day, you're going to remember that and it is going to hurt me so much more when you leave me then than if we just . . . if we just . . .' She swallowed, gulping against the wave of sobs. 'If we just end it now.'

'Do your worst, Shaw.'

She looked at me.

I spread my arms wide. 'Try it. Take a shot. Scream the worst things you can think of at me. You think I'm going to leave you? Try and make me.'

Her breath was coming fast and uneven, white fog in the night air. My wife was a dragon tonight.

'Here, I'll start,' I said. 'I'm a snob. I'm a mansplainer. I have obscene amounts of privilege and a spotty record when it comes to recognising it. I cry about my horrible dad even as I take advantage of being his son. I pick fights for the sake of picking fights. I'm all the worst things about university made flesh.'

She didn't say anything.

'Come on,' I said. 'That's just a warm-up! A mere tasting platter of things you've said to me before. If you're such a terrible person, you must have a whole well of them to draw on. Hurt my feelings, Sadie. I dare you.'

'You're not listening to me!'

'I am listening to you. I always listen to you. I'm just not agreeing with you.'

I closed the distance between us, taking her shoulders in my hands. 'You want to know why I'd never tell Fiona that being loved by her can be exhausting? It's because our foundation isn't strong enough to handle a fight yet. I don't know her well enough.' I smoothed my left hand over her hair. 'Maybe one day, Fi and I will get to a place where I feel comfortable enough to fight with her, but we're not there yet. It's still too fresh. Too fragile. Not like what you and your sister have.'

Sadie closed her eyes. Tears kept streaming down her cheeks anyway.

'I'm not going to pretend I know what the fuck Chess is thinking,' I said. 'But this silence between you . . . I thought it was my fault, for a long time.'

'No. It's—'

'And it's not your fault either.'

I slid my fingers through her hair, thumb beside her ear, and made her look at me. 'It's not your fault,' I repeated.

'Yes it is.' Her face was crumpling again. 'All Chess has ever done is fight for me. She's sacrificed so much for me. Everyone – everyone – left, but she stayed and she loved me even harder to make up for it, and then I threw it back in her face.'

'Respectfully, Shaw,' I said, 'being loved like that *does* sound absolutely fucking exhausting.'

She bit her lip, hard, trying to hold back more sobs.

I slid my fingers down to her jawline. Gently, I traced the pad of my thumb against the divot of her chin.

'I'm sure it was hard for her to hear,' I said. 'I'm sure it hurt. I understand why she'd be angry. I understand why she might want some space.'

Sadie closed her eyes again. Her whole body was shaking.

'But it doesn't mean it wasn't true,' I said, 'and it doesn't make you a bad or a fundamentally unlovable person to say it. That's ridiculous.'

'She sent me a letter.'

'With the wine?'

'No. Last month.'

I did the mental calculations. Had Chess got that email I sent her back in April? Had it finally spurred her into action?

'She said,' Sadie added, opening her eyes again, 'that she needs to work out what her life looks like without me in it.'

Oh no.

'And if Chess can leave me,' she went on, 'then anyone can.'

The look on her face was heartbroken and confrontational all at once. And there was only one way I knew how to respond to confrontation.

'You're wrong, Shaw,' I said. 'And I can prove it.'

'How?' she demanded.

'I want you to think carefully about whether you want to have this argument.' Every line of my body was taut. 'Because once I say this to you, it's not a thing I can unsay.'

For a moment, the night was perfectly still. We were the only two people in a vast, dark universe, the only sound the ragged intake of her breath, the thudding beat of my heart.

'How?' she repeated.

I threaded my fingers through her hair again, combing it out of her face. If I was going to do this – if I was going to say these words that would change reality, that would end the companionate comfort of our little life together, one way or another – I wanted to look her in the eye.

'I will concede,' I said, 'that you said a pretty mean thing to your sister. But you've spent *fifteen years* saying mean things to me and I have loved you every second of them anyway.'

I took her hand in mine and pressed my lips to her knuckles, just below the rings I'd put on her finger.

'I'm not telling you this because I expect anything from you,' I said. 'I never have. I never will. I certainly don't deserve anything from you. If you want to walk away from me, I'll let you go. But I need you to hear me when I tell you that I'm not going to walk away from you. I love you, Sadie – and there is nothing you can say or do that will ever make me want to leave you.'

Chapter Twenty

Sadie

Once, several years ago, when Jonah and I were still PhD candidates, I gave a paper in the ESU student seminar series about declarations of love. Essentially, I was arguing that declarations of love in a romance novel were a major step towards the ultimate eucatastrophe of the happy ending and, when executed well, they made the world's most overused phrase – 'I love you' – feel like it was being said for the first time.

Professor Fisher hadn't bothered to turn up to this particular seminar (a pleasant surprise) but one of his students – a smug prick named Peter – had. 'I just don't think the language of *catastrophe* is useful here,' he'd said. 'Isn't the whole point of romance novels that they're pink and fluffy and nothing bad ever happens?'

I'd opened my mouth to speak, but Jonah got in before me. 'You're misunderstanding what a catastrophe is, Peter.'

He was sitting in the second row, tweed-clad arms stretched across the backs of the empty seats on either side of him. 'It's not a disaster, it's a dramatic term. It's all through the literature on ancient theatre. Four stages: prologue, protasis, epitasis, catastrophe. The catastrophe is the moment when it all hangs on the precipice. If it goes one way, it's a tragedy, and everyone will probably die; if it goes the other, it's a comedy, and everyone will get their happy ending.'

'If I could answer the question for myself, thank you,' I said sharply, 'Peter, there is in fact plenty of rising and falling action in the romance genre. These books are not set in a static world where everything is pink and fluffy and nothing bad ever happens. Eucatastrophe is *joy poignant as grief.* The joy cannot be truly felt in a world where the grief isn't possible.'

'And the catastrophe is the narrative fork between the joy and the grief.'

'Fisher, who exactly is giving this seminar paper?'

'You are, Shaw, of course. But I'm right, though, aren't I?'

He was right, but I squared my shoulders for a fight – because *of course* he'd take me agreeing with him as some kind of victory, and I was not going to let him have it.

The argument we were in the middle of now, though, he had just emphatically won.

'I love you, Sadie Shaw,' Jonah said to me, looking me dead in the eyes, one hand twined tight in my hair, 'and there is nothing you can say or do that will ever make me want to leave you.'

Those words – somehow both words I had heard before and words I had *never, ever* heard before – were catastrophic.

Two paths were before me, snaking away into the moonlit darkness. *Everyone leaves in the end,* whispered the ghost of Chess, a flash of red hair, walking away from me.

But then there was Jonah, arms spread wide, an invitation, an embrace. *You think I'm going to leave you? Try and make me.*

'Say it again?' I asked, my voice croaky from crying. 'Please?'

'Sadie,' he said. 'I love you.'

I was on the precipice.

I could believe the evidence of thirty-two years. I could run. He would let me.

Or I could believe him.

I could—

I could—

Jump.

'Jonah,' I said, 'will you please kiss me?'

His breath caught in his throat. His hand tightened reflexively in my hair. He leant his forehead against mine and the world narrowed to a single point.

'You've been crying, darling,' he said desperately, running his thumb along my cheekbone. 'You . . . I don't want to take advantage.'

I curled my fingers into his lapels, the way I had on our wedding day. My knuckles rested against his chest, and I couldn't tell if it was his heart or my heart that was racing.

'You can't just tell me you love me,' I whispered. 'You need to show me. If you mean it, you need . . . I need you to prove it.'

His breath was as ragged as mine. It – he – was the only warm thing in the cold of the night, and his eyes were wild as he tried to find the hole in my argument.

'Oh fuck,' he whispered, as he realised he'd lost this time. 'Oh God, Sadie.'

And then his lips were hot and hungry against mine and his fingers were twined painfully tight in my hair and Jonah Fisher was kissing me like he would never, ever let me go.

I wound my arms around his neck, desperate to feel every line of him pressed against me, real and solid and here, here, here with me. 'I love you,' he gasped into my mouth. 'I love you so fucking much.'

We stumbled towards our apartment, stopping halfway up the stairs so he could press me back against the railing. 'Hold these,' he said, taking his glasses off and pushing them into my hand, 'they're in the way,' and buried his face in the curve of my neck, kissing his way up my throat, one thigh between mine.

His hands were at my waist, pulling me into him. My free hand snaked under his blazer, and when I dug my fingernails into his shoulder blade and he groaned into the place where my jaw met my hairline, I felt the vibrations of it in every cell of my body, goose-bumps rippling up and down my arms.

'Inside,' I breathed. 'Please.'

I gave him his glasses back so I could find the keys, fingers scrabbling in my handbag as his arm banded around my waist, my back against his chest, my earlobe caught between his teeth. His erection was pressed hard against the small of my back, and his heartbeat thrummed through my body, fast but even, a rhythm that was also a promise. I nearly dropped the keys three times before I managed to unlock the door.

He was already kissing me again as it slammed closed behind us, one hand snicking the lock shut before it was back on me, palm against the nape of my neck. I dropped my handbag on the floor and shoved the blazer off his shoulders. He put his glasses back on so he could help me with the buttons of his shirt, but his fingers were shaking even worse than mine, so, 'Here,' he said, 'let's try this,' and took his glasses back off again, putting them on my head and using them to push my hair out of my face like a headband, kissing me once tenderly before pulling his half-unbuttoned shirt off over his head.

I twisted my fingers into the hair that dusted his chest, letting my forehead fall to his shoulder. I traced the darker line of it that cut down the centre of his body, fading away almost completely as it passed his navel and then thickening again as it disappeared under his waistband.

'Sadie,' Jonah said, as I unbuckled his belt. 'Oh God, Sadie.'

I licked along the line of his clavicle.

His hands tightened on my hips, then slid down to my thighs. '*Sadie*,' he gasped, and hoisted me up against him, lifting me off the ground and pushing me back against the wall.

It was an inherently sexy position and I wrapped my arms and my legs around him instinctively, but the fear that suddenly pulsated through me was just as instinctive. 'Please don't drop me.'

He pressed gentle, featherlight kisses up my throat until he got to my lips. 'Shaw,' he said into my mouth, 'I've got you.'

He kissed the tip of my nose. 'Do you trust me?'

I let out a long, slow breath.

I love you, Sadie. There is nothing you can say or do that will ever make me want to leave you.

'Yes.'

I kissed him, long and slow and deep, tongue licking against his, the tongue with which he'd made that promise to me. He made a sound, deep in his throat, and I fisted my hands in his hair harder, pulling him closer, grinding myself against him.

'Oh, shit, I actually might drop you if you keep doing that,' he choked out, followed by another wordless moan as I did it again. 'Your room or mine?'

'Mine's closer.'

The difference was all of five steps, but Jonah didn't argue or hesitate. He paused only to hit the switch on my fairy lights as he carried me into my bedroom, kicking the door shut behind him and setting me down. 'Take your clothes off,' he breathed into my ear. 'Please.'

He toed his shoes off as I managed to undo the side zipper of my dress, nearly dislodging his glasses from the top of my head as I pulled it off. He hooked the fingers of his right hand under one of my bra straps and pulled it gently off my shoulder, kissing his way along my collarbone as he sketched a line up my spine with his left hand, fumbling for the clasp.

I undid it for him after a few failed attempts. He smiled at me sheepishly, that Cardigan Jonah smile that made everything feel warm and golden. 'Sorry. I can't really see.'

I traced my fingertips along the little indentations his glasses had left on his cheeks, drawing his face down to mine so I could kiss them too, one after the other. Beneath my lips, his beard was soft, just as it had been that night when he'd told his dad I was one of the most brilliant early-career researchers in the country.

'You can touch, though,' I said, guiding his left hand to my breast.

He needed no further encouragement.

We fell back onto my bed, his weight almost knocking the wind out of me as we landed, his mouth ravenous against mine but his fingers careful, caring, caressing on my skin. He kissed his way down the column of my neck, and when his lips fastened on one of my nipples I almost shrieked, heels pressing into his exceptional arse as my legs tightened around him.

He grinned up at me, a brilliant flash, then did the same thing to my other nipple. The sound it tore out of me was even louder and more high-pitched, and his second grin was even wider. 'Filing that data point away,' he said, 'for significant further exploration.'

Then he blinked, one hand curling around behind him to settle on my ankle. 'How are you still wearing shoes?'

'I don't – ah! – fucking know, Jonah.' I almost sobbed as he bit down lightly on the side of my breast, nuzzling his beard against it. 'I . . . just . . . oh God.'

He pressed a kiss between my breasts, right over my pounding heart. 'Let me help you with that.'

He drew back, unzipping one of my ankle boots and then the other, pulling them gently off my feet, peeling the socks I was wearing under them off too and dropping them to the floor. He feathered his thumb over the tattoo on my left foot, once, twice, three times, before he looked me in the eye, gaze not leaving mine as he kissed it.

I knew he couldn't see it in the dim lighting, but he knew what it said. He'd seen it many times, as I sat barefoot next to him on the couch. *Joy beyond the walls of the world, poignant as grief.*

I nearly burst into tears again.

His hands smoothed up the sides of my legs. 'Can I?' he asked, fingertips resting on the waistband of my underwear.

'Yes. Please, yes.'

I lifted my hips up to help him. He slid them down slowly, fabric gliding agonisingly over my sensitive skin, before he cast them aside.

I was desperate for him to touch me. But Jonah just stood there, looking at me, for a long time.

'What's wrong?'

'Nothing. I just can't . . . Can you give me my glasses, please?'

I'd forgotten they were still on the top of my head. I handed them to him, disentangling them from loose strands of my hair.

He put them back on, and he looked at me again, and the strangest sound came out of him – like someone being strangled halfway through the most contented, satisfied sigh of their life.

'Oh fuck, Sadie,' he breathed.

He wrapped his fingers around my ankles, bending to kiss my tattoo again before he pulled my legs gently apart. '*Oh fuck, Sadie,*' he choked again. 'You're so beautiful.'

I didn't know how to process the way he was looking at me. He seemed stunned, awestruck, spellbound, like some sacred treasure was spread out on the bed before him.

Tears welled in my eyes. 'Jonah . . .'

His hands tightened on my ankles. He yanked me suddenly towards him, falling to his knees at the edge of the bed. 'Hold these,' he said, pressing his glasses roughly into my hands again, and then he buried his face between my legs.

My head snapped back and my back arched, but his hands were firm on my thighs, holding me open, holding me down, holding me close. 'Jonah!'

He smiled against me, his laugh a gentle hum as I only just managed to put his glasses on my bedside table without dropping them.

Then he got to work.

It takes a lot of time and a lot of effort to become an expert at something. No one knew that better than an academic. I had let so many things fall by the wayside in my pursuit of scholarly mastery.

But Jonah was clearly better at time management than me, because on top of becoming an expert in his own field, he'd clearly found time to do a second PhD in eating pussy.

He might have looked at me like I was sacred, but the things he did to me were profane. His beard brushed against my inner thighs as he licked a long line up the centre of me, making me sob. He nudged my clit with the tip of his nose, making me inhale sharply, and then, when he pulled it into his mouth, sucking gently, then sucking harder, he made me scream, and scream, and *scream*.

He grinned again, looking up at me. 'I'm going to use my fingers,' he said, pressing a chaste kiss to my hip bone, 'if that's okay.'

'Please, please, please,' was all I was capable of saying, the thought of it turning my brain inside out. 'Please.'

His grin widened. 'When you blush,' he said, smoothing a hand over my lower belly, 'it starts right – here.'

He kissed just below my navel. 'Look at it go,' he said, kissing his way up my body. 'Even I can see it. Has this been happening, all this time, under all those pretty dresses of yours?'

I yanked his hair and pulled his face to mine, before he could fasten his lips around my nipple again and completely turn my brain to liquid. I could taste myself on him as he kissed me, and it filled me with a sense of possessiveness so strong it almost overwhelmed me.

This was my husband.

Mine.

And he wasn't going to leave.

'Well, when you blush, Fisher, it all goes straight to your face,' I said, and grabbed his cock.

Jonah went completely still.

I stroked him through his pants. He made that half-strangled, half-satisfied sound again. It was my turn to grin.

'I'm assuming your little experiment failed,' he choked out at last, 'because I definitely don't have enough blood anywhere else in my body to blush.'

I undid the button on his pants and slid my hand inside them, wrapping my fingers around the length of him. 'I didn't manage the full scarlet special,' I said, kissing the apple of one cheek, then the other, 'but I got you to turn a tiny bit pink.'

I stroked him again, and he collapsed onto me with a groan. 'If you keep doing that,' he said, voice muffled in my breasts, 'this is going to be over quickly and disappointingly.'

I stroked him once more and then let go, scratching my nails up the line of hair on his belly. He panted into my skin for a few seconds, like an athlete at the end of a marathon, before he nuzzled the hollow at the base of my throat and kissed me again, lovingly, lingeringly.

'This is like co-writing with you, Shaw,' he said. 'I lay out a perfectly good plan of attack and then you insist on including a bunch of tangents.'

I was about to protest, but then his fingers dipped between my legs and I forgot every word in the English language except *yes* and *fuck* and *please* and *Jonah*.

He played me like a violin, coaxing the first orgasm out of me with two fingers, thumb against my clit as the entire world turned white; the second assisted by his mouth, laughing against me as I quaked uncontrollably. 'It's not funny,' I panted, as he chuckled, forehead pillowed on one of my thighs. 'It's not fair, that you can completely steal my powers of rational thought like this.'

'Shaw, you've been stealing my powers of rational thought for fifteen years, every time I look at you,' he said fondly. 'Strictly speaking, I think it's your turn.'

'That's cute, Fisher, but I don't think you understand the extent of the problem.' I tugged lightly at his hair, which I hadn't managed to uncurl my fingers from yet. 'You should have tried seducing me before we both applied for this job. If you'd fucked my brains out then, you wouldn't have had to go to all this trouble.'

'Hey.' His tone was sharp. 'No. None of that.'

He crawled back up my body, bracing his elbows on either side of my head. He'd lost his pants at some stage, and his skin was hot against mine, everywhere our bodies were pressed together. 'There is nowhere in the world that I would rather be than here with you.'

He slid his nose against mine, then kissed me, just once, tenderly. 'If some angel descended from heaven and told me I could live my life over again, go back, make different choices – I would do everything exactly the same,' he said, 'if it meant I could end up here.'

Then he looked thoughtful. 'Well, maybe not *exactly* the same. There are a few revisions I'd make. And—'

'Jonah,' I said, 'shut up.'

I shoved at his shoulders, pushing him onto his back. I pulled open the drawer of my bedside table, sending up a quick prayer of thanks to whatever higher being had been looking out for me during the move when I'd contemplated throwing out the half-empty box of condoms I had left over from my last partner but had ultimately decided against it.

I glanced at the expiry date as I tore the packet open. They were still good for a few months. Thank fucking God.

Jonah tried to swallow his groan as I rolled the condom onto him, but he couldn't. It lit something up, deep inside me, and suddenly, of all things, I was thinking about the first time I read 'On Fairy-Stories', and how it had struck that chord in me that had never stopped reverberating.

Outside this room, we still had problems. Problems that would not be solved easily. The hollow place Chess had left in my heart could not be filled by anyone else. Jonah would always be his father's son. The university would probably always be a cruel, cut-throat, neoliberal institution that would do its best to bleed us dry.

But despite all of that, in here, in the starry glow of my fairy lights, in this tiny world inhabited by just the two of us, something good *could* happen.

I straddled Jonah, knees on either side of his hips. I laced the fingers of my right hand through his left and brought it to my lips, kissing the second cheap wedding ring that I'd put on his finger just that morning.

'Do you know why I asked you to marry me, Jonah?'

He was barely breathing. 'Tell me,' he rasped.

'I didn't know it, when I asked you.' I took his cock in my free hand, rubbing myself against the head of him, feeling him quiver beneath me. 'I didn't know it, when I was fighting with Chess about why marrying you was actually a good and sensible and reasonable and not completely insane plan. I didn't even know it when Fiona said it straight to my face. Like, literally, she said it to me, and my brain skated right over it, like it was obscure French theory.'

Jonah's face was so white and bloodless he looked like he was about to faint.

'I don't know when I figured it out. What is it that Darcy says to Elizabeth in *Pride and Prejudice*? "I was in the middle before I knew that I had begun"?'

Jonah made a choked sound that might have been a laugh. I slipped the head of his cock inside me and he made a choked sound that was definitely a gasp.

Thank you, Fiona had said to me, that day in Tsundoku. *Thank you for loving my brother enough to do this.*

'I don't know who I am without you beside me, Jonah,' I said, sliding all the way down onto him, feeling him long and hard and solid inside me. 'I love you too.'

He tugged at my right hand, pulling my face down to his. I rocked my hips against him as he kissed me, the fingers of his other hand tangled in my hair. 'Sadie,' he murmured into my mouth, 'fuck, Sadie . . . Sadie, darling.'

The endearment made me smile. He made another choked sound as I rocked against him again, and I drew back slightly.

Then I paused. 'Jonah, are you crying?'

'No!'

I dipped my head and kissed the tears off his cheeks.

'It's because I'm in *pain*, Shaw,' he insisted. 'I'm so hard it feels like I might die.'

I laughed. 'I think we might be able to collaborate on solving that problem.'

I rose up, but he grabbed at my thigh. 'Wait, wait, wait. Can you give me my glasses again?'

His cock slipped out of me as I reached over for them, but he guided me straight back onto it the second they were on his face. 'If my beautiful bride is going to ride me,' he said, fingers digging hard into my hips, 'then it would be rude not to watch.'

I braced my hands against his chest. 'Are you ready?'

'I hope *you're* ready,' he replied, 'for the fact this might last about nine seconds.'

'A whole nine?' I ground down into him and was rewarded with an almost agonised cry. 'I need to work a bit harder, if you can hold out that long.'

He shifted one of his hands. His thumb brushed across my clit, and every nerve ending in my body sparked to life again.

'Don't think,' he panted, thumb moving against me as I started moving against him, 'that I'm going to let you do – oh my God, Sadie, holy fucking hell you feel incredible – all the work.'

'Shut the fuck up, Jonah,' I managed to say, third orgasm already starting to build with the perfect dual pressures of his thumb on my clit and his cock thrusting up to meet me, matching my rhythm, 'and let me do some of it – oh fuck, yes, yes, there, like that.'

Later, afterwards, when he'd finally managed to get up and get rid of the condom, we lay snuggled in my bed together in the soft glow of the fairy lights, his head on my shoulder. 'Don't let me forget to change the sheets before Thursday,' I murmured, carding my fingers through his hair. 'We absolutely *cannot* let the girls sleep in here otherwise.'

He chuckled. 'You'd better change them *on* Thursday, because I plan on messing them up several more times before then.' He glanced up at me. 'If that aligns with your plans. Obviously.'

I pressed my lips to his temple. 'I made my best argument for why we should split up tonight,' I said, 'and you dismantled it.'

'In that case, we better add condoms to the grocery list, because that box isn't going to get us very – oh God, Sadie, I love you so much.'

He turned his head suddenly into my shoulder. His voice was breaking when he spoke again, directly into my collarbone. 'I love you,' he said. 'I love you, I love you, I have always loved you, I don't entirely understand how we ended up here but I love you so fucking much.'

'You need to understand who I am, though.'

My voice was cracking too as I tugged at his hair, made him look at me. 'You might have won the argument, but I made some valid points,' I said. 'I'm still all fists. I'm still all teeth. And—'

'I like your fists.' He found my hand and bit down gently on one of my knuckles. 'I like your teeth.'

It was hard not to laugh as he strummed his finger over my lips like a guitar string, pulling the bottom one down slightly before leaning in and lining my front teeth with the tip of his tongue.

I bit his lip in return. 'I mean it, though,' I said. 'Some days I'm probably going to be a real bitch to you. No matter how well and how frequently you dick me down, that's not going to change.'

'I wouldn't want it to – although that does sound like a challenge I'd be interested in attempting.' He kissed me. 'Do you know Shakespeare's Sonnet 130?'

'Is that *Let me not to the marriage of true minds admit impediments*?'

'That's 116. Also very appropriate, my darling, but not the one I mean.'

He got up, putting his glasses back on and finding his phone in his pants pocket. 'This is 130,' he said, settling back in next to me and bringing it up on the screen.

I leant my chin on his shoulder so I could read it. '"*My mistress's eyes are nothing like the sun*".'

'It goes on like that for most of the poem.' He gestured briefly down the first three quatrains. 'There are some pretty sick burns in there about Shakespeare's dark lady mistress, to be honest – like, "*In some perfumes is there more delight / Than in the breath that from my mistress reeks*"? Not terribly romantic.'

He scrolled to the bottom. 'But I really like the end. Lines eleven to fourteen.'

I started at line eleven. '"*I grant I never saw a goddess go; / My mistress, when she walks, treads on the ground*".'

'"*And yet, by heaven*,"' Jonah said, looking at me, not the screen, '"*I think my love as rare / As any she belied with false compare*".'

I melted into him. As far as declarations of love went, it was entirely citational – quite literally someone else's words – but it was somehow also entirely personal.

Then Jonah snorted with laughter.

I looked up. 'What?'

'Van just forwarded us both an academic jobs digest,' he said. 'You'll never guess what they're recruiting for back at ESU.'

He showed me. *Lecturer in Literary Studies, Level B.*

'Look who the chair of the hiring committee is.'

Direct all enquiries to: Professor Christian Fisher.

I snorted too. 'Well, that rules me out,' I said, 'unless you wanted to take me on partner hire.'

Then, unbidden, a bolt of fear shot through me. What if Jonah decided – what if he wanted—

'Stop,' he said, flicking my nose with his finger. 'I see your mind piecing that argument together, Shaw, and I'm here to tell you that it's completely without foundation. I'm not going anywhere.'

He tightened his arm around me and kissed me. 'When it comes to blithely walking into academic jobs I don't deserve, I have *extremely* high standards.'

'You do deserve—' I started, but then he was hitching my leg over his lap, and his fingers were sketching a fiery pathway up my inner thigh, and as he closed his mouth over my nipple again, all the words in the world fell away from me.

JULY

Chapter Twenty-One

Jonah

The next month was the best of my life.

As a scholar, I had been trained not to make big claims like that – the reality was always more complicated – but the evidence in this case was entirely overwhelming.

It wasn't perfect, of course. Even though it was mid-year break, we were still wildly overworked. Sadie was still profoundly sad about her sister. Despite everything that had changed, we were still ourselves, and thus still had our arguments.

'No!' Sadie exclaimed, as we were going through the first round of peer review revisions on our old-married-couple article. 'Absolutely not, Fisher. Do you want the journal to actually accept this article? Have you forgotten how badly we need these research points? We can't just handwave away that query like that!'

But now we had a powerful new strategy for working through our disagreements. 'I'm sorry for yelling,' she purred later, unbuckling my belt, pushing me down in my desk chair and then going to her knees in front of me. 'Reviewer 2 is the problem, not you.'

I didn't subscribe to the idea that men had *needs*, sexually speaking. That was just something they said to excuse cheating on their partners. I had gone long stretches of time before with only my work and my hand as companions and I'd survived just fine.

If it were true, though, and there had been even the remotest chance of my eyes wandering, it would have been completely obliterated. Sadie looked after me and my needs like I was some prize vegetable she was growing in her garden.[48]

We were having so much sex. *So much* sex.

It didn't take us long to christen every room in our apartment.[49] Given it was mid-year break, we were already spending most of our time working from home, but we cut our campus time down to the absolute bare minimum, taking the Zoom option for meetings whenever we could. 'Oh God, this is – oh! – so unprofessional,' Sadie gasped into a pile of notes as I took her from behind, bent over her desk. 'I'm supposed to dial into a love studies research network meeting in four minutes.'

'Do you want me to stop?'

'Don't you fucking dare,' she panted. 'Maybe hurry up, though? Julia always – ah! – starts on time, and I need at least – oh God, there, there, there, that's it, that's so good – sixty seconds to fix my hair.'

I reached around and stroked her clit. She screamed into her notes. I got her to the meeting with a topknot that was only slightly listing, a love bite blooming on the side of her neck, and about ten seconds to spare.

Thursday nights, when we looked after the kids, were the hardest. Neither of us were particularly quiet in bed,[50] which should have

---

48 It was ridiculous, how adamant she was that she was one of the world's most selfish people. 'I have to at least be in the top ten,' she'd insist, while simultaneously doing something to me that made me feel like I was levitating. I loved her to distraction, but sometimes she left *terrible* holes in her arguments.

49 A day and a half, specifically. It was a small apartment.

50 It probably wasn't surprising that two passionately argumentative people with PhDs in words tended to be coitally, ahem, chatty.

made us restrain ourselves, but we had fifteen years to catch up on – and just in case that stat about how couples had more sex in the first year of their marriage than in the rest of it combined was accurate, we needed to get our numbers up if we were going to balance out our late start.[51]

'Did you know Uncle Jonah and Auntie Sadie like playing games?' Georgia announced one night, when we were having dinner at Fiona's.

'Really, Georgie-girl?' Fi said, cutting up some of her lasagne for her. 'What games did you play?'

I was already beetroot-red. The blush was swiftly rushing towards Sadie's face too. 'Fi—' I started.

'We played Taco Cat Goat Cheese Pizza,' Rosie said. 'I won!'

'Not that game!' Georgia said. 'They play games with each other. I had a bad dream the other night and I went into their room and Uncle Jonah was tied up because he was losing.'

I wanted the floor to open up and swallow us whole.

'Poor Uncle Jonah.' Fi was visibly shaking with how hard she was trying not to laugh. 'Good for Auntie Sadie, though.'

Sadie's blush deepened. My desire to fall into the molten heart of the earth intensified.

'Does Daddy like to play games too?' Rosie asked. 'I heard Madison's mum say that he played games with you.'

'Different kinds of games, Rosie-girl,' Fi said. 'Eat your dinner.'

Lex snorted derisively. Fiona shot them a half-warning, half-pleading look. For a moment, the lines of exhaustion were carved deep on her face.

So yes, things weren't perfect. Not even close.

But they were still better than they had ever been.

---

51 Science.

We'd had vague intentions to head into campus for the pre-Semester Two faculty town hall, feeling like it might be a chance to connect with some of the colleagues we still only barely knew. However, on the morning of the meeting, Sadie had made the complex and convoluted case that we could simply not do that (*The school meeting next week is mandatory in-person. Why should everyone be blessed with our presence at* two *long boring meetings?* she'd said, an argument that would have been thoroughly convincing even if she wasn't wearing one of my cardigans and nothing else), and so we sat curled together on the couch, her laptop on the coffee table, a slide with the Lyons University logo and *this meeting will commence shortly* on the screen.

I teased Sadie's earlobe between my teeth. She made a satisfied sound, deep in her throat.

'The video and audio are definitely off, right?' I murmured. We were both fully clothed now, in a gesture towards professionalism, but we were also well aware that this meeting was probably going to be stultifyingly dull and that there were far better things we could be doing with our precious time.

'Mm-hmm,' Sadie said. 'I checked. Four times.'

I slid my nose against her cheek. 'I've always admired your rigour.'

I was making a solid start on demonstrating my admiration when the dean's executive assistant popped up on the screen and introduced the dean, who called the meeting to order. 'Here are the agenda items for today's town hall,' he announced.

I had my face nuzzled into Sadie's neck, but she stiffened. 'Shit, Jonah.' She tapped me on the knee. 'The last item. Look.'

Item Six on the agenda on the slide was *Renewniversity: Phase Three.*

'They're firing people,' she said. 'That's what that means.'

Blood was starting to drain away from her face. My own felt like it was slowly being replaced with ice water.

'Not necessarily,' I said. 'Maybe it's about unit cuts. Like your popular fiction unit. They could be trying to save money by streamlining the majors or something.'

I had years of practice in playing devil's advocate, but I wasn't even close to persuading myself, let alone my brilliant wife.

Still, if I could make her feel better, even for a second, I had to try. 'And if they are firing people – we're *cheap*, Sadie. We're the cheapest continuing staff in the whole department, and we do so fucking much of the teaching. If they're going to cut people, they're not going to cut their Level Bs. It'll be Cs and Ds. Maybe even Es.'

'You mean the people that bring in all the grant income?'

'Vargas was an E. That must be a huge salary saving. And her home department was Lit Studies. Maybe that'll be enough of a cut from our departmental budget to placate the suits.'

Sadie let out a long breath, her forehead falling to my shoulder. 'Okay. Okay.'

I kissed the top of her head. 'How about I make us both a cup of tea?'

'Is eleven am too early for wine?'

She was only half-joking but I laughed it off anyway, kissing her hair again and then getting up to put the kettle on. I had a feeling that alcohol-wise, we were going to need to pace ourselves. There was a dark, cold, hollow feeling in the pit of my stomach.

We *were* the cheapest people in the department. We *did* shoulder far more than our fair share of the teaching. As far as value for money went, Sadie and I were an extremely good investment, especially given the way they were gaming our workloads.

But they'd still only wanted to hire one of us.

We were on our third cups of tea by the time they got to Item Six. I'd switched to ginger, but Sadie was still drinking caffeinated, and I could feel her shaking, her fingers twined through mine so tightly it was almost painful.

'For this last agenda item, I'm going to hand over to the faculty managers,' the dean announced.

'Fucking coward,' Sadie muttered.

'They'll outline the steps we'll be taking in Phase Three of the Renewniversity plan, which, as you all know, is a redefining and re-envisioning of Lyons for a better and more productive future – a future that will let us best support our people and our wellbeing.'

Automatically, Sadie and I clinked our tea mugs together and drank.[52]

It took several moments for the suits to start speaking, as they first tried to figure out how to share their screen and then how to unmute themselves. 'I can't watch this,' Sadie said, turning her face into my collarbone. 'This is excruciating.'

I pressed my lips to her temple.

'All right,' one of the suits said. 'Thanks for bearing with us there – Zoom gets the best of us all sometimes, hey?'

For a moment, I wished we had gone into campus for this town hall. It would have been nice to be in a room full of people and hear that joke fall completely flat.

'On the slide, you'll see the two prongs of Renewniversity Phase Three, which is designed to put the faculty back in the black and build a healthy budgetary surplus for the years to come.'

---

52 Julia had taught Sadie the 'our people' and 'our wellbeing' drinking game and we played it every time the dean spoke. I felt slightly guilty endorsing a game created by the woman who had very obviously broken my brother's heart, but there was no denying that it was piercingly accurate.

The first prong was a ten per cent increase across the board in teaching allocation. 'For example, if you're on a 40-40-20 contract, this will shift to a 50-30-20 split between teaching, research and service,' the suit said.

Sadie and I exchanged horrified glances. Even in the best-case scenario, where they didn't give us yet more lectures, that was going to mean so much more teaching.

'We recognise that research is the core business of the university,' the other suit said, in response to an audible outcry from the people in the room. 'This is a temporary measure, in order to protect as many jobs as possible. By increasing permanent staff members' teaching allocation for the next two years, we can claw back deep savings from the casual budget.'

In other words: they were going to get rid of *astronomical* numbers of casual staff.

'Oh, those fucking arseholes,' Sadie said. 'Casual academics—'

'Are always the first casualties,' I finished heavily.

'We've got to work out how to protect Lin and Veronica,' she said. 'They work so hard. They're so good at what they do. We can't lose them.'

'Agreed.'

'Unfortunately, though,' the suit went on, 'in order to protect the faculty's financial future, it will be necessary to also streamline our number of permanent staff.'

We tightened our grip on each other's hands simultaneously. Sadie's engagement ring had twisted around backwards, and the stone dug into the flesh of my palm.

They changed the slide to a website screenshot, *Renewniversity* written at the top in script they'd probably paid a graphic designer a casual academic's semester wages to design. 'At the conclusion of this meeting, you will be sent a link to the Renewniversity Phase Three website,' the suit announced.

'If your name appears in the revised org chart, then your position is not in scope for Phase Three,' the other suit said. 'If your name does not appear, however, then it means a position at your level has been eliminated. You will be required to reapply for your role and at the end of the semester, the applicant not selected will be transitioned out.'

'It's a spill and fill,' Sadie breathed. 'It's the fucking academic Hunger Games!'

The only response I could make was to squeeze her fingers even tighter.

The outcry in the room was audible again. The suit held up a hand. 'I'm sure you all have many questions, but rest assured these are answered in the FAQ section of the Renewniversity Phase Three website.'

'Fuck the rest of this meeting,' Sadie said, grabbing her laptop off the table, closing the Zoom, and opening her email.

I got up and got my laptop too. Sitting cross-legged beside each other, we both frantically refreshed our email until the message with the link appeared. 'Here, here, here, I've got it,' I said, opening the website.

The server is busy, came the error response.

It took ten agonising minutes of repeated refreshing before the website finally opened on Sadie's screen. She hit ctrl-F and typed *literary s,* which took us to a side-by-side of the current departmental org chart and the revised one.

On the current one, there were two Level B positions at the bottom of the chart. *Lecturer: Dr Sadie Shaw. Lecturer: Dr Jonah Fisher.*

But I knew, without even looking – deep in the pit of my stomach, in my bones, in every fibre of my being – what the revised org chart said.

'No,' Sadie said, a sob in her voice. '*No.*'

Just one position. One little Level B square on the chart, under all those Cs and Ds and Es. *Lecturer: by application.*

She pressed the heels of her hands into her eyes, digging her fingers into her hairline. 'This can't be happening.'

I set my laptop aside and put my arms around her. She set hers aside too and wound her arms around my neck, burying her face in my shoulder. There was a lump in my throat the size of a melon as I stroked her hair.

Sadie pulled back suddenly. 'Oh fuck, Jonah, the reuse policy,' she said, eyes wide and wild. 'That's why they got us to write all the lectures! And do them all together!'

It took me a moment to join the dots. 'Christ,' I groaned.

The reuse policy meant that the university was not allowed to pay a casual academic to give a lecture in one semester, and then reuse it in further semesters without paying them.

The fifty-two lectures Sadie and I had written in our first semester of employment, though – and the further fifty-two we were in the process of writing for our second semester – as well as all the materials we'd prepared for my Shakespeare unit and her shelved popular fiction unit: all of those were prepared by *permanent* staff members, and were thus owned by the university, who could reuse them with impunity for as long as they wanted.

'That's why they let us get away with partner hire, even though all they can talk about is how broke the faculty is.' Sadie's face was a mask of pure horror. 'So they could bleed us both dry for a year – and then cut one of us loose, leaving the other one to give those lectures over and over again.'

Part of me wanted to push back. *I don't know if their intent was that diabolical. Vargas wouldn't have masterminded that, surely.*

The intent didn't matter, though. Someone – Petrovski, probably – had concocted this scheme at some point, and the impact was what counted.

'I can't believe this is happening, Jonah.'

Tears were starting to stream down Sadie's face, her shoulders shaking. 'After everything – I can't believe they're pitting us against each other again.'

'Shhh, shhh, shhh.'

I pulled her to me. 'It's okay,' I said into her hair. 'It's okay, my darling.'

'No, it's not!'

I framed her teary face between my fingers. 'There's only one way this goes, Sadie,' I said, tracing her cheekbones with my thumbs. 'There's only one way I'll let this go.'

'Jonah, no!'

Her fingers came up to curl around my wrists. 'I can't take this away from you,' she said. 'I *won't* take this away from you.'

'It was never mine to begin with.' I kissed the space between her eyebrows, the tip of her nose, her lips. 'This is your job. This has always been your job. There's not a chance in hell I'm going to fight you for it.'

'But you'd win!' she exclaimed. 'You know you'd win this time, Jonah!'

I did know that.

'I already have everything I could ever want,' I said, leaning my forehead against hers.

'No!' she insisted. 'What . . . what about that job back at ESU? Applications are still open. You could—'

'You're my *wife*, Sadie. I love you. I'm not going anywhere.'

Despite my best efforts, tears were welling in my eyes too, moisture starting to collect under the lower edges of my glasses. 'We'll figure something out,' I said, trying and failing to stop my voice from cracking. 'I survived as a casual for years. I can do it again.'

'They're firing most of the casuals!'

'Maybe I could go professional, then, try and get a job in the research office or something,' I said desperately. 'Or hey, maybe this is finally my chance to audition for *Superchef*. I could see if I could work in the kitchen at Tsundoku in the meantime. Satoshi's always offering Fi a job.'

'That's because he's in love with her, you idiot,' Sadie sobbed.

Her hands came up to cup my face too. 'I can't let you do this,' she whispered. 'I can't drag you down like this. I can't let you throw your career away.'

'Darling,' I said, tasting salt as I kissed her, her tears and my tears mixing together, 'you can't make me do anything else.'

For the first time in a long time, neither of us were in the mood for sex. We should have been working, but neither of us were even remotely in the mood for that either.

Instead, we just lay on her bed together, me on my back, Sadie half-draped over me, head tucked under my chin.

'I hate this so much.' Her voice was hoarse from crying, her fingers still slightly shaky in mine where our joined hands rested on my chest. 'I can't imagine – I don't even know how to conceptualise – a world where you're not an academic anymore.'

'Neither can I.'

It was starting to sink in, the weight of it, what it actually meant. *What's Dad going to say?* the part of me that was still a kid, terrified of disappointing him, whispered.

I adjusted my position slightly, tightening my grip on Sadie, burrowing my face into her hair like she was a teddy bear.

'I don't know how to be an academic without you,' she said softly.

'You won't be without me.'

I brought her hand to my lips so I could kiss her knuckles. Everything else in the world might change, but that point was not and never would be up for negotiation. I was hers, and I was never going to leave her.

'I know' – she kissed mine in return – 'but it won't be the same.'

She tilted her head up so she could look at me. 'You *are* university to me, Jonah,' she said, 'for better or worse.'

I brushed my nose against hers. She shivered. I let go of her hand for a moment so I could reach for a cardigan of mine hanging on the end of her bedpost, draping it over both of us.

She turned her face into my throat and pressed her lips to my Adam's apple. 'I love you so much,' she whispered. 'The thought of them taking this away from you – of *me* taking this away from you . . .'

'You're not taking anything away from me. You got this job, not me. And there's no universe in which I would fight you for it.' I tucked the cardigan tighter around us both. 'Besides, even if I wanted to fight you – which, to be clear, I don't – I wouldn't. I made a promise to your sister.'

Sadie pulled back and looked at me.

'That day at the airport,' I said. 'She told me that you were an adult and you could do whatever you wanted, but if I did anything to drag you down or hold you back, she would ruin me.'

She was quiet for a long moment before she spoke again, voice low. 'Why didn't you tell me this before?'

'I didn't think I needed to. You saw her grab me by the collar. What else would she have been saying?'

Something about the line of her jaw changed. Her nostrils flared.

'I'm sorry. I should have. But—'

'No.' Sadie sat up, twisting her hair up and tying it back severely in a bun on the back of her head. '*No.*'

'I'm sorry.'

'Not you.' She leant down and kissed me quickly. 'You haven't done anything wrong. I mean – *no*. I'm not going to be responsible for you losing your job. I'm not going to drag you down. I'm not going to hold you back.'

'You're not—'

'I know it's not my fault, Jonah.' She pulled my cardigan around her shoulders. 'But if I just roll over and let them do this to you, I'll never forgive myself. What the university is trying to do is outrageous, and we're not taking it lying down. Not without a fight. Not without even trying.'

Her phone was sitting on the bedside table. She picked it up. 'I'm going to call Julia. This whole Renewniversity thing is bullshit. The union must already be moving on it and if there's a campaign to be a part of, I want to be front and centre.'

'Are you sure?' I sat up too. 'What if it makes things worse? I know things are different now, but the way I got this job was pretty fucking scammy.'

'It was partner hire. You're my partner.'

'Yes, but if anyone found out—'

'Fisher,' my bonfire of a bride said acerbically, 'just because I didn't know what I was actually proposing when I proposed to you doesn't mean this wasn't always real.'

My love for her had been a constant background hum for the last fifteen years, but every so often it flared up so intensely it caused me genuine physical pain.

'I have a couple of calls to make, actually,' she said. 'There's one other card we might be able to play.'

🖊

We'd skipped lunch in our post-town hall paralysis, so I made us an early dinner. I left it simmering on the stove while I waited for Sadie to get off the phone. I opened a bottle of Bibliophile cab sauv to let it breathe and took it out to the balcony, half-sitting, half-collapsing into one of the chairs, despite the icy winter chill.

It was really sinking in now, the implications of what was happening. The wine was breathing much easier than I was.

Sadie was a force of nature. I trusted her – I believed in her – but the university was a brutal neoliberal institution, with very little incentive to listen to anything or anyone.

So no matter how hard she fought it, there was every chance that come the end of semester, I would be saying goodbye to academia. Farewell to my life's work, the only thing I was even remotely qualified to do.

Who would I be, without it? Who was Jonah Fisher, without the tweed?

'Oh, you opened some wine,' Sadie said, stepping out onto the balcony. 'Bless you, brilliant man.'

I pulled her onto my lap. She kissed me twice, fingers brushing along my beard, before she leant over to fill our glasses.

I let out a long breath. I would be Sadie Shaw's husband. No matter what happened to me professionally, I would have that. I would have *her*.

'What did Julia say?' I asked.

'There's a plan,' she replied, clinking her wine glass against mine. 'I'm not sure how much you're going to like the plan, but there's a plan. Cheers.'

'Cheers. Tell me.'

I would go along with anything she said. Here, sitting on my lap in the dying winter sunlight, wearing one of my cardigans, surrounded by the lush greenery of her herb garden, she was so beautiful.

'Well, there's two parts to the plan.' Sadie took a sip of her wine. 'The union wants to take this to the media, really whip up some public outrage. We need to take this wide. We need to get coverage into every media outlet there is. TV. Newspapers. Online stuff. Everything.'

She kissed the tip of my nose. 'But, like, the *Daily Mail* hasn't historically been particularly interested in workplace relations stories – people get unjustly fired all the time, right? – so the campaign needs a hook. It needs a narrative. It needs—'

I realised where she was going. 'Us.'

She nodded. 'Julia asked her ex-husband for advice on a strategy – he's some media bigwig – and he suggested that a married couple being torn apart by unjust bureaucracy is a great narrative hook.'

'Star-crossed lovers,' I murmured.

'Exactly.' She kissed me again. 'I don't know how you feel about that – going from kind-of-fake-married to sort-of-real-married to extremely-publicly-married, but—'

'Sadie, there's no *sort of.*'

I stroked some of her hair behind her ear. 'If you'll have me, my darling,' I said, 'I'm in this forever.'

For a long moment, she just looked at me.

'Really?' she said at last.

'Come the fuck on, Shaw. You've been paying attention the last month, haven't you? Do you really think any part of me was planning to pack up and disappear once three years were up?'

'My head knows that, I think,' she replied. 'But my heart . . .'

I ran my knuckles over her chest, then bent to press a kiss to it, lips brushing against the top of her left breast. 'I'll tell your heart this as many times as it needs to hear it,' I said. 'If you want to get rid of me, you're the one that's going to have to leave, because I'm not going anywhere.'

'Oh, Jonah . . .'

Sadie softened against me. I kissed the top of her other breast, then the hollow at the base of her throat. She twined her fingers in my hair and pulled me up to kiss her lips. 'I'm not going anywhere either,' she whispered into my mouth. 'And I'm going to make sure you don't lose your job, darling. I promise.'

It wasn't quite a bucket of ice-cold water over my head – the world could never seem too bleak when I had Sadie Shaw sitting on my lap, promising me forever – but it was at least somewhat chilly.

I rested my chin on her shoulder and tightened my arms around her. 'So, the first half of the plan is for us to become the main characters of the union media campaign,' I said. 'What's the other half?'

'We sue.' She let out a long breath. 'I don't know if Phase Three is illegal, exactly, but it's certainly not ethical. And if there is a legal case to be made here, then I know who could make it.'

I blinked. 'Sadie . . .'

'I called Chess,' she said. 'And she's going to help.'

Chapter Twenty-Two

Sadie

I couldn't sleep that night.

Jonah, bless him, let me pretend I was asleep, although given he spent the night spooning me, he had to know I hadn't done more than uneasily doze. This was something I needed to work through on my own.

I'd finally showed him Chess's letter yesterday, sitting on his lap out on the balcony. I'd thought he might be angry, or maybe even protective – *I could* never *imagine a life without you, Sadie,* I'd imagined him saying, when he read the part where Chess said she needed to redesign her life without me in it – but instead, his brows had just furrowed behind his glasses.

'What did she say when you called her?' was all he'd asked.

'I didn't speak to her,' I said, tugging his glasses down his nose a little so I could press my lips to those two lines between his eyebrows. 'A man picked up. Some friend of hers. He sounded familiar – I must have met him at one of the Sydney Law Society functions she dragged me to. He said he'd tell her that I needed her and that she'd be here tomorrow morning.'

Then, Jonah didn't ask, *do you think she'll actually come?* and in that moment, I loved him more than I ever had. The last thing

I needed was for someone to put that thought into the universe when it was already taking up so much space in my head.

Jonah was fully dressed when he brought my coffee down to me in the garden that morning, tweed blazer under his winter overcoat. 'I thought I might go around to Fi's and help her get the kids off to school,' he said, stroking some hair behind my ear. 'Maybe sit her down and tell her about the work situation. Explain that no matter what happens, I'm not going anywhere.'

I nodded, wrapping my fingers around my coffee mug. 'That sounds like a good idea.'

'But if you need me . . .'

'Then you'll be right around the corner,' I finished. 'I know, Jonah. I know that if I need you, you'll come.'

He kissed my temple tenderly. 'Always.'

He was gone by the time I went back upstairs, but he'd left breakfast for me – a jar of overnight oats in the fridge. There was a Post-it stuck to it. *I know no ways to mince it in love, but directly to say I love you*, he'd written. *Henry V 5.2. Also me. xx*

I looked at the note for a long moment, then I folded it up and slipped it in my bra. I had to do this by myself, but I wanted his words against my skin just in case.

Because if Chess didn't come . . .

I started pacing.

I'd imagined three separate knocks on the door by the time the real one came, four quick raps that sent me jumping out of my skin. I'd changed my outfit twice and put my hair up, taken it down and put it up again, but I was second-guessing everything as I raced to the door. What if having my hair up made Chess think this was just a business meeting? What if I was taking too long to answer the door and she left? What if it wasn't even her and she'd sent the lawyer friend who'd answered the phone to help me instead? She'd said that I could call her, not that she'd *come*.

'Hi, Sadie,' Chess said, when I opened the door.

She looked . . . exhausted. Drained, the way Fiona did some-times when the kids were really putting her through it. There were dark circles under her eyes that I hadn't seen since her early days climbing the legal ladder. Her hair was pulled back so severely it was tugging at her skin.

I wanted so badly to hug her. I wanted to put my arms around her and not let go, the way I used to when I was a little girl. I wanted her to laugh and hug me back, and say, *oh, sweetie, it's so good to see you.*

But she didn't move. And so neither could I.

'You must have had an awful flight,' I blurted out. 'It's so early.'

She had no luggage, I realised. Just her handbag. She wasn't planning to stay.

I balled my fist, resisting the urge to rub my hand over the ache in my chest. 'Come in.'

'Thank you.'

So polite. So formal. So un-Chess.

I bit my lip hard as I closed the door behind her, trying desper-ately not to cry. At least she was *here*. That was something. That was a start.

'Cup of tea?' I asked her. 'Or coffee?'

'Coffee would be great. Thanks.'

'I'll warn you, Jonah usually makes the coffee,' I said, going on tiptoes to get the beans down from the cupboard. 'We bought this new machine about a month ago and I'm not entirely sure how to use it yet. Sorry if I fuck it up.'

'That's all right.' Chess was looking out the window. 'Your view is beautiful.'

'I know, right? Imagine how much this kind of view over the water would cost in Sydney. Although this place should really be costing us a lot more than it does, given how shit the Hobart rental market is. Our landlord is way too nice to us. I told you about him in my letters, right? Isamu? The winemaker from Bibliophile?'

She didn't say anything.

'You did . . .' I hesitated. 'You did read my letters, didn't you?'

'Of course I read your letters, swee— Sadie.'

The brutal way she cut herself off from saying *sweetie* was like a knife between my ribs.

Chess set her handbag down. 'What do you need?'

Just that. *What do you need?*, like I was one of her clients, about to be billed in six-minute increments.

'Um, well, I was really hoping you could help us with some legal advice,' I said. 'There's this whole situation at work, and . . . no.'

I closed my eyes for a second. It was a cold, clear morning, but it felt like that night in the garden with Jonah, when he'd told me he loved me and two pathways had snaked away into the night from me as I stood frozen, caught between grief and joy in equal measure.

'I need a lot of things,' I said. 'But the most important one . . . I need to know why, Chess. I need to know why you – why you abandoned me.'

I opened my eyes again. She was staring at me, a stricken, almost horrified look in her eyes.

'*Abandoned* you?' she said at last.

'I said some awful things to you,' I said. 'I know I did. And I totally understand that you needed some space. I'd need some space too, under the circumstances. But all I wanted to do was make it right, and you were gone. I needed you and you were *gone*.'

I hated the way my voice sounded, high-pitched on the last word, the petulant cry of a child, the child I'd been so insistent I wasn't.

If Chess had noticed, though, she didn't say anything. She was still staring at me, as if I'd spoken in some other language and she needed to translate it in her mind before she responded.

'Then why didn't you call?' she asked.

'What?!'

I had to clutch at the edge of the kitchen bench to keep myself tethered to reality. 'Are you seriously asking why *I* didn't call *you*?' I demanded. 'I tried! So hard! I called *constantly* those first few weeks! And then I tried to give you space, because that's what you asked for, but . . . I wrote you all those letters!'

'And I wrote back,' she said. 'I know it took me a while to be ready, but I wrote back and I told you, if you needed me, you could call.'

'That is not what you fucking said!'

The coffee machine started making an ominous whirring, grinding sound, but I ignored it. 'You said that you needed to work out what your life looked like without me in it!' I exclaimed. 'You basically said, *ugh, fine, call me if you need bail money!*'

'Sadie, no!'

Chess crossed the kitchen in two steps and put her hands on my shoulders. 'No,' she repeated, looking into my eyes. 'That is not what I said at all.'

I pressed my tongue hard to the roof of my mouth. I was so, so close to crying.

'I said I needed to work out what my life looked like when it didn't revolve entirely around you, not that I wanted a life without you in it,' she said. 'Everything in my life has been about you for so long, Sadie. Ever since we were kids, it's been baked into me, bone deep. *Look after your sister. Protect your sister. Everything'll be all right if you can just make sure your sister's okay.*'

Her fingers were digging into my shoulders, almost painfully hard. 'But those things you said to me were absolutely right,' she went on. 'It was a kick in the guts, but you were right. I've been so focused on looking after you that I've spent all these years treating you like a child, when you're ... God, you're so much more of a functional adult than I am.'

'No, I'm not.' I sniffed.

'You've got a whole life here,' she said. 'I could see it in your letters. You've built this whole world for yourself, a whole, happy, complete life, and ... and I think I was stopping you from doing that before. My world revolved around you, so I made yours revolve around me.'

A tear slipped down her cheek. 'The last thing I wanted was space from you, but after you went through with the wedding, I realised that was what you needed. I needed to give you a chance to live your own life. To be the grown woman that you are, without me forever treating you like a child. To work out what you really want, without me interfering. Because I loved you so much it was smothering you.'

'Chessie, no,' I whispered. '*No.*'

She let go of my shoulder with one hand so she could wipe her tears away. 'I ... It took me a lot to write that letter,' she said quietly. 'I thought – well, I'm still a mess, but I could see from your letters that you were flourishing. You kept saying that you missed me but I thought ... I thought maybe it was habit, or guilt, or something. So I wrote ... well ... if there was still room for me – still a place for me – if you still needed me in your life, still actually really, truly needed me ...'

'No. No, no, no, Chessie.'

'And then you didn't call.' Her voice cracked. 'You stopped sending me letters—'

'I didn't think you wanted them anymore!'

'—and then your birthday ... God, I had so many plans for your birthday. I wanted to see you so badly, but you hadn't written and

334

you hadn't called, and I—' She swiped her wrist across her eyes. 'I completely chickened out. All I could make myself do was send you that wine and hope that even though I wasn't brave enough to call you, you might call me, even just to tell me that you got it, but—'

I flung my arms around her, as tight as I could. 'Chess, I'm so sorry,' I gasped into her hair. 'I thought . . . I thought . . . I've got a fucking PhD in English and *I read everything all wrong!*'

She didn't reply. She was too busy crying, her face pressed into my shoulder, and the joy of her being here and the grief of the past few months were all mixed together, and it was absolutely, deeply, profoundly eucatastrophic.

✏️

A little while later, we sat on the couch with the cups of coffee I had eventually got round to making. She was drinking out of one of Jonah's mugs. The sight of it in her hands made me feel something I couldn't quite explain.

There were a lot of things I couldn't quite explain, if I was being honest. There were so many things I wanted to say that it was hard to know where to start.

Chess met my eyes and smiled, a little awkwardly. Clearly I wasn't the only one.

'So,' I said, sipping my coffee, 'um . . . how've you been?'

The awkward smile turned into an awkward chuckle. 'Did the bursting into tears before not give it away, or . . . ?'

'Well, I thought I should probably check,' I said, 'given I seem to have recently become very bad at reading.'

Chess sighed, setting her coffee cup down. 'No, Sadie. No. I don't want you to think you've done anything wrong. I fucked up, not you. This is all my fault.'

'Forgive me if I'm wrong,' I said, 'but I don't think it was you who came to me and said, *surprise, I'm marrying my nemesis tomorrow, you must be cool with it or else.*'

'I'm the one who immediately tried to steamroller over you without listening, though. I'm the one who didn't even turn up to your wedding. I'm the one who—'

'Chess, we're both adults, okay? Please let me take some of the blame.'

She exhaled audibly. 'One of us is an adult,' she said, 'but I don't think it's me.'

'Then listen to me.' I put my coffee cup down too. 'Let me be the big sister for a minute. *Listen* to me.'

She closed her eyes and bit her lip.

'I need you, Chessie,' I said. 'I'm always going to need you. That's never, ever going to change.'

Tears started to bead on her lashes again. She blinked them away.

'There's no version of my life without you in it,' I said. 'I am who I am because of you. You raised me. You *made* me. You shouldn't have had to – fuck knows no one else wanted to – but you did, and I'll never stop being grateful to you.'

'I didn't know how to stop doing it, though,' she said. 'I still don't know how to stop. I don't know how to . . . it's been months, and I still don't know how to live my life without putting you right at the centre of it, Sadie. Every time I think I'm making progress . . .' She shook her head.

I reached over and took her hand. 'How about we figure it out together, then?'

Chess paused for a few moments, and then she nodded. I tugged at her fingers and pulled her into me, putting my arm around her so that her head rested on my shoulder, the way she always used to do for me when we were kids.

'I've missed you so much,' I whispered. 'Going all these months without talking to you – it's been so awful.'

'You've done all right without me.'

She gestured at the three things hanging on the wall – mine and Jonah's doctorates, separated by our wedding photo. 'It's real now, isn't it? You and him?'

'Yes,' I replied. 'It wasn't, when that photo was taken, but it is now.'

Even as the words were coming out of my mouth, I knew they weren't quite the truth. I might have been too proud and too stubborn and too stupid to admit it, but *something* between Jonah and me had been real ever since I'd turned up at his bedroom door and asked him if he wanted to marry me.

'I need Jonah too,' I said, resting my cheek against Chess's hair. 'Not the same way I need you, but I've needed him for a long time, even if I didn't really know it. I think . . . I think that was why I was so scared to tell you we were getting married. I knew you hated him – and I knew you'd talk me out of it, if I gave you enough time to do it – but something in me knew I needed him.'

'I'm sorry. I'm sorry I made you feel like you couldn't tell me that. Like I wouldn't listen to you.'

'That part *really* isn't your fault. I didn't even know it myself.'

I let out a long breath. 'Jonah and I have always been on a level playing field,' I said. 'It's . . . different, the way I need him. The way I've always needed him: to keep me sharp, to challenge me, to push me when I need to be pushed. He made me too, in his own way, over the years, for better or worse, and now . . . now he's made me really happy. He's the best thing that's happened to me in a long, long time.'

Gently, I pushed Chess away from me, so we were both sitting upright again and I could look her in the eye.

'But none of this,' I said firmly, 'changes a single thing about how much I need you, Chessie. How much I love you.'

I took both her shaking hands in mine. 'You will always be the first best thing that ever happened to me,' I told her. 'I will always love you to the end of the universe and back again. And yes, I'm an adult now, with a job and a husband and a whole full life, but that doesn't mean I have no place for you in it. I'm an adult who knows what she wants – and what I want is my sister back.'

There was a long pause before Chess spoke. 'Did you . . .' She swallowed. 'Did you really believe that I'd cut you out of my life? Just like that?'

'Yes,' I replied. 'Turns out all that therapy you helped pay for is yet to fix my abandonment issues. We should really lodge a complaint.'

The sound she let out was short and sharp, but it was recognisably a laugh, and the knot inside my belly loosened, just a little.

'I think I need to spend some serious time of my own in therapy now,' she said. 'I just . . . I can't describe what happened to me, Sadie. It's like I've been frozen. I got it stuck in my head that I had to stay away from you, that I needed to let you go, to give you space, that it was for your own good. I knew after that day at the airport you'd keep calling and texting, and I knew eventually I'd give in, and this panicked voice in my head was shrieking that that would be bad for you, because then I'd just smother you again – so I told work I was taking leave, got all my mail redirected, and I just . . . left.'

She folded a knee up, resting her chin on it. 'I meant it when I said I was trying to figure out what my life looks like when it doesn't revolve around you,' she said. 'But I haven't been making much progress. The fact that I had to have someone else hold onto my phone so I didn't obsessively check on you . . .'

'Who was that, by the way?' I asked. 'He sounded so familiar, but I couldn't place him.'

She shook her head. 'Just a friend. It doesn't matter. The only thing that matters is that you know you'll never, ever lose me. That I love you too much for that, even if you don't want me to.'

'I'm so sorry I said that to you, Chessie,' I said. 'I do want you to love me. As much as you want. To the ends of all the universes.'

'I couldn't stop if I tried,' she said, voice cracking.

I swallowed, trying to get rid of the lump in my throat. 'Drink your coffee before we both start crying again. I'm sure you have to get back to Sydney sooner rather than later and I don't want to waste all our precious time together on tears.'

Chess obeyed, picking up her cup, taking a deep breath, a long sip of coffee, and then another deep breath. 'So you mentioned something about legal advice,' she said. 'What do you need?'

'How do you feel,' I asked, 'about helping mastermind a big, public, messy unfair-dismissal case?'

Chapter Twenty-Three

Jonah

Just like on our wedding night, Sadie spent the evening crying, but this time it was with happy tears. 'She's back,' she wept into my chest. 'I've got her back.'

I had a few deeply uncharitable thoughts about how long it had taken and how thin Chess's reasoning seemed to me,[53] but I wasn't about to articulate them. I still had a long way to go before I became an authority on being a good sibling – and in any case, this was not a situation that needed a devil's advocate.

Instead, I just held my wife close and stroked her hair and let her have this. No matter how angry I was about how Chess had made Sadie feel these last few months, I would not be poisoning this particular well.

'How are you feeling?' Sadie asked me, turning her face into my skin and pressing her lips to my collarbone. 'I've been so wrapped up in my own shit that I haven't been giving you the attention you deserve, even though you're literally on the brink of sacrificing your career. Are you doing all right?'

---

53 *I thought I was smothering you, so the only other alternative was completely exiting your life* – really? That would get some stern words in the margins about logical leaps and a profound lack of nuance if it were an assignment I was grading.

I thought about it for a second, fingers drifting over her skin. 'I'd be lying if I said yes,' I replied, 'but I'm doing better than I thought I'd be.'

It had helped, spending the morning with Fiona while Sadie was with Chess. We'd sat at her kitchen table with a pot of ginger tea after the kids had gone to school and we'd talked it out. *No matter what Dad's drilled into you, there is life for Fishers outside academia*, Fi had said to me. *If we need to, we'll find yours, Jonah. I promise.*

Then she'd smiled and said, *I'll help,* and something in my heart had swelled so much it was almost painful, because I believed her.

'You're not going to lose your job, though,' Sadie said, kissing my jawline. 'We're not going to let it happen. I don't know if I've really properly communicated how good Chess is at being a lawyer, but if you think I'm a good scholar . . .'

'*Brilliant* is the word I believe I like to use.'

'Sorry for paraphrasing when I should have quoted, you pedant.' She nipped at my earlobe. 'Anyway, however brilliant you think I am as a scholar, she's a million times more brilliant as a lawyer.'

Then she sighed. 'I can't believe I misread her letter like that.'

I repressed a snort. I absolutely could believe it.

There was a narratological phenomenon called overreading, where people read things into a text that weren't really there.[54] When Sadie had shown me Chess's letter yesterday, it had been reasonably clear to me that she – caught in her months-long spiral of grief and guilt – had overread it.

It hadn't been *totally* clear, though. The blame did not sit entirely on Sadie's shapely shoulders. I didn't know if Chess had intended

---

54 If you've ever sat through an amateur dramatic society production of *Hamlet* set in an insane asylum – of which I've somehow seen three – you know exactly what overreading is.

her letter to be ambiguous or not, but she had certainly left a lot of room for interpretation.

Not that I would be saying any of this to Sadie. *Wife not actively crying, Jonah doesn't feel like he's dying.*[55]

'For someone with a PhD in reading things, you'd think I'd be better at it.' Sadie traced circles over my heart. 'Look at how egregiously I misread you, for years and years and years.'

This time, I did snort. 'You didn't misread me. Not the whole time, anyway. I deserved a lot of the disdain you threw my way. Just like cooking and cleaning, I learnt how not to be an annoying arsehole embarrassingly late.'

Sadie smiled into my throat. 'You've left me such an opening there,' she said, 'so I want you to read the fact that I'm not taking it as a sign of how much I love you.'

'Yes, yes, I'm still an annoying arsehole.' I kissed her temple. 'No one is more restrained than you, wife.'

She chuckled.

I tightened my arm around her. 'If you want an example of someone catastrophically misreading a situation, though,' I said, 'let me tell you about how you broke my heart when we were nineteen.'

To Sadie's chagrin and my well-hidden relief, Chess had declined the offer to stay at our place while she was here, opting instead to stay in the hotel room she'd booked. She did, however – to Sadie's delight and my well-hidden chagrin – extend her stay so she could spend some time working with Julia and the union on the first

---

55 Happy tears excepted. All good mantras should have fine print in the footnotes.

steps of the anti-Renewniversity Phase Three campaign, and Sadie insisted we take her out to dinner.

'The Jonah in Chess's head is the tweed bro I spent a solid decade shit-talking to her,' she said, standing in the kitchen as we took a quick tea break the following afternoon. 'I want her to get to know the real Jonah. Cardigan Jonah. Teddy Bear Jonah.'

'Just do me one favour,' I said. 'Please don't refer to me as Teddy Bear Jonah anywhere she – or, indeed, anyone in the world – could overhear you.'

'Fine, fine.' She went up on her toes to kiss me. 'I hear you. You're a very manly man. You have your pride.'

Then she smiled against my lips. 'You *are* a teddy bear, though. My teddy bear. And I'm not going to let you go.'

'Oh yeah?' My fingers trailed down her sides and she yelped and then laughed as I hoisted her up against the fridge. 'Prove it.'

Sadie wrapped her arms around my neck and her legs around my waist. 'You're on, Fisher.'

She proved it. I still had the half-moon marks of her fingernails carved deep into my shoulder blades when we left the house for dinner a few hours later. She had *clung* to me.

We met Chess in front of Tsundoku. 'I'm so excited to show you this place, Chessie,' Sadie said. 'You're going to love it.'

'I'm sure I will. Hello, Jonah.'

I kissed both her cheeks European-style in greeting – air kisses, my beard only barely brushing her skin. 'Hello, Chess.'

Unusually, Isamu, not Satoshi, was behind the bar. 'Nice to see you, Sadie, Jonah,' he said. 'And—'

'This is my sister.'

Sadie was always beautiful, but radiating joy like this, she was incandescent. I couldn't resist pressing my lips to her hair. She smiled up at me.

'Francesca Shaw,' Isamu said. 'An extremely valued customer.'

'This is Isamu, our landlord,' Sadie explained. 'He's the wine-maker. He's usually down at the vineyard, but—'

'I had some business to discuss with my brother,' Isamu said, beckoning to Satoshi, who was emerging from the back. 'He'll get you seated and pour you something special. Welcome, Francesca.'

'Thank you,' Chess said simply, twining her fingers together in front of her.

Sadie had told me many times that Chess had a lot of opinions about wine, but she was relatively quiet as Satoshi talked us into a bottle of their new non-vintage sparkling. 'I know, professionally, Jonah and my lives have gone to shit, but still – we need to cele-brate!' Sadie declared. 'I'm so glad you're here, Chessie. So, so, so glad you're here.'

'I'm glad too, sweet—Sadie,' Chess said, as we all clinked our glasses together. 'Cheers.'

Unable to keep the smile off her face, Sadie carried the bulk of the conversation, telling Chess everything about everything, from what a cartoon villain Petrovski was, to our misadventures in babysitting, to all the new things she'd learnt about wine from our acquaintance with the Tsukamoto brothers. 'You'd be so proud of me,' she said, leaning over to top up our glasses. 'I used the word *terroir* in a conversation the other day – and I'm, like, ninety per cent sure I used it accurately.'

'I'm always proud of you,' Chess said, 'but well done. Very impressive.'

'We'll have to go out to dinner with Fiona sometime – Jonah's sister. I think you two will really get on. I'm only ever going to be an enthusiastic wine amateur, but she really knows what she's talking about. You can fight over who loves Bibliophile more.'

Chess chuckled. I did too, keeping what I was actually thinking – that if she ever said anything even remotely combative to Fi, then we would have a capital-P Problem – off my face.

'This is where I got all the books I sent to you,' Sadie said, gesturing at the bookshelves around us. 'I have no idea how Satoshi keeps the romance section so well-stocked – like, who keeps bringing in all these second-hand books and why aren't they keeping them for themselves? – but he does such a good job.'

'Of course I do,' Satoshi said, overhearing her on his way past our table. 'This is not a snobby establishment, my friend. It is a business! I love to make money! I make a point of keeping that section well-maintained.'

'You're a prince,' Sadie said, as Satoshi grinned and headed back up towards the bar.

Her phone started vibrating on the table. 'It's Julia,' she said. 'It's probably about the campaign. I should take it.'

'Go,' Chess and I said at the same time.

'I'll grab some food menus on the way back, so we can order dinner,' Sadie promised, and disappeared.

Which left Chess Shaw and I alone, for only the second time in recorded history.

I took a sip from my champagne flute. This was my sister-in-law. For Sadie's sake, I needed to exhibit some restraint. I needed to shove down every bit of toxic argumentative programming my dad had ever jammed into my head. I needed to let it go.

'Spit it out,' Chess said.

I looked at her.

She took a sip from her own flute. 'Don't give me the mock innocence. I know there are things you're dying to say to me. So spit them out.'

'I have no interest in starting a fight with you,' I said. 'Sadie would hate that, and the only thing I care about is her being happy.'

'On that,' Chess said, 'we can agree.'

'Sadie loves you,' I said. 'If you're important to her, you're important to me. I know you've never particularly liked me, but we're family now, and . . . I don't know how much Sadie's told you about this, but I've been rebuilding my relationship with my own sister, and that means a lot to me. I want Sadie to have a good relationship with you. *I* want to have a good relationship with you. Genuinely.'

'We can agree on that too,' she said. 'You've been good to her. You're clearly good for her. Keep doing that, and you and I will be absolutely fine.'

'That goes for you too, though.'

My grip on my restraint slipped. I was only hanging on with one hand now, dangling over the cliff as I stared her directly in the eye.

'I want us to get along, Chess,' I said. 'But if you ever do something like this to Sadie again – if I *ever* hear my wife crying herself to sleep over you again – I will ruin you.'

How I would do that, I had no clue. I was a tweed-wearing academic on the brink of unemployment with precious little experience of the world outside the ivory tower. I had no idea how one went about ruining someone.

But I was an intelligent man. If I had to, I would figure it out.

'That's fair,' Chess replied. 'If I hurt her like this again, I deserve to be ruined.'

Her gaze went far away for a moment, as if she were looking into some other world just over my shoulder, misery flashing across her face. Part of me wanted to turn around and see what she was looking at. Another part wanted to reach across the table, touch her arm, and ask her if she was all right.

'It sounds like we have a deal, then,' I said instead, as lightly as I could, offering her my hand.

Chess shook it. It was obvious where Sadie had learnt her assertive handshake. 'Deal.'

Then she let go, leaning back in her chair and taking a sip of sparkling. 'I got your email.'

'I figured. The timing of when you sent your letter to Sadie . . . it checked out.'

She teased her bottom lip between her teeth for a moment. She didn't bite it, but the mannerism was still so similar. 'There were some things in there,' she said at last, 'that I needed to hear.'

And yet you chose to respond in a way that was unbelievably easy for her to misinterpret, I did not say. No one would benefit from me arguing the point, even if there *had* to be more to the story than she was saying.

'I love Sadie more than anything else in the world,' she said. 'I might never stop being angry about you riding her coat-tails, no matter how much she insists that you deserve this job as much as she does.'

That was fair enough. I might never be over the guilt of that myself.

'But the fact that you're willing to give it all up for her if you have to – that means a lot,' Chess said. 'That goes a long way with me.'

My grip on my restraint slipped again. 'Don't thank me for loving her.'

'I wasn't going to.'

Chess met my gaze. Even subdued, it was easy to tell this was a Shaw I was sitting across from, all fists, all teeth. 'I would never thank anyone for loving her, like it was some favour, some hardship, something they had to go out of their way to do,' she said. 'She deserves all the love in the world.'

'Agreed.'

'So I want you to know that I'm going to fight like hell to make sure you can keep your job,' she said, waving past me as Sadie approached our table again. 'What the university is doing is in a grey area between legality and illegality, but even if we don't get a ruling in our favour, I can absolutely fucking bury them in paperwork and red tape. If nothing else, I can make it much more expensive for them to fire you than to keep you on.'

'Plus,' Sadie said, sitting back down, putting her phone on the table and then lacing her fingers through mine, 'according to Julia, we're already getting a ton of interest on the media side of things. Lyons is going to look like they're trying to fire you so they can fund a brand-new major in kicking puppies. If we pull enough public heartstrings, the pressure on the university will be so intense they'll have to back down.'

I nodded. I didn't think it would be that easy – years of growing up with Professor Christian Fisher as a father had shown me that universities did not particularly care about anyone's feelings – but I was hardly about to say it.

Sadie drew our joined hands to her lips, kissing my knuckles. 'We're about to become the nation's most extremely married couple,' she said. 'I hope you're ready for that.'

I used my free hand to tip her face up to mine. 'What do you fucking think, Shaw?'

She grinned. I kissed the tip of her nose. Opposite us, Chess took a sip of her sparkling and almost certainly shoved down about a thousand things she wanted to say.[56]

That, at least, I could respect. 'Thank you, Chess,' I said, turning away from Sadie to look her in the eye. 'For helping us fight this.'

---

56 Could this be an overreading? Sure. Was it? Definitely not.

She gave me a tight-lipped smile. 'You're welcome, Jonah.'

One day, I might push Chess harder. Much as I'd meant everything I'd just said about wanting a good relationship with her – and much as it would make me a giant hypocrite, given my own track record as a sibling – it was difficult to set aside how angry it had made me, watching my wife suffer for all those months. One day, I might ask why she'd really done it.

But tonight, Sadie was so happy sitting there with both of us, fingers squeezing mine in approval, and that was more important than anything else – so even if that day might eventually come, it was not going to be today.[57]

'Now, talk me through this food menu,' Chess said, businesslike. 'Tell me what's good.'

She and Sadie got into a discussion over whether we should order a cheeseboard before dinner or after – 'I mean, we're obviously getting the cheeseboard,' Sadie said, 'it's just a matter of when.' I let them talk, speaking only when spoken to.

Chess and I might never truly see eye to eye, but on the most important point, we were in clear and firm agreement. If Sadie was happy, then that was good enough.

'No!' Satoshi barked suddenly. 'Out!'

He pointed a finger at the man who had just come into the bar. 'You are not welcome here. You will never be welcome here. Out!'

'Excuse me?'

'You heard me.' Satoshi was shaking.

Isamu put a warning hand on his shoulder and said something quietly to him in Japanese. Satoshi snarled something back.

---

57 It was amazing, really, the amount of restraint I was able to employ now that I wasn't spending most of my mental energy on keeping my love for her hidden in the footnotes.

Isamu looked at the man and folded his arms. Even under the white dress shirt he was wearing, his biceps bulged ominously. 'It would be best,' he said, 'if you left.'

'Fine,' the man said curtly. The door swung closed behind him.

'Jonah, what's wrong?' Sadie asked me. She must have felt my arm stiffen around her.

'That was Matt.' I drained my water glass. 'Fiona's piece-of-shit husband.'

'Oh, shit, darling. Are you all right?'

I nodded. 'Fi might not be, though. The one upside of him not paying child support is that she doesn't have to deal with him. If he's back in town . . .'

'What's her legal situation?' Chess asked. 'Does she have a decent lawyer? Because if they're not protecting her and her rights properly, I can help. I don't do family law myself, but I'll find you a shark.'

I glanced at her, surprised.

'I have a soft spot,' she said, 'for sisters.'

OCTOBER

Epilogue

Sadie

'Oooh, that sounds promising,' I said to Chess, phone wedged between my ear and my shoulder as I tried to pry the cork out of the wine bottle without breaking it. 'Do you have any time in your calendar in the next couple of days? I can set up a Zoom with you, me and Julia, and we can talk about next steps.'

'Tomorrow's a fourteen-hour day for me, but I've taken Friday off,' Chess replied. 'I was thinking about flying down to Hobart Thursday night. Maybe we can all have lunch on Friday?'

'Absolutely. I'll text Julia. And I'll make up the Bunbury Suite for you.'

'Don't do that. I'll stay in a hotel.'

I did my best to suppress a sigh. Chess had visited Hobart several times over the past few months, working with us and the union on the anti-Renewniversity campaign, but she was so intent on this *Sadie is an adult who needs space* thing that she'd steadfastly refused to stay with us, no matter how many times I told her that I wanted her to.

Well, either that or she was terrified she'd hear me and Jonah having sex and didn't want to admit it to me. That, I supposed, I could understand.

'You're not getting out of Friday night dinner at Fiona's, though,' I said, finally managing to get the cork out of the bottle. 'She tells me to thank you every time I see her.'

Chess snorted. 'She's probably spent more time thanking me than I've spent working on her case.'

That definitely wasn't true. Chess had found Fiona an incredible family lawyer to represent her in the divorce, but she'd also gone digging into Matt's finances personally. Fiona had nearly fainted when Chess had revealed to her what she'd be entitled to in child support once the divorce was finalised.

'And yet you will be thanked again,' I said. 'In words, and probably in wine. Thank goodness you like Bibliophile.'

'Thank goodness,' Chess echoed.

There was a knock at the door. 'Jonah, can you get that?' I called. 'It's the pizza!'

'On it!' he called back.

'He's not cooking tonight?' Chess asked.

'I ordered him to take a night off,' I replied, pouring the wine – a Bibliophile syrah – into two glasses. 'We just finished writing the last of our lectures for the semester and we're both completely exhausted. Plus, we've got our workload meeting next week and fuck knows how many more Petrovski is going to heap on us in retribution.'

It hadn't taken much for the university to back down on laying Jonah off. Chess had barely begun to terrify the university lawyers when the media campaign started rolling out, portraying us as a sort of academic Romeo and Juliet, two lovers being torn apart by cruel institutional forces outside their control. *A clerical error led to Dr Sadie Shaw and Dr Jonah Fisher's positions being considered in scope for the Lyons University 'Renewniversity' major workforce realignment project,* came a swiftly issued public statement.

The Faculty of Arts looks forward to employing both Dr Shaw and Dr Fisher for many years to come.

They'd clearly been hoping that with Jonah's job saved, the media campaign would fizzle out and they could go on their merry way with Renewniversity Phase Three. And, to an extent, it had – we'd kept juicing it all we could, but there was only so long you could keep the public interested in stories about layoffs, particularly ones in an industry they didn't really understand or care about.

But there was no tiring Francesca Shaw, The Lawyer Who Eats Lawyers.

She'd been as good as her word. I didn't understand half the things she'd done – give me academic jargon and I'll tell you exactly what it means; give me legal jargon and I'm completely lost – but she'd done exactly what she'd told Jonah that night in Tsundoku. She'd buried them in red tape.

With her help, the union got the first arm of the Renewniversity agenda thrown out. There would be no adjustments to 40-40-20 contracts, which meant that Veronica, Lin and all the other people in the Lyons precariat would still have work next semester. Casual academics were *not* going to be the first casualties, not this time.

Now we were working on getting the other arm – the academic Hunger Games arm – tossed too. The end of the academic year was coming up, so we were running low on time, but given Chess had begun this phone call tonight with, 'so I have an idea', I was pretty sure we were going to make it happen.

'I should let you go and eat,' Chess said. 'I'll see you in a couple of days, okay? I love you.'

I had a sudden vision of her pacing around her high-rise apartment in Sydney, and for a moment I felt profoundly sad. I hated to think of her being there every night, all on her own.

'I love you too,' I said. 'To the end of the universe and back again. Always.'

✎

Jonah and I ate dinner on the couch in our pyjamas in front of an episode of *Superchef*, the pizza – pesto chicken with a side of garlic bread, same as always – on the table in front of us. 'I know this is very easy for me to say from here on the sofa, and I know I no longer need this show as a backup career plan,' he said, nudging me with a socked foot, and then nodding at the screen, 'but I genuinely think I could take some of these people. You can't tell me that I couldn't make a better attempt at coq au vin than whatever that guy's trying to do.'

'Do you want me to play devil's advocate and tell you that you absolutely could not take that guy, and then let you convince me that you could?' I asked, swallowing. 'Or do you want me to be your devoted wife and tell you that you're the best chef in the entire universe and there's not a person in this country who could defeat you?'

'Wife,' he said instantly.

'Jonah Fisher,' I said seriously, licking a finger clean of grease so I could hook it under his chin and turn his face towards mine, looking him dead in the eye, 'you're the best chef in the entire universe. There's not a person in this country who could defeat you.'

He grinned. 'Why the fuck did I waste so many years arguing with you?'

'It wasn't wasted time,' I said, taking another bite of garlic bread. 'How would we have written a hundred and four battle lectures – and counting – without spending all that time becoming the masters of bickering like an old married couple?'

Our first journal article about our pedagogical approach had come out last month in *Studies in Higher Education*, a prestigious journal that would score us some decent research points. We were working on a second one, but now the semester had ended, we were daring to dream that we might actually get to return to our own individual research at some point.

'Oh my God, I forgot to tell you.' He swallowed. 'My dad texted me today. He asked me if *that man* had given us our workload allocations for first semester next year yet and if I needed any advice on how to push back if he did anything unreasonable.'

That man was new Professor Fisher code for Petrovski. Jonah hadn't said as much, but he'd been terrified about how his dad was going to react to the media campaign and the news that he might give up his future in academia for me. It had turned out much better than expected, though. Instead of jumping straight to *You have shamed this family! Death, dishonour, disowning!*, Jonah's dad had latched onto the fact that Petrovski was responsible for the fact his son might lose his job and had sworn blood vengeance. I didn't think it was the *main* reason the university had backed down on firing Jonah, but it was almost certainly *a* reason and, for the first time in my life, I'd found myself feeling somewhat warm about Christian Fisher.

. . . Right up until Jonah had admitted, cheeks pink, that his dad had also said *why don't you just knock Sadie up like I did your mother, that'd solve your problem*. Professor Fisher would forever have to be graded on a curve.

'What did you tell him?' I asked.

'I said that we don't have our workloads yet and that we won't meet with *that man* without our union rep present, but if we need his advice, we'll ask for it.' He nudged me with his foot again. 'Emphasis on the *we*. What's mine is yours, and that goes for unfair advantages as well as all my worldly possessions.'

'I'm glad to hear you think that way,' I said, nudging him back, 'because you know that grey cardigan of yours? You're never getting it back.'

✏

A while later, after the show had ended and we'd put the remnants of our dinner away – 'You know I love you, but this really is unacceptable,' Jonah grumbled, 'pizza is just not an appropriate breakfast food, Shaw' – we curled back up on the couch, with Jonah's head resting in my lap.

'When you do that, it makes me think I should have just let the uni get rid of me,' he said, making a satisfied noise as I scratched at his scalp. 'This is my real dream career. Lying on the couch while my wife babies me.'

'The pay is pretty shit.' I combed my fingers through his hair.

'Mmmm, but the perks are great.' He found one of my hands and pressed it to his lips.

He tried to let go, but I wouldn't let him. 'The finish is coming off your wedding ring,' I said, running my thumb across it. 'We're going to have to swap it out again.'

'We should just bite the bullet and get real ones.' He kissed my hand again. 'We've got some money saved up. We're both employed. I know there's still two years until our probation is up, but Petrovski wouldn't fucking dare fire us now. And we can't keep wearing fake rings forever.'

Forever.

A warm, honey-golden feeling started to bloom deep in my belly. 'Okay,' I whispered, leaning down to kiss the tip of his ear.

Then I shoved at his shoulder. 'Up.'

'No,' he groaned.

'Come on, up,' I said, pulling him into a seated position and then tugging the ring off his finger. 'I'm not having you go around with a wedding ring in this condition, Fisher. I have my pride. We need to swap this one out until we can get real ones.'

The idea came to me as I was rummaging through my underwear drawer for the last of the three-for-$12 pack of rings. It wasn't a sudden realisation; nothing sharp, nothing piercing. It settled over me gently, like one of Jonah's cardigans wrapped around my shoulders, and it left in its wake not the ecstatic joy of eucatastrophe, but something more akin to satisfaction, contentment. It was a different, gentler, more everyday form of joy, but it was nonetheless deeply profound.

I put a pin in that thought, deciding to interrogate it later. That sounded like a concept I needed to theorise.

'So, about that money we have saved up,' I said, tossing the last of the wedding rings up into the air and catching it again as I came back into the living room, 'I have a thought.'

'House deposit?' There was something slightly nervous in Jonah's expression.

We'd talked a little about starting to save up for a house of our own. *I love this apartment, but it really is so small*, I'd said to him a while ago. He'd agreed, and replied, *especially if we decide we want to . . .*

And then we'd both blushed and looked at each other for a long moment, the memory of his dad making that crack about him knocking me up hanging awkwardly over us.

'Before we start seriously saving for a house deposit,' I replied.

We weren't ready for the rest of that particular conversation yet. It was a *when*, not an *if*, and I was pretty much positive we were on the same page, but we were still so new, in so many ways, and that could wait.

I perched on the edge of the couch beside him. 'How would you feel,' I asked, 'about having a wedding?'

He blinked. 'A wedding?'

'Don't get me wrong, our first wedding was lovely, but I wasn't exactly in the right headspace for it,' I said. 'And I didn't realise what I was actually proposing, when I proposed to you. Why I was even doing it. What I really felt. That I couldn't live without you.'

'Oh, Sadie,' he said softly.

'Plus, neither of our sisters were there, which feels like an obvious omission.' I took his hand and pressed it to my lips. 'I know Fiona still doesn't know that our first wedding wasn't exactly for romantic reasons, so we might have to think a bit about how to explain it, but . . . it'd be nice to do it again. To choose this – to choose each other – properly, and forever, instead of kind of doing it by accident.'

'*Sadie*,' Jonah choked.

I glanced at him. He took his glasses off so he could wipe the tears away from his eyes.

'Oh, darling.' I wrapped my arms around him and he hugged me tightly.

'I love you so much,' he whispered into my hair.

I stroked my fingertips against his beard and drew back so I could kiss him as I slipped the ring on his finger. 'Then hopefully,' I said against his lips, the clever lips of this brilliant man who had bound himself to me with the most unbreakable bonds in the world, 'you'll say yes.'

Acknowledgements

There are two questions you get asked a lot of as an author: 1) are any of these characters based on people you know? and 2) are any of these characters based on you?

My answer to this has always been no, and that remains true for *An Academic Affair*.[1] However, the world of the book is based on one I know very, *very* well. If you read this book and were like 'Oh, being an early career academic can't be *that* brutal, can it?': yes, it can. Just about everything that happens has either happened to me or someone I know.

Like Jonah and Sadie, I moved to Tasmania to take up my first academic job in my early thirties – although mine was a short-term contract, not permanent. I was very grateful to be employed, but until I finally secured my permanent position at Deakin University in Melbourne a couple of years later, that job insecurity was a source of constant stress. The one thing in this book I've never heard of anyone trying is the marriage of convenience – but if someone had come to me with a proposal like that when I was in the precariat, I probably would have considered it.

---

1 Even if Jonah and Sadie's couple name is actually my name. What a horrifying realisation that was.

Unlike Jonah and (especially) Sadie, though, I was very lucky to have some senior scholars in my corner. I would not have an academic career now without them – which gave me, among many other things, the experience I needed to be able to write this book. To Professors Hsu-Ming Teo and Lisa Fletcher: thank you for having my back. Your ongoing support has meant so much to me, and who knows what I would have done without it.

Thank you also to all the scholars I've met over the years as part of the International Association for the Study of Popular Romance and the Romance Area of the Popular Culture Association (of which Sadie is definitely a member). Thanks similarly go to my colleagues, past and present – this is, perhaps, my most research-y non-traditional research output yet.

I was quite nervous about writing a book so close to my own experiences. However, everyone at Simon & Schuster Australia held my hand and talked me through it. Huge thank you to Anthea Bariamis and Lizzie Levot, who provided constant support (and wisely prevented me from naming this book *Higher Yearning*); to my lovely publicist Gabby Oberman, who is an absolute star; and especially to Cassandra Di Bello, who has been a stalwart champion for my work for many years now.

I've also been blessed to work with Atria Books in the US. To Ifeoma Anyoku and Kaitlin Olson – thank you so much for taking a chance on this little Australian romance. To Camila Araujo and Aleaha Reneé – thank you for taking on the very difficult task of marketing a book when the author lives on the other side of the world.

Someone I've always had in my corner, and who never gets enough credit for all her hard work, is my literary agent Alex Adsett. I could not do this without you, Alex – I know I say this to you all the time, but *thank you*.

I am lucky to have an excellent group of friends who show up for me all the time, even when I've disappeared into a work spiral and haven't showed up for them quite as much as I should have. Kate, Adele, Steph, Anna, Meg, Katie, Claire, Rashmi, Mabel, Sonya, Mel, Hannah, Monique, Athena, Amy – you're all wonderful, and I adore you.

I also have to acknowledge the very important contributions of some people who – literally and metaphorically – have held me together. One of my own attributes that I gave to Sadie was her persistent jaw-clenching issues: my myotherapist Natalie Holmes is the reason they're not a whole lot worse. Similarly, good wine is very important to me and to this book (and will be even more important to what comes next, wink wink). A huge thank you goes to sommeliers James Er, Chris Parker and Aaron Crothers of the wine bar Our Terroir, who have answered an incredible amount of wine questions for me and poured me some beautiful drops after long days. Anything the Tsukamoto brothers get wrong about wine in these pages is on me.

Finally, I'd like to acknowledge everyone who's picked up this book. Sadie and Jonah are so dear to my heart. The world they live in is my world. Thank you so much for letting me take you on a journey into it.

And if this world is your world too – if you're in the brutal world of early career academia?

I see you. I've been you. This book is for you.

About the Author

Jodi McAlister, PhD, is an author and academic from Kiama, Australia. Her academic work focuses on love, romance and popular fiction. It means that reading romance novels and watching *The Bachelor* is technically work for her. She is currently a senior lecturer in writing, literature, and culture at Deakin University in Melbourne. She is the Vice President of the International Association for the Study of Popular Romance.

For more, visit JodiMcAlister.com.au or find her on Instagram @jodimcalister.